DANGEROUS LOVE

You've abused and threatened me, you've used me badly under false pretenses, and my career is in shambles—not that I can hold you solely accountable for that. You have created a very dangerous person in me, Mr. Macalester, a person with nothing left to lose."

Macalester did not even flinch, although her tirade had been intended to shame him.

"You want to know what dangerous is?" he countered, his tone deliberate. "Dangerous is a wanted man, worth five thousand dollars to a bounty hunter who doesn't much care whether he takes you in sitting in your saddle or across it. Dangerous is knowing for dead certain that your partner will go to prison for twenty years and that you've got another five years of running ahead of you if you don't deliver. Dangerous is doing business with Garland Humble in the first place, and, lady, dangerous—and stupid—is falling in love with his wife!"

Macalester was breathing hard, and his dark eyes fairly bored into her soul. He had lied to her before, she knew, but he was not lying now. Her heart hammered loudly in her chest. He was magnificent in his rage, and in his declaration. In spite of everything, she knew, with an awful certainty, that she loved him as well, as she had never loved, or ever would love, any other man.

Other *Leisure* and *Love Spell* books by Carole Howey:
NOBLE AND IVY
SHEIK'S GLORY
TOUCHED BY MOONLIGHT
SWEET CHANCE
SHEIK'S PROMISE

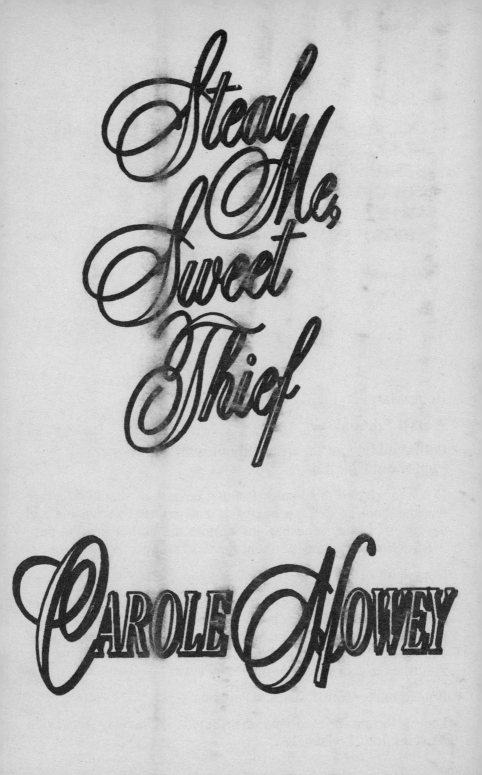

Steal Me, Sweet Thief

CAROLE HOWEY

Book Margins, Inc.

A BMI Edition

Published by special arrangement with Dorchester
Publishing Co., Inc.

Printed in the United States of America.

Digest format printed and distributed exclusively for Book
Margins, Inc., Ivyland, PA.

For Florence Berggren:
Musician, Mentor, Friend
and
Riders of The Outlaw Trail
(You know who you are!)

Chapter One

Billy Deal was almost too good-looking to be a man. With his baby-blue eyes, fair skin, dimpled chin and a crop of curly blond hair, he had the look of a cherub, of a Botticellian image perfectly preserved and perpetually youthful. He smiled easily, and his smile left a string of broken hearts in its wake. Women, his friends were fond of repeating, didn't know whether to mother him or take him to bed. And, as he himself was fond of replying, he was fortunate that the result was usually the latter. Just now, in fact, the two fairest tarts in the Fort Worth Saloon, who were only average as most of the outlaw's conquests went, dangled from his arms like Christmas tinsel.

Kieran Macalester smiled at the sight. In spite of the fact that his friend's good looks drew women like flies to manure—maybe even because of it—Macalester did not envy the younger man. Billy Deal possessed, in equal measure to his outward appearance, a quick

9

mind, a quicker temper and an even quicker hand to the trigger, all of which his friends and adversaries alike tended to overlook, to their eventual misfortune. Still, each of these attributes, Macalester reflected, sipping his whiskey, had worked to his own advantage more than once: having a partner who drew a lot of attention tended to leave one free to operate in obscurity.

Macalester finished his whiskey and stood up slowly to his full six feet, shaking his head at a girl who approached him, a young whore who couldn't have been more than fourteen. His tastes ran to older women, women who had better sense than to trifle with the likes of Billy Deal.

Deal was singing a bawdy song with the piano player in his staunch, tone-deaf fashion. Macalester approached him and struck him lightly on the shoulder.

"Business, William." He cut through the improbable harmonies.

Deal leveled surprised azure eyes at him, and Macalester could see that he'd had more red-eye than was good for him.

"Humble business. Remember?" Macalester went on patiently. "Dinner. You can serenade these ladies when it's finished. Unless they find their ears, meanwhile."

Billy scowled. Even his scowls were pretty.

"Your damned watch is fast again," he grumbled, but gingerly disengaged himself from the attentions of the giggling, somewhat slovenly girls, who looked to Macalester as though they were but mischievous children who had gotten into their mothers' powders and rouges on the sly.

"I'll be along later," Billy promised them, bussing each of them full on the mouth while his hands slid to their ample backsides.

"You ain't goin' anywheres, mister." A new voice growled from a shadowy corner of the saloon. Billy's sharp eyes instantly focused on the corner from which the bearlike sound had emanated.

"It's right kind of you to invite me to stay," he replied, and Macalester recognized his polite tone as a precursor of trouble. "But I did say I'd be back."

From the shadows emerged a rangy man about Billy's age, which was several years younger than Macalester's own, clean-shaven and wearing jeans and a denim shirt similar to Billy's. Macalester noticed that the man's gun was tied down. He was sure Billy noticed, too. A man with Billy's reputation didn't live to Billy's age without keen powers of observation, among other talents.

Macalester felt a small tightening in the pit of his stomach, with which he was all too familiar. He'd lost count of the number of times Billy had faced men like this one. They were old, young and everywhere in between. So far, miraculously, Billy hadn't killed anyone. He had merely injured his opponents enough to make them think long and hard before challenging anyone again. But it was only a matter of time, Macalester reflected. Only a matter of time until Billy Deal actually killed someone. Or until someone killed him. And then he, Macalester, would have to find himself a new partner—a tedious and uninviting prospect.

"And I said you ain't goin' nowhere," the other man insisted.

The challenger's grammar, Macalester noted with wry amusement, was deteriorating with the passage of time. He further noted the man's wet shirtfront rising and falling with each shallow, rapid breath he drew. His lips, which he licked frequently, were parted, and revealed bad teeth. Macalester pursed his mouth and backed away from Billy, who was displaying no such anxiety.

"Finish this up and let's get going, Deal," Macalester said in a purposely loud and clear tone.

11

The two girls, at least one of whom had no doubt been the cause of the debacle in progress, retreated behind the piano, their young, painted features slack. Macalester leaned his broad back against the faded wallpaper not far from the door, and far enough, he hoped, from the action. Sometimes these would-be heros shot wide. Once one had even put a bullet through the crown of his own hat, ruining a perfectly good twelve-dollar Stetson, not to mention adding a gray hair or two to his mahogany locks. He crossed his arms in front of his chest and felt his jaw clench as he watched the adversaries, standing but ten feet apart. A .45 could do considerable damage at that distance, even if the aim wasn't too good. The challenger was angry, and scared. Billy, to all appearances, seemed more bored than annoyed.

"You . . . Billy Deal?" The man tried his voice.

"What if I am?" was Billy's casual, drawling response.

The man licked his lips again. He did not move, except to glance at Macalester.

"Then that makes you . . . Kieran Macalester?" The bravado waned from the challenger's voice.

Macalester shrugged, not taking his eyes from the man who was now dangerously close to drawing his weapon.

"Man like you ought to know better than to ask a question like that," Macalester replied quietly.

Macalester noticed several things at once from the corner of his eye: the bartender slowly ducked down behind the bar; two men who had been drinking at the bar sidled behind the piano near the terrified girls; and an old man who had been sitting in the back had, with remarkable stealth and agility, slipped out the back way, no doubt to summon the sheriff.

Billy cleared his throat, drawing Macalester's attention again. The younger man was as motionless as an

12

ivory statue, his sky-blue eyes unblinking.

"Well, mister? I ain't got all day," he remarked lazily.

Macalester wanted to close his eyes, but he dared not. He was aware of movement and noises in the street outside. If the sheriff got in there, he reflected grimly, they would never make it to Humble's.

In the instant it took him to blink, a shot was fired. The stranger's gun clattered to the floor, and he was gripping his bloodied hand with a raw cry of pain. A curl of gray smoke issued from the muzzle of Billy's .45.

Macalester did not concern himself overmuch with the condition of Billy's latest victim. The foolish man would live. Not well, and not happily, without the use of his right hand, but that was his problem. After all, he had challenged Billy, and what was Billy supposed to do—let the fellow shoot him? Macalester sprang forward and seized Billy's arm, pulling him quickly toward the door.

Outside, in the September twilight, Macalester deftly unlashed the horses, Billy's and his own, as Billy mounted.

"Wait." Billy hesitated, looking about. "I gotta—"

"That's them, Sheriff!" It was an old man's voice across the street. "I saw 'em! They—"

"Too late," Macalester told Billy, his pulse accelerating. "Save it till we're out of town."

Before he was completely in the saddle, he reined his Appaloosa away at a gallop without looking back. Billy would follow. The sheriff probably would not, satisfied that the outlaws had left town without further threat to the well-being of his community, or to his own life. There were, Macalester reflected, certain advantages to an unsavory reputation.

A few miles out of town, Macalester finally reined to a halt. They were only a mile or two from Humble's, and it was nearly dark already. There was little chance that they had been followed. The local sheriff would be content to report that he had run the infamous duo of Kieran Macalester and Billy Deal out of town without ever having fired a shot.

"You okay, Billy?" Macalester turned his mount to see Billy Deal leaning over the side of his bay mare, retching over an unlucky juniper bush. The sight did not surprise Macalester. He had witnessed it after every showdown in which Deal was involved.

"Damn," he heard Billy swear softly. "Damn." And the gunman's stomach heaved again.

Macalester waited, saying nothing. He knew it was not fear that prompted so violent a response from his partner. It was something involuntary, as though Deal's own body were rebelling against the danger in which his mind had placed it. Of course, the red-eye probably didn't help, either. Billy's somewhat petulant stomach was a standing joke among compatriots past and present, although none had ever dared to tease him about it. Macalester himself had certainly never felt the urge to taunt him. In fact, he thought it to be one of Billy's finer qualities, proof of his partner's deeper sensitivity. Besides, he suspected that such a joke would not wear well, even coming from him.

In a few minutes, Billy appeared at his side, mopping his face with his wadded-up kerchief.

"Damn," he said again, and Macalester could smell the sour reek of bile around him like a rancid cloud.

Macalester chucked to his mount and started them on their journey again. Billy, beside him on the bay, stuffed a pinch of tobacco into his cheek. Macalester suspected that the object of this exercise was for Billy to rid himself of the foul taste in his mouth, although the idea of replacing one foul taste with another seemed rather strange to him.

"What do you guess Humble wants?" Billy asked after

a time, his humor apparently restored.

Macalester swore. "That's only the tenth time you've asked me that since we got his telegram. And I don't know any more now than I did then."

"Well, hell," Billy grumbled, then spat. "I'm just tryin' to make conversation. Talk. Say something. You're good at it."

Macalester smiled to himself.

"Do you remember the last job we did for old Garland Humble?"

"Don't remind me." Deal sniffed, his gloved hands tightening on the reins. "I thought Wichita was a right nice town, up till then. Now I never want to see it again. Senator, what the hell are we doin' here, now that I think about it? That old bastard's got more money than God, and every dogshit job he hires us for, he tries to welch on. Why do we keep comin' back for more?"

"Because, William, he has more money than God. And just about as much influence. And he's the best chance we have of getting that amnesty we want."

"The one *you* want, you mean." Deal was disparaging. "Seems like it don't much matter now, anyway. How long since our last job? Two years? Three?"

"Two years and four months." Macalester was laconic. "But the statute of limitations on armed robbery is seven years. In five more years, I'll be closing in on forty. My life's more than half over now, Billy. Hell, in five years, I could be dead."

Billy grinned at him, an expression he could barely make out in the growing Texas darkness.

"You could at that, the way you shoot."

Kieran Macalester did not mind the insult to his marksmanship. It was the truth, after all.

"I'll be all right, I guess, as long as nobody cuts out my tongue."

*   *   *

15

Garland Humble's home was anything but homey. The Texas palace rose from the landscape like a pagan temple, complete with devotional lights burning in all of its windows. It always reminded Kieran a little of Monument Valley, where monoliths of rock rose hundreds of feet from the canyon floor like gargantuan pillars rammed into the earth by angry gods. The overdone edifice before them, however, was hopelessly out of place, whereas the Utah version was nothing short of majestic.

A groom approached to take their horses as they dismounted. Kieran offered a mild jest to the effect that he'd thought slavery to have been abolished, but the man did not respond, whether through insult or lack of understanding, Kieran did not know. In either event, their horses were led away to be cared for as he and Billy Deal were admitted to the house by the butler, an impeccably dressed and utterly humorless man of perhaps fifty, whom Billy enjoyed tormenting at every opportunity.

"Howdy, Alice!" Billy greeted the man in a jovial tone. "Still whorin' for Gar?"

The man's name was Hallis, but Billy preferred to drop the H, a habit since adopted by more than one member of Garland's extensive household, no doubt to the butler's dismay. Hallis did not offer a reply, except in the form of a disparaging scowl. He led the two men through the cherrywood-paneled foyer to the accompaniment of such remarks as "Did your mother have any sons, Alice?" and "When are you gonna marry and break my poor heart?" Kieran offered no comment, preferring not to interfere in his partner's fun. Hallis, he had discovered, was capable of holding his own against the younger man.

The butler paused before a pair of ornately carved oaken doors, knocked softly, then opened them, announcing, "Mr. Macalester and Mr. Dull to see you, sir."

The dining room was a dozen yards across if it was an inch, and featured a banquet table nearly its equal in length. At the far end of the rosewood behemoth, partially obscured behind a towering silver candelabra through which he peered like a duck hunter, sat a large man who compensated for the dearth of hair on his head with a full beard the color of new steel.

"You're late," he complained in a strident yet lilting voice that had surprised both men the first time they'd heard it, for its lyricism was at odds both with its owner's appearance and personality. "Don't you two ever dress for dinner?"

Macalester stepped forward in an easy swagger, unmoved by the older man's irritation. He snapped his fingers once.

"Damned if I didn't leave my opera cape at the Ritz Hotel." He mocked his host's protocol. "Your sheriff had other plans for us. That steak looks good, Gar. But we could do with a wash first."

"Make it fast," Garland Humble growled. "I don't expect I'll live past a hundred. Hallis!"

It was not until dinner was well over and the three men sat before a roaring fire in Garland's sitting room with Napoleon brandy and Havana cigars that any serious conversation took place. Garland Humble seemed to enjoy lavishing a fine dinner and all of the amenities upon them before asking—that is, telling—them what he needed them to do, in strictest confidence and for comparatively little compensation.

Kieran watched the old man over the rim of his Waterford brandy snifter. Humble was like an old, fat spider—a spider spinning web upon web, snaring his hapless prey. Were he and Billy his prey, as well? Kieran preferred not to think about that. Predator or quarry; where Humble was concerned, neither prospect pleased him. Watching Humble and Deal laugh together over some jest to which he had not been a part, he grew suddenly apprehensive. Garland Humble would ask much, this time. The stakes would be high. Perhaps too high. Kieran swallowed his brandy and poured himself another from the bottle that Humble had, uncharacteristically, left open on the inlaid table between them.

"I expect you'd better tell us what this is all about, Gar, before I drink much more of this fine swill."

Humble seemed to take his measure, his watery blue eyes demonstrating no hint of amusement or camaraderie. Kieran was equal to his gaze.

"All business, eh, Macalester?" The older man's voice was low and reedy. "I like that. Just what I need, this time."

"We're always just what you need," Billy interjected, his own voice shaded with sarcasm. "Cheap labor with a reason to keep our mouths shut. Ain't that right, Senator?"

Garland started.

"Senator?" He stared from Billy back to Kieran. "Why'd he call you Senator?"

Kieran shrugged. "Ask him."

"Well?" the old millionaire demanded of Billy, who was examining the amber hue of his brandy by the fire's glow.

Billy took a long look at Macalester, then did the same at Humble. "Because he's such a damned fine liar," he said at last, lifting his glass in tribute.

Garland Humble stared at both men for a long moment. Then he laughed as loud and hearty a laugh of profound enjoyment as Kieran had ever heard. It was not a pleasant sound. Neither he nor Billy joined their host in his mirth, and after another moment, Humble lapsed again into a somewhat awkward silence.

"That's good." He poured himself another generous brandy. "It's always nice to learn of your unsuspected talents, Macalester. You'll need every one of them this time, I think."

The large man shifted his bulk, straining at the seams of his gray linen suit as he reached two fingers into his inside breast pocket. He withdrew a small rectangle, which he tossed across the narrow gulf to Kieran. Macalester caught it and turned it over, holding it up to the light of the brass lamp on the table.

It was a photograph. A mere four inches high, it was a full-length picture of a woman—by all measures a damned attractive one—who might have been any age between eighteen and thirty. She was not dressed in regular clothing, he noticed. She appeared to be wearing a costume of some sort, which revealed all of her shapely arms, much of her charming bosom, and even a trim ankle. And he couldn't swear to it, but Kieran thought, for a capricious moment, that he suddenly caught a faint trace of something exotic in the air. Jasmine. He shook his head hard.

"Fine-looking woman," he said at last, tossing the picture to his partner, who offered a long, low whistle.

"Who'da thought an ornery old bastard like you could have such a looker for a daughter!" Billy exclaimed.

There followed a deathlike silence, chilling enough to cause Kieran to stare at their host. Humble's features were rigid, and his steel-gray eyebrows met over his bulbous red nose.

"She is my wife."

19

Chapter Two

The silence following Garland Humble's revelation was shattered by an explosion of riotous laughter from Billy. Garland bore the insult with almost superhuman restraint. Macalester was flooded, inexplicably, with a sense of dread. He wished Billy would shut up. He kept his features bland and said nothing, waiting for the story to unfold naturally, or as naturally as it could, given its bizarre beginnings.

"She's an actress?" Billy's question demonstrated both his keen powers of observation and his utter lack of tact.

Garland grimaced.

"Worse. A singer. Opera."

Opera! This melodrama was becoming more intriguing by the moment. Kieran was forced to restrain a laugh himself at the thought of the aged curmudgeon Garland Humble wooing a beautiful young woman, actually luring one away from the lively world of the stage to the comparatively prosaic world of the altar. Certainly Garland's almost legendary wealth must have played some part in the woman's decision to marry him. Garland Humble was reputed to be one of the richest men in Texas. Possibly the entire country.

"Never took you for an opera lover, Gar." Billy's continued amusement was beginning to irritate his partner. "Or the marryin' type, either. How'd she get you to the al—"

"Billy, if you don't shut up, I just may have to kill you," the old man growled, looking more than capable of the deed. "I'm going to finish this story, if you don't mind, and I'm only going to tell it once."

Billy, for once, seemed nonplussed. Kieran remained silent.

"Her name is Geneva Lionwood." Garland's gruff tone softened. "I met her in New Orleans three years ago."

He shifted his immense bulk in the leather wing chair, which groaned in protest.

"She was beautiful, Macalester." Kieran did not need the use of his name to tell him that Garland Humble was speaking only to him. "And she had—has—a remarkable soprano voice like nothing I've ever heard. And I've heard them all: Nilsson, Calve, Fursch-Madi, Sembrich—"

The names meant nothing to Kieran, although Garland recited them as though they were the names of the books of the Old Testament, and he, Macalester, were a Sunday school teacher. It was a little unnerving.

"—understudying for Lucia di Lammermoor at the time. Understudying! With that voice!"

"Incredible," Macalester interjected politely, although he had not the faintest idea of what Garland was talking about.

"I spoke to the management. I paid them ten thousand dollars to let her sing the role. I sat in the box for every performance. She was brilliant. She was . . . grateful. More than grateful, I thought. Or hoped. When she said 'yes,' I thought I'd died and gone to heaven."

My God, he's serious. Kieran saw the old man's eyes glisten in the pale light of the dying fire. Billy, mercifully, remained silent.

"For six months, I was the happiest man alive." Garland's voice went a shade darker. "Then one morning, she'd gone. Vanished. Packed up and left during the night, without so much as a by-your-leave. I was—" He paused, breathing a deep, broken sigh.

"I want her back, gentlemen," he said finally in a sharp voice.

"And," Billy ventured at last, sounding doubtful, "you want us to get her for you."

Kieran felt a knot in his stomach, around which the brandy twisted like a mean snake. Garland sent a measuring look his way.

"Not exactly." The old man looked straight into Kieran's eyes.

Kieran did not look away. There was more to this story, he sensed, but Garland's bright eyes, the color of robin's eggs, gave him no satisfaction.

"Where is she?" he inquired, laying a finger beside his cheek as he rested his elbow upon the arm of his chair.

"New York City," Garland replied promptly, tugging on the silken cord that hung beside his chair from the ceiling. "You can leave tomorrow. Naturally, I'll pay your expenses."

"I never been to New York." Billy sounded impressed. "I hear tell ladies walk the streets in their nightgowns."

Hallis entered the room quietly, carrying something. In the darkness, Kieran could not make out what it was. Billy, facing the other way, did not seem to notice him.

"You're not going to find out, Billy," Garland remarked in a casual tone. "Leastwise, not this trip. I want Macalester to handle this alone."

"Why?" Kieran wondered why he was not surprised by this news.

Garland waved a fat, impatient hand. "Because this job calls for finesse. Tact. Intelligence."

Kieran could not resist sending a smug grin in his partner's direction. Billy scowled.

"Besides," Garland seemed unaware of the looks exchanged by his audience, "you're not as good-looking as Billy is. Hell, if I send him up there, the two of them might just up and run off together."

It was Billy's turn to gloat. Kieran looked away from his partner, annoyed at the warmth in his own face. Garland Humble would pay for that remark, all the more insulting because of its offhandedness, as though Humble need not concern himself with Kieran's feelings. Kieran didn't mind that Billy was better looking than he, but he did object to having his nose rubbed in it in so careless a fashion. He did have his pride, after all.

"What's it worth to you, Gar?" He ran his finger across his lips as he considered his host.

"Ten thousand."

From the corner of his eye, Kieran saw Billy sit bolt upright in his chair and gulp. Kieran felt a faint smile trace his mouth.

He shook his head. "Not enough."

Garland's eyes widened, then narrowed again.

"What are you after, Macalester?"

"A letter." Kieran responded promptly. "A real nice letter to Governor Roberts, all about how Billy and I have gone straight, and how we deserve amnesty, and how you're going to help him get reelected."

"And the ten thousand dollars," Billy added. God bless Billy's larcenous heart.

23

Garland's hairy jaw dropped.

"That's outrageous!"

Kieran settled back in his chair, crossing his right boot over his left knee. "That's the price."

Garland Humble stared in open-mouthed astonishment for a full half-minute, but Macalester knew it was all a show. Ten thousand dollars was pin money to Humble, and that letter, along with its inference, wouldn't cost but a few thousand more. No doubt Garland considered himself more than fortunate to get off so cheaply. At last, he closed his lips, sealing the hole that had appeared between his mustache and beard.

"You're a pair of bold rogues." Garland folded his fat, white hands upon his chest, displaying a thick diamond-and-gold ring on his index finger, a sure sign that he was satisfied with the deal. "I'll add a condition of my own."

"That being?" Kieran inquired patiently.

Garland sent a glance Billy's way.

"Mr. Deal stays here with me. As my guest. And my insurance."

"Your hostage, you mean!" Billy declared hotly, rising in a menacing fashion.

Hallis, who had been standing unobtrusively several feet behind Billy's chair, came forward, quick and quiet as death. Before Kieran could utter a warning, the butler swung a hard blow to the back of Billy's head, and the younger man crumpled instantly to a heap on the floor. Too late, Kieran realized that the object Hallis had been carrying was a blackjack.

"Damn it, Hallis!" Garland snapped, even as Kieran leaped up. "I told you not to—now he's probably bleeding all over my Ispahan."

Kieran knelt to examine his friend. Billy was out cold, and there was a sizable welt forming on the back of his head, staining those blond curls with a thin line of crimson. He was still breathing. Slowly, Kieran looked up at the butler, whose satisfied expression changed to one of terror. The older man took several steps backward.

"Mr. Macalester." His voice quavered. "I didn't mean to—"

"Stop whimpering, Hallis." Kieran cut him short. "I'm not going to do anything to you. But you'd better steer way wide of Billy from now on. And if anything bad happens to him while I'm away, I'm holding you personally responsible. If he has so much as a hangnail when I get back, there won't be any place where you can hide from me. Just remember that. Billy Deal may have his faults, but he never sucker-punched anybody. He's no damned coward."

"Get out of here, Hallis," Garland ordered the butler. "I'm sorry about this, Maca—"

"Like hell you are." Kieran spun on his host, his anger rising like molten lava in the core of a volcano. "Hallis was acting on your order. I bet you told him to take Billy out if he showed any signs of resisting. Damn you, Humble. If I find out that this is a setup—"

Garland gripped the arms of his chair, his fat knuckles turning white. "Calm down, Macalester." Kieran had to admire the irritability in the old man's voice, which contradicted the terror in his eyes. "Nobody's setting you up. It isn't you I don't trust. It's her. I just want to be sure that you don't forget your job when she bats her eyelashes at you."

Macalester did calm down, almost against his will.

"I thought you weren't worried about that, being as I'm such an ugly old cuss."

Garland chuckled, getting up slowly from his chair. The chair, Kieran reflected, had to be relieved.

"Take him upstairs." The old man gestured to the pile on the floor that was Billy. "Your rooms are ready. And you have a train to catch in the morning."

25

Kieran looked the fat old spider straight in the eye.

"I'm going to catch it with that letter in my pocket, Garland. You may trust me, but I don't return the favor. You can date it a month from now, if you like, but that letter is mine, as of this moment."

This was not negotiable. Garland nodded slowly, not averting his gaze.

"All right, Macalester. As a gesture of good faith. But—"

Here it comes, thought Kieran, clenching his jaw. Humble's caveat. With Garland Humble, there was always a caveat. And it was always pricey.

"You have one month to return my wife to me. Thirty days. After which time, William Deal becomes my property to dispose of as I choose, including, but not limited to, turning him in for the reward. At least it'll make up for my out-of-pocket. We'll see just how deep your loyalties run."

Kieran laughed, more amused than alarmed by what the old man no doubt had hoped was an ominous warning.

"I hope it takes me considerably less that thirty days, Gar. The idea of spending that much time with any woman who would marry you is about as appealing as playing 'keep away' with a pint of nitroglycerin."

Garland smiled faintly. "You just keep on thinking that, Macalester."

Now that, thought Kieran, staring hard at the old man again, did sound like a threat.

Chapter Three

"He is stupid!" Soprano Geneva Lionwood wrenched the startled, inept tenor's music from his trembling hand and hurled it to the stage before her.

An *obligato* of colorful Italian insults ensued.

"You are stupid," she spat back at the red-faced man across from her, this time in flawless Italian. "This is the fifth time you've walked on my cadenza in this rehearsal alone. If you do it one more time, I'll have you skewered and roasted for the pig you are!"

Another vituperative recitative of scathing Mediterranean insults followed, this time from the orchestra pit. Italo Campanini, the world-renowned tenor who brought crowds to their feet at La Scala, Covent Garden, the Academy of Music and dozens of other opera houses throughout the world, had walked on her cadenza. Again. And now the conductor, Campanini's countryman Vianesi, was berating *her* for it. This was insupportable. Abbey must know. And Blaine must back her up.

"But he is wrong!" Still in Italian, Geneva pleaded with the conductor, although she could not see him for the footlights. "Tell him! There are a full three measures of three there, with a *fermata* and *ritardando*. Even if the direction wasn't specific, it makes no sense musically or dramatically for him to take a single step before I finish my cadenza!"

"*Disgraziata!* How does she expect me to change my costume for the next scene if I am standing here with my thumb up my fundament waiting for her to finish?" Campanini, obese, perspiring, appealed to the invisible conductor. "I remind Signorina Lionwood that it is Campanini's name above hers on the handbills!"

"And it is Gounod's name above yours!" she retorted, giving the luckless score on the stage a little kick. "And Mr. Abbey's! I very much doubt that a man of Mr. Abbey's reputation wants his premier production literally trampled to death by a selfish oaf of a—"

"Miss Lionwood!"

Henry Abbey, new director of the even newer Metropolitan Opera House, halted the commotion from the wings with his stentorian exclamation. He was a paragon of grace and diplomacy as he strode smoothly out onto the stage, and Geneva was relieved. She didn't like him personally, but that was not important. Abbey was a man of musical integrity at least, and was, moreover, an American, like her. His will must supercede Campanini's. Even Vianesi's. This round was surely hers. She smiled at his approach.

"Mr. Abbey—"

He held up a hand.

"Not another word, if you please, Miss Lionwood." He turned to Campanini, and Geneva could scarcely contain her delight at the dressing down that the tenor was about to receive. If she was lucky, Abbey would give the conductor a courteous but firm rebuke, as well.

"Please accept my apologies on behalf of Miss Lionwood, Signore." Abbey spoke in Italian and bowed low to the tenor. "She is young, and she does not yet know the way of things."

Geneva felt as if she'd been punched in the stomach. Over Abbey's bent back, Campanini sent her a triumphant sneer. Before she could recover, Abbey straightened and turned to her, wearing the look of a stern, scolding papa.

"Let us have no more of these outbursts," he cautioned, still speaking Italian, shaking a finger at her. "Signores Campanini and Vianesi are busy and important men who have been performing opera since you were a child. Neither of them needs the instruction of a young snip with a wealthy patron."

Geneva bit her tongue and waited. It was all true: She was hardly the headline performer, all those present were far older and more experienced than she, and she did enjoy the patronage of Blaine, Lord Atherton, which was largely responsible—all right, then, *wholly* responsible—for her having been granted the role of Marguerite in the Metropolitan Opera House's premier performance of Gounod's *Faust,* although her ability to perform the role in her own right was unquestioned. But surely Abbey could not mean to allow these proud, pompous asses to make a gross mockery of Gounod's genius!

Without another look at Geneva, Abbey started off.

Mind yourself, now, girl, Audrey, her friend and wardrobe mistress, would warn her, Geneva knew—if she were there. But Audrey was dressing Calve across town at the Academy of Music.

Pride, and a sense of fairness, got the better of Geneva's instincts for self-preservation.

"But Mr. Abbey—"

"Look here, miss." Abbey spun on her and spoke in cold, crisp English. "We both know that the only reason you stand here at all is because you have the favor of a prominent patron of the art. I cannot dispute your right insofar as the music is concerned, but I, and the opera house, stand to lose far more by angering Campanini and the others than by catering to your whims, right or wrong. I have kept silent as to the means by which you have secured the favor of Lord Atherton," he said with a knowing leer, "and thus the leading role for this production. I expect you to keep silent in the matter of how I manage it. You are expendable. I wanted Nilsson for the role. If you cause me any more trouble, I'll see to it that I get her, and Lord Atherton's bequest be damned."

Abbey nodded toward the score, still on the stage. "Pick it up," he ordered her. "Give it to Signore Campanini. And apologize to him. While you're about it, apologize to Signore Vianesi, as well."

Geneva stared. She suspected that Abbey's angry commands had more to do with her recent rebuff of his unwanted advances than with his desire to appease either the tenor or the conductor. He wanted to shame her in front of all of them, and to show her just how much power he had.

She hated him.

In the folds of her gown, she squeezed her hands into fists. *Use your head, girl.* Audrey's constant, wise admonition was like the ring of a hammer on an anvil. The problem was, the anvil, in this case, was her head. And it was hard.

"Do it, Miss Lionwood." Abbey was impatient.

"Very well." She thought she'd choke on the words.

Pick it up, a naughty voice in her head encouraged. *Pick it up and give it back to the pig. And tell him how sorry you are.*

She stooped to retrieve the mistreated score. Abbey gave her his fingers to help her stand again, but when she glanced up, she saw that both he and Campanini were taking advantage of her position to look down her neckline.

But even if they hadn't taken such an advantage, she'd still have thrown the score at Campanini's head, anyway. And her aim was true.

"Disgraziata!" the tenor roared again. *"Disgraziata! Cretina! Dio mio!"*

"Cretino!" she hurled back at the injured tenor, fighting tears of anger and frustration as she stormed off stage. She would have said more, but she had to reach her dressing room, quickly. She refused to allow these men to see that they had reduced her to tears.

This business was so wicked, so cruel to anyone without the proper connections: European ones. And Geneva was as American as the town of Hoboken, where she'd been born. The opera world was amazed—and probably annoyed—that, with such inauspicious roots, she'd made it as far as she had. Abbey should have supported her. He would be sorry, someday. She swore it.

Abbey was screaming something else at her, but she could not hear him. Her head ached, and water filled her eyes. Her hands to her ears, she made her way to her tiny dressing room. Once inside, she slammed the door so hard that the mirror above the vanity fell to the floor with a crash, shattering into dozens of jagged shards on the wood floor.

Her dressing room was the size of a closet, while Campanini enjoyed the luxury of a veritable suite! Abbey would not dare to treat another soprano of, say, Nilsson's stature, in this shabby fashion. She seized the first handy object, which happened to be a Limoges vase of cobalt blue trimmed in gold leaf, full of the red roses that had arrived from Blaine that very morning, and threw it, with all of her strength, against the wall that had lately supported the hapless mirror. The result of her tantrum was a spectacular explosion of blue china slivers, water and roses, which left its residue upon everything in the room, herself included. Fortunately for her, she was unhurt by the event. Her slight relief, however, was momentary. Spent, she collapsed upon the worn brocade chaise, heedless of broken china and roses, and at last sobbed uncontrollably.

"Geneva!"

Not Blaine, she pleaded with her inner god. *Please, not Blaine. I couldn't bear him, just now . . .*

"Geneva!"

The summons from the wings was louder and more distinct. She recognized the voice, to her chagrin: It was Blaine, Lord Atherton. She allowed herself a small groan. *Let him look for me,* she thought, hoping he would fail in his quest. She pushed aside an errant rose that lay near her cheek. God, the musty odor of the upholstery, mingled with the sickeningly sweet smell of strewn roses, was nearly intolerable!

Blaine called to her a third time. He was getting nearer to her dressing room. Geneva sat up and scrubbed her face with her skirt. It would not do to allow him to see that she'd been crying. Where was her gremlin?

She liked to pretend that there was a gremlin who appeared whenever she needed him, a gremlin whose task it was to take all of her unwanted emotions, usually anger and frustration, and keep them in a little box. She'd invented him in her childhood to help her deal with disappointments and other cruelties of life, and she discovered that he was as effective in her adulthood as he had been then. Perhaps even more effective, especially during her brief tenure as Garland Humble's wife. Her eyes dried by the gremlin's magic. Or was it the thought of Garland Humble?

"Geneva!" Blaine burst into the room like more shattering glass. "What in bloody hell has happened in here?"

Blaine was intolerably stupid at times.

"Go away," she said woodenly, not even granting him a hostile glance. She was no longer hurt and angry, just weary. The gremlin exacted a price, always.

"Gen—"

"Don't even think of scolding me, Blaine!" she warned him from her prone position on the chaise. "I can't tolerate any more. That stupid, stupid Campanini—he's still using the score—can you imagine? He walked on my cadenza. Not once. Not twice. But every time. Every time! And *Faust* opens next Friday!"

"*Faust,*" Blaine began in a truculent, singsong tone that infuriated her afresh, "will not open until October twenty-second."

Her fury forgotten, she sat bolt upright. "What!"

Blaine might have been considered handsome at one time, with his blue-gray eyes and his softly dimpled chin. But time and good living had softened his features rather than hardening them, like a loaf of white bread left too long to rise. He was smiling his indulgent, condescending, Peer-of-the-Realm smile, which she detested.

There were many things about Blaine Atherton that she detested, not the least of which being his atrocious teeth, ridiculously short hair the color of old hay, and the fact that he was nearly twenty years her senior. The last he could not help, of course, but the first two were easily remedied—that is, if one took the time and the trouble. Her experience with titled English gentlemen, however, was that they devoted neither money nor attention to their personal grooming with the exception of their haberdashery, which often bordered upon fop-

33

pishness. Blaine, Lord Atherton, was no exception to this paradigm.

"The building is not completed." Blaine seemed delighted to impart the news. "Abbey has told me in strictest confidence. Which reminds me: He has also fired you."

"Blaine, this is no time for jokes."

Chuckling, Blaine brushed away slivers of the broken vase with his gloves to sit beside her on the chaise. He smelled of verbena and rotten teeth.

"I am in earnest, Geneva," he whispered, wearing an expression suggesting that he had just bestowed upon her the world's largest precious gem.

Geneva swallowed more tears.

"You—you promised me Marguerite." She choked out the words, trembling. "You promised me the Metropolitan, Blaine!"

If this was one of his wretched jokes, she would kill him for it. If it was not, she would simply die. The ripest, sweetest fruit always seemed to hang just beyond her reach.

"I promised you the Metropolitan, my darling girl," Blaine breathed, taking her two hot hands into his own cool ones. "But it pleases me to give you Covent Garden, instead."

Covent Garden! Geneva forgot her disappointment. Set in London like a dazzling jewel in common clay, the famed opera house had launched many an illustrious career. Chosen by numerous composers to premier new works, the Garden's reputation rivaled La Scala's in certain circles as a showplace for the very finest music and musicians in all of Europe—nay, the world! And, having conquered the critical and exacting European audiences, she would, surely, find many new doors opened to her here at home. . . .

She paused in her calculating: Henry Abbey had

opened the Metropolitan's as-yet untried doors to her that very spring. She had been delighted at the unexpected honor of being invited to perform the lead in *Faust* at the opening of the brand-new opera house on Broadway, even though she knew she had not been the director's first choice. The mercurial Abbey was known to have a predilection for the Swedish soprano Christine Nilsson, but clearly had been unable to ignore Blaine Atherton's obscenely large bequest, which was tied to the selection of herself, Geneva Lionwood, as premier diva.

Geneva had nevertheless been gratified that she, an American-born singer with no European reputation, had even been considered. American audiences were historically unkind to their own, and were known and disdained throughout Europe for preferring the name to the talent. This prospect had alarmed her, but Blaine had reassured her, saying that audiences would come to hear Campanini, but would leave praising Lionwood.

Campanini, the grim reality. Campanini, the tenor who, by all measures, was a true musician's nightmare, with only the blessing of a God-given natural voice, which his renowned father had not managed to ruin.

Vianesi, another grim reality: a brilliant, impossible conductor who considered opera to be Italy's gift to the world, and himself to be the Almighty's bequest to opera. His musicianship—and his tantrums—rivaled her own.

Perhaps the grimmest reality of all had been Henry Abbey himself. He had proven to be distressingly yet cunningly lecherous, suggesting to her on more than one occasion that he might easily be persuaded to extend greater favors to her, were she to extend certain favors to him. Her continued rebuff of his attentions had earned her the humiliation of this afternoon as well as this very miserable box of a dressing room in which she now stood staring at Blaine, who had just handed her the moon.

But could Blaine do it?

True, Lord Atherton did hold a seat on Covent Garden's Board of Governors. Besides, he was embarrassingly wealthy, and money, she knew, held powerful sway in the expensive business of opera. She pulled her hands from his and clutched the claret-colored silk of his coat sleeves.

"Blaine, if you are joking, or lying to me, I will kill you. I swear it."

His expression was mildly rebuking. "My dear Geneva," he chided her in a murmur, holding her chin between his thumb and forefinger, "have I lied to you yet? About anything important, I mean?"

She grimaced and jerked her head away from his touch. "Your wife, for example?"

He waved his hand. "Unimportant." He kissed her lightly upon the nose. "Entirely unimportant."

Geneva disengaged herself from his attentions, not in the least aroused by them. She never quite knew why she was bothered that Blaine had a wife in England. She should really be grateful, after all. Certainly, she would never entertain the notion of marrying him herself.

Besides, she was already married, although Blaine probably did not know that. Sometimes, Geneva even managed to forget about it herself. It seemed as though that event was something that had happened to another Geneva Lionwood, very long ago. She had achieved much in her attempts to forget it during these last three years. Although for some reason, Garland had been much upon her mind in the past few days.

Perhaps it was because of all the patronizing men in her life at present.

"It's late, Blaine," she said at the end of a sigh. "I'm

due at the Academy. Mapleson will be livid."

"Why, so you are, and so he will," her would-be lover replied softly, sliding his arms down around her, pulling her closer. "My Zerlina. My Violetta. My Lucia, my Susannah, my Marguerite . . ."

Unwillingly, she felt a thrill course through her—at his words, not his gentle touch. She felt a familar surge of power. She was all of those women, and more. Her musical talent and superb voice made her so. She smiled. Blaine, for all of his shortcomings, knew the way to appease her.

"Not your Marguerite," she reminded him, with no small twinge of regret that she would not, after all, open New York's Metropolitan Opera House. "Not yet."

"In November." He sounded so sure of it that her spine burned. "In London. I promise it."

She pushed aside her disappointment, draping her arms about Blaine's silk-ascotted neck like a wreath. "When do we sail for England?" She could not contain her excitement.

He sought her lips for a brief kiss, his plain, soft features crinkling into a grin that was almost attractive. "Mmm. Can we not first set aside this silly rule of yours, about not making love while you're involved in a production? I know you perform tonight, but, darling, I've waited for you forever, it seems—"

"Mmm, the patience of a saint, you exhibit," she murmured, trying to accept his ardent kisses anywhere but on her mouth. "Oh, that's right; I forgot. You celebrate no saints in the Church of England."

"Hmmhmm." His chuckle was muted by his continued attempts to kiss her. "My darling, no one amuses me as you do . . ."

And laughing often kept Blaine's attention directed to matters less amorous, which was why Geneva always endeavored to keep him as diverted as possible. Time, however, was obviously taking its toll. Blaine's hands slid up her bodice, and his thumbs teased the neckline of her dress. How much longer could she fend him off and still keep him interested?

"London, Blaine." She disentangled herself from his embrace. "When do we leave?"

"Let's talk about it tonight, after your performance," he suggested, nuzzling her neck. "*Don Giovanni* is sold out again!"

Geneva suspected that her success was as desirable to him as her body. She pushed him away and made a face at him.

"They come to hear Calve," she grumbled, hoping he would rise to the bait.

"Ah, but they leave in raptures over Lionwood's Zerlina!"

He did not disappoint her. She smiled, grateful for his predictability.

"I'll blow you a kiss," she assured him, fingering his lapel. "Will you be in your box?"

"I might be late," he replied, taking her hand and pressing a kiss onto her fingers. "But I shan't miss your *'Batti, batti.'* Depend upon it."

She sniffed and pulled her hand away. "Not my favorite aria."

Blaine laughed aloud. "Understandable. You are not exactly the type to invite your lover to beat upon you while you quietly yield."

She slapped his hand lightly.

"Don't be impertinent," she said coolly. "Drive me to the Academy to make up for your cheek."

Blaine seemed to enjoy her playing the role of a queen granting favors, and it was certainly no trouble at all for her to indulge his whim.

"This way, My Lady." He bowed low with a sweep of his arm. "Your carriage awaits. As does your adoring audience." He kissed her fingertips.

Yes, she thought, with no small contentment, bestowing a fond glance at the Englishman. For all his shortcomings, and shortsightedness, Blaine Atherton knew, as no one else, the circuitous route to her heart. And as long as she could hold him in the palm of her hand without welcoming him into her boudoir and still maintain his patronage, especially as he was taking her to London, it was all to her good.

Something told her that at least one of those things was an impossibility. Perhaps it was that fickle gremlin of hers.

Chapter Four

Geneva peeked through the hole in the blood-red curtain into the noisy, crowded audience of the Academy of Music. The house lights from the behemoth central chandelier were still up; patrons were making for their seats in the annoyingly leisurely manner of the privileged class: showing off jewels and furs, husbands and lovers, looking for an opportunity to scrape one up on their friends and to snub their enemies. Sometimes, not even the overture silenced them. It was said that Mozart had scribbled the overture to *Don Giovanni* in under three hours in the dark morning before its premier, with his wife prompting his muse by telling the brilliant young composer bawdy stories. If this legend were true, it was certainly a tribute to Mozart's boundless abilities, and a good joke on ignorant and unappreciative audiences.

Blaine was not in his proscenium box borrowed from the Beekmans, who were on holiday in Europe, and were probably enjoying Blaine's own box at Covent Garden. Tardiness was not unusual for Blaine, but it never failed to annoy Geneva. It seemed to her that the more one paid to hear an opera, the less regard one had for the spectacle. Having great respect for the music for its own sake, she often found herself resenting the cavalier attitudes of the so-called patrons of the art.

"Your wig is all wrong," a tart, nasal voice behind her scolded. "It will be off before the second scene. Here, let me."

It was Audrey Stancil, the wardrobe mistress, fussing with her hair. Audrey was a diminutive yet leonine woman who had been costuming productions for nearly thirty years. She was also the closest thing to a friend that Geneva had had since she was a child.

"Ouch!" Geneva, whose scalp was inordinately sensitive, pulled away from Audrey's deft ministrations as the latter expertly applied hairpins.

"You should have waited for me," Audrey remonstrated. "Turn around."

Geneva did so. Audrey, in her plain gray dress with a crisp white pinafore, was like a general reviewing her troops. She surveyed the ersatz Zerlina from hemline to hair ribbon, tugging a pleat here, tucking a blouson there. The wardrobe mistress shook her head, making a clucking sound.

"You will display your ankles, won't you, child?"

Geneva winked at her and glanced toward the closed curtain.

"I must give them something to remember me by, Audrey."

"As if they will forget your voice!" Audrey wagged a finger at her. Audrey, Geneva thought, would have made a wonderful mother to her. No doubt a much better one than her own.

"Well, at least they're pretty ankles." Audrey was

brisk. "Do you know, that Flemish Cow was jealous of your costume, and wanted me to shorten hers, as well?"

"Calve?" Geneva was amazed. "Emma Calve? Jealous of me?"

Calve, a beloved Belgian soprano, was singing Donna Anna in the production, and was but a few years Geneva's senior. Her broad, farm-girl features and physique had earned her the catty nickname among jealous rivals, including Geneva, of "the Flemish Cow."

Audrey nodded. "And her with tree stumps for legs! Some women have no common sense. None at all."

"Not like us, eh, Audrey?" Geneva teased.

Audrey did not chuckle.

"Humph!" The wardrobe mistress fussed once again with the placement of each golden curl of Geneva's blonde wig. "You're one to talk. I hear Abbey fired you today."

Bad news traveled like an epidemic.

"Who told you?" Geneva knew it was useless to ask, because Audrey never told. Audrey was the soul of discretion. That's why everyone told her everything. "Never mind. I can guess. Calve was looking at me in that snide way of hers."

"You'll never learn to hold your tongue, will you?" Audrey stepped back and surveyed her work with critical satisfaction. "Or did you expect that fancy Lord What's-His-Name to stand up for you? You're not warming his sheets yet, are you?"

"No." Not that Blaine hadn't pressed her. Not that he would wait much longer, as he was paying for her lavish accommodations at the Biltmore. He surely meant to share a stateroom with her if he paid her way to London.

"Well, thank heaven for that, at least." Audrey sounded mollified. "He's not for you. Never mind that he's married; you need a different sort of man."

Henry Abbey was a different sort of man, but he'd just fired her. Geneva was not disposed to think of him favorably.

Garland Humble had been a different sort of man, too. Geneva shuddered.

"I shall never marry." *Again*. Once was enough.

"Bosh. You'll marry quickly enough, when the right fellow shows himself. Hold still. This paste buckle is loose. Those lazy seamstresses!" Audrey pulled a needle and thread from the pincushion fixed like an apron about her waist and took a stitch.

"I'm married to my career," Geneva murmured. *Because a man expected more than I was willing to give.* She could still see Humble's face as he'd said "I do." And he really thought he'd bought her.

"Others, maybe. Because they can't love anything else but. But not you. You'll be wanting a man's love. Wanting babies, too. You're more like me than you think, and when I was your age, miss, I'd been married for six years and had three children."

Geneva forced a chuckle. This was a familiar tirade.

"Why is it that we adore to have others repeat our mistakes?" she wondered aloud. "I shall never marry, Audrey, and I shall certainly never have any children. Men are nice to have about occasionally, but they do get in the way of things."

"That's only because you haven't found the right one yet." Audrey wore a look of unmistakable complacency on her papery face. "Or he hasn't found you."

"But Blaine is . . ." Geneva began in half-hearted protest, because she knew she should.

Audrey merely shook her head of tight, gray curls and took Geneva's face into her two gentle, grandmotherly hands with a sureness that baffled Geneva into silence.

"Be honest with yourself, Geneva Lionwood," she said with tenderness that threatened to bring tears to

43

Geneva's eyes. "Be honest with your heart, and it will never lead you astray."

The strains of the overture could be heard from the other side of the curtain. Geneva glanced away at the sound, and when she looked back, Audrey was gone again. Probably off to fix Calve's hemline.

Zerlina was, for the most part, a delightfully capricious role demanding vocal agility and brilliance as well as considerable acting ability. A mediocre Zerlina could ruin an otherwise sterling production, whereas a brilliant one could save what would otherwise be an exercise in tedium. It was a role Geneva enjoyed and performed with gusto. True, it was only the third leading female, but it offered great exposure, and the cast assembled by Mapleson for this performance was competent, if not exceptional.

The show went off without so much as a missed cue. Geneva was pleased by her performance, her third Zerlina that week at the Academy, and was thrilled that the audience demanded a curtain call for her, as well. Proud, grateful, she curtseyed as low as she dared in her low-cut costume, retrieving roses thrown from the boxes lining the stage. One large bundle of exquisite long-stemmed red roses, which she took to be a favor from Blaine, caused her to direct a look toward his box with the intention of blowing him the kiss she had promised. Her stare, however, was diverted by a markedly tall, shadowy aspect in Blaine's very box, a silhouette that seemed to acknowledge her attention with a slight bow before disappearing from view.

Geneva was not a believer in things occult, nor was she superstitious in any way. Therefore she could not fathom why such an occurrence, certainly not in the least threatening or even unusual, should send a shiver—of excitement or trepidation?—along her spine. She blinked, and the shadow was gone. Chiding herself for her foolish thoughts amid the din of an adoring audience, she gracefully gathered the offerings thrown at her feet, touched her fingers to her lips and exited the stage.

She enjoyed the glares Emma Calve sent her way as she slipped back behind the curtain, but did not acknowledge them. She was both charged and exhausted by her performance, and sought her dressing room for a few moments of peace before Blaine came to claim her for the evening.

With the door closed behind her, Geneva was able to shut out the backstage uproar somewhat. She deposited her bundle of botanical tributes onto her dressing table, wishing to scrape the makeup from her face and to free her scalp from the hot wig. Like a falling leaf, a scrap of white paper fluttered to the carpet from the largest bouquet, catching her eye. She picked it up, smiling to herself, thinking of Blaine's tiny, cramped scrawl and the trite but sincere words of praise she often found on such notes.

But it was not from Blaine.

In a bold, unfamiliar hand was the single word: Delmonico's. Geneva frowned. She thought of the tall specter in Blaine's box. Could there be a connection between the two?

Delmonico's. An invitation? She laughed, admiring the fellow's cheek. Well, she was not fond of Delmonico's, since the opera stars tended to frequent the place. She preferred Sherry's, where she was seldom outshone by any other luminaries, save for New York society itself.

Delmonico's. The note in her hand seemed to burn her. Its boldness excited her, even frightened her a little. *You shall be disappointed*, she thought primly, tracing the letters with her finger, *whoever you are*.

"A triumph! Perfection! The standard by which all future Zerlinas should and must be judged!"

Blaine was outside of her dressing room, although there was no telling whom he might be addressing. Quickly, she tucked the small white card into her bosom and sat down at the vanity. She was busy withdrawing hairpins from her wig as Lord Atherton burst into her dressing room, followed closely by the bearlike figure of Colonel James Henry Mapleson, whose stern, forbidding countenance was a stark contrast to Blaine's ecstatic one.

"Was she not brilliant, Colonel?" Blaine breathed, seizing her hand, kissing it several times. "Was she not—"

"Begging your pardon, Lord Atherton." Mapleson was barely civil to Blaine. Geneva felt a spear of ice through her heart as the director of the Academy of Music sent his piercing stare her way.

"Never," he began, his Oxford accented bass shaking with anger, "on my stage has Zerlina taken a solo curtain call. And she never shall again. Do I make myself clear, Miss Lionwood?"

After Covent Garden, she thought, lowering her gaze in a show of humility, *I will make you regret this, you overbearing, pompous ass.*

"Perfectly, Colonel." She kept her tone light and pleasant.

Mapleson stared at her a moment longer. She could see, without looking directly at him, his barrellike chest rising and falling rapidly in a heavy pant and his bushy amber whiskers working furiously as his jaw clenched and unclenched. It was as though he had gotten hold of her like a furious, mindless bulldog and was chewing her up.

If you are waiting for an apology, she thought, not moving, *you will stand there until Hell freezes.*

"Very good," he said finally and, begging Blaine's pardon once again, turned and left them alone together.

The dressing room was suddenly stifling, and the smell of the multitude of roses nauseating.

"Geneva, my love." Blaine's cultured tone was low and conciliatory. "He had no right to speak to you so, after such a glorious accounting—"

"Why didn't you tell *him* that?" She yanked the wig from her head, sending hairpins flying, and threw it at Blaine's startled face. "Instead of standing there like a whey-faced ninny! How could you, Blaine? How could you let him upbraid me like some common chorister? Is that all I mean to you, that you could allow that pitiful excuse for a director to—to—"

She was on the verge of tears yet again. She was too easily moved to weep, even with her gremlin about to assist, and it never failed to annoy her. It weakened her position in any argument, and caused men, important ones, to dismiss her as overly sensitive, high-strung and emotional. It was a trait she had inherited from her mother, and she regularly cursed that woman for it.

Even now, Blaine was patting her arm in a patronizing, infuriating manner. "There, there, Gen," he murmured. "Pay no mind to the colonel. The man has his hands full, what with all of these temperamental divas about. Calve probably threw a fit when you drew such applause . . ."

Blaine was going on, but she did not hear him. She took several deep, slow breaths in an effort to command herself, and gradually the urge to cry receded. She was still angry with Blaine. But she had already, in one day, angered two men who were very important, not to say crucial, to her career. She could not afford to drive this one off as well, if she had any hope of avoiding a future in vaudeville like her mother. She sighed, and the sigh, she was relieved to note, only caught once.

The gremlin obligingly popped her tears into his box,

47

like precious, silver-white pearls.

". . . that she was jealous." Blaine seemed to be warming to his tirade. "It's plain the woman sees you as a threat to her own position, as well she should. But there. You feel better now? Good. Where shall we go, my pet? Sherry's?"

Geneva cast aside thoughts of the unpleasantness moments beforc. The note beside her breast burned her.

"Delmonico's, I think."

Blaine was surprised.

"Delmonico's?" He flopped into her chaise, elevating one leg. "I thought you hated the place!"

"I—I do," she answered, applying cream to her makeup. "But I should love to see the Cow's face one more time as she remembers my curtain call. Please, Blaine?"

Blaine chuckled, and she knew she had successfully deceived him. A small triumph, actually: Blaine was alarmingly easy to deceive.

"Of course, my love," he assured her, adjusting his bold sky-blue cravat.

Geneva sponged the heavy makeup from her face.

"Thank you, darling." She nursed her victory as she watched him in her mirror. "And thank you for the lovely bouquet."

Blaine's eyes widened, and his mouth opened. Then he shut it again and swallowed. "I—you are more than welcome, my precious," he stammered, straightening in the chaise.

Easily deceived, thought Geneva, watching him in the mirror with satisfaction. But not easily deceiving. Blaine was not the party responsible for the flowers, or the bold note.

But she might shortly discover who was.

Chapter Five

Geneva Lionwood made an entrance at Delmonico's
that was no less dazzling than her performance in *Don
Giovanni,* and possibly more audacious than her sub-
sequent curtain call. The statuesque soprano descended
the white marble staircase like a goddess visiting mere
mortals. She wore—rather, she displayed her figure—
in a silver-and-white creation accented by a gay white
ostrich plume in her upswept chestnut hair. Her white
satin gloves came nearly to her shoulders, and from one
arm dangled a rather nondescript (save for an outrageous blue cravat) gentleman, like an old fan she no
longer used but kept around out of fond habit. She
smiled at the waiters and the maître d', who bowed and
scraped like an enthralled minion. This woman, reflected Kieran Macalester, smiling in spite of himself as
he settled back in his chair, was going to be one huge
handful.

Garland Humble's three-year-old tintype had not

done her justice. Neither had that ridiculous blonde wig she had worn onstage. Geneva Lionwood was graceful, lovely and extraordinarily talented. Ignorant as Kieran was of the sophistication of opera, he knew at least that much. Her performance had inspired him to fetch a spray of roses from a street vendor during an intermission, and even to attach a brief, bold, anonymous note to them. He had watched from the box as she took them from the stage, pleased to imagine that she'd looked directly at him. Her appearance at the celebrated restaurant might be mere coincidence, he knew.

Or it might not.

The sparkling vision that was Miss Lionwood was led to a table not far from his own, causing a mild but not unwarranted commotion among the patrons. She was seated amid scattered applause and even a cry or two of *"La Divina!"* all of which she acknowledged with serenity and regal élan. Her escort seemed pleased by the attention as well, but his annoying expression was one of "see what I have caught!" Kieran disliked him instantly.

Suddenly, for reasons not immediately apparent, the big room became hushed. Frowning, he looked about and discovered the cause: another woman, whom he recognized as the leading lady—what was her name? Calf?—no, Calve—had entered the room.

The woman was, quite literally, larger than life.

The entire room burst into spontaneous applause and all the patrons in the place were on their feet, except for Geneva Lionwood and her escort. Kieran stood as well, and had a sudden inspiration. Unnoticed, he breached the short span between himself and the miffed Lionwood contingent, and bent to whisper in her ear:

"Go on; stand and applaud. Don't give her the satisfaction."

All at once she was looking at him. Her eyes were an exotic dark green, like some lush tropical forest. Her rose-petal mouth smiled briefly. He felt a surge of warmth along his spine, and he was surrounded by the faint, intoxicating scent of jasmine.

"I'll do better than that," she whispered in that rich, thrilling voice of hers. "Watch."

She rose. He straightened, backing away from her chair. Her escort seemed not to have noticed their fleeting conversation.

Geneva Lionwood fixed a dazzling smile upon her arresting features and applauded even as she snaked through the adoring crowds toward the very object of their attention. She walked boldly right up to the large, plain, square woman in a black satin gown that was a bit too tight, and even as the latter glared at her, Geneva seized the broad diva's shoulders and kissed her soundly upon each cheek. This demonstration was greeted by still greater applause, and Calve, not to be outdone, had no choice but to return the favor. *A real piece of work*, thought Kieran, unable to smile any wider.

Geneva headed back to her seat, her smile as innocent as a baby's, her eyes, those smoky emeralds, glimmering. Kieran laughed.

"Sir! Have we been introduced?" There was a chilly edge to the man's cultured English accent.

Startled, Macalester wrenched his attention from the gloriously theatrical Miss Lionwood to her considerably more prosaic escort. In Texas, or any place west of the Mississippi, Kieran would have been vindicated, he realized with amusement, for introducing his closed fist to the man's aquiline nose. But this was New York: slights real or imagined were punishable in far more civilized, and more dangerous, ways. Kieran reached into the inside breast pocket of his jet-black dinner jacket for his newly acquired gold card case and one of several fine forgeries contained therein.

"R. Hastings McAllister, San Francisco, sir," he responded, his blessedly glib tongue easily losing its natural east Texas twang and finding educated address. "Colonel Mapleson recommends me, as a representative of the San Francisco Opera and Light Theater Company."

The man scrutinized the forged letter and calling card by holding both right up to his nose. Kieran did not look away from him, although he was acutely aware that Geneva Lionwood had returned to the table. Geneva Lionwood Humble, he reminded himself. Although certainly, he had seen precious little evidence of humility displayed by her so far.

Geneva, exhilarated by her most recent performance, managed not to look directly at the ruggedly attractive stranger with the bold, dark-eyed gaze as she resumed her seat with his self-assured assistance. She ignored the look of displeasure on Blaine's face, keeping her smile politely interested.

"San Francisco!" she interjected, having heard that portion of the tall stranger's remark to Blaine. "Your friend has come a long way, Blaine. Introduce us."

She allowed herself to look at the man at last. Barely half a yard away from her, the stranger rose from his bent-over position, slowly, to his full height. She felt a rush of warm wind, like the beating of wings of a large, predatory bird. He wore an elegant evening suit not unlike Blaine's own, or, for that matter, every other man's in the room. But it was not his finely tailored suit that arrested her attention.

His wide-set dark eyes, very nearly the color of anthracite, met her gaze with a boldness she found both intriguing and unsettling. His mouth, almost crudely wide, widened still farther to the corners of his very square, smoothly shaven jaw, displaying even, white teeth. His dark hair shined in the glow of Delmonico's fabulous chandeliers, and it was overlong, curling slightly about the stiff white collar of his shirt and jacket.

His was a face that commanded attention, a face one could call sensual, if not exactly handsome. Coupled with his tall, powerful build, which not even the finest tailoring could camouflage, the man's presence was compelling, at least. She found herself wondering what the exquisite tailoring *did* hide . . .

Blaine issued perfunctory introductions with little warmth, his tone flatly implying that he hoped this interloper would leave. His annoyance delighted her.

"You've come a long way, Mr. McAllister," she remarked gaily. "You must join us. Mustn't he, Blaine? I am amazed that the reputation of Delmonico's spans the continent."

R. Hastings. McAllister sank his frame into a chair between Geneva and a frankly scowling Lord Atherton. She probed his steady gaze, hoping the attorney would betray himself into confessing that he was responsible for the rose bouquet and the accompanying note. He, however, met her challenge without even a flicker of that bold stare.

"Not so much the legend of Delmonico's as the legend of Lionwood" was his smooth response.

Flattery always found favor with her, and this San Francisco lawyer's was no exception. His voice was a lovely baritone, his accent utterly unplaceable. There was an intimacy to his words, though, that made her cheeks warm, and she found herself looking at his hands on the white damask tablecloth. They were fine, strong hands, neatly manicured, if somewhat rough-looking to belong to an attorney. Powerful hands. Exciting hands. Geneva shivered at the thought of them touching her.

McAllister was as charming as Blaine was sullen. Clearly younger than the English peer, the lawyer demonstrated a certain brashness, taking charge of their evening with an authority that left her breathless. She and Blaine were to be his guests, he insisted, and he proceeded to order steaks and duckling and napoleons and Champagne and brandy, all the while relating the tale of his interesting odyssey.

He was charged, it seemed, with the duty of securing a cast of the finest musicians for the Bay City, and had been successful thus far save in the quest for a diva. San Francisco audiences, he declared, would brook no foreigners, preferring, as befitted that brassy and totally American city, a homegrown soprano. He was to find such a soprano and lure her by any means necessary to the far coast to be the jewel in the crown, as it were. And he was pleased to announce to them, lifting his own Champagne goblet, that he had, this very evening, uncovered that jewel.

Geneva was silent, even as the loquacious and charming California attorney toasted her with his bottomless dark eyes. It was Blaine who relieved her of the necessity of asking, and his host the need to reply.

"Geneva? In the 'Wild West?' Hah! Unthinkable. Quite funny, actually. She's afraid of horses and cannot, I am quite certain, handle a six-shooter."

Blaine had consumed a quantity of the Champagne, thanks to McAllister's application. McAllister chuckled. It was a warm, indulgent sound that tickled the base of Geneva's spine like a teasing, caressing finger.

"I'm not much with a gun, myself," he remarked self-deprecatingly. "But San Francisco is civilized. Why, it's so civilized that there are almost as many politicians behind bars as there are bank robbers."

Geneva laughed, more at the tone McAllister had used than at his amusing remark. Suddenly the attorney was looking at her again with that direct, probing gaze, the like of which gentlemen in New York did not subject a lady. The laugh died in her throat. Overcome by a desire she knew was dangerous, she could neither find a remark nor avert her own stare from his.

"I am prepared to offer excellent conditions, Miss Lionwood," McAllister went on seriously. "Please say that you'll come."

Geneva prayed he could not detect how very much she wanted to. She felt a hard weight in the back of her throat as she gazed steadily into the dark, compelling eyes of R. Hastings McAllister. She swallowed.

Blaine Atherton, Earl of Trent and the key to Covent Garden, sat across the table with a studied look of utter boredom on his features, his eyes glazed and drooping from too much drink. How many more mistakes could she afford to make with men?

"I imagine—" she measured her words carefully, keeping her tone soft and even in spite of her inner tumult—"I would be even more valuable to San Francisco having conquered Covent Garden."

McAllister's brow rose. "Covent Garden?"

Geneva nodded, granting Blaine a fond glance. To her surprise, the peer registered alarm.

"Lord Atherton has arranged for my debut in London in November, haven't you, darling?" she announced, sipping the last of her Champagne.

"Damn it, Geneva!" Blaine snapped. "That was not for publication!"

"Why not?" Geneva was startled by his outburst.

Blaine, still scowling, sent a pointed glare in their host's direction. McAllister pursed his wide mouth, surveying his guests.

"With your permission, Miss Lionwood, Lord Atherton." He rose. "I will return shortly."

"How dare you, Geneva?" Blaine's voice was ugly and overloud. "I resent being placed in a position of—"

"Of what?" Geneva, furious, kept her own voice low. "Of being forced to acknowledge publicly what you so earnestly promised me in private? Debuts are seldom well-kept secrets, Blaine. How is it that the world is to be ignorant of my performance at Covent Garden?"

Blaine's angry expression became, to her disgust, one of confusion.

"No, don't answer, Lord Atherton." She stood up. "It is all too plain to me, now. How convenient it would have been for you, to set me up in the chorus at Covent Garden with the promise of things to come, while keeping me as a pet in a little house in St. John's Wood."

Conversation at adjoining tables had ceased, and Geneva felt the eyes of society upon them. Blaine seemed helpless, looking about himself like a wounded animal. Geneva drew herself up, contemptuous of his inability to form even a graceful lie for her.

"You are despicable, Blaine," she remarked through a smile. "And I don't know which is the greater: your vanity, or your stupidity."

Kieran Macalester, lately known as R. Hastings McAllister, watched the tableau with no small satisfaction from the archway of the Gentlemen's Grille. He was always pleased when his instincts were proven correct: Lord Atherton was a phony. Not taking his eyes from the regal figure in white that was the exiting Miss Lionwood, he handed the waiter one of Humble's hundred-dollar bills and aimed himself in the direction she had taken.

Predictably, it had begun to rain. Geneva stood under the canopy outside of Delmonico's and pulled her flimsy silk stole closely about her shoulders. A futile gesture, she realized bitterly. The garment offered precious little defense from a New York autumn night, and a rainy one at that. The doorman, in a warm topcoat of blue with gold braid, returned to his station, having safely ushered an elegant, if slightly tipsy, couple to a cab.

"Madam?" He addressed her, his features devoid of expression.

"I—I require a cab," she replied in an exasperatingly faint voice. Her scene with Blaine had left her weak and shaking, and more than a little upset. Her gremlin had apparently taken the evening off.

"May I see you home, Miss Lionwood?"

The warm baritone behind her belonged to none other than the intriguing California attorney. She wanted to take refuge in that voice.

"Yes, thank you, Mr. McAllister," she murmured. He gazed at her with a startling expression of tenderness. Through an odd trick of the light and shadow of objects behind him, he appeared to have a small pair of horns upon his head, very much like a gremlin or a devil, until he applied his top hat. Through her despair, she smiled at the sight.

"You are shivering," he reproved. "Here."

Before she could protest, he had removed his own cape and placed it about her. His hands lingered on her shoulders for a moment as she fastened the buttons about her neck. It was a gallant gesture that rendered her numb with gratitude. The garment smelled like the tailor shop from which it had, no doubt, recently come. It was heavy and warm, and it made her feel very safe.

The doorman readied the cab and Geneva climbed inside with the help of the solicitous attorney, who seated himself across from her. She knew, by the fall of the light, that he could see her face. But she could not see his.

"Your destination, sir?" the doorman prompted after a moment.

"Miss Lionwood?" McAllister's polite tone was respectful of her state.

"The Biltmore, please," she barely whispered, and McAllister relayed the same to the doorman, who nodded.

"Very good, sir."

He closed the door, and the cab lurched off.

"The Biltmore!" McAllister repeated, sounding pleased. "By some coincidence, my own destination as well."

Geneva said nothing. She breathed a sigh—a broken one. She had done it, after all. Three important men in her life, and, for one reason or another she had alienated each of them in the space of a day.

"Miss Lionwood, if I may." McAllister's smooth baritone broke the silence. "I take it there will be no debut at Covent Garden?"

Disappointment knifed her. She wished, desperately, to be alone. To cry, to rage, to scheme with her gremlin and to piece her career back together as best she could, without Blaine, as pitiful as he had proven to be, to champion her. Henry Abbey would never take her back. Mapleson had not dismissed her, but after *Don Giovanni* she knew that there would be little hope of his keeping her on for the rest of the season, even in the chorus, much less as an understudy. There remained only the courteous and charming, if mysterious, R. Hastings McAllister and his offer of San Francisco.

"No," she answered at the end of another long, deep sigh. "There will be no debut."

"I am sorry." He allowed a moment of silence out of respect, she assumed, for her devastation.

"However, may I hope that Covent Garden's loss will be San Francisco's gain?"

He was a shrewd one, this McAllister. Brassy. And persistent. Ordinarily, she admired such qualities in men, but tonight her heart was heavy with the thought of New York and London having trickled through her fingers like the very rainwater that beaded down the isinglass windows of the cab.

But what about San Francisco?

"It is unchivalrous of you to seek to take advantage of my late misfortunes, Mr. McAllister," she replied coolly, hoping he could not detect the devastation in her voice.

She heard him sigh. "You're right, of course," he allowed. "I'm not as patient as I might be. I beg your pardon."

McAllister was a refreshing change from the men in her life so far. He was polite without being obsequious. He was like an uncut gem. That was allowable, even desirable, in men from the West, she decided. Their refinement should always have some hard edges, like the Rocky Mountains compared with, say, the Adirondacks. Her poetic and topographical simile improved her spirits a little.

"My ill humor is not your doing," she remarked by way of forgiveness. "In fact, your bouquet was the highlight of my otherwise abysmal day."

He chuckled again. It was a rich, comforting sound, the verbal equivalent of the cape he had so gallantly offered to her. "You're alarmingly perceptive, Miss Lionwood. Or am I hopelessly transparent?"

She could not help smiling at the compliment. "As to that, Mr. McAllister," she responded, hoping to be mysterious, "only time will tell."

The cab jolted to a halt. They had reached the Biltmore. McAllister alit first and helped her down, holding onto her hand a moment longer than was needed. She did not object. She liked the feel of his hand, strong and sure. He did not wear gloves, and he did not apologize for that. It seemed as though he wanted to demonstrate his power, or at least to give a glimpse of it. She found herself searching his face for—what? He smiled at her, that wide, honest grin accented by deep, teasing clefts in each cheek.

"Tomorrow," she said, wanting to smile, herself, "*Don Giovanni* closes with the matinee. I'll give you my answer after that."

He seemed satisfied with her response. "May I take you to dinner, then?"

Brassy, she thought again with an unwanted shiver of excitement. Considering him, she feinted. "No, I have dinner in my rooms after matinees. But," she added, pulling her hand gently away from his, "you may join me there. Suite 20G."

With a graceful gesture, she removed his cape and handed it back to him. "Good evening, Mr. McAllister."

The doorman admitted her to the building. Kieran did not follow her. He was aware of a faint aroma about the cape Geneva Lionwood had lately worn: the scent of jasmine. He watched after her and presently heard a long, low whistle. The sound startled him until he realized that he had issued it.

New York City suited Kieran Macalester more than he would ever have guessed possible. He had arrived by train four days earlier, having spent nearly that long in transit. He'd used his time wisely, however, studying the books on opera he had borrowed from Garland Humble. He'd poured over New York newspapers as well. They fed an eager public reports of the greater and lesser doings of opera's personalities.

It had been ridiculously easy to pinpoint Geneva Lionwood's whereabouts, and subsequently to formulate a plan to insinuate himself into her company. He had, with little trouble, procured several fine forgeries, among them a letter of introduction to Colonel Mapleson from a member of the Beekman family (in Europe and unavailable for confirmation). With it, he gained entrance to the Beekman box at the Academy of Music to experience for himself what he had only read about.

Geneva Lionwood was everything Humble had represented, and more. For once, the spider had not exaggerated. She was lovely beyond any faded old tintype, beyond anything Kieran could imagine. But more than that, she possessed a vulnerable quality that had reached right into his chest and wound itself tightly about his heart from the first moment her gaze met his.

She was a living, breathing catastrophe waiting to happen to him.

"Sir?" the cab driver interrupted his thoughts.

Kieran pulled at the end of his black silk bowtie until the accessory hung in two black strands from his collar. Geneva Lionwood Humble was also no fool. There was a reason for her postponement of an answer to R. Hastings McAllister regarding the San Francisco venture: He was certain she intended to check his story. He patted his breast pocket, where he kept Humble's letter, listening for the reassuring sound of crinkling paper. It was there, as always.

"Fifty dollars in gold," he said to the driver, without looking at him. "You take me wherever I need to go, you don't ask questions and you never saw me before in your life."

"Yes, sir!" The driver was enthusiastic. "Where to?"

"The nearest telegraph office," he replied, climbing in again.

"But isn't there one inside the ho—"

"Is that a question?

"No, sir."

And the cab rolled off into the waning night.

Chapter Six

Macalester's work kept him busy until nearly mid-morning, when at last he retired to his rooms at the Biltmore. He intended to peruse some additional literature on opera that he had acquired—anything to take his mind off of the captivating soprano—and to catch a short nap before attending Geneva's matinee performance, but his body had other plans for him. Overcome by weariness from his late-night missions as well as four previous days of much work and little rest, it was not hard, as the words on the pages before him blurred, to succumb to the overwhelming temptation of sleep.

He awoke abruptly to the sound of knocking and he started in his chair. The open book on his lap fell to the floor with a thud, and for an uneasy moment, he did not remember where he was.

A second round of knocking made him aware, in the pale gray light of dusk, that he was in his suite at the Biltmore. Instinctively, he felt at his breast pocket for the letter, Humble's letter to the governor, petitioning amnesty for himself and Billy. He knew an instant of terror when he realized it wasn't there.

Damn!

He stood up so quickly that he upset his chair, and it wasn't a small chair. His eyes focused on the coat that fell as the chair toppled. A long white envelope slid half out of the inside breast pocket.

The letter.

Relief made him weak.

"Western Union, Mr. McAllister," a brisk, young, male voice paged him from the hall with the third round of knocks.

What time was it? Groggily, Mac stumbled to the door, rubbing his eyes with the heels of his hands. Wordlessly, he opened it to an annoyingly fresh-faced young man in a crisp gray uniform and cap. He signed for the man's offering and fished in the pockets of his rumpled pants for a tip. If the messenger wondered why he was half-dressed in evening clothes, which by this time hung about him like rumpled old sacks, he did not ask. He merely thanked him, and Mac closed the door again, lighting a lamp before opening the note.

"Set up dummy office San Francisco Opera and Light Theater Company immediately Stop Purpose to confirm R Hastings McAllister as representative seeking soprano to curious party GL Stop Do it and don't ask questions Stop Reply"

That had been his message to Garland Humble in Fort Worth in the small hours of the morning. Humble surely had the contacts and the resources to accomplish such a deed. If he did not, well, procuring his wife would be more difficult. More difficult, but not, Macalester was certain, impossible. He read on.

"Done Stop Better be worth it you SOB Stop"

He grinned. That, he supposed, would depend entirely upon the value Garland Humble placed upon his very charming wife.

The mother-in-law clock on the mantle chimed the quarter hour.

Six-fifteen.

Damn! Dinner with Geneva! He had forgotten. He quickly fed the telegram into the lamp, watching it combust into a brief, bright flame. Regrettably, he had no time to bathe and, having slept in his evening clothes, he would have to settle for one of the two additional new suits Garland Humble's expense money had provided. He washed, shaved and changed in fifteen minutes, then decided that a further delay to the hotel florist in the lobby might be worth the extra time. It was only money. And Garland Humble's money, at that. Certainly, he'd buy the largest bouquet he could carry.

Geneva ignored all of Blaine's notes, which had been arriving with flowers and chocolates and even a diamond hat pin since before breakfast. The humiliation she had suffered at his hands at Delmonico's before McAllister, a complete stranger, was more than her ambivalent personal feelings for the English lord could endure. She shunned his repeated attempts to see her, both in her rooms and at the Academy, in favor of her personal mission to verify the mysterious R. Hastings McAllister's credentials and offer.

Indeed, McAllister's offer was looking better and better with the passage of time. The telegram awaiting her in her dressing room after the matinee was a positive response to her query sent earlier. Mapleson's personal assistant at the Academy and Audrey Stancil had confirmed the arrival the day before of a tall, ruggedly handsome man bearing credentials that had impressed even the colonel, a man who, aware of his own importance, did not impress easily.

And Geneva was tired. Since her arrival in New York more than two years before, she had worked and studied, had trusted and been betrayed, had been promised and been denied more times than she could count. It was not her abilities that held her back, she realized: It was merely her tragic flaw to have been born and raised on the wrong side of the Atlantic Ocean.

The opera world was crammed with singers less talented and less musical than she, but because their names were Patti or Calve or Nilsson or Sembrich or Campanini or LaBlache, they were embraced by an American public starved for a link to the Continent. It was all so very discouraging.

She sighed, rifling her closet for something suitable to wear while entertaining a strange man in her rooms for dinner. The blue? No, too dull. The red? Too flamboyant.

She might, had she been born to money or to a family with wisdom greater than her mother and father displayed, have had the immeasurable benefit of European training to recommend her. But as it was, she had only her looks, her voice, her nearly photographic memory and her God-given ability as a musician.

And these assets had not been enough to gain her what she so desperately craved.

In San Francisco, though, she might at last have an audience. After so much time and so many disappointments, she didn't dare allow herself to hope too much. And this shrewd attorney, old enough to know the way of the world yet still young enough to enjoy it, might very well hold the answer to her future. But she would have to be canny, play her cards close to her breast.

Geneva smiled to herself, passing her hand over the dresses, selecting her green velvet dressing gown with gold braid at the collar and sleeves. It was magnificent and careless, and always made her feel regal and sensuous. Slipping her arms into its sleeves, she was invigorated, even anticipating the challenge before her. Her money was running out. Blaine's support would cease, and she had no prospect of legitimate work on the opera stage in New York for the remainder of the season. But she must not allow Mr. McAllister to suspect any of this: It might lessen her desirability to San Francisco, and it would certainly weaken her bargaining position.

She allowed McAllister to wait for several minutes after his knock without even calling out in answer. She examined her reflection in the full mirror critically, hesitating only a moment before unbuttoning the collar at her throat, then another moment to release her chestnut hair from its severe pinnings. McAllister, she knew instinctively, found her attractive. Let him be as distracted as possible as they discussed their business. Caveat emptor.

She opened the door. As it had last night, McAllister's sheer animal magnetism struck her like a tidal wave. He had not the least look of impatience or uncertainty about him. How she envied his confidence!

"You are late, Mr. McAllister," she greeted him, watching his eyes as she ushered him into her foyer with a graceful sweep of a green velvet sleeve. "Dinner is cold."

He offered her a ridiculously huge array of botanical wonders. His eyes, dark, penetrating yet impenetrable, yielded nothing but mild amusement at her rebuke.

"But not the company, I hope?" was the bold reply that passed for an apology.

She found herself smiling at him as she relieved him of his floral offering. She reigned herself in; she could not afford the luxury of so dangerous an attraction. Not yet, at least.

"Do come in," she went on obliquely, leading the way

into the parlor, where a cart set with white damask and silver-domed dishes waited like an idle but patient lover. "Sit down and pour the wine. I must find a vase for these. Or perhaps a bucket."

Men, she had learned early, tended to follow simple, direct instructions when these orders were properly issued. Her practiced delivery was neither overbearing nor cajoling, and she was pleased to note, upon her return, that McAllister had, indeed, seated himself at the portable table and poured two goblets of the ruby beverage. He began to rise as she approached, but she waved him back, seating herself across from him, brushing her long, wavy hair from her neck with a quick gesture designed to attract attention without appearing obvious.

"Your business detained you, and kept you from the matinee," she intoned, watching him.

He pressed his lips together in what she took to be a shamed expression. It was far more attractive than any such look had a right to be.

"Unfortunately, yes," he lamented. "I missed your performance. But I hope I'll have many more opportunities soon, in San Francisco."

He lifted his glass in tribute, obliging her to do the same. She did not drink, though, but stared into the bowl of the goblet.

"Mr. McAllister, your persistence is most disarming," she observed, setting her wineglass back upon the table. "You leave me with the distinct impression that you won't accept 'no' for an answer."

McAllister's sensuous mouth widened to a smile.

"Miss Lionwood, I assure you that if you make it necessary, I'll carry you off bodily."

An interesting thought.

"Let us hope that will not be necessary," she murmured, uncovering the dishes so that she did not have to meet his disconcerting, bright-eyed gaze. "I do hope you like pheasant."

During dinner, McAllister outlined to her, in an unhurried fashion, the terms he was authorized to lay before her. She very nearly choked on her biscuit when he named the figure: one thousand dollars a week during the season, which ran from October through April. Combined with a suite in the Hotel San Francisco and five months out of the year to travel and to study, it was a queenly ransom. She removed her hands from view, clenching them as tightly as she could under cover of the table.

"A persuasive offer," she congratulated him, managing her tone. "And a generous one. May I suggest, however, that monetary compensation alone is not what attracts an artist to a situation such as yours?"

She was very aware of the many implications of her question, and she was curious to see how he would respond to them. She arranged her features into a carefully bland expression and watched him toy with the stem of his empty wineglass, his generous mouth slack and his dark eyes thoughtful.

"I take it you refer to artistic discretion," he said smoothly. "Word your addendum any way you like, and we can debate the particulars at a later time. Does that answer your concern?"

How very neatly he handled that, she thought, conscious of a twinge of admiration. He had left the innuendo entirely up to her without denying his own interest. She smiled.

"Admirably," she replied. "Now there remains the matter of my relocation to San Francis—"

She was interrupted by his indulgent laughter. Her cheeks, maddeningly, grew warm.

"You are delightful, Miss Lionwood," he declared, his eyes twinkling. "Naturally, we'll handle all of the arrangements. And," he added, his gaze seeming to penetrate her very soul, "I would consider it an honor and a privilege to escort you personally."

Her heart, ever rebellious, fluttered. She swallowed hard and looked away from him. "That—that won't be necessary." She toyed with her spoon.

He cleared his throat. "Will your sponsor be traveling with you?" His inquiry was quiet, as though he was concerned that someone might overhear.

How discreet he was! Of course, he was referring to Blaine.

"No." She examined the shell pattern on the silver. "He and I are . . ."

What was it about R. Hastings McAllister that made her want to tell him everything?

"I made my way from New York to New Orleans and back again; I'm sure I can find my way to San Francisco with little trouble," she wound up, hoping he would not pursue the subject of Blaine Atherton further.

"But Miss Lionwood." Suddenly his hand was on hers, warm and strong. "I insist."

His gentle, quiet tone compelled her gaze to his.

"San Francisco is civilized enough." He went on as though he had not marked her sudden confusion. "But there're some pretty rough territories between the Mississippi and the Pacific. I feel personally responsible for your safety until I deliver you."

Geneva's heart fluttered at the sound of that, but she nevertheless felt obliged to protest.

"But surely on the train—"

"There are train robbers," he remarked, settling back in his chair as he considered her.

She laughed. "I should like to meet one. I find it hard to imagine that a handful of men could intimidate a whole trainload of people."

McAllister's grin was enigmatic. "I daresay one would

69

think twice before trying to intimidate you, Miss Lionwood," he murmured, shaking his head. "But you would be amazed."

She was intrigued. "Have you ever witnessed a train robbery?" She realized that she would be surprised if he responded in the negative.

He hesitated over his answer. "Yes," he said at last, cupping his hands before his mouth in a gesture approximating prayer. "A long time ago. I—"

He was interrupted by a loud, sharp knock upon the door. Geneva's face grew warm, and she prevented herself from uttering an unladylike expletive.

"Excuse me," she muttered, rising.

If it was Blaine, she would kill him.

It was. And worse: He had been drinking.

"Geneva!" he bellowed beyond the door. "Damn you, let me in!"

"Go away, Blaine!" she whispered through the door, mortified.

"Go to hell, Geneva!" he shouted back. "I pay for this bloody room. If I want to shout, I'll bloody well shout! Open the door!"

There was a warm rush of air, a ripple of power. McAllister was beside her. "Would you like me to—"

"I'll handle this!" She interrupted his whisper fiercely, unable to look at him. "This is my affair."

"Who's in there with you?" Blaine demanded, and the doorknob rattled as if tested by a ghost.

"Blaine, I am not opening the door. I have nothing to say to—"

"It's McAllister, isn't it?" he bellowed. Geneva closed her eyes. She might have expected Blaine to behave badly. San Francisco Opera and Light Theater Company stood inches away from her, and Blaine Atherton was stomping all over it with hobnailed boots. Tears stung her eyes.

Damn it, not now! she thought, feeling a sob of despair rise in her throat. *Not tears, in front of McAllister!*

"Geneva, you bloody trollop! You'd better—"

"Excuse me, Miss Lionwood." McAllister gently moved her aside. Geneva could not even protest as he opened the door.

Blaine was a mess. His collar was open and his ascot loose. His shirtfront was stained and wrinkled, and his small gray eyes were red-rimmed and puffy. Were she not so furious with him, she might even feel sorry for him.

"Let's take a walk, Atherton." McAllister's baritone was soft and conciliatory as he clapped a heavy arm about the shorter man's shoulder.

Blaine wrenched himself clumsily away from the younger man's grip.

"Take your hands off of me!" he demanded. "And it's 'Lord Atherton' to you!"

Blaine started back to Geneva's door, but McAllister kept his hand on his shoulder.

"I wouldn't." The attorney's tone was light, but faintly warning.

"I wouldn't' be damned to you, you bloody whoring Yankee bastard!" Blaine fairly spat.

"This—" McAllister's baritone was almost pleasant— "is how we bloody whoring Yankee bastards handle rude drunks."

With that, he dealt the peer an efficient blow to the side of the head with his fist, rendering him instantly unconscious. Geneva watched in wonder as McAllister caught the slumping figure of Blaine Atherton and hoisted him upon his shoulder with astonishing ease, like an oversized sack of produce.

"I'll put him in a cab and send him around the park a few times." McAllister was laconic. "When he comes to, he'll have quite a headache, but he probably won't remember any of this."

Geneva nodded mutely, unable to meet McAllister's pitying gaze.

"I think it best if we leave New York as quickly as possible," he went on in a gentler tone, a tone that made her feel like crying again. "My business here is finished, and if you can be ready tom—"

"I can be ready by morning." She made her voice hard to mask her emotions, but it shook once, and she suspected that McAllister was not fooled. "Early. I'd like to leave as soon as possible."

McAllister was silent.

"I'm sorry about all of this," he said finally in a husky voice. "But I enjoyed our evening. I look forward to many more. I'll make the arrangements, and we'll discuss them at breakfast. Say, eight o'clock?"

"Seven would be better." Her eyes stung. She wished he would take Blaine and leave. She couldn't hold back much longer.

"Seven, then." McAllister's voice was soft as a kiss, the kiss she might have had, if Blaine hadn't interrupted. Disappointment joined her other emotions. The gremlin would have a feast tonight.

She nodded quickly, still unwilling to look at McAllister, unwilling to see the dissolute lump of humanity that was Blaine Atherton dangling down McAllister's broad back like a bulky black shawl. She did not wait for McAllister to carry him away, or even for a "good-night." She escaped behind her door as quickly and quietly as she could, closing and locking it behind her. Finally, she allowed herself the dubious luxury of a flow of unrestrained tears.

Macalester lost no time depositing his burden into a cab. It was nearly ten o'clock; he had much to do. But the evening had taken its toll on him, as well. He rejected the idea of starting the departure arrangements right away. He felt as though he needed to lie down.

His room was dark. He lit a single lamp, unable to shake off a growing turmoil in his stomach. Dinner had gone so well. Better, even, than he had hoped. He had talked Geneva Lionwood into his trap so neatly that it had seemed almost too easy. Given her seductive behavior, he might even have talked her into bed, unless she talked him into it first. Atherton's untimely interruption could not have upset him so much as to unsettle his stomach. Or perhaps it was something else.

After checking his pocket once again, he pulled off his tie and removed his coat, dropping both carelessly onto a chair. He closed his eyes, hoping to clear his brain, but saw only the distressingly lovely Geneva Lionwood Humble, her dark hair loose about her white neck, her dusky green eyes regarding him with a keen and sensuous intellect . . .

He felt hot. He opened his eyes again, aware that he was breathing hard. His mouth watered, and he swallowed a lump in his throat. He brushed his arm across his forehead; he was sweating. He went to his washbasin and turned on the water. The sound of it rushing into the bowl was cooling and soothing. He looked up into the mirror before him at the man who had just engineered, brilliantly, a monumental deception that would alter at least one innocent life forever.

He could not fight it any longer. Gripping the edges of the basin, he vomited.

Chapter Seven

The logical route to San Francisco would of course have been New York to Philadelphia to Chicago on the Pennsylvania Railroad, then the Central Pacific for the remainder of the trip. But Macalester was not going to San Francisco. He was taking Geneva Lionwood, without her knowledge or consent, to Fort Worth, Texas.

The next lie in this elaborate scheme was to convince Humble's wife that he had urgent business in Memphis before they could continue to the coast. In the two days it would take to reach Memphis, he was sure he could devise further lies that would get them pleasantly by train to Little Rock. After that, he could lie no more. She would surely be suspicious, being so close to the home of her estranged husband, and might even try escaping from him. No, the train to Fort Worth was out of the question. The last leg of the journey would have to be undertaken by wagon or on horseback, probably under very unpleasant circumstances.

He pretended to read his newspaper and willed his stomach to stop churning. Unlike Billy's capricious digestive system, which seemed to recover instantly, his own had not stopped nagging him since the night before, when he had acknowledged his monstrous deed to himself. Across from him in the roomy first-class compartment sat the serene and trusting Geneva Lionwood, in a mauve traveling suit complete with parasol, picture-frame millinery and bone-colored kid gloves and shoes. She was reading a musical score, her face rapt with attention as her bewitching emerald eyes scanned the pages before her.

Two days. Two days he had known her, and he had foolishly—stupidly—allowed himself to develop feelings for the woman. How had it happened? And when? Could it have been at Delmonico's, when she had boldly answered his challenge regarding the rival soprano? Or perhaps it had been later, when she'd accepted his cloak in the rain, wearing a woeful, waiflike expression that tugged upon his heart. Or maybe it had only been the night before, during their tantalizing verbal foreplay . . .

Macalester shook his head hard. He had to admit to himself that his charade had been challenging, and yes, fun, but had at last become so real to him that he had to catch himself, every once in a while, and remind himself that they were not going to San Francisco. That he was not the emissary of the San Francisco Opera and Light Theater Company, and he was not here to make Geneva Lionwood the toast of the coast.

He was the very worst thing that could happen to this woman. He literally had to shake himself and force himself to recall that she was Garland Humble's wife, that he was returning her to her husband, and that Billy Deal's future depended on his not forgetting these things.

75

He sighed involuntarily. She looked up at him and he realized, abashed, that he had not even known that he had been staring at her. Her perceptive gaze sent a shiver along his spine.

"You're very quiet, Mr. McAllister," she observed in her soft, melodious voice. "And I doubt you've said a dozen words to me since we left New York this morning. Is anything troubling you?"

They had just pulled out of Pennsylvania Station in Philadelphia, where they had changed trains. Macalester had acquired the newspaper that now rested, open, upon his lap. He managed a smile in the face of those treacherously lovely verdant eyes and shook his head.

"No." He breathed deeply, searching for a lie that was not too far from the truth. "I think I'm just tired." His celebrated silver tongue needed a serious polishing, if that was the best he could do.

"Why do you do that?"

He was startled. "Do what?"

"Pat your lapel that way." She demonstrated with gloved fingers on her breast.

He felt his face heat. She'd caught him checking for Humble's letter, probably more than once. She was too canny. Or he was becoming careless.

"I—no reason," he hedged. "A habit, I suppose. Why? Does it bother you?" If he put her on the defensive, she might change the subject, or at least give him an answer that would give him more time to think up a plausible lie.

"No," she replied, but the look in her green eyes told him she'd thought about it more than once. Damn. "I thought you kept the train tickets there, or perhaps some money pinned to the inside of your coat. Many people do that, in the city."

"Oh?" Keep her talking. Obviously, she liked to talk. What woman didn't?

"They're afraid of pickpockets," she informed him. "You don't strike me as being a man who would fear such things, though."

"I don't?" He couldn't help being amused. "What kind of man do I strike you as?"

She gave him an innocently flirtatious look that sent a bolt of heat lightning down his spine. "A man with secrets," she said without hesitation.

He resisted an odd and dangerous urge to touch his pocket again, resolving not to be so obvious about it in the future. He tried to laugh. Her expression did not change. "A man who's tired." He repeated his earlier excuse and hoped he was more convincing than before. "I've been traveling for a long time, and I'm anxious to get back."

"Have you a sweetheart waiting for you? Or a wife? You never said," she murmured, with a most fetching droop of her eyelashes.

"Neither," he replied, then could have choked on his tongue. If he'd said yes, a wife and several fine, fat children, he might have discouraged her attention and given himself another lie upon which to focus. But it was too late. He had, with one unguarded response, removed all barriers to her affection, with the one huge exception of the fact that he knew her to be the wife of another man.

To his dismay, she laughed. "Why, Mr. McAllister! You're blushing!"

Maddeningly, his tarnished silver tongue cleaved to his mouth. He could not answer her, nor did she release him from her probing gaze. Finally, he thought of something to say that might give her cause for reflection.

"Perhaps I've been waiting for you," he said slowly, aware that there was more truth to those words than to any others he had yet spoken to her.

"You're teasing me." Her laughter was musical, but brittle.

He did not answer, except to shrug.

She quickly looked away from him into her lap. If she was aware of the appealing nature of her response, she gave no sign of it. Macalester, watching her, felt his stomach tighten into a knot once again. It was going to be a long trip to Little Rock.

Mr. McAllister was a bewildering gentleman, Geneva reflected. They were speeding southwest through the darkness toward Roanoke, and she had been unable to engage him in any conversation for more than half a dozen sentences. He seemed reluctant to talk about himself and politely uninterested in topics she introduced. She had taken his earlier remark as a jest, or possibly a remonstrance for her bold curiosity, but now she was completely at sea. The idea that he might, indeed, have been flirting with her was an intriguing one. Still, men had flirted with her in the past; men like Blaine Atherton . . .

Blaine. His very name made her grimace. All of that time, wasted. All of his promises empty as eggshells, and just as brittle. McAllister, she was sure, was not like that. She did not know why, exactly; she just felt it. If only there were some way to break through the barrier he had constructed! But perhaps there was.

Geneva Lionwood developed a mysterious illness somewhere between Philadelphia and Roanoke. She tried to hide it, but when she collapsed to the floor of the compartment five minutes before the train pulled into Roanoke, Macalester knew he had to get her off of the train. She needed a doctor, and a proper bed.

He collared a conductor and arranged to have their baggage taken off. There was no telling how long Geneva's condition would necessitate a delay, but it was best to assume the worst. As the train came to a stop, he left her lying upon the bench in the compartment while he arranged for a cab. A light rain was falling, but it was not cold. Returning to the compartment, Macalester found that Geneva, flushed and disoriented, was trying to get up.

"What—what is happening?" she murmured, sounding weak and alarmed.

He knelt beside her, pressing his hand against her hot cheek.

"We're in Roanoke," he replied, trying not to sound too concerned. "We're going to get you to a hotel. You need a doctor."

"Oh . . . I don't want to be the cause of a delay—"

"Shh." He quieted her protest, lifting her into his arms. She was so light, she was no burden at all. "It's all right. It's all right . . ."

Poor brave thing, he thought, fighting a knot in his chest. *She's even trying to smile.*

The doctor concluded his examination, his gray whiskers twitching into a frown. He removed his spectacles and crossed his arms before him, regarding his patient doubtfully.

"What is it, Doctor?" Macalester demanded, just above a whisper. He had watched the man for a quarter of an hour, poking, palpating, thumping and listening to Geneva, and the man had uttered nothing more than a few terse questions. Now he merely stood beside the canopy bed in the largest suite in the most expensive hotel in Roanoke, shaking his graying head over the motionless female form on the bed before him.

Suddenly, the doctor gave him a direct, unsettling look. "She could be in a family way."

Macalester nearly fell down. "No, she—"

What did he know? She could be, he supposed, although the notion that Geneva Lionwood might be carrying that phony English lord's child wasn't a pleasant one, on several counts. Humble wouldn't be happy about it, for one thing.

Chagrined, he realized the doctor was waiting for him to finish his sentence.

"I suppose she might be," he allowed at last. "But I doubt it."

He couldn't figure why the doctor gave him such a queer look. It was hardly reassuring.

"You do, huh? Well, then, I'd say exhaustion." His refined Virginia drawl was not convincing. "Dehydration. She seems healthy enough, otherwise. Unless there's something I can't detect."

His voice trailed off. Macalester grimaced. He had scant respect for the medical profession anyway, and this man's clumsy diagnosis only served to confirm his disdain.

"Can't you give her something?" he persisted, watching Geneva's shallow, uneven breaths. "A tonic, or—or something?"

The doctor glanced at him. "I'd rather not," he said, shaking his head again. "Not tonight, at least. Watch her tonight. Get her whatever she wants to eat. Make sure she drinks plenty of fluids: tea, consomme, whatever. If she's no better when I check back in the morning, perhaps we'll have to take her into the hospital."

The hospital!

"Has your wife ever had a spell like this before?"

It was a long moment before Macalester realized, abashed, that the doctor was addressing him. "She—" he began, then hesitated. "Not that I'm aware of," he finished, uncomfortable. He had registered them merely as McAllister, even though he had secured a room for himself adjoining the suite. He was beginning to sense, to his dismay, that he was slowly losing con-

80

trol of this very tenuous situation, and he had no idea how to regain it.

He straightened, rallying. Geneva was sick, that was all. It would pass. And what if this obscure country physician did think she was his wife? In a day or two at most, they would be on the train again bound for Memphis. That is, if Geneva recovered sufficiently.

If she recovered.

He helped the doctor into his coat.

"If she takes a turn for the worse, drive her right over to the hospital and have them summon me. And don't worry, Mr. McAllister." The doctor smiled at him, clasping his hand. "I'm sure she'll be just fine."

Macalester realized, annoyed, that his concern must have been evident on his face. He withdrew his hand abruptly from the doctor's and led him to the door, thanking him as politely as he could. Relieved to be alone again, he returned his attention to Geneva Lionwood, who was trying to sit up.

He was by her in an instant, taking hold of the hands with which she had begun fumbling with the fastenings of her jacket. They felt cooler, but she still seemed weak as a kitten.

"Too warm," she murmured, regarding him through half-closed eyelids. "Can't breathe."

His fingers turned to lead. He would have to undress her himself. He muttered a brief curse under his breath and, the room having become suddenly quite warm, he removed his own jacket and tossed it onto a chair near the bed. She lay perfectly still as he worked the fastenings of her jacket. That accomplished, he paused, looking down at her, utterly confounded as to what to do next.

The only women he'd ever undressed before were whores, but whores never wore much anyway. Geneva's frilly ivory blouse completely baffled him, with its rows of pleats and folds, long, straight lines of covered buttons and impossibly tiny loops. Suddenly her hand was on his, warm and gentle. He looked up and found her regarding him with sleepy serenity. His legs turned to jelly.

"You are so kind, Mr. McAllister," she said, barely above a whisper. "And I am such a bother!"

She sat up weakly with his help, slipping her arms from the jacket. With astonishingly deft movements, she undid her blouse. He helped her to lift the voluminous garment over her head, willing himself not to think as she lay back against the pillows like some mythical goddess in her charming corset and snow-white chemise. She stretched her lithe, bare arms above her head with a small sigh that sent a surge of hot metal through his core. Damn, he thought uneasily, finding the fastenings of her skirt and petticoat. Both yielded without a struggle along her nicely rounded hips, revealing shapely, silk-stockinged legs. It required all of his will to prevent himself from stroking those long, shapely limbs, and they continued to distract him as he unbuttoned and removed her shoes.

The tight shoes made him think of something else.

"Guess you'd better—uh—loosen up that—uh—"

Lord, he was tongue-tied as a boy, and he couldn't look up.

"Oh, that's so sweet of you!" she said with a weak little sigh. "Would you? Please?"

Oh, Lord. He couldn't. Not without—

Billy. Prison. Twenty years hard labor.

If she wondered why he performed his task so quickly, and maybe a little roughly, she didn't ask. He got to his feet and gathered her things into a bundle. She smiled drowsily, easing onto her side.

"Mr. McAllister," she pronounced in a soft, inviting tone, "however can I repay you?"

82

Kieran discovered, to his alarm, that he could not move. He could not even breathe. He wanted her so badly that if he dared to react to her question, or even to blink, he would be there with her on that big, wide bed, completing the job of undressing her, with far less caution and care than when he had begun. That chemise would be a memory, those stockings and pantalets shreds. A hair's breadth stood between him and his desire; any movement would make her his.

Garland Humble's image played before him suddenly like a taunting court jester: *I want to be sure you don't forget your job when she bats her eyelashes at you.*

Kieran closed his eyes. *Damn Garland Humble.*

"I'll get you some tea," he managed, turning away from her. It was only four or five steps to the door, and he congratulated himself that he negotiated the distance in a cool, unhurried gait. Once outside, however, he closed the door and leaned his entire weight against it to keep her dangerous allure trapped behind it. Sweat crawled down the small of his back, and he heard his heart pounding in his ears like a loud warning.

The time had come and passed. There was no point in Geneva belaboring her feigned illness in Roanoke. By morning, she made a miraculous recovery and was pronounced healthy and fit by the doctor, who seemed to want full credit. By noon, they were back on a southbound train heading for Memphis.

Geneva was disappointed at, but not discouraged by, the ultimate failure of her first plan. It had been so easy to persuade McAllister that she was ill on the train. He had fallen into her carefully laid trap like a felled oak, hard and heavy. It was a glorious sensation, to realize that she possessed that kind of power over people in general and men in particular. McAllister, prepossessed and remote, was an especially satisfying conquest and, having achieved her aim of spending the night in a hotel instead of on the train, she had thought the rest—the seduction—would be a mere formality, if necessary at all.

But McAllister had, at last, eluded her snare, or perhaps she had played her earlier part too well. Indeed, McAllister remained by her bedside throughout the night, as far as she knew. She had grown tired of watching him watch her from the chair across the room, his long legs spread out before him and his hands crossed upon his expansive chest. She had fallen asleep, the covers drawn up to her chin thanks to McAllister. And when she had awakened to the bright morning sunshine streaming through her windows, he was still there, snoring softly, in exactly the same pose.

She was undeniably disappointed, but touched at the same time. He seemed to have no expectations of her, and she found that refreshing. Men had always wanted something from her, often in return for very little. But McAllister had merely handed her San Francisco in a jewel-encrusted chalice and offered himself as escort. How very perverse, she thought with some wry amusement, that she should at last meet a man who attracted and intrigued her so much as to want to make love with him, and find that she was obliged to virtually force him into the situation!

Well, she mused, holding her cards close to her breast, tomorrow would be another day. And tomorrow. And tomorrow. Buoyed by the thought of imminent triumph, she played her cards with a flourish.

"Rummy," she pronounced gleefully, relishing McAllister's look of rueful amusement. He threw in his cards and leaned back against his seat, rubbing the back of his neck with one hand.

"Let's play something else," he declared, grinning at her. "I don't like losing."

The sun was setting on the Tennessee River Valley. Geneva collected the cards with her gloved hands, smiling to herself.

"I never met a man who did," she felt obliged to remark.

Her escort chuckled.

"Oh? And what about women?"

She sat back in her own seat, folding her arms before her. He regarded her expectantly. She liked the expression.

"Women are accustomed to losing," she began, shuffling the cards for another hand. "We don't like it, but at least we are prepared for it. We can cope with it. And every time we lose, we learn something. What does one learn from winning all of the time? Merely that one enjoys winning. Being able to accept the disappointment of losing makes the joy of winning all the sweeter."

"You sound as though you speak from experience."

She sighed. *How little you know of me,* she thought.

"My mother was a vaudeville actress, Mr. McAllister," she said, looking out of the window, determined to keep this brief and unsentimental. "My father, a piano player in a saloon. I learned from both of them how to lose. But winning . . . that was something I had to teach myself. Shall we play some poker?"

Macalester's luck was decidedly better at poker, although the graceful soprano was capable of holding her own. He amused himself, and his lovely companion, by spinning tales of San Francisco far into the night. He and Billy had traveled through the town several times, so it wasn't hard for him to turn one of the most elegant fancy houses he'd ever seen into an opera house nearly as grand as New York's Academy of Music. Her questions were broad enough to be satisfied by his sketchy responses, and when they became too specific, he shrugged them off with the excuse that he was just an attorney—an agent for the facility and not involved with the artistic aspects.

The conversation was therapeutic for him. It kept his mind off of things he preferred not to think about as well as those about which he was forbidden to think. As the night wore on, the conversation gradually lapsed into the peaceful silence of sleep.

By evening of the following day, they arrived in Memphis. Geneva hadn't mentioned his "odd little habit" again; Macalester had taken pains to break himself of it. Now, he scarcely remembered to check for the important letter at all, except in private, but as it was still there every time he did, he decided he'd been behaving like a worried old grandmother about it.

Macalester planned to spend the night there in the comfort of a hotel, and to make the last leg of their train journey to Little Rock the following afternoon. It was his intention to deposit Geneva Lionwood at the hotel with the excuse that he had business to conduct and arrangements to make. He did not trust himself to spend too much time alone with her under circumstances that might lead to a compromise of his loyalties, if not of Mrs. Humble herself. On the train, he was largely safe from opportunity, if not temptation. And it would do neither of them good to become involved: she would hate him when she at last discovered, as she must, the true nature of his mission.

The Memphis station was busier than Roanoke's had been, but not nearly so chaotic as Philadelphia's Pennsylvania Station. Macalester took Geneva by the arm, guiding her through the crowd to a bench near the cab stands.

"I'm going to arrange for your luggage to be held here at the station until we depart," he explained, gesturing for her to sit. "I want you to—"

"Macalester!"

It was so distant that at first, he was not even certain he had heard it. Geneva stared at him expectantly. Had she heard it, too?

"Macalester!"

This time, it was louder. Closer. Geneva looked beyond him. His mouth going dry, Macalester straightened and looked about, but he could see no one he knew among the crowd. He resisted the overwhelming urge to lead Geneva quickly out of the train station, electing to rely on his ability to handle whomever might be calling him without giving himself or his mission away.

"Howdy, Macalester." The voice, reedy and low, was at his shoulder. He still could not place it, although it was distressingly familiar. "Travelin' in better comp'ny these days, I see."

Macalester caught his breath, realizing at last who was standing beside him. His heart sank into his fancy dress boots as he turned to meet the steady, measuring gaze of the enemy.

Chapter Eight

Lennox, the only name by which the bounty hunter was known, was tall and rangy and smelled of buffalo and buckskin in spite of his new-looking mail-order suit. His hair, no particular shade of brown, was literally waxed to his head like the ends of his long mustache, which drooped on either side of his hollow, stubbly cheeks like the tails of a couple of dead rats. His eyes, a kind of golden brown often found in half-breeds, did not blink as he regarded Macalester without smiling.

Macalester felt as if he'd just been hamstrung and trussed like a prize turkey.

"Out of your grazing territory, aren't you, Lennox?" He purposely ignored the man's remark.

Lennox merely shrugged, accentuating the ill fit of his cheaply made coat. "No more'n you, I guess."

Lennox glanced at Geneva a few feet away and nodded to her. "This your wife?"

"This is none of your damned business," Macalester

warned him in a low tone. "We're a long way from home, Lennox, both of us. Don't even think about it."

"Got some business of my own." Lennox, unaffected by Macalester's threatening manner, spat a stream of tobacco juice. It landed on the platform and splashed onto the shoes of a lady who had passed too close. Macalester looked up from the shoes at a macabre funeral procession: a plain pine coffin strapped upright to a creaking dolly, pulled by a Negro porter. The parade passed before him, close enough to touch.

"Billings," Lennox volunteered in response to Macalester's unvoiced question, and the latter could smell the reek of the wiry man's chaw. "He got careless in Abilene. Like you did, in Wichita. Only you're still alive, and Billings here is gonna eat worms."

Billings. Sam Billings. A likable fellow whom Macalester and Deal had come across a few times, wanted in Tennessee for shooting the carpetbagger who had run his family off of their own land after the war. They used to joke about the five-hundred-dollar reward for his capture, dead or alive. And now he was dead. Killed by a man who'd as soon pay the portage on a casket as the train fare for a living captive. The casual manner in which Lennox dismissed a human life sickened Macalester. He remembered Geneva, sitting somewhere behind him, but he could not worry about her right now. They were a long way from Texas, but if Lennox would bring a corpse from Abilene to Memphis for five hundred dollars, he wouldn't hesitate to trade a bullet and a ticket to Austin for five thousand.

"I'll settle your bacon when I'm through here, Macalester," Lennox said, backing away in the wake of Billings's coffin. "Count on it."

He found a bitter smile for the unpleasant man.

"Memphis isn't Wichita, Lennox," he called after him. "And I'm not Billings."

"No. And you ain't Billy Deal, neither," Lennox rejoined, causing several heads to turn at the mention of that name. "See you around, Macalester."

He was gone. Macalester drew a deep breath, wondering if he could get enough air into his lungs to stay alive.

"Who in heaven's name was that?"

Geneva's melodious voice sounded awed, if not horrified. A lie found him quickly, in spite of his agitation.

"Just an old enemy of mine," he replied, hoping he sounded less worried than he felt. "I sent his brother to prison a few years ago, and he's had it in for me ever since. Nothing to worry about. Shall we go?"

He effected a grin but, looking at last into Geneva's steady, green-eyed gaze, he had the uneasy sense that she was not deceived, at least not completely. He recalled an old expression suddenly, about being between a rock and a hard place.

The fact that McAllister had not introduced the man spoke volumes to Geneva. She herself had formed an instant dislike for him: He had had the cheek to stare at her and then to make a remark in reference to her as though she might be no more than a piece of McAllister's luggage. She was filled with a morbid curiosity about him as well, and the puzzling exchange between him and McAllister, of which she had heard only bits and pieces: Billings. Wichita. Abilene. And Billy Deal. That last name had a familiar ring to it, although she could not quite recall why. And McAllister himself, effecting a casual demeanor, seemed nevertheless disturbed by the encounter, so much so that she refrained from voicing her questions during their brief ride to the hotel.

The lobby was a spacious area decorated by polished-walnut furnishings, a large red Persian rug, clean but worn in spots, and lamps with umbrellalike shades, hung with gaudy yet pretty fringes of garnet-colored beads. It lacked the elegance of the hotel in Roanoke, but it was charming and clean and very close to the train station. Geneva waited for McAllister, who was arranging for their rooms, in an overstuffed brocade chair.

"There are no suites available," he reported when he returned, his features thoughtful. "We have adjoining rooms. I have my business to attend to; I'm sorry I won't be joining you for dinner. Please have it brought up to your room. I'd rather you stayed there for the evening."

He was ordering her to stay put. And in an abrupt tone, thinly camouflaged with words of courtesy. She searched his face, but his handsome features, carefully bland, yielded no clue as to his deeper meaning. Question upon question sprang up in her mind like ducks in a Coney Island shooting gallery, but she put them aside in favor of one.

"Will you be out all evening, then?"

McAllister opened his mouth and even started to reply. Then he seemed to find her a smile, not merely with his wide and sensuous mouth, but with his warm brown eyes as well, the kind of smile she had not seen upon his face since New York. It made her feel as though someone had lit a fire in an otherwise damp and chilly room. In another instant, she felt a warmth against her cheek, and she realized, stunned, that it was his hand.

"Don't worry about that man," he said softly enough for her alone. "He won't trouble you. And I'll be back as soon as I can."

Her cheek grew cool again. He had withdrawn his hand. She felt dizzy.

Perhaps, she thought moments later, when she was able to think again as she followed the porter upstairs, tomorrow had come tonight, right here in Memphis.

*   *   *

Geneva awoke hard from a sweet dream she could not remember. It was still dark, and she was chilly. Annoyed, she sat up, massaging her bare arms with the flats of her hands. Fumbling in the darkness, she lit the tiny lamp by her bedside. Its light was small, but adequate to her task. *Must have left the window open,* she thought, slipping her legs out from under the covers. Rubbing her eyes, she made her way across the room toward the window. The sheer white curtains billowed with the night breeze, and the same breeze caught her nightgown, sending the white lawn garment rippling like a gentle wave.

All at once she was aware of a strange and unpleasant odor, like the smell of a wet animal. She paused in her quest, suddenly afraid—of what, she did not know. She did not want to go nearer to the window, but at the same time she did not want to turn her back on it. Something was wrong.

She thought of calling to McAllister, who, if he had returned from his business, would be asleep in the room next to hers. She rejected the idea at once: It was probably nothing. She would cause herself needless embarrassment. She stood there a moment longer, shivering in the nightdress, and forced her irrational fear aside. This was silly. She would close the window and get back into bed, where it was warm.

She took another bold step forward and remembered, feeling a cold shaft of sickening realization through her chest, that she had closed that window before she had retired. It was then that she became aware of a large shadow in the window alcove, not half a dozen feet from where she stood.

Her scream was a loud and lusty reflex that forced the shadow from its hiding place and through the open window into the night. Geneva was overcome by wave upon wave of terror; she could not seem to stop her scream. It possessed her like a demon, even after McAllister had crashed into the room like some avenging angel, shoeless, shirtless, with a big Colt revolver drawn and poised for action.

Paralyzed by shock and fear, she was reduced to sobs as she watched the attorney look about, then out of the window, for the unseen intruder. He closed the window and locked it, drawing the curtains. She felt herself begin to shake as he turned to her, his features distressed.

"Are you all right, Geneva?" she heard him ask in a hoarse voice.

She caught her breath.

"I—" She tried to speak, but barely a sound came out. Her eyes filled with tears she tried desperately to hold back. She could only nod, biting down on her lip to keep from crying.

"Was it him?" Macalester looked about as though searching for evidence. "Was it the man from the train station? Lennox?"

He crossed the few feet between them, his expression becoming one of amazement.

"My God, you're trembling like an earthquake!"

Was it instinct that made him draw her to his breast and enfold her in those magnificent, strong arms? She did not know. She did not care. She was in his arms, and she could no longer prevent the flood of tears. Only these were tears of relief. She felt cold, so cold, and his touch was warm and unbearably tender. She laid her head against his shoulder, trying to quiet her sobs as he held her tightly.

"It's all right," he said, barely above a whisper. "He's gone now. I'm here. Everything's all right."

He loosened his hold. When his arms fell away from her, she thought she would faint. "Please," she managed in a whisper, clutching his arm. "Don't leave me alone!"

She looked into his eyes and found him gazing down at her with a rapt expression that made her quiver with sudden desire. She knew, she could see very plainly, that he wanted her. Fear was gone, having vaporized quite as rapidly as it had advanced. McAllister did not blink. He seemed to be searching her face, and she saw him swallow hard.

"Don't leave me," she repeated in a breathless whisper, feeling a burning deep within her that, she knew, could only be satisfied by one thing.

He seemed paralyzed before her, but she could not wait for him. She needed him now. On her toes, reaching, she sought his wide mouth with her parted lips, brushing against them slowly once. And again. She felt their softness, and their strength. Another swell of desire spread from her loins upward through her breasts, and his lips stirred as she grazed them a third time.

He tasted her, and she felt a surge of energy pass between them. He seemed to falter, then he sampled her lips again, and again. She slid her hands up along the contours of his pectoral muscles and along his broad, unyielding shoulders, and she felt his hand, firm but gentle, at the back of her neck. His kiss deepened as he held her, and he explored, to her delight, every aspect of her lips and her mouth. She felt him tug at the delicate capped sleeve of her nightgown, and she sighed as, with delicious slowness, he tugged the garment down the soft, willing flesh of her arm.

In a moment her breast was exposed, and as he cupped it in his hand, caressing her hardened nipple between his thumb and forefinger, he began to devour her mouth as a condemned man might relish his last meal on earth. And she was happy to be the repast.

Step by step, she drew him to the bed. He seemed strangely reluctant, but that reluctance served only to heighten her already strong desire to get him there. He was one of those men who preferred to keep himself under the most superb control, she supposed, and in her limited experience, they were precisely the sort who, once they lost that control, were the most wonderfully sensual of partners.

At the edge of the bed, he drew away from her again, his dark eyes bright with heat, his angular jaw set and grim.

"Gen, I can't—"

She pressed her mouth to his, and her body against him. He couldn't mean it. His body told her so, in no uncertain terms. She slid her hands down along his sides, and slipped her fingertips into the waistband of his trousers. A low moan escaped his throat, and she knew he could. He would.

Buttons dissolved, and in moments it was just her and him. She drew him down with her, down to the sheets. He pressed himself to her, as if every part of him wanted every part of her. Men had wanted her before, but never like this. She loved the feel of him, the bigness, the warmth, the fierce gentleness of his touch. And more, she loved that he could not seem to get enough of her. He teased the joining of her legs with his erection, and she opened for him, wanting to feel, wanting to know.

"Oh, Mr. McAllis—"

He stopped her whisper with a finger on her lips.

"Call me Mac," he said, with a strange, compelling sadness in his eyes. "But don't talk. Please. Just don't . . ."

He was frightening. He was wonderful. His sadness and his power drew her in a way no other man had. He seemed to want more from her than her body, her responses, yet he seemed to fear to take it, even though she wanted to give. His strokes were measured, as if he meant to pleasure her but to deny himself, for some reason she couldn't fathom. She couldn't allow that. Her climax neared, heightened for her by his silent, deliciously maddening control, and just before he drove her over the edge, she fastened her legs tightly about him like a trap so that he had no choice but to remain still within her as she came all around him. Her loins cried out with the joy she would not allow to pass her lips, and she looked up to see his features, betraying that she had broken him at last.

When it was all over, he fell on her with a shudder. His weight was thrilling, all the more because she knew he'd meant to deny himself but had at last been unable to hold out against her. He whispered something beside her ear. It sounded like "God help me."

In another minute, he tried to leave, but Geneva would not let him.

"Stay," she urged, and pushed him gently onto his back. Laying her head upon his broad chest, she listened to his quieting heart and his deep, shuddering breath, her own body ringing like a newly cast bronze bell.

Trust your heart, Audrey had advised her in New York. Her calculating had led her astray; her single-minded goal of achieving the adoration of a decidedly fickle public, and her use of people, especially men. McAllister was new. He was the symbol of her rebirth and renewal. He represented a new phase, not only in her career, but in her life. *Perhaps,* he had told her two days ago, his dark eyes reading and yet unreadable, *I've been waiting for you.*

And perhaps, she thought, nestling closer to him, she had really been waiting all of this time for him, as well.

Kieran Macalester wondered, holding the world in his arms, whether he was dead or alive. He could not recall ever being happier, or more profoundly sad, in his entire life. Geneva had fallen asleep beside him, her lovely face half-buried against his chest. He brushed a stray lock of soft chestnut hair from her cheek, allowing his finger to trace the outline of her jaw. He was filled, suddenly, with such pain that he was obliged to leave her bed.

What had he done?

What was he, after all? An outlaw, hired by Geneva's own husband to bring her back to a home she had left and had no wish to return to. A notorious and deadly bounty hunter was stalking him, even as they lay together. He pictured, in the darkness, the huge, impossible, deadly web Garland Humble had woven about him.

He found his trousers and put them on. Geneva slept, rolling onto her stomach, settling in for a long and peaceful slumber. How she would despise him, he realized, swallowing the rock that had abruptly risen in his throat, when she discovered, as she surely must, what his true mission was! He closed his eyes, unwillingly visualizing her anger and her disdain. How could he have placed himself in the untenable position of falling in love, and falling hard, for a woman who, under the *best* of circumstances, would be completely wrong for him, but under these conditions could prove to be a foolish, even fatal, mistake?

He shook his head hard and flexed his back. This was ridiculous. There had to be a better way out of this whole damned mess. He was no fool. He'd gotten himself and Billy out of more than a few ticklish spots in the past.

But none of them had included all of these elements: Garland Humble, Lennox and a beautiful woman whom he loved to distraction . . .

A small sigh behind him brought his thoughts back to the moment with a jolt. Geneva was stirring, and the very sound of her stretching in bed was sufficient to

97

reawaken a keen desire in him.

"Mac?" he heard her murmur, and against his will, he smiled. How fortunate that he had chosen so ambiguous an alias. The nickname was perfect. Perhaps, he thought, rolling his tense shoulders, he would share with her the nickname that Billy preferred. He pushed aside his dark, troubling thoughts and turned to her again. The pale light of the lamp beside the bed revealed her drowsy, sensuous smile, and she drew back the covers invitingly.

"Come back to bed," she coaxed, her rich voice husky with renewed desire.

He was drawn to her, like a moth to a bright and deadly flame. Before he even meant to move, he was back in the bed, his body eager for hers. She took him this time, and that was even more exciting than before. She straddled him as he lay upon the bed, working him until his loins ached to deliver their essence, but then she cleverly held him back, even as he'd tried without success to hold back from her, before. The torture was exquisite and poetic. His hands spanned her waist, wanting to make her go on and on.

"Lord," he moaned, sliding his hands down to her thighs. "Oh, sweet Lord . . ."

Just at the very moment when he thought he could no longer bear the pleasure, he felt her begin to tremble. Her body arched and her head fell back, sending her hair cascading down her shoulders like a mahogany waterfall. A hoarse and primitive cry issued from her throat, and it triggered his own climax. In another moment, they were crying out and clinging together as she fell upon him, covering his chest with her soft, warm, slender body. As the glittering waves subsided, Kieran wondered if he would ever move again. Geneva was still warm and all around him, and the faint suggestion of jasmine in her soft curls was like a paralyzing drug. She had drawn his climax from him like the most cunning of thieves. Twice. He slid his fingers along her back, tracing her narrow shoulders and ribs, to that sumptuous swelling of her backside. He breathed a deep sigh and held her as tightly as any lunatic would cling to his slim thread of reality, whispering "I love you, Geneva" so low that he felt certain she could not have heard it.

Chapter Nine

Every time Macalester started to tell her his tangled tale of deceit during the brief trip to Little Rock, Geneva would look at him with those infinitely trusting green eyes and rob him of his tongue. He had rehearsed the scene dozens of times in his mind and decided that any way he tried it, it sounded shabby at best and unconscionable at worst. Either way, she would never forgive him for it, even if he swore to help her escape from Humble again.

Could Garland Humble really hold Geneva in his magnificent Fort Worth prison if she was of a mind to leave it? Macalester, knowing what he did of Geneva Lionwood, doubted it. Surely, he ruminated further, staring out of the train window, Geneva's gloved fingers entwined in his, Humble must know it, too.

Then why did the spider want her back?

That question, among others, troubled him. Geneva herself might know the answers, but of course it was impossible to ask her, for now.

Little Rock, Arkansas, rumbled closer as the unrelenting wheels of the train chewed up the ground beneath them. Lennox would never expect them to head for Little Rock, Macalester figured, and by the time the bounty hunter had worked it out, they would be well on their way to Fort Worth, traveling as inconspicuously as possible. Stagecoach and wagon were unthinkable: The ruthless and wily Lennox could easily overtake them, poking along on four wheels. They would make the three-hundred-mile journey on horseback in less than a week, if they rode hard.

Kieran willed himself to feel nothing as they debarked from the train. His aim was to find a hotel and get a good night's sleep before buying horses and provisions—and breaking the news to Geneva Lionwood about his master design.

If the diva noticed his dark humor, she did not remark upon it. She remained tranquil and pleasant, commenting on the rustic charm of the town as they traveled the short distance to a hotel.

His habit had been to secure two adjoining rooms for their use, and his conscience would not allow him to alter that, even though Geneva exhibited mild amusement at the arrangement. And indeed, after they had dined and retired for the evening, he had neither the will nor the inclination to stay away from her. She slept soundly in his arms afterward while he, perversely, could not lure sleep. He lay in the darkness, wide awake, counting the hours until morning.

Geneva stretched alone in her bed, blessing her good fortune. It was daylight and McAllister was gone, off, she supposed, to make further arrangements for their continuing journey. She sat up in bed and pushed the covers down to her knees. McAllister was very good for her. Aside from being an exceptional lover, he was also wonderful company, if somewhat reserved. Still, she mused, they were a long way from San Francisco. There would be ample time to learn all of his secrets.

She got out of bed. The coolness of the polished pine floor beneath her bare feet was a welcome jolt, awakening her even more. She washed, but did not dress. Perhaps she could lure the quietly passionate attorney back to bed when he returned from his mission. She smiled to herself, feeling an unexpected warmth wash over her at the memory of the night: his hard, lean body against hers; his wide, talented mouth touching her all over. Remembering these things, she was confident she could entice him.

To pass the time until his return, she puttered about the small room, picking up articles of clothing she and McAllister had, in their fevered haste, carelessly abandoned the night before. She sorted her own things, determining which required laundering and which could be salvaged for an additional wearing. Next, she turned her attention to his.

His trousers were heaped upon the floor. She giggled, feeling a ripple of excitement surge through her as she thought of him undressing. His body was like a Michelangelo sculpture, although he seemed disarmingly unaware of that fact. His shirt lay upon the vanity bench like a dissolute guest, and she picked it up, shaking the wrinkles from it. She recalled that he had carefully hung his coat in the armoire. Odd that he should treat that one article with such care, having so recklessly discarded the others.

She remembered his peculiar quirk of patting his lapel. Come to think of it, she hadn't seen him perform that little ritual ever since she'd mentioned it on the train several days ago.

A man with secrets.

A quiet man, a thoughtful man, a man carefully in control, except between the sheets. She shivered with delight. If she could find some clue to him, perhaps she might breach that control at other times, as well.

Should she?

How could she not?

The armoire door stuck as if Mac had tried to lock it, but the lock failed and the door creaked open. His coat was inside, a sentry at its post, ready to be seduced into desertion. She giggled at her foolish fancy and fingered the lapel.

To her surprise, she felt something in an inside pocket.

One of your secrets, Mac? she wondered, slipping her fingers inside.

There was a long, white envelope that looked as if it had been carried about for some time. It was not sealed. A love letter, perhaps? She could not deny a stab of jealousy at the thought. Perhaps she was better off not knowing, after all.

No. What harm could it do? At the very worst, the contents of the envelope were irrelevant. At best, they might give her a glimpse of, and therefore an advantage over, R. Hastings McAllister, Esquire. With careful, deft fingers, she slipped the paper from its casing and unfolded it.

It was, to her bewilderment, addressed to the Honorable Oren Roberts, Governor of the State of Texas. The handwriting was a coarse scrawl that was vaguely familiar to her. She skipped past the salutations to the second paragraph. The black words on the page seemed to move, like ants over spilled honey. Several of them leaped at her:

". . . Kieran Macalester and Billy Deal, whom I personally know to have recanted their crimes and who have proven to be of invaluable assistance to me in several delicate matters of business which have also affected the welfare of the State of Texas and most recently in the recovery of my wife. It is for this reason that I respectfully request you consider granting them amnesty . . ."

The paper began to shake. Geneva realized, feeling her insides recoil as though she'd been kicked, that her hand was trembling. She skipped down to the closing to confirm what she now already knew: It was signed by Garland Humble.

Against her will, she remembered Garland. Garland loved to buy things. To own things. His Louis Quatorze desk. His bust of Julius Caesar. His preposterously expensive Napoleon brandy, and the one-of-a-kind Waterford crystal goblets in which he served it. He had a ridiculous piece of machinery called a Welte Forsetzer, a German gadget that worked like a sort of inside-out player piano, when it worked at all. She remembered he'd tried to get a rather prominent pianist to record piano scores of operas and songs on its cylinders, so she might have some accompaniment to sing with, just for him.

His very own bird in a gilded cage.

Her gremlin had been busy indeed while she'd lived under Humble's roof.

No time for reverie. San Francisco evaporated like a mirage. McAllister. Macalester. The San Francisco attorney was in fact a wanted criminal in the employ of her estranged husband. The letter fell to the floor as her hands went to her mouth.

Deal and Macalester. The names came back to her from the past. Although she had never paid much attention to the stories, she recalled enough about them to know that the two men were wanted in Texas and perhaps elsewhere for their parts in a score of train and bank robberies during a five-year period that ended abruptly over two years before.

McAllister. Macalester. No emissary of the San Francisco Opera and Light Theater Company; no more than a common criminal.

A common criminal she had taken to her bed.

Geneva sank to the bench, feeling faint. She must think. She must concentrate. She must fight the urge to shed useless tears of anger, fear and hurt, and look beyond the present to her immediate future.

She steadied herself. Could there be a simple explanation behind the letter? She was given to flights of fancy; hadn't she believed Blaine Atherton when he'd offered her Covent Garden? It was possible that the similarity of names was merely a coincidence. After all, McAllister was an attorney. She recalled, then, the man in the train station in Memphis. Lennox, McAllister had called him. *You ain't Billy Deal*, he had remarked.

The notion that Garland Humble had gone to all of this trouble to bring her back to Fort Worth was preposterous, yet it would be in perfect harmony with his wicked, possessive, manipulative style. Briskly, she reviewed her alternatives.

She could confront McAllister with her discovery and demand an explanation. Of course, he could lie. And if he had lied to her from the beginning, as she suspected, then why would he admit the truth now? She could demand that he return her to New York, but that, she realized grimly, could be much more difficult than it sounded. After all, Garland had no doubt offered the man a reward, of which the amnesty letter was very likely only a part. And even if the felon did nurse any tender feelings for her . . . Well. Any man who had no compunction about making love to a woman under such appallingly false pretenses would hardly be moved by the pleas of his victim.

Against her will, she recalled his touch, its gentleness

and urgency. The sadness, the infinite tenderness in his face. God help me, he had said against her throat.

Her eyes were wet. *Mac, how could you do this to me?* She choked back a sob and shook herself into action. How could she have done this to herself? Trusting the wrong man? Again?

You were wrong, Audrey, Geneva thought, tasting the bitterness in her mouth. *Oh, how very wrong you were! If only I could tell you!*

There was movement outside of the door. No time to summon the gremlin. She must act, and act now. Shaking, ice cold with fear, she quickly seized the lamp from the table beside her bed with both hands. Praying that she was strong enough, both physically and emotionally, she positioned herself behind the door. As she heard the key slide into the lock, she lifted the lamp high above her head.

"Geneva, I—" Macalester entered the room, his back to the door. He was dressed in jeans and a dark chambray shirt, looking, at last, more like an outlaw of the Wild West than the reserved San Francisco attorney he had pretended to be. Geneva steeled herself, planting her bare feet firmly. The outlaw paused for a moment, not moving. She held her breath.

"Geneva?" he called again, as if to himself.

She resisted a compelling urge to hurl invective at him, satisfying herself with bringing the big, heavy lamp down hard upon the back of his head. The sound of the crash was awful. The lamp shattered, and there was broken glass everywhere. She watched Macalester crumple to the floor in a solid heap and dropped the remains of the appliance on his back.

She dressed quickly and stuffed a few of her belongings into her valise. The rest of her luggage would be sacrificed, admittedly a small price to pay for her continued liberty. She rifled Macalester's pockets and

106

found, blessedly, three hundred dollars, more than enough money to buy her way back to New York, or anywhere else she might decide to go. She paused at last at the door, staring down upon the immobile outlaw with a strange mixture of loathing and longing.

Mac's angular features were softened by his state of unconsciousness. His wide mouth, the mouth in which she had taken such delight mere hours before, hung slightly open, pressed against the polished pine floor. A sob rose in her throat, and she quickly turned her back on him. He had played her for a fool and had very nearly won. In a last, parting gesture, she placed the letter that had betrayed him in his open hand, closing his long, slack fingers about it. Then she stepped over him and out of the door, closing and locking it behind her as if shutting her heart securely inside of a solid steel vault.

Macalester's first conscious thought was of pain. His head felt as if it had been used as a blacksmith's anvil. With effort, he opened his eyes. It took a moment or two for his vision to clear. There were bits of broken glass spread out like a carpet across the pine floor before his eyes.

He tried to think, but the wall of pain prevented it. Then he tried to sit up and discovered the soft parchment in his left hand. He did sit up then. Broken glass ground under his legs as he curled them up beneath him for support. Bewildered and disoriented, he unfolded the paper.

The pain did not subside, but his mind cleared instantly as the import of his predicament struck him, as surely as had the lamp that lay in pieces on the floor around him: Geneva had found the letter. She had found him out. And then she had gone.

Damn, he thought, reaching back with one hand to

107

touch the painful knot rising on the back of his head. Geneva Lionwood did nothing by halves.

He leaned his back against the door, willing the pain away. It did not vanish completely, but it did subside. Then he totaled the situation.

Late-morning sunshine filled the room; she could not have been gone long. An hour, two at most. Her aim would have been to put as much distance as possible between them, and the best ways to do that were by train, stagecoach or flatboat down the Arkansas to the Mississippi.

He raked his fingers through his hair, closing his eyes against the throbbing pain radiating from the lump on the back of his head. There was a burning in his gut that made the pain in his head seem inconsequential: Maybe he should just let her go. Return to Humble empty-handed. Tell the old spider that she had given him the slip. Slowly, he struggled to his feet, leaning against the door until the room stopped spinning. No, that was unthinkable. Garland Humble, master of trickery and deceit, would take one look at his face and know that he was lying. And he would probably know or guess why, as well. And he, Macalester, could watch his amnesty slip further out of reach, and would probably never see Geneva again to explain himself, or to apologize.

He concentrated on placing one foot before the other and managed to stumble to the washstand. He poured water into the bowl from the pitcher, and it slopped over the sides. He leaned over and splashed it onto his face, then wrung out a washcloth and applied it to the wound on the back of his head. Holding the cool, damp cloth against the bump, Macalester stared at his reflection. His hair was disarrayed, his dark eyes vacant and his angular jaw clenched. Cursing his monumental stupidity, he turned away from the image and kicked a broken piece of the lamp. The fragment skittered across the floor and banged against the door. It clattered back to the floor and presently came to rest. The room settled into silence again.

Time was wasting. Tossing the washcloth aside, Macalester gathered a few of his belongings, including the damned and damning letter, electing to leave the excess behind. Seldom in his adult life had he owned more than two changes of clothing, and it looked as if his masquerading days were at an end. The hand-tailored suits would not be needed anymore; they would merely weigh him down. He preferred not to ruminate upon the deeper ramifications of such a sentiment, haste being the order of the moment. Time enough for philosophical reflections after he had gotten Geneva Lionwood back.

He did not even bother to lock the door upon leaving the room. His barest belongings slung over his shoulder in saddlebags, he started down the hall toward the stairs, his heart as heavy as his throbbing head. Just as he was about to begin his descent to the lobby, voices drifted up the stairwell.

". . . last night." That was the clerk, his faint drawl a combination of nasal Midwest and Southern transplant.

"What room are they in?" another voice, gravely and low, asked. "I'd like to surprise them."

Macalester froze.

Lennox!

Backing quietly away from the stairs, he moved up the hallway toward the window, careful to walk close to the wall but on the carpet. His heavy boots were a liability, but he was able to negotiate the short distance without causing so much as a creak of a floorboard.

The window was closed and locked. Macalester looked outside, assessing his chances. The slanted roof of the wraparound porch was right below the casement, and from its edge there was, he judged, about a ten- or twelve-foot drop to the yard. He had wanted to question the clerk about Geneva, but that would be impossible now. He would have to gamble on the window and trust his luck in tracking her down on his own, and staying one jump ahead of Lennox.

Resolutely, he unlatched the window. It gave way with an unoiled squeak of protest. Instantly, he was aware of a heavy, running step upon the stair: He had given himself away. Muttering a brief curse, he eased himself out of the window, flattening his broad back against the green wooden shutters as he drew his revolver from the holster at his hip. His situation drew some curious stares from passersby, but he waved them on with the muzzle of his gun. They did not require additional warning. His gesture and, he knew, his grim expression persuaded them that undue curiosity might be injurious to their continued well-being.

Inside, in the hallway, he heard the running footsteps of someone, probably Lennox, approaching the window. He prayed that the bounty hunter would make a mistake, even a simple one such as poking his head out of the window to have a look around.

Lennox was so near that Macalester could hear him breathing, inches away from him, just inside the casement. Macalester held his breath, not daring to move. There was a creak of old wood as Lennox leaned a heavy hand upon the sill. In another moment a shadow moved slowly across the shutter.

"You, there!" a voice from the house across the alley shouted.

Macalester looked up sharply to see an old matron in a second-story window, her plain, hard features expressing annoyance, her tightly corseted bosom, in white linen, heaving with outrage.

"What are you doing, on that—"

What happened next happened in the twinkling of an eye. Lennox shoved his head out of the window and had just turned it in his direction when Macalester landed the butt end of his gun upon the back of the bounty hunter's neck with enough force to pull him from the window and send him tumbling over the porch roof and down, with a hard thump, to the ground below. To the accompaniment of continued vituperative shouts from across the way, Macalester negotiated the roof to the rear of the building. He blessed his fortune in finding a handy downspout, which he used to lower himself easily to the ground. He peeked around the corner to see that a small cluster of curious onlookers had already gathered about Lennox, who lay as still as death. Macalester hoped, briefly, that he had not killed the man: Murder did not sit well with governors contemplating amnesty.

But he could waste no more time. Geneva Lionwood was on the loose, and he could not afford to let her slip away. There were but two weeks left in Garland Humble's timetable, and Billy's future, as well as his own, depended on him sticking to it.

He guessed he had thirty minutes, possibly an hour, before Lennox would be on his trail again, and he needed to use the time wisely. On the big roan he had purchased earlier that morning from the livery, he rode the main street of Little Rock inquiring as to Geneva's whereabouts. He let out that she was his wife, and that she had run off after an argument. His story met with sympathy, ridicule and even admonishments to beat her when he recovered her, but very little in the realm of solid information. Of course, Geneva was no fool. She would have expected him to look, and look hard, and so would have made herself as inconspicuous as possible among the populace of Little Rock.

111

The stage depots yielded nothing. Scanning the schedules, Macalester could see why: Geneva would have missed the early departures, and no further ones were scheduled until the afternoon. That left the train and the flatboat.

Flatboat was what his gut told him. She would want him to think train, but flatboat was really the best. They weren't but a hundred miles from the Mississippi, and two days on the Arkansas could have her on a riverboat to New Orleans as cozy as she pleased.

The docks yielded the answers he was looking for. Yes, the harbormaster told him, surveying him with a critical eye that told Macalester that the man would remember him when Lennox came calling later. The woman he described had been there, and she had booked passage on a boat due in Pine Bluff, forty miles downriver, around eight that evening. Thanking him, Macalester fished in his pocket for his money, hoping to make an offering designed to help the sharp-eyed man to forget him. It was then he realized that almost all of his money was gone, as well. Cursing God for making women clever, he departed, heading southeast for Pine Bluff, riding hard.

Chapter Ten

The Arkansas River was neither wide nor straight, but the boatman guided the craft along her banks like an experienced seamstress working an elaborate pattern. The river had a musty smell to it, but it was a clean smell, a wild smell. Geneva, sitting on her valise along the gunwale in the stern, could almost have enjoyed the idyllic journey along the tree-lined waterway were it not for the uncomfortable accommodations and her nagging worry that Macalester would dog her trail.

Macalester. She could not think of him without a host of painful and ambivalent emotions. She hated him, surely, for his treachery, and for the fact that he had more than taken advantage of her, both emotionally and physically. His deception was unforgivable. And yet—and yet . . .

What harm had he really done? She had burned her own bridges in New York without any assistance from him at all. And Blaine, who supposedly cared for her,

113

would have taken her all the way to London for far less of an excuse than the masquerading outlaw's. Still, she mused, he might have been honest with her. She would not have gone with him willingly, of course, but it would have been nice, for once: a refreshing change, for a man to be honest with her.

But Macalester was an outlaw, and she knew little of the breed. Perhaps he was incapable of being honest.

The small flatboat was crowded with goods, livestock and passengers bound for Pine Bluff or the Mississippi. The journey of one hundred miles would take two days, she had been told, with the overnight stop in Pine Bluff. With grim amusement, she looked about at the assortment of humanity and domestic animals. The facilities on board were as far removed from a first-class train compartment as Arkansas itself was from New York. After two days under these conditions, she promised herself in silence, there would be a hot bath, a laundering of her pink and gray traveling suit and a real bed in a real hotel. Not to mention decent food. She had neglected to ask about provisions on board and had not thought to bring any with her. It was nearly noon now, and her stomach was reminding her, none too gently, that she had not breakfasted that morning: She had been in too much haste to remove herself from Macalester's company.

A young woman, even younger than herself, wearing a an outrageously cut satin gown of a sunset hue, eventually sat down on her own luggage beside Geneva. She had perfect skin the color of bittersweet chocolate, an absurdly long feather boa that seemed perpetually inconvenient, and a large, overdone piece of millinery with golden plumes standing proudly a foot or more in the air.

"At least it ain't rainin'" the girl offered by way of a greeting as she adjusted her skirt hem. "I'm Camilla.

Camilla Brooks. Most folks call me Brooksie; I guess 'cause I run off at the mouth."

Geneva nodded to her in acknowledgment, quickly readying a lie.

"I'm Eve Lyons," she told the girl, who had settled into her place with the easy grace of one accustomed to a variety of circumstances.

"Eve Lyons," the girl repeated, flashing a smile of white-toothed brilliance. "Well, Eve, I guess you're a schoolteacher. Am I right?"

Geneva silently blessed the girl for providing the story.

"Yes," she murmured, smiling tentatively. "Yes, you are."

Brooksie's own smile broadened triumphantly.

"I knew. I can always tell. It a gift. My mama had it, too. She used to tell me, 'Chile, it unnatural, how we knows things.' She used to make me get down on my knees with her on that dirt floor and pray to Jesus to take the devil outta us. But I knew it wasn't no devil. It just a gift. Like singin'. I'm a singer, you know," Brooksie went on proudly, nodding her head until the plumes bobbed like huge birds priming for flight. "I got that from my mama, too. I'm gone to New Orleans. Gonna make my way in this world. Yes, ma'am. You gonna teach school at Pine Bluff?"

Geneva found that she could not help smiling at the woman's breezy, open manner.

"No," she replied, keeping her voice low in contrast to the other's bold and strident tone. "I'm bound for New Orleans, myself. Have you ever been there before?"

Brooksie stared at her for a moment, then laughed. It was such a joyous sound that Geneva very nearly laughed herself.

"Me? I ain't never been past my church, till today.

115

You ain't from around here, are you?" Geneva shook her head.

"I'm from—" She thought for a moment. She did not think it wise to tell too many lies. After all, she might have to recall what she had said at a later time. On the other hand, Geneva had the distinct impression that Camilla Brooks would allow her no rest if she told her she was from New York City.

"I'm from Albany," she said finally, looking askance at the other passengers. "Albany, New York."

Was it her overactive imagination, or were those men staring at her, those rough-looking men of undetermined years who dressed as though shoveling manure would be a step up for them in this hard world? She faced Camilla again, whose aspect was much easier on the eyes than anything else on the vessel, including the five shabbily dressed children who were running about shoeless, or in shoes that did not fit, with no stockings. Geneva shuddered. What would these people do, she wondered—Camilla Brooks included—if they knew she had three hundred dollars pressed against her bosom?

Brooksie was prattling on about something, but Geneva was no longer listening. From the corner of her eye, she could see one of the men approach, wearing a most unpleasant expression upon his granitelike features. His black beard was thin and wiry and looked as though it had encountered neither comb nor scissors since it had begun to grow upon its wearer's chin—and by its length, that was probably a long time ago. Geneva looked away from him, holding her breath, hoping he would move on.

He did not. He stood before them, planting his heavy, muddy boots firmly. Camilla stopped talking and stared openly at him. She seemed, miraculously, at a loss for words.

"What's a nigger girl botherin' this lady fer?" His

116

voice was incongruously high and nasal.

Geneva very nearly laughed, both at the sound of it and with relief that he apparently did not mean to rob her.

"Oh, go away and mind your own business," she told the man, shooing him off with a wave of her gloved hand. "Nobody's bothering you."

The man's small mouth opened, creating a dark hole in the beard, and his narrow, pig eyes widened.

Simple, direct commands, Geneva reminded herself, forcing herself to return his stare blankly.

"Go on," she urged again, gesturing to the cluster of men on the other side of the boat. They had ceased their cackling conversation and were now, to her dismay, watching the events unfold before them as though they were audience to a failed comedy.

For a full two minutes there was neither sound nor movement, except for the dipping of the rudder and the gentle slap of waves against the bulkhead. Then the man stared them both up and down, as though memorizing their features for future use. The notion was not comforting.

To Geneva's astonishment, he turned away and sauntered back to his contingent in a heavy, shuffling step. Geneva said nothing but remembered to draw a breath, unable to take her eyes from the taciturn party of men across the deck. Camilla Brooks, too, was silent, as though the man had taken her tongue back with him as a prize.

"There gonna be trouble, sure," the dark-skinned woman said under her breath, and indeed, Geneva could not even be certain she had been meant to hear it. She felt a sudden chill and drew her cloak more tightly about herself, although the afternoon breeze was not cold. She wished, unexpectedly, for the imposing presence of Macalester, remembering his tidy treatment of the drunken Blaine Atherton outside of her suite at the Biltmore. She reproved herself immediately for such a foolish fancy: Macalester, when he awoke, would have no reason to want to protect her from the likes of these ignorant and loutish men.

Beside her, Camilla gasped. Geneva looked up to see the five men approaching them, their thin, oatmeal faces grim. The grisly quintet stood before her and Camilla for a minute, staring. Geneva resisted an urge to place her hands over her blouse where the three hundred dollars nestled snugly between her breasts.

Before she knew quite what was happening, the men seized her and Camilla Brooks and lifted them over the gunwale, dropping them unceremoniously over the side, in spite of their cries of protest, into the dark, slow waters of the Arkansas River.

Geneva bobbed to the surface after a few awful swallows of river water. Its smell was not unpleasant, but its flavor was ghastly. She coughed and sputtered for breath. The river pulled at her clothing, and she discovered quickly that movement was difficult. Surprise and dismay gave way in a moment to indignation.

"How dare—come back and—oh—"

She saw the boatman cast a backward glance over his shoulder and return to his task, apparently with no intention of assisting. The five men who had executed the unscheduled dunking stood silent and still, like paid mourners at a funeral. The other passengers had already begun rifling the women's belongings, which the men had not bothered to send overboard. Camilla's hat, plumes incredibly untouched, floated along behind the boat like a frigate in full sail, swirling gaily in the wake.

Camilla!

Treading water, Geneva looked about for any sign of her talkative new friend. A few feet away, the water churned, and she caught a glimpse of flaming orange tinted with brown just below the surface. The younger woman was struggling for air. Clumsily, Geneva reached down into the water for her and missed. Fighting a sense of panic, she stripped off her ruined jacket and skirt underwater. She was able to move more easily then, but she sensed she would tire quickly.

Taking a deep breath, she tried again, diving into the dark water. This time, blind, she seized a handful of saturated satin and came up for air. Camilla's dark head appeared beside her, and she coughed, struggling in Geneva's grip.

"Be still; I've got you." Geneva panted, hooking her elbow beneath the other's chin. Miraculously, Camilla did stop thrashing.

"We ain't gonna die in this muddy old river," Camilla managed to say. "We too young."

Inspired by her spirit, Geneva found a reserve of strength. She wanted to answer her friend to reassure her, but she suspected she would need all of her resources to get them both to the river's bank, some twenty feet away. Camilla talked for her, encouraging and praying aloud as Geneva's aching limbs and throbbing chest worked inexorably to draw them to the shore.

At last her shoes touched the slick bottom. She had come but half a dozen yards; still it had seemed a mile. Struggling against the soaked remnants of her clothing, she pulled Camilla in behind her. The other woman gained her footing and in turn took Geneva by the arm, pulling her along as she negotiated the muddy bank. Geneva's knees gave out at last as her ruined boots touched dry land and she collapsed to the ground, certain that she would never move again.

She lay perfectly still, coughing up river water occasionally. Camilla had dropped down beside her in like circumstance, and they remained thus for a long time.

It seemed hours to Geneva, who ached so in her limbs and in her chest that she could not even cry. The sun was westering, and they were in the shade of oaks and cottonwoods whose leaves were just beginning to fade.

It was getting cooler. By nightfall, when they should have been comfortable in an inn at Pine Bluff, they would be chilled in their damp clothing in the Arkansas woods, unless they could find shelter. Of its own volition, Geneva's hand went to her breast: she breathed a painful sigh of relief. The money was still there. She sat up with effort, shivering as a brief breeze blew in from the water. Her blouse and her petticoat, all that remained of her tidy traveling suit, were still wet, and they clung to her like whining, spoiled children.

"We must be miles from Pine Bluff," she observed presently, her voice faint. "God, I wish I were dry. Come on, Brooksie. We've a long way to go."

In response, Camilla sat up, brushing her hair out of her face with a muddy satin sleeve. Geneva laughed weakly at the sight, although it pained her to do so.

"You're a picture," she told her companion, who was streaked over every inch of her once-grand dress with brown river mud.

"At least I'm still wearin' my clothes," the other retorted, gesturing to Geneva's dishabille. "We can't take you no place decent, gal. That's sure."

Geneva looked down at herself, grimly assessing the damage wrought by their ordeal. Her fine silk blouse, once the color of fresh cream, was now a translucent gray-brown and bunched about her hips like a shift. Her petticoat, stained the same color, barely reached the tops of her soaked and soiled boots. She could feel her hair pulling loose from its pins, and she knew there were traces of mud on her face and neck as well.

"That won't be much of a liability, for the time being," Geneva grumbled, "since there aren't any decent places in these woods. Anyway, there's no help for it."

She stood up and extended her arm to Camilla, who accepted it although she did not seem to need any assistance. The dark-skinned woman held onto her hand for a moment, until Geneva, startled, met her gaze.

"You saved my life," Camilla stated, her sable eyes thoughtful, her pretty mouth unsmiling.

Geneva shook her head.

"We saved each other, I guess." She shrugged, feeling a little uncomfortable under the other woman's unabashedly admiring gaze. "You talked me to the shore. I couldn't have made it without that."

Camilla smiled.

"Then it was Jesus," she pronounced. "That was my mama's special prayer. I ain't never knowed it to fail."

Jesus, Mama or Camilla, it made no difference to Geneva. She was there, in one piece. She was wet, and she was cold and hungry, and she had a long way to trudge in wet boots, but she had money, and she had her life. And, it seemed, by accident or Providence, she had made a friend, as well.

The two women followed the river until dark, then they huddled under a tree, trying to keep warm. It was October; the nights, even in southern Arkansas, were cool. Without a fire, and without blankets or even dry clothing, it seemed a body could near freeze to death in the woods at night. Geneva shivered with more than the cold. Could Macalester have trailed her? Would he have made Pine Bluff by this time, and somehow learned of her unscheduled stop? Knowing what she did of the clever and unprincipled outlaw, she believed it to be entirely possible.

Given her present circumstances, she nearly wished for it. Anything would be better than freezing under a tree in the black night of an Arkansas forest, even if it involved being taken once again into Kieran Macales-

121

ter's custody. She had escaped from him once; she could do so a second time.

Beside her, Camilla slept, snoring softly. Geneva envied the younger woman's ability to sleep under these conditions. Every noise, every strange animal sound startled her, and she was certain that a variety of snakes, insects and other unsavory pests were taking up residence in her hair, or in her petticoat. Besides, she was unable to shake the cold. Her whole body ached with the chill. Her feet were freezing inside of the wet boots and her hands were like ice. She tried to sit on them to warm them up, but Camilla lay against her in such a manner as to make it nearly impossible for her to move without disturbing her. To make matters worse, her stomach was painfully empty and growled with indignation each time she managed to doze.

It was the longest night of her life, and it did not end until the sky began to lighten to a pale, misty gray. The fog was wet and cold and did nothing to lift her dismal spirits. She resented, finally, her companion's apparently peaceful slumber, and she awoke her at last with a rough shake.

"Wake up, Camilla!" she said briskly, and her voice echoed in the trees. "We'd best be on our way. Maybe we'll make Pine Bluff in time for breakfast."

Camilla stirred and groaned.

"Don't let's talk about food, until we can eat some," she mumbled, straightening.

Geneva's back and legs informed her of their displeasure at the night's accommodations as she attempted to stand. She felt as though her limbs had rusted in the damp and cold. She was surprised that they did not squeak as she moved to an upright position. She drew in a breath and sneezed. The sound reverberated through the fog like cannonshot, reminding her, with a jolt, of their lonely and perilous circumstances.

"Come on, Camilla," she urged again. Suddenly there seemed to be a shadow behind every tree and she wanted, desperately, to be quit of the place.

The river was nearby. They followed it again, heading southeast, slowly but steadily making their way toward Pine Bluff. Camilla's loquaciousness had lapsed to an occasional remark, or a fragment of a song, or an exhortation to the Almighty. Geneva simply trudged along, conversation being more of an effort than she cared to make. Her feet hurt. Her back hurt. Her head hurt. And her heart ached.

She proceeded several yards downriver before she realized that Camilla was no longer following her. Annoyed, she turned to her companion with a tart remark that never left her lips. Camilla stood perfectly still, her head cocked to one side. It struck Geneva, not lightly, that the woman was listening for something.

Camilla seemed to anticipate her question. She raised a finger in a request for silence.

"A horse," she said quietly. "Comin' hard. Comin' this way."

Geneva felt what little warmth there was leave her cheeks. "Quick!" she whispered. "Let's hide."

Camilla frowned. "Why?"

Geneva seized her by the arm and led her to a cluster of bushes.

"Shh," she told her perplexed companion, pulling her down to a crouch. "I'll explain later. Stay down!"

She heard the sound then. A dull, steady thrum. It grew louder, gradually overpowering every other sound except for the pounding of her heart. The unseen rider slowed to a trot, then a walk. A roan appeared from the trees, and Geneva could not restrain a small gasp: Kieran Macalester dismounted, pulling his brown Stetson down over his brow. She watched him crouch low over the ground, examining the footprints she and Camilla

123

had carelessly left all over the landscape like pieces of a puzzle, and not a difficult one, at that. He was not dressed in a suit, or in the evening clothes he had worn at their first meeting in New York. On this occasion, he wore corduroy pants and a freshly starched black shirt with a dark kerchief at his throat. Her breath caught in her chest: He looked every inch the outlaw she knew him to be.

She felt an urgent tug on her sleeve.

"Who is he?" Camilla barely whispered.

"Shh!" Geneva hissed again, and instantly Macalester's head jerked up. She held her breath as, for a moment, he seemed to look directly at the bush behind which they were hiding. She felt exposed. She did not move.

Presently he straightened to his full height. He stared long enough for Geneva to envy him his clean, warm, dry clothing. To her amazement, he turned away, leading his mount back to the road. In another minute, she heard the horse depart at a canter, and the sound diminished against the fabric of noises in the awakening forest. Geneva sighed as though she had not drawn breath for several minutes.

"Who was that?" Camilla repeated her earlier question in the same whispered awe.

Geneva did not look at her. She felt compelled by the memory of his tall, hard form crouched down in the mud not ten feet from where she was hiding. Surely he had known of her presence. Why had he ridden away?

"Listen to me." Geneva was panting, and she ignored the question again as she reached into her blouse. "That man is looking for me. Take this." She found the tightly folded wad of bills in her blouse and pressed it into Camilla's hand. "He'll leave you alone, and I don't want him to have it. If we make it to New Orleans together, we'll split whatever's left. If anything happens to me,

124

just keep it. Do anything you like with it. I'd be happier knowing he doesn't have it."

Camilla's pretty face clouded with concern, but she seemed to sense that Geneva did not want to tell her any more. Without looking at the folded paper notes, she nodded and tucked them into her own dress. The gesture was, to Geneva, like the closing of a metal door.

Macalester dismounted about fifty yards down the road and tied his snorting roan to a sapling. His relief at having located Geneva Lionwood was tempered by— there was no other word for it—his dread of what must surely follow. His head had stopped hurting him late the day before, but the lump had remained and would be a reminder to him, not only of his own treachery but of Geneva's determination. He had forgiven her in his own mind for dealing so harshly with him: After all, would he not have done the very same thing, in similar circumstances? In fact, he had done the same thing to Lennox, in Little Rock. He could forgive it, but he could not forget it, not if he valued his life and his freedom.

He doubled back quietly on foot, his boots making little sound on the damp forest floor as he negotiated his way to the riverbank. He found a broad old oak tree behind which to conceal himself, and waited.

He did not have to wait long. In minutes, he saw not one but two women, Geneva and a dark-skinned companion, as muddy and bedraggled as a couple of orphans, making their way awkwardly in cumbersome, clinging skirts and boots with impossibly tiny heels. Geneva's chestnut hair was matted and coming loose from its pinnings, and her lovely face was streaked with mud and lined with such determination as he had never before seen on anyone's face, let alone a woman's. Her clothing, or what was left of it, was utterly ruined.

125

She was, nevertheless, the most beautiful sight he'd ever seen.

When the two women were within a few yards of where he stood, he came out from behind the tree and placed himself directly in their path.

"Good morning, Miss Lionwood," he said gravely, but he could not prevent a smile from crossing his lips, both at her ridiculous state and at his relief that he had recovered her.

Chapter Eleven

The two women stopped short, each of them appearing to have taken root like one of the trees around them. For an instant, Geneva's wide eyes, greener than ever among the like colors of the forest, demonstrated fear. Then she seemed to notice his smile. She looked away from him, but made no move to run.

"If you dare to laugh," she intoned, her voice low and shaking, "I will kill you."

He'd had no intention of laughing, but her empty threat did induce a chuckle from his throat, hence a glower from her. Her eyes narrowed at him in an unpleasant expression. She gestured to her companion with an elegant sweep of her small, fine, dirty hand.

"Camilla Brooks," she began by way of introduction, "Kieran Macalester, my kidnapper. Have I pronounced your name correctly?"

Her polite tone was liberally laced with sarcasm. He bit his lip to prevent further laughter from escaping, hoping to ward off further abuse.

"It'll do," he replied evenly, restraining himself from reaching for her mud-streaked cheek. "Come on. Let's get you some dry clothes. Oh. One more thing."

He held out a gloved hand, his palm outstretched. She stared at him blankly.

"The money," he prompted her.

He was treated to a brief, derisive laugh.

"Would I be wandering in the woods in my wet underclothing if I still had that money?" she scoffed, her hands on her hips.

Macalester curbed his annoyance. It was Humble's money; he didn't really care about that. He could wire the millionaire for more from the next town. It was Geneva's display of temper that was beginning to play upon his nerves, and with everything else on his mind, he did not need a fractious woman working on his patience as well. He shrugged, feigning indifference, hooking his thumbs into his gun belt.

"We'll be living lean for a while, then," he told her, hoping the news would sober her. "And you'll have to wear my extra clothes. Had your breakfast yet?"

The two of them immediately took on expressions resembling those of hungry she-wolves. Macalester could not prevent another wry laugh.

"I guess not. Well, come on, then. I have some grub in my saddlebags, if you don't mind eating from a can."

By the look of them, he doubted they would mind eating off of the ground.

Macalester's clothes were an ill fit for Geneva. The trousers were too long, too tight in the hips and too big at the waist. Even his belt was too big, and had to be cinched and looped over itself. The shoulder seams of his scratchy wool flannel shirt came down almost to her elbows, and the shirt itself was nearly long enough to be a shift. But the unlikely ensemble was warm and dry and clean, even if it did smell of the leather on the inside of Macalester's saddlebags. She was still wearing her ruined shoes, since her only other choice was to go barefoot.

She had washed the mud off of herself and out of her hair, while Camilla, in her own petticoat, had worked on her orange dress. The gown would never be the same again, but it did look much improved, drying in the light breeze on an evergreen shrub. Geneva brushed her dark hair dry with Macalester's hairbrush and used a scrap of ribbon from her camisole to tie it back into a thick tail that fell to the middle of her back.

Macalester had disappeared nearly an hour before, leaving them his horse and a cheery fire. The idea of flight occurred to Geneva again, but she rejected it at once: She did not know how to ride a horse, and Camilla, too, had confessed to a fear of the animal. They were still a long way from Fort Worth. The opportunity to escape would surely arise again.

"You're a half a day from Pine Bluff, Miss Brooks," Macalester announced upon his return, striding unexpectedly back into camp at last. "Just keep following the river."

Geneva's heart sank.

"Aren't we going to—"

"I was in Pine Bluff last night." Macalester cut her off, his angular features grim. "There's a man looking for me." He did not elaborate.

Geneva could not maintain his hard gaze. Where he had been so gentle and loverlike in Little Rock, he was now cold and nasty. She suddenly felt the annoying urge to cry. Oh, why had she allowed herself to fall in love with R. Hastings McAllister? Trust her, she thought miserably, to fall in love with someone who did not even exist.

The time had come for her to part company with Brooksie, who had proven to be a prudent as well as courageous companion. The younger woman, her dress now cleaner and dry, seemed surprised when Geneva drew her close for a hug.

"Keep that money," Geneva advised her in a whisper so Macalester would not hear her. "Use whatever you need. I'll look for you in New Orleans as soon as I can. And if you hear of a man named Lennox, tell him that you saw us. Godspeed, Camilla."

Camilla's large brown eyes filled with tears.

"I'll be fine." She cast a glance in Macalester's direction. "You take care. I bet it wouldn't take much to charm that big old handsome fella to take you anywheres you want."

Geneva did not answer her. She merely watched as Camilla headed down the path, following the river toward Pine Bluff. Did she imagine it, or did the forest grow a little colder, in spite of the bright midday sun? Soon Camilla Brooks disappeared in the curtain of trees. She felt a gentle hand upon her shoulders and she turned, startled, to see Macalester before her, regarding her with a contrite expression on his undeniably handsome face.

"I'm sorrier than hell about all of this, Geneva," he said, his dark eyes compellingly serious. "Maybe I should have been straight with you from the start."

Geneva kept her features emotionless and glanced after Camilla, who was long gone.

"I wouldn't have come along." She forced an indifferent tone into her voice. "I'm only sorry I didn't see through your plot. And, of course, I despise you for taking undue advantage of the situation. That in itself was unforgivable. Unspeakable, really. Still, one can't expect anything more from an outlaw and a liar, I suppose."

She turned away from him, not wanting him to guess her own chaotic emotions.

"I am both," he admitted, with no trace of pride or amusement in his quiet baritone. "But I swear I never meant to hurt you, Geneva. Your husband is a scheming old bastard, and I think he knew I was going to— that you and I would—oh, damn," he ended up finally, sounding flustered and completely disgusted with himself.

"I can't imagine why Garland wants me back after all of this time." She elected to ignore his awkward apology. "But as I have been brought this far, I may as well go quietly the rest of the way."

In a pig's eye, she thought, tossing her head.

Geneva's legs, back and buttocks ached from endless hours bouncing on the back end of a horse without benefit of a saddle. She would rather have died than admit to Macalester either that she was terrified of horses or that she was in real pain, so she held tightly to his narrow waist and bit her lip to prevent herself from crying out. She was sore, as well, from the constant rubbing against the insides of her thighs, but Macalester did not stop. He did not even speak to her again until it was nearly dark and he finally reined the tireless animal to a halt.

"We'll camp here for the night," he remarked, using the six words she had dreaded hearing. She had hoped for a soak in a hot tub, and a soft, warm bed in a cozy hotel, but it seemed the hard ground and a warm plate of beans were the best she could expect.

Macalester held his arm out, and it was a moment before she realized he was trying to help her down. She took hold of the arm with both of her hands: It was like steel beneath velvet. She tried to swing her leg across the horse's tail, but the burning pain of the chafe was so sharp all at once that she cried out and let go of his arm. Her feet touched the ground and her legs collapsed beneath her. She fell to the earth, feeling as though her legs were on fire.

Macalester was by her in an instant, his handsome, angular features perplexed and concerned.

"What's wrong?" he was asking her, and through the stars that danced before her eyes she was aware of a vague desire to strike him.

"Go away," she managed to whisper, closing her eyes. "You have very nearly killed me today. I refuse to allow you to gloat over me, as well."

But he did not leave her.

"Damn," he muttered, and she felt his hands upon her legs. "You're bleeding, Gen. Bleeding bad. We'll have to get these clothes off. Why didn't you say something?"

He began to undo the belt that cinched her into the trousers. *Don't touch me,* she wanted to shout. She even tried to pull away from him, but the stars in her head grew brighter, and harder, and began to whirl, and it was easier to surrender to them that to fight Kieran Macalester's ministrations.

A small but cheery fire greeted Geneva's eyes when she opened them. The tiny flame crackled and shimmered and laughed at her. There was a small tin cup set upon a rock near the flame. She felt warm, and the pain she remembered so clearly had eased somewhat. She did not want to move.

The object beneath her head was neither hard nor particularly soft, but it was not uncomfortable, either. There was a blanket beneath her body and a blanket on top of her, and between the two, except for the shirt that did not fit, she was naked.

She drew in a deep, shuddering sigh. She had been through too much in the last week to feel any embarrassment. She was thankful to be still, not to have a powerful, relentless beast beneath her like an ever-rolling ship. She wanted never to move again.

"Feeling better?"

It was Macalester. His voice was quiet and gentle. She turned her head slightly, surprised at the effort it required, and saw him sitting on the ground just across from her. One long leg was stretched out before him, the other crooked at the knee, supporting his elbow. In one hand he held a tin cup. He appeared to be relaxing against a rock, or a cluster of rocks. His hat was gone. His handsome features were sharply defined in the orange glow of the small fire, and they were etched with worry.

"Uh huh." She was surprised, even amused, at the weak quality of her voice.

With a small grunt he got up from his repose. She watched as he retrieved the cup that had been warming by the fire and brought it over to her. She tried to sit up, but was reminded sharply of the reason why she lay there in the first place. Macalester, seeming to sense her discomfort, knelt beside her and, without a word, gently lifted and supported her head as he offered her the beverage in the cup.

She drank. It was warm, and that was good, but it was also bitter. After a few swallows, she grimaced and refused more.

"You make terrible coffee, Macalester," she told him, feeling a little stronger.

She heard him chuckle, that deep, rumbling sound that warmed her even more than the fire, or the coffee. He gently lowered her head again.

"That's what Billy always tells me. I guess that's why he usually makes it."

Billy Deal. She was reminded, unpleasantly, of her situation, and with whom she was conversing. She tried to turn her body sideways, but a shaft of pain from her knees to her back convinced her that the effort was not only unnecessary, but foolish as well. She breathed a small sigh in lieu of a cry of pain.

"I guess this is God's punishment to me for lying in Roanoke," she said, half to herself.

"What do you mean?"

In spite of her condition, she relished the proof that he had been completely deceived by her performance in Virginia.

"I wasn't sick at all. I just wanted to get off of the train for the night."

But I needn't tell you why, she added to herself, a sin of omission rather than commission. She heard him laugh once, a harsh and hollow sound.

"If this is how God punishes liars, then I guess I'm in for a heap of trouble," he declared under his breath.

Geneva did not answer him. The stars in her head were beginning to pulsate again.

When Geneva next opened her eyes, it was daylight. Not bright, but light enough for her to realize that the sun was probably up, somewhere beyond the cool morning mist of the Arkansas woods. A single songbird sang high up in the tree above her head. A lark? A bluebird? She did not know. She could not tell one bird from another, except to look at. Nearby a twig snapped, and she turned her head. It was Macalester, up and about, tying something to the saddle of that enormous red monster that had been the source of her wounds the day before.

She caught a slow, shimmering movement in the grass out of the corner of her eye. Curious, she concentrated her attention upon it. In a moment, watching the long gray band slide through the grass and early fallen leaves, she realized it was a snake.

Her scream echoed in the canopy of trees like an alarm, and she jumped up from her makeshift bed, clutching her blanket about her, unable to take her eyes from the terrifying sight. Macalester bounded through the clearing as quick as the wind, carrying a shotgun.

"What is it, Geneva?" he demanded. "What's wrong?"

In reply, she pointed with a trembling hand to the spot where the reptile had been.

"A sn—a snake," she gasped. "It was—it was right in my face!"

Macalester poked the ground with the barrel of the shotgun like a baker testing a huge cake for doneness. He reached down into the grass and brought up a wriggling rope about two feet long.

"A garter snake," he explained curtly, looking around as though expecting important visitors at any moment. "Harmless. And I'll bet half of Arkansas knows we're here now."

He tossed the creature back into the grass and eyed her with annoyance. She felt the small hairs rise on the back of her neck, and she made herself as erect as she could.

"I would like to know how I am to be expected to know the difference between a snake that is harmless and one that is not. It is roughly the equivalent of someone expecting you, as an outlaw, to sing the role of Rigoletto. One finds few snakes of either variety on the stage of the Academy of Music. Although I must confess that my recent education in snakes of all types has been rather enlightening."

"We have to move now." He ignored her remark, looking around again. "Lennox is probably close enough to have heard you."

Geneva sat down on her blanket, folding her arms across her chest and raising her chin in defiance.

"Mr. Lennox is *your* problem, not mine," she pronounced with a lift of her nose. "I refuse to get on that beast again."

135

"You won't have to." Macalester, staring down at her with his thumbs hooked in his gun belt, was laconic. "I've rigged a litter for you. We can't be more than a few miles from a little town called Camden, where we can find you a doctor. You need some kind of salve for those legs, not to mention some decent clothes. I can't take you back to Humble looking like some half-dead squaw, now can I?"

"And you plan to steal the money for all of this?" She mustered as sarcastic a tone as she could, ignoring his implied disparagement.

He grinned at her infuriatingly. "No, I plan to wire Humble for more."

He bent down and, to her astonishment, scooped her easily into his arms, blankets and all, and carried her to the makeshift litter lashed to the horse's saddle and ready to go. He set her on her feet. She was annoyed that the effort seemed not even to have winded him.

"How much is my husband paying you for my return?" she asked in a quiet voice, staring squarely into his frank, unsmiling brown eyes

Macalester did not answer her right away. In fact, for a moment while he stared back at her, she thought he had not heard her question. His gloved hand reached for her face, then he seemed to think better of his gesture, for his hand returned to his side.

"It isn't the amount so much as it is the conditions." His tone was far gentler than his earlier remarks. "I need amnesty from the governor of Texas, and Garland Humble has the kind of power to guarantee that. Besides, your husband is holding my friend Deal hostage. If I don't bring you back, he claims he'll turn Billy in for the reward, and Billy'll spend twenty years at hard labor."

Macalester sighed, unable, it seemed, to meet her gaze any longer.

"It looked so easy when he laid it all out." The outlaw's rugged features were thoughtful. "When I agreed to it, I never expected you to be so—"

He stopped, pursing his wide mouth as though wanting to prevent further words from escaping without his permission.

"Get on the litter." His eyes grew empty of emotion. "It'll be a bumpy ride, but—"

"Macalester." She seized the lapels of his brown flannel shirt, sensing that he might, in this unguarded moment, be vulnerable once more to her charm. "Kieran. Don't take me back! I don't know what Garland wants, but it can't be good. I—I'm afraid of him. Please, just let me go! I'll give you—"

Macalester's strong hands suddenly covered her own, so tightly that she cried out.

"You're good, Geneva," he told her in a hoarse whisper, his eyes burning into her. "You're very good. But this has to be my way. You got away from Garland Humble once; you can do it again. If I can help you, I—"

"You fool!" Her frustration at last overwhelmed her patience. "Garland knows more ways to cheat and to steal than you or I have ever dreamed! He moves people about to suit his whims like pieces in a game of chess! If you imagine he'll ever let you and your Billy Deal go—"

Kieran's mouth covered hers unexpectedly with a bruising strength that nearly suffocated her. She clutched his shirt, wanting, for a wild moment, to remain in his arms forever. His kiss consumed her, made her feel as though the ground had fallen away beneath her feet. He released her, and she nearly fainted as his strength and warmth withdrew from her like a receding wave. He held on to her arms again, and her surroundings stopped reeling. In his dark eyes, she read an infinite sadness that was like a blow to the stomach.

"I'll help you any way I can," he repeated, his voice a shadow of itself.

She had failed. She beat upon his chest with her fists, weak with frustration and despair.

"Damn you, Macalester!" She sobbed. "I hate you!"

She wept in silence as she was bumped relentlessly along in the litter behind Macalester's roan. The gremlin apparently had no liking for the woods, for he was nowhere in evidence.

Chapter Twelve

Macalester's heart rode to Camden, Arkansas, in the heel of his boot. His chest hurt where Geneva had struck him, although the blows had not been hard. He was glad she was not riding with him: The feel of her arms around him would be more than he could bear. With Geneva on the litter, he was able to put her behind himself literally as well as figuratively and, through his own bitterness, concentrate on keeping them both out of the hands of Lennox.

By midday, traveling at an excruciatingly sluggish pace, they reached the town. It was a modest assortment of clapboard structures: houses, stores, saloons, a bank, a livery, a telegraph and post office, a jail, a small hotel, a whitewashed church and, blessedly, a doctor. Macalester was aware of the stares that his odd little procession drew, but he did not acknowledge them. His policy had been, for some time, to hide, as it were, in plain sight. So far, it had worked for over two

139

years. He saw no reason to alter the strategy here.

Macalester dismounted from the roan, and as he tied the reins to the hitching post, a young man emerged from the low building, coatless, the sleeves of his starched white shirt held in place by a pair of black garters. He removed his spectacles and ran his slender, smooth, white hand through his curly brown hair. Macalester noticed all of this while completing the task of securing his horse.

" 'Afternoon," the man offered in a congenial tone, shoving his hands into the pockets of his gray pinstripe trousers.

Macalester touched the brim of his dusty brown Stetson.

" 'Afternoon," he replied. "You the doc?"

"That's me."

Macalester glanced down the street. He was looking for Lennox, and was relieved that he did not see any evidence of the bounty hunter. He approached the young physician, adjusting the brim of his hat against the glare of the midday sun.

"My wife," he began, effecting a sheepish and unsophisticated demeanor, "she's hurt. Can you take a look at her?"

The younger man scrutinized him for a long, hard moment. Then he nodded and went into the building, leaving the door open behind him.

Macalester approached the makeshift litter. Geneva was asleep, or unconscious, but she was gripping the side of the litter with whitened knuckles. Her hair was strewn about her captivating face like fallen leaves. Gazing down at her, he was stricken by a painful feeling he did not care to name. Crouching down beside her, he whispered, "We're here, honey. Put your arms around my neck."

She did not answer him, but she did hold onto him

as he lifted her and the blankets into his arms and followed the doctor into his infirmary.

It was quiet and clean inside, and it smelled of some pungent antiseptic. The doctor, scrubbing his hands in a washbowl, motioned to one of two empty, white-sheeted beds. When Macalester laid Geneva down upon it, he realized, mortified, just how dirty and neglected she looked. He uncovered her as the doctor approached.

"What in the name of God has this woman been doing?" he demanded in quiet outrage.

Macalester did not answer him right away. He watched as Geneva half-opened her eyes. He could not swear to it, but he thought he saw her smile. A wicked smile.

"Riding," he answered the doctor's question at last, preparing his speech and his accent. "She's a city gal, Doc; you know, you can't tell them nuthin'. Thought she could ride bareback all the way from Fort Smith. She ain't a complainer, though, thank God, so I didn't know a thing about it till last night. Well, I couldn't go nowheres till mornin', so I rigged that litter and moved her as soon as it got light."

The doctor glanced at him critically, rolling up his sleeves. "Where's her horse?"

He sounded skeptical. The doctor, Macalester realized grimly, was no fool. Dutifully, the outlaw issued a self-shaming grimace.

"I was so mad when I saw what happened," he lied smoothly. "I up and shot the sumbitch. It was stupid, I know," he went on with a wave of his hand. "Waste of a good horse. But I couldn't help it."

He moved closer to the doctor, who took a half step backward in return.

"I'm plum crazy about that woman, Doc," he wound

141

up just above a whisper. "It would kill me if anything bad happened to her."

Macalester was sorry as soon as the words left his lips: the doctor looked more doubtful than ever. The irony of the situation, Macalester realized, bitterly amused, was that it was the first remotely true thing he had said to the man. He glanced at Geneva, who bestowed a loving look upon him, a look that had trouble written all over it.

"You promised me a sugar cake," she intoned in a fawning whine, aping his own feigned accent. "Go get me a sugar cake, Sugar Cake. And some coffee. Not that awful stuff you make. Some real coffee."

Macalester hesitated. He needed to send a wire to Humble for more money, and he couldn't very well take her with him. But he hated the idea of leaving her behind with the very suspicious doctor. He looked from Geneva to the doctor and back again. Geneva said nothing more but continued to smile in a double-edged way that made him want to choke her. *Damn you, Geneva,* he thought, smiling back at her. Well, if she could take advantage of a situation, so could he.

"Behave yourself, Honey Bunch," he murmured, bending over her for a kiss. "I mean it, Geneva," he whispered, hating the feeling of helplessness she had forced upon him. But there was nothing for him to do but leave her in the skilled hands of the doctor, and leave himself in the treacherous hands of Geneva Lionwood.

Outside, Macalester moved quickly. The telegraph office was a short way down the street. A tersely worded message to Garland Humble in Fort Worth from R. Hastings McAllister regarding diminished funds was, he was sure, sufficient to the moment. Confident of Humble's prompt response, he informed the telegraph operator that he could be reached at the doctor's office when the reply came. He then proceeded to the livery across the street, where he stabled his roan and picked out a gentle old mare for Geneva and some tack. He could pay with cash when Humble contacted the bank.

His stomach growled. He stood in the street fishing in his pockets and came up with a dollar and forty-seven cents. He could buy himself a steak dinner at the hotel for a dollar, he was sure, but he was reluctant to leave Geneva alone with the doctor that long. It was with no small regret that he detoured to the general store, where he bought tins of tea and hash and a packet of tea biscuits to share with Geneva. He slipped a couple of small apples into his pockets on the way out, feeling only a little guilty about his petty larceny. If he remembered, he would leave the store an extra nickel after he got the money from Humble.

He did not knock when he returned to the doctor's infirmary; he merely opened the door and admitted himself to the ward. The doctor, whose name, Macalester realized with some embarrassment, he still did not know, was mixing a concoction in a tall beaker with a long glass rod. He looked up from his medicines, his gaze still critical. What had Geneva told him?

"How's my wife?" Macalester offered by way of greeting, searching the man's face for any sign of betrayal.

"Remarkably well, all things considered," was the doctor's terse reply. "She's soaking in a tub. Go on back. Maybe she needs some more hot water. The kitchen's through there."

Macalester nodded and took a step in the direction the doctor had indicated.

"When will she be able to travel?" He risked the question.

"She shouldn't ride until those sores heal up. I wouldn't even want to see her in a wagon. But I expect you're in a hurry, aren't you?" The man sounded as though he'd heard those words before, more than a few times. Macalester, annoyed, felt his face grow warm. He refrained from another lie, though, not knowing what tales Geneva might have already spun for the doctor, true or otherwise. Instead, he merely stared at the younger man and nodded mutely.

The doctor smirked. "Never knew of anybody passing through Camden that wasn't in a great big hurry to leave it. They always have someplace more important to go."

His remark did not demand an answer, so Macalester gave him none. Satisfied that there was no nervousness or deceit in the doctor's demeanor, Macalester removed his hat and hung it on a peg on the wall behind him before continuing on back to the closed door at the end of the narrow hallway.

He entered without knocking. Geneva lay motionless in the small tub, her bare feet dangling out of the end of it and her wet head pressed against its curved back. Her slender white arm hung limp over the side, her fingertips barely touching the floor. Her eyes were closed and her rose-petal lips were slightly parted for her shallow, regular breaths. Looking at her, Macalester could hear his very blood coursing through his veins. He closed the door behind him and cleared his throat to announce his presence.

"I have never been so sore in my entire life," Geneva remarked in a light, quiet voice, without moving. "And I've never heard a more preposterous tale than the one you told Dr. Thorpe."

Macalester did not answer her. He was thinking about the parts of Geneva Lionwood that he couldn't see. On the stove, a kettle hissed a warning.

"That's my hot water." She yawned, then stretched a little in the small tub. "Do you think you can pour it in here without scalding me?"

Macalester found his tongue at last. "That depends on what you told Dr. Thorpe." He forced a casual tone. He put his parcels on the sideboard and, using a dish-towel, seized the handle of the hot vessel.

Geneva sat bolt upright in the tub, and as he carried the kettle of boiling water toward her, he was wickedly amused by her look of undisguised terror.

"Mac, you wouldn't!" She gasped, crossing her arms in front of her chest. Her green eyes were wide as she edged away from him.

He knew he would never do such a ghastly thing to anyone, let alone her, but he thought it just as well, for the moment, that she was not privy to the same information. He smiled, standing directly over her.

"Well?" He took perverse pleasure in her obvious anxiety. "What does Dr. Thorpe know about Mr. and Mrs. McAllister?"

He saw her gulp.

"Mac, please—" she begged in a whisper.

"This pot's getting awful heavy, Gen," he teased, shaking his head slowly.

"I didn't say anything, Mac; I swear it," she babbled, her green eyes filling with tears.

The sight made him deeply regret his empty threat, although he did not recant it.

"I hardly spoke to him," she went on quickly. "He was more concerned about my injuries than he was about us. I just repeated what you said. I swear. Mac, please don't . . ."

Macalester set the kettle down upon the floor. He kneeled beside the tub, steeling his gaze to hers.

"Do you really think so little of me as to believe me capable of such a thing?"

Tears had worked their way from the corners of her emerald eyes, and he felt them burn him as they crept down the curve of her cheeks.

"I thought I knew you in Memphis," she told him, her voice a faintly whispered reproach. "But I was wrong. I don't know what to believe anymore. I only know I can't afford to make the mistake of trusting you again."

Her words were like sharp arrows delivered to his vital organs from velvet bowstrings. The only answer he could give was to pour the water slowly and carefully into the tub to warm her.

A night in a soft, warm bed, free from the fear of being set upon by marauding insects and other unnamed creatures, was like a night in heaven. Geneva realized, with some grim amusement, as she stretched in the small bed, that little more than a week ago she would have turned up her nose at such mean accommodations. But today was a different day, an entirely different universe from that time. Then, she had had San Francisco, the gem of the Pacific, at her feet, and New York and London in the palm of either hand. She wondered idly, watching the dust particles form a beam of light from the sunshine brightening the small room, if any of them—Blaine, Mapleson, Audrey, Abbey—any of them, cared about what might have become of Geneva Lionwood.

She thought of Camilla Brooks, on her way to New Orleans with three hundred dollars in her bosom.

She thought of Garland Humble, waiting in his Fort Worth fortress for her return.

A shadow crossed before the window, erasing the beam of glistening dust and shattering her reverie. Kieran Macalester: outlaw, abductor, charlatan, abuser and savior; the charismatic, enigmatic man of both her dreams and her nightmares of late, entered the room bearing a small wooden tray covered with a checkered napkin and a large bundle wrapped in brown paper under his arm.

"Bought you a present," he announced in greeting,

adroitly balancing the tray with one hand while tossing her the bundle with the other.

She was amused by her childlike sense of anticipation as she pulled at the strings of the package. Macalester set the tray down upon the table beside her and sank his long, muscular frame into the small wooden chair by the bed. He smelled of horses, and leather, and faintly of the smoke of a wood fire. The combination of scents was arousing.

Inside the package was a black broadcloth riding habit, a crisp white linen blouse, stockings, undergarments and a pair of supple leather riding boots with matching gloves. Stunned, she held up each item, amazed by the quality and detail, and surprised that each garment seemed to be very nearly perfect in size.

"Humble wired the bank," Macalester offered conversationally. "We have enough to finish the trip. But just enough. As soon as you eat breakfast, we'll be on our way. I'm sorry to rush you like this, you not being healed up yet, but—"

"You're always sorry, Macalester." Geneva mustered her most disparaging tone as she sat up to partake of her morning meal. "Why, you're the sorriest man I ever met."

"Geneva!"

Macalester stood up quickly, knocking over his chair. His features were a study of patience worn to the bone. She did not blink as she stared hard at him in return.

"I've done everything I can do, short of letting you go, and the only reason I haven't done that is because I can't," he told her, his baritone low and as hard as steel. "Maybe it would have been better if I'd just tied you to a horse and rode you willy-nilly to Fort Worth. Not that there'd have been much left of you, after that."

"And am I supposed to be thankful that you've chosen a more humane method of abduction?" Geneva curbed

147

her own anger, clenching her hands under the blanket. "You've abused and threatened me. You've used me badly under false pretenses, and my career is in a shambles, not that I can hold you solely accountable for that. You have created a very dangerous person in me, Mr. Macalester: a person with nothing left to lose."

Macalester did not even flinch, although her tirade had been intended to shame him.

"You want to know what dangerous is?" he countered, his tone deliberate. "Dangerous is a wanted man, worth five thousand dollars to a bounty hunter who doesn't much care whether he takes you in in your saddle or across it. Dangerous is knowing for dead certain that your partner will go to prison for twenty years and that you've got another five years of running ahead of you if you don't deliver. Dangerous is doing business with Garland Humble in the first place, and, lady, dangerous, and stupid, is falling in love with his wife!"

Macalester was breathing hard and his dark eyes fairly bored into her soul. He had lied to her before, she knew, but he was not lying now. Her heart hammered loudly in her chest: He was magnificent in his rage, and in his declaration. In spite of everything, she knew, with an awful certainty, that she loved him as well, as she had never loved, or ever would love, any other man. She was obliged to look away, unable to bear the import of his statement, and unwilling to allow him to guess her own feelings.

"Eat your breakfast," Macalester muttered at last. "It's the best you're likely to have between here and Fort Worth. And get ready. We leave as soon as I get back."

"Where are you going?"

Was that her voice? It sounded like a small, petulant child's. Macalester must have thought so, too, for he offered her a grin, in spite of his pale and serious countenance. She felt her own face grow warm.

"Just over the livery, to get the horses. Think you can manage until I get back?"

"I will manage far better," she replied coldly, "if you never get back."

He seemed more amused than hurt by her response. "Use some of the ointment Thorpe gave you," he advised, striding toward the door. "And wrap up your legs in some of that gauze. That'll stop the rubbing. We'll be traveling fast from here on out."

Geneva's heart was chilled. "But I don't know how to ride," she said faintly. "I—I'm afraid of horses."

Macalester treated her to a skeptical look, as though he suspected a lie.

"I mean it, Macalester," she warned him, unable to keep a tremor from her voice.

The outlaw paused at the door, his gloved hand on its lever.

"My ma used to say, 'You're never too old to learn something new.' " Then, tipping her a brief, mocking smile, he was gone.

It seemed to Macalester as though the quiet little town on the Ouachita had somehow shrunk, overnight, to an uncomfortable fit. He resisted a powerful urge to walk in the shadows of the morning. The livery stable was just across the street. In less than an hour, he told himself, they would be on their way, and Camden, except possibly for Dr. Thorpe, would quickly forget them.

Macalester, in his idle moments, sometimes amused himself by imagining that towns did not really exist except as he required them, appearing out of the earth when one needed a soft bed, a soft whore, or even just a beer, then quickly being swallowed up again as soon as he rode out. He wished, lately, that this was true, for if it was, Lennox wouldn't have a prayer of finding him.

The livery proprietor came out to greet him, a man

older than himself; older, possibly, than any other man he had ever met. He looked as though he had been born in the patched denim trousers, green suspenders and worn, stained undershirt he was wearing, and would probably die in them. His derby, no doubt once black, was covered with dust and salt stains, and his gray whiskers looked like a layer of ash upon his weathered face. The three teeth remaining in his mouth appeared to exist for the sole purpose of holding the two-inch stub of cigar that, unlit, made a ludicrous ornament to the man's already comical visage.

"Settlin' up?" was his only remark.

Macalester nodded, reaching into his pocket.

"Seen any new faces?" he inquired of the man conversationally, peeling off the appropriate denomination.

The man said nothing. He did not reach for the bills Macalester extended to him. Chagrinned, Macalester added another dollar.

"Nope," the man cackled cheerfully, taking the money with a lightning quick gesture and turning away, as though worried that Macalester might try to get his extra dollar back.

A dollar for good news was not a bad trade, Macalester reasoned, leading his roan and the little bay mare, saddled and packed, out of the stable. There remained evening accounts with Dr. Thorpe and getting Geneva into the saddle, and the last leg of this bizarre odyssey could continue. Nine days remained in the original month Humble had allowed him, although now that seemed so long ago. Somewhere during that time he had lost his heart, and he was doubtful he would ever reclaim it again.

Glancing up the street, he saw the young doctor striding purposefully along the walk toward the infirmary. Macalester quickened his own pace, glad of a happenstance that would eliminate the need for him to go looking for the man.

"We won't be taking up any more of your time, Doc," Macalester greeted the man, who pulled up short as though he had been caught filching a penny candy. His soft brown eyes had the look of a cornered doe. Macalester grew uneasy watching him.

"Already?" The man seemed to make several attempts at the word before it actually came forth.

Macalester nodded, glancing once up the street in the direction from which Thorpe had come.

"What's wrong, Doc? You seen a ghost?" His genial tone, he knew, was laced with suspicion. He took the man firmly by the arm. "Let's walk around back with these animals, and you and me'll settle up inside."

Macalester wanted to get off of the street. Something had scared the doctor, and he had a sneaking suspicion he knew what that something was. Leading the doctor and the two horses up the alleyway, he made a rapid decision. He tethered the horses to the railing of the back stairs and ushered the nervous physician in the back door of his infirmary with one of his best self-assured smiles.

"I paid sixty dollars for that mare," Macalester remarked, silently drawing his gun as Thorpe preceded him into the kitchen. Deftly, the outlaw slipped the bolt on the door, locking it.

Dr. Thorpe made a lunge for the cupboard, but Macalester leveled his Colt and cocked it. The sound alone was enough to stop the nervous young physician cold.

"What are you going to do to me?"

The man's voice quivered. Macalester was satisfied that Thorpe would do anything he was told.

"I'm going to give you the mare," Macalester replied, enjoying his dual role of tyrant and benefactor. He gestured with the muzzle of the Colt, and Thorpe followed

151

his direction, backing slowly away from the cupboard, his fresh features a study of bewilderment.

"What?"

"All you have to do," Macalester went on, not taking his eyes from his quarry, "is ride her."

With his left hand, he opened the drawer Thorpe had gone for and withdrew the gun. Satisfied, he tucked the weapon into his own belt. The doctor, as Macalester had hoped, continued to be amazed.

"Tell me who you talked to this morning," the outlaw ordered.

"There was a man," the doctor seemed almost eager to reply, "in the general store. I didn't talk to him, but I heard him asking about a man and a woman."

"What else did he say?"

It might have been a coincidence; it was possible, Macalester knew, that he was worried over nothing. But more than likely it was Lennox who had dogged them here.

"He said the woman was a looker. And he described you pretty well, too." Thorpe seemed less nervous now, but he remained perfectly still. Macalester was pleased by his cooperation: The idea of killing, or even hurting the man, was repugnant to him.

"What'd the fellow look like?"

As though reading from a textbook, the doctor described Lennox to the tips of his waxed mustache. The doctor, unfortunately, had a sharp memory, coupled with an unsettling ability to conjure a mental image. This was not a comforting prospect to Macalester, who would eventually release the man to tell his story to anyone who would listen. With a few brief words, Macalester ordered his hostage into the next room.

Geneva, luckily, was dressed, and she sat upon the bed brushing her chestnut hair. She dropped the brush and stood up abruptly, her eyes wide at the sight of Macalester's gun.

"Oh, God, Mac—"

"Be quiet and listen," Macalester interrupted her tersely. "Don't talk, either one of you. We're going out the back. Gen, tie the doctor's wrists with that gauze. Not too tight."

For a moment, Macalester thought the diva was going to rebel. His countenance must have persuaded her against the folly of such a course, for she hesitated only a moment before complying with his request.

Weight. He needed weight. He glanced about quickly and spied something in a corner.

"What are those?" he demanded of the doctor.

"Sandbags," the young man replied. "I use them to stabilize fractures."

Macalester tested one. He judged it to weigh about fifty pounds.

"Grab one of those and drag it on out back," he ordered the man, who managed nicely in spite of his imposed handicap. Macalester himself hoisted two of the bags over his shoulder and gestured to Geneva to precede him up the short corridor.

"I don't trust you at my back anymore," he told her.

"What are you going to—"

"I'll explain later." He cut off her question, straining his ears for any suspicious noise from outside.

Lennox was a few hundred feet away, and perhaps moments from learning his whereabouts, if he did not know them already.

Chapter Thirteen

The fear of God. Somewhere, somehow during the course of his life, Kieran Macalester, through accident or will, had divined the secret of instilling such dread in other people, mastering its mysteries to his unending benefit. He did not even require his gun to support the implied threat of his countenance; in fact, had any of the objects of his intimidations been privy to his singular lack of skill with the implement, he was certain the result would be considerable diminishment of his effectiveness. Geneva Lionwood and Dr. Thorpe both stood patiently by as Macalester, his gun holstered, secured the three sandbags to the mare's saddle. He needed to provide a distraction for Lennox, and a convincing one. It was his intention to send Thorpe, on the weighted mare, south-southeast on a parallel course with the Ouachita, while he and Geneva, on the roan, would double back northeast before striking southwest again.

154

At best, his strategy would throw Lennox, who was only a fair tracker, off of their trail for a few days. At worst, it would buy the outlaw a few precious hours to think of something else.

With mixed sentiments as to the chances of success for his plan, Macalester sent the frightened young doctor off. The doctor, he knew, was smart, and would not ride very long, perhaps half a day at most, before he realized that he was not being followed by them, as he'd been told. But maybe by the time he returned to Camden, Lennox would be gone again, having missed the valuable information that might have helped him.

Geneva, for a tall, ample woman, was astonishingly light. His hands spanning her waist, he lifted her easily onto the roan, on a blanket he had secured as a makeshift seat about the horn before him. He was startled to discover that she was trembling in his arms as he held her fast before him.

"Mac, I'm frightened," she ventured, her voice muffled by the collar of his jacket, into which she had buried her face.

He was momentarily crippled by a painful spasm of tenderness for her.

"Don't be," he advised her, nudging the roan to a trot as he held her firmly with his right arm. "Lennox won't catch us."

She lifted her head suddenly, an expression of disdain apparent on her heartbreakingly lovely face. "I don't give a damn about Lennox." She sniffed. "I hope he does catch you. I'm afraid of this animal, and I'm scared to death that you'll let me fall off at a full gallop!"

Macalester laughed. "Don't worry, honey. You're worth far too much to me to drop on the road, much as I might be of a mind to do it."

He held her tighter, cantering out of town, heading back the way they had come.

155

They rode hard. Geneva was as tense in his embrace as a ball of string wound too tightly, and soon his arms began to ache with the effort of securing her in place and managing the powerful beast who carried them effortlessly through the Arkansas woods. He had not anticipated the task to be so tiresome. That, he assumed, was because a part of him had been looking forward to the duty.

It was mid-afternoon before he stopped. He had been heading north, as far as he could tell, since leaving Camden and he thought it safe to head back toward Texarkana and Fort Worth. The afternoon had clouded over, and the weather had gone cool and damp. Macalester wanted to slide off the roan and into a soft, warm bed for a nap. He dismounted, feeling the small pulls and aches in his muscles that reminded him that he was thirty-five years old, not a young man anymore. On solid earth once more, he helped Geneva slide to the ground, where she nearly collapsed before him until he caught her arms.

Thank God she ain't a complainer. He recalled his earlier words to Dr. Thorpe in his affected backwoods drawl.

She drew in a hard, shuddering breath. "Where are we?" she murmured, still holding onto his arms as she arched her back.

He resisted an urge to pull her close to him for a comforting embrace: Her comfort, or his own? He could not be sure which.

"You don't want to know," he replied lightly. "Because we aren't anywhere near where we should be. Are you hungry, or do you—need to do anything?"

He was looking into her eyes all at once, unexpectedly. He felt trapped in a lovely emerald prison. He felt as though the earth had mysteriously evaporated into a cloudy mist at his feet. He swore he heard the ocean in his ears.

"We should go back to Pine Bluff," she said, sounding exhausted. "We could take a steamer all the way to New Orleans, and then either take the train to San Antonio or sail to Galveston. I won't make it this way, Kieran, and I suspect you won't, either."

Macalester knew, feeling an ache in every joint, that she was right, even if it was merely her intention to get to New Orleans so she could try to escape from him again. But time and money were running out. The route she was suggesting would add days to their journey, and would cost far more than the meager recent allowance advanced to him by Humble. Frowning to himself, the outlaw walked about, working out the kinks. He was not hungry, even though the day was nearly over and he had not eaten since early in the morning. He was taut as a barbed wire fence, and could no more think of eating than of making love . . .

"I wish we could, Gen." He flexed his stiff shoulders. "But we can't. We have to make it this way as far as Texarkana. If Lennox doesn't catch up to us, we'll take the stagecoach to Fort Worth. I promise."

"And if Lennox does catch you?"

Macalester stared at her. Her gaze was matter-of-fact, if not disparaging. He was certain her change from "we" to "you" was intentional.

"How did you get away from Humble?" He changed the subject, taking his canteen from his saddle.

"I had six months to make my plans," he heard her say in an even tone as he swallowed the tepid, tasteless water. "I knew every way out of Fort Worth."

He offered her the canteen, and she accepted it with graceful, gloved hands. He watched her press its collar to her mouth and take a few small sips, then blot the corners of her lips with the back of her glove as she handed it back to him. She wore a carefully blank expression, and he wanted, oddly, to change that. Even a scowl would be preferable. There was something disturbing about the faraway look in her clear green eyes.

"I bet old Gar didn't put up with your temper," he teased, but did not laugh.

Geneva focused her gaze on his, but did not answer right away, although her look seemed to be speaking to him in a very distinct language that he, unfortunately, could not comprehend.

"Old Gar," she said in a faint, passable mockery of the jovial tone he had used, "is a monster."

Her quiet, clear words fell like drops of acid upon silk. Were it not for the hissing burn afterward, Macalester would have sworn she had not spoken them at all.

The canteen fell to the ground at his feet, and before he quite knew what he was doing, he had taken hold of her arms with his two hands.

"What do you mean? Geneva, what did he do to you?"

Her jaw tightened and her mouth narrowed to a thin line, as though she did not intend to allow further words to escape without a struggle.

"What does it matter?" Her chin went up an inch. "You'll have your amnesty, and your Billy Deal. And I've beaten Garland Humble before. I—I'll do it again."

Macalester, stunned, was powerless to do anything more except to stare at her. He perceived, all at once, something he had not noticed before, although he could not now see how he had failed to recognize it: Geneva Lionwood was as strong-willed as any man he had ever known, indeed, stronger than many. She would tell him nothing more now. Gazing at her impassive yet undeniably lovely features, he knew that. There was something magnificent about her expression. Defiant. And more than a little unsettling.

She turned her head, looking into the forest. "What's that noise?"

Macalester, startled out of his rapt contemplation, released her arms. "What?"

He heard it then, as soon as the word left his lips: a slow, regular thrumming, coupled with distant shouts, erratic as random gunfire.

"Damn it!" he ejaculated.

Kieran Macalester had been on the wrong end of enough wildcat posses to recognize one when he heard it. Damn that doctor! He couldn't have ridden more than an hour down the Ouachita before hightailing it back to Camden to rustle up a few locals with nothing better to do than hunt down five thousand dollars. That in itself was some comfort: The doctor, he realized, was smart enough to know that sharing his information with Lennox would be far less lucrative than running him down themselves. Chances were that none of these men, however many there might be, had Lennox's know-how. Certainly none of them knew him as well as Lennox did.

But could Lennox be far behind such a large and conspicuous gathering?

Macalester could waste no time being disgusted with himself. He had already allowed himself too much distraction. He should have heard the posse sooner, and he would have, had he not been so consumed by Geneva Lionwood Humble. By now, it might be too late. Already, the sounds were all around them. To slip by this posse now would be like threading a needle in a dark room. Unless . . .

He retrieved his canteen and swung quickly into the saddle, lifting Geneva before him without giving her a moment to protest. Securing his arms tightly about her, he whispered, "Don't make a sound," and nudged the eager roan to a trot.

Geneva, crushed against Kieran's broad, unyielding chest, could hear his heart beating in a strong, accelerated pace. She was frightened, too, but not by the same things that caused the outlaw's heart to race. She was frightened by what she had been forced to remember, and by the thought of meeting Garland Humble again, face to face, after so much time.

Macalester pressed onward, toward the very core of the noises. His strategy became clear to her: In the confusion of many scattered riders, he hoped to pass in their midst, slipping by in plain view, posing as one of them. It seemed an audacious, almost foolhardy plan, and Geneva prayed it would fail. If these men, however many there were, could take Macalester, then she would be free—free to return to New York, or New Orleans, or anywhere else she desired to go.

"We just passed a couple of them," she heard him whisper hoarsely. "There's a cave up ahead. We'll hide there until dark, and try to move out then."

Macalester knew, as they neared the entrance, that they could not ride the animal inside. He reined up and allowed Geneva to slide off the saddle. He dismounted as well, and took hold of the rein, pulling the roan toward the cleft in the rocks.

The horse resisted, whinnying, tossing his mane and eyeing Macalester with real distrust. Beside him, he heard Geneva utter a small, bitter laugh.

"It's over, Macalester," she said, her tone rising in pitch excitedly. "They're not going to let you get by. I'm only sorry I won't get to see you—"

Macalester clasped his hand over her mouth, none too gently, to stop the sound. He pulled her close.

"Be quiet, Geneva. You don't know what you're saying! Do you imagine these men are fine, upstanding pillars of the community? They won't listen to anything you have to say! As far as they know, you're my wife!

160

Or my whore. Nothing would make them happier than to rape you before my eyes, and maybe leave you to die in the woods. Is that what you want?"

She twisted her head away from his grip, her hair coming loose from its knot and falling across her angry features.

"You're lying," she accused, her voice shaking. "You've lied to me from the very beginning. I don't see why I should believe you now. You only want to save yourself!"

She tried to break away from him, but he pulled her back, holding her defiant face in his hands; wanting to make her see the danger that she herself was in. She was so reckless that she broke his heart.

"I have lied," he told her, his voice a hoarse whisper. "But I'm not lying now; I swear it. Geneva, if you ever believed me, if you ever believed that I love you, believe me now!"

She stared at him, amazed. Her expression changed rapidly to disbelief.

"You don't love me," she sneered elegantly. "You loved the idea of possessing the wife of Garland Humble. How dare you speak to me of love! You can't even begin to comprehend the meaning of the w—"

His mouth covered hers. He had to stop her words. He could not allow her to alert the posse with her tirade, and he could not bear to hear her malign his feelings anymore. Her lips yielded to his, filling him with the pain of the realization that she would never understand, that his desire would henceforth go unfulfilled, and that he had no one but himself to blame for all of it.

She wrenched away from him, and the damp stillness of the Arkansas woods was pierced by her scream. It was a sound that surely must have rivaled any the young soprano had ever executed upon a stage. For an instant she froze in Macalester's embrace, her green eyes wide with wonder at the Pandora's box she had willingly opened.

Move, Mac! a voice inside of him urged. *Move now!* But he gazed a moment longer at her face, wanting never to move again. He released her at last from his embrace and seized her wrist in one hand and the bridle of the roan in the other. Scrambling, he pulled them both toward the narrow mouth of the cave. Behind them, the shouts of the posse closed in upon them.

Chapter Fourteen

The inside of the cave was dark, damp and cold. There was no way to tell how large or how small the space might be, except for the sound of their combined footfall, echoing like restless souls in a graveyard. Geneva hated it, but she was too frightened to protest further. Macalester's pronouncement had shaken her; there was no denying it. As much as she knew Kieran Macalester to be a rogue and a liar, she also knew that, in some incomprehensible way, he did care for her, and would not, with the exception of restoring her to Humble, see her come to harm.

Macalester held tightly to her hand, hurting her. In the thin shaft of light that slipped like a sprite through the entrance of the cave, she could see his angular features, tense and straining. He was listening hard.

"They've lost us," he whispered presently, and she could not tell whether he really believed it, or was trying to convince himself. "They've trampled all over our

163

trail; they'll never guess that we slipped right by . . ."

From outside the cave came the sounds of men and horses. Geneva stifled a gasp.

"Shh." Macalester's admonishment was barely audible.

"Hollis, why don't you and Ed take a short look in the cave?"

"Hell," said another voice. "Go look yerself, Orin, if yer so interested. We'll give you a right fine burial, after Macalester puts some daylight through ya."

Two other voices laughed. The sound made Geneva shudder. She felt a gentle pressure about her shoulder, and she realized it was Macalester's arm. The gesture was so protective that she stared at him, wondering how deeply he'd had to dig inside of himself for the quick, reckless grin he flashed her.

Suddenly the roan snorted. The sound was like an explosion, echoing off the walls of the cavern. Macalester's smile disappeared. After a deathly still moment, there was a chorus of laughter from outside.

"I allus thought that cave was haunted," one man chortled, "but not by no horse ghost!"

"Best come on out, Macalester," another voice encouraged. "There ain't but one way outta there, and this is it. Four of us is waitin' for yuh, so don't try nuthin'."

Macalester's face, in the darkness, turned grim. Geneva started to move, but he held her fast to him. What could he be waiting for? she wondered, more curious as to the possible outcome of this situation just now than she was frightened by it. They had reached a stalemate. It remained only to see which side would tire first.

A shot was fired. The bullet ricocheted off the walls of the cavern like a crazed and deadly insect. All at once she was on her back on the floor of the cave and Macalester was on top of her, his weight crushing her so she could scarcely breathe. It had happened so quickly that she did not even know how she had gotten there; she assumed Macalester had pulled her down to protect her.

"Guess we won't know if we hit 'em till we hear 'em fall," one of the men opined.

Macalester said nothing but lifted his head, listening. Geneva tried to think, but all she could envision was being out of that clammy and inhospitable cave, where there was less of a chance that a random bullet might end her life prematurely.

"Why don't we all jest fire away?" another voice suggested. "It's five thousand, dead or alive. He's one hell of a sight less dangerous dead."

Choruses of righteous agreement ensued. Geneva felt a stirring within her like an embryonic volcano.

"No!" she cried out as the eruption surfaced.

Macalester, still on top of her, stared at her, his features stricken. Her heart hammered loudly. There was no retreat, now.

"Who's there?" one man demanded. "Come on out here with your hands up! And don't try nuthin' funny!"

Funny! Geneva trembled. There was nothing whatever remotely funny about this predicament!

Wordlessly, Macalester eased off of her.

"Don't shoot!" she called out, willing her voice to stop shaking. "I'm coming out."

She got to her feet unsteadily, and the outlaw stood up with her. He took hold of her arms, gazing down at her, and she could see him in the dim light from the entrance. She wanted to speak to him, but the words would not come. He nodded quickly, as though responding to an unvoiced question. He pressed a kiss against her forehead, like a blessing, and then released her, silently. She wanted to cry.

Taking the roan's lead from Macalester's outstretched hand, she walked away from him to the

165

mouth of the cave. She held up her arm against the
contrasting brightness of the outside, but was seized in
a ruthless grip that made her cry out in shock and pain
as her arm was wrenched behind her back.

"Where's yer man, bitch?" A low, gravelly voice
sounded near her ear.

Pain snaked across her shoulders, making her dizzy.
She wanted to speak but could not form the words. The
sounds went forth in little gasps.

"Let 'er go, Orin," one man advised, with no particular enthusiasm. "She ain't gonna tell us nuthin' if she
cain't breathe."

"That's a fine-lookin' horse she's got there," another
offered.

"Horse, hell, Ed!" the fourth man exclaimed. "That's
a fine-lookin' woman that horse's got there!"

The man they called Orin released her abruptly and
she fell to her knees, still reeling from the sudden pain
he had inflicted upon her. She willed the small patch of
ground around her to stop moving, and presently she
saw four pairs of boots in the mud before her eyes.

"You his wife?" a hard voice challenged her from
above.

"Whatsa matter with you, Hollis? Doc already told
you she was!"

"Get up," a third voice ordered.

Geneva was filled, suddenly, with disdain for these
men, whose faces she had not even yet seen. Slowly,
and with no assistance, she got to her feet. She stood
erect and, one by one, met each man's unpleasant gaze
full in the eye. Each of them was taller than she, and
each seemed to measure her in a most distressing way
as they met her gaze boldly.

"Where's Macalester?"

The one who had hurt her, Orin, addressed her again.
He was a thin, balding man whom she guessed to be in

his forties. The passage of time had apparently left the
man with a strong, wiry build and an undeniably mean
disposition. She drew in a deep, broken breath and
prayed that the four men, standing close enough for her
to detect their dire need to bathe, would believe the
story she was about to spin.

"Macalester," she began, managing a low and even
tone, "is not my husband. He took me as a hostage. He
abandoned me here when he learned we'd been followed. I think he's heading for Pine Bluff. I—"

She was on the ground again, and her jaw throbbed
so that she saw stars.

"Jesus, Orin, you're a mean bastard!" The other man's
tone was envious.

"You're lyin'." Orin ignored the compliment. "Doc
said you two was real cozy. You're lyin' to protect him;
I think the sumbitch is still here. He in that cave?"

"Not anymore, he's not." Macalester's casual, insolent
drawl caused five heads, including Geneva's, to turn in
his direction. Macalester looked cool and incredibly
self-assured. Indeed, he dared to grin at the party,
pointing his revolver at the self-styled leader, Orin.

"Throw down your guns." He circled the group
slowly. "Nice and easy."

Geneva watched in wonder as the surprised men did
as they were told. She got up again, slowly, touching
her jaw to be sure Orin had not broken it with his blow.
Macalester had been right, after all, about the posse.
She had no desire to find out exactly how right. She
caught the roan's lead as Macalester ordered the men
into the cave from which he himself had lately emerged.

He moved quickly after that, picking up each gun,
emptying the chambers, then throwing them as far as
he could in different directions. The bullets he pock-
etcd. Geneva watched him in silence, wondering how
many times the outlaw had performed these tasks be-

fore. She was filled with an odd mixture of dread and relief at being back in his hands again, and it would take her some time to sort through these emotions. She waited for his instruction.

He glanced up at her finally, as though he had forgotten about her.

"Scatter their horses," he said, checking the roan's saddle. "The rest are likely to be here any time. We have to move, and we have to make it tough for them to follow us."

Scatter them? Geneva turned to the large, placid animals doubtfully. They stood huddled together, swishing their tails to flick away insects. She realized, chagrinned, that she had no idea how to accomplish the task.

Behind her, a twig snapped. Turning, she saw that Macalester had broken off a willow switch. He applied it sharply to the flanks of two of the animals and made a noise to frighten them further. Instantly, the creatures bolted into the woods. When he faced her again, he was grinning.

"See how easy it is?"

He did not wait for an answer. He mounted the roan quickly and reached for her hand.

"Don't move, Macalester!"

From several locations, the sound of cocked shotguns stopped the outlaw cold. Geneva held her breath. Into the clearing came five more men, including Dr. Thorpe, all with long-barreled weapons leveled at them.

"Don't shoot!" she heard Macalester say, his baritone clear and strong. "She's worth more alive than I am dead."

"Damn you, Macalester," she whispered, sending a glare his way.

Geneva ran toward the doctor. "Dr. Thorpe, make them listen to me!" she began, trying to keep her wits about her. "I'm not Macalester's wife! I—"

The doctor, his eyes cold, leveled his gun at her chest. She stopped short where she was, five feet in front of him.

"You had plenty of chances to tell me that yesterday, and you never did," he told her. His words were like icicles driven into her breast.

"She's telling the truth, Thorpe." Macalester's voice was steady behind her. "Her husband is Garland Humble, in Fort Worth. He hired me to bring her back. She's worth a lot of money to him."

"They're lyin', both of 'em!" Orin, newly emerged from the cave with his compatriots, added his opinion with a savage scowl.

The members of the ragtag posse, to a man, looked at Dr. Thorpe. Geneva's heart lifted: There was a chance she could win him.

Thorpe ordered Macalester off the roan, a command the older man promptly obeyed. Macalester raised his hands slowly, demonstrating that he would not try to resist. Geneva saw, but could not react to, Orin stealing up behind Macalester, deftly taking the outlaw's gun from his holster and, before Macalester could turn, thumping him handily over the head with the butt of the weapon. A cry escaped Geneva before she could prevent it, but she made no move toward the fallen man. She faced Thorpe again, knowing, with a grim certainty, that she would not get another opportunity such as this.

"Dr. Thorpe." She strove for the kind of cool composure Macalester had demonstrated minutes earlier. "Please. You must listen to me. I must get to Pine Bluff, to the steamboat. Macalester—he—"

"Shut up," the doctor ordered peremptorily, looking distracted.

"But—"

169

"Somebody gag her." He cut her off, turning away. "And tie up Macalester, too. It's getting dark. We won't make it back to town tonight. We may as well make camp here."

Geneva felt the rough, bruising hands of a man only too happy to oblige the doctor's request. She lowered her head, cursing Macalester, and herself.

Chapter Fifteen

Macalester thought that when he opened his eyes he would find himself on the floor of the hotel room in Little Rock. He was surprised, therefore, to find his face pressed against the dirt and debris of the Arkansas forest floor, although he was not surprised by the burning, throbbing pain in the back of his head. His eyes focused on a fire and the men seated around it. The air was filled with the sounds of their voices, laughing, talking about the many ways to spend the reward they would split, and the sound of spoons scraping tin plates.

Macalester tried to sit up but discovered that he could not move. His wrists and his ankles were securely bound behind him in such a way as to make movement nearly impossible. He was able, however, to move his neck, if he didn't mind the excruciating pain, and he discovered that Geneva was beside him, similarly bound, and gagged, as well. She was staring at him, her green eyes reproaching him. He knew, with a sinking

171

heart, that the look would haunt him for the rest of his days, especially if those days were spent splitting rocks in prison.

"Are you hurt?" he got out in a whisper, not sure whether he could have managed a louder tone.

She stared at him a moment longer, then glanced at the assemblage of men. He could tell that she was thinking that it was just a matter of time . . .

"Hey, Thorpe!" he called, and all heads turned in his direction.

"What do you want, Macalester?" The doctor, seated a little apart from the rest, sounded weary. Macalester guessed the man was wondering, about now, why he was sitting out in the damp, chilly woods with a bunch of good old boys eating canned beans instead of sitting by a warm fire in an easy chair with a good book and a glass of brandy. Macalester didn't answer him, so the man got up, with effort, and ambled over to the captives on stiff legs.

"These ropes are awful tight," he said when the young doctor stood over him. "And I'm mighty tired of eating dirt. Help me up?"

He could feel Geneva's eyes upon him, but he did not even glance at her. Sighing, the doctor bent down. This adventure, Macalester could tell, was beginning to wear on the man. In moments, he felt the ropes give a little. Then the doctor took him by the shoulders and righted him, leaning him against a tree.

"She's not my wife, Thorpe." Macalester kept his voice low, hoping not to attract the attention of the others. "Don't let anything bad happen to her. Wire Garland Humble in Fort Worth when you get back to town. He'll back me up; I swear it."

The doctor sighed, backing away from him. "I'll see what I can do," he said, rather lamely, Macalester thought.

"Can't you untie her?" He had to push for as much as he could get from the man. "At least take the gag off of her. She's mouthy, I know, but . . ." He shrugged as best he could, under his constraining circumstances.

Thorpe grimaced and glanced at Geneva.

"If she doesn't keep her mouth shut, I can't be responsible for what happens to her," he warned, shaking his head as he looked back at Macalester. "These boys're pretty worked up. It doesn't take much to turn some men into wild animals, if you know what I mean."

Macalester did. He risked a look at Geneva, but could gain no clue to her thoughts from her blank stare.

"Hear that, Gen?"

She nodded slowly. She heard: but would she heed?

Thorpe stepped over Macalester and removed Geneva's gag.

"What're you doin', Doc?" Orin challenged him, accepting a jug from his neighbor.

"They have to eat," Thorpe answered tersely. "Hand me a plate of beans."

"Damn you, Macalester," Geneva hissed as the doctor walked away.

"You already played that song, honey." He sighed. "Don't you know any others?"

"Shut up," someone at the fire told them.

"Oh, leave them alone, Hollis," Thorpe chided the man. "They're human beings."

"Not for long, if they make any trouble," another piped up. Several of the men laughed.

"They ain't human," Orin growled, looking right at Macalester with real dislike. "They're just an outlaw and his whore. They're nuthin' to nobody."

There were choruses of grunts that Macalester, with growing apprehension, took for agreement with Orin's unpleasant sentiment. He glanced at Geneva, who stared blankly at the assemblage, the fire gleaming in her eyes. Her lower lip quivered.

"That's enough!" Thorpe, agitated, turned on the men. "I won't have these people treated any worse than they have been. I'm beginning to think this woman is telling the truth, after all."

"He's a fancy talker, Doc," Hollis warned. "I wouldn't put no stock in anything Kieran Macalester has to say. Or his whore, neither."

"Who put you in charge 'a this trip, anyway, Doc?" Orin drawled, leaning back on his elbows.

Macalester did not like that one. He was trouble.

The doctor then made his mistake. Standing in the center of the ring of men, he drew his gun, demonstrating to Macalester, and no doubt to the rest of the assemblage, his lack of skill with the weapon as well as his lack of diplomacy.

"I'm the one who put you all wise to Macalester." Thorpe's voice, and hand, shook. "If it hadn't been for me, that bounty hunter would have gotten him, and we'd never have seen any of the money. Now let's all calm down and—"

He was cut short by Hollis, who had arisen stealthily behind the naive and foolish younger man and clipped him behind the ear with a rock before Macalester could even summon a warning.

"Damn, Hollis!" One of the men sat bolt upright.

"Whatsa matter, Ed?" the man with the rock sneered. "Your liver turnin' white, too?"

Macalester's mouth went bone dry. This was not good. He licked his lips, looking from face to face, trying to find a reasonable man. His search was in vain.

Orin stood up and swaggered over to the captives. He paused first by Macalester and grinned down at him with a leer that sickened the outlaw.

"She must be pretty good," he opined hungrily, "for you to lie like that for her. Think I'll have me a taste."

"Orin, you ain't gonna . . ." Ed laughed nervously.

"Her husband's the most powerful man in Texas," Macalester heard himself say, although he hardly recognized his own voice; it sounded as brittle as glass. "He'll hunt you down like dogs, and kill you, every one of—"

"You're a damned liar." Orin punctuated his casual rejoinder with a savage kick that caught Macalester in the side, just above his hip bone. "You're just tryin' to protect your property. Well, a man like you got no right to property. None at all. So you can just lay there and watch while we make your property our'n."

Macalester barely heard him. He nearly blacked out from the pain, but he fought to remain conscious. When he opened his eyes again, Orin was standing over Geneva, wearing the look of a rutting animal. Geneva was staring up at the man with a blank expression. Her body was rigid. Orin glanced once more at Macalester, as though to be sure the outlaw was watching him.

" 'Sides." Orin grinned. "This ain't Texas. This here's Arkansas."

With that, Orin was upon her, tearing at her clothing. She struggled against him valiantly, although her hands were still secured behind her back. Her scream was silenced by Orin's mouth upon hers, but in another moment Orin jerked as though he'd been bitten by a snake, and he sat up, straddling her.

"Sumbitch!" he howled, and blood dripped from the corner of his mouth. He struck her hard with the back of his hand, turning her face to one side. "She bit my tongue!"

Good for her, Macalester thought.

The other men gave him no sympathy either.

"Best stick it where she got no teeth, Orin," one advised, ambling over to join his injured companion.

Geneva lay still beneath Orin, her blouse torn and the

175

round white flesh of her breast exposed nearly to the nipple.

"I'll see you all in hell," Macalester heard her say in a remarkably steady voice, "before I let you take me!"

"Shut the bitch up! Where's that gag?"

Macalester did not want to watch. He felt helpless to prevent what was about to happen, and it sickened him to think he had brought it upon her.

A distraction! That was what he needed.

"If this ain't the sorriest excuse for a posse I ever saw in my life!" He managed a laugh that, he was sure, only sounded unnatural to himself. "A bunch of randy old men who let their peeters do their thinkin' for them! Hell, I'll be free again before morning!"

"Is that a fact?" one of them huffed, swaggering past Geneva to where he sat, bound and defenseless. *Here is where I get the shit kicked out of me*, Macalester thought. Well, at least that would take their minds off raping Geneva. For a little while, anyway. The thought encouraged him, and he laughed again, louder.

"You fellas are pretty stupid," he declared roundly. "The best piece of ass in the world ain't worth five thousand dollars!"

His comments, he was pleased to note, seemed to have taken some of the heat out of the men. Orin, still straddling the ravaged soprano, was livid with rage. He and Hollis joined the man who stood before him, along with the other men who had, until now, watched events from the campfire.

"You got a big mouth, Macalester," Hollis remarked with a scowl. "Somebody needs to shut it for you."

Macalester managed a shrug. "Anybody think he's man enough?"

Orin snickered. "You'd like for us to untie you to find out, wouldn't you? You're a smart sumbitch, Macalester, but we ain't quite as stupid as all that."

176

Macalester didn't know about that. In fact, returning the older man's derisive sneer with one of his own, he began to think it entirely possible.

"Maybe you're not stupid," Macalester allowed in a most condescending fashion, "but you sure aren't smart, either."

He opened his mouth to go on, intending to press Geneva's case with the men, but he closed it again, deciding it was best not to return their attention to the woman. All eyes were upon him now, and he did not wish to remind them of her presence.

Staring hard at Macalester, Orin withdrew a long, shiny hunting knife from its sheath on his belt. Macalester hated knives. The fact was, he hated guns, as well, and any other kind of weapon that might bring him to serious harm. He forced himself, however, to maintain Orin's stare without blinking.

"Orin, you ain't gonna—"

"I'm gonna cut out his tongue!" Orin hissed, holding the knife in an underhand position. "His bitch near bit off mine; I'll take his for payment!"

A nearby blast deafened Macalester, and Orin flew back a good five feet into the air, a gaping, bloody hole in his chest and a look of surprise on his ugly face.

"Anybody else want to die, tonight?"

Lennox walked into the camp, the dirty fringe on his buckskin leggings bobbing gaily to and fro, the shotgun in his left hand smoking, and a long-barreled Colt primed in his right. The posse from Camden, to a man, backed away toward the campfire, their expressions belying their shock.

Macalester breathed again.

"I never thought I'd be glad to see *you*," he muttered, half to himself.

Lennox granted him a glance.

"Shut up, Macalester. I ain't doin' this for you. I still

177

owe you one for Little Rock." Then he addressed the posse. "All right, boys. Toss your guns over here. Easy."

The men complied with no hesitation, waiting expectantly for the bounty hunter's next command.

He ordered them to turn around and walk away from the campfire and away from one another. The first man to turn around, he promised them laconically, would get a bullet for his pains.

Macalester could not help admiring the coldblooded manner in which Lennox then proceeded to shoot down each man, pausing only long enough to take his other Colt from its holster so he did not have to bother reloading. Beside him, he heard Geneva gasp. The sound directed Lennox's attention her way, and he stared at her dishabille blankly. Presently he holstered both guns and unsheathed his own hunting knife, a weapon similar to the luckless Orin's, but somewhat broader. He moved toward her, demonstrating no temperament to abuse, but Geneva nevertheless shrank away from him, her eyes wide with speechless horror. Macalester was not too surprised when the bounty hunter nudged Geneva onto her stomach with the toe of his boot, then, with one neat, efficient gesture, sliced the bonds of her wrists, freeing her hands.

"Fix yourself, ma'am," Lennox told her in his slow, quiet way. "We'll be ridin' now."

He walked over to Macalester then, looking him up and down. Macalester fought the uneasy sense that he was being measured for a coffin and maintained his adversary's cool, unsmiling gaze.

"Howdy, Macalester," was all the man said before severing the cord about the outlaw's ankles.

"What about my hands?" Macalester dared to ask him as Lennox replaced the knife in its buffalo-hide sheath.

"I like 'em right where they are. Now shut up and get on your feet."

Macalester shut up. With some effort, he got to his feet, wincing from the sharp pain in his side where Orin had kicked him. Orin lay in the dirt now, not a dozen feet from where he stood, his glassy eyes staring heavenward, his dirty shirtfront, what was left of it, soaked with his own blood. Macalester, who had gone to check on Thorpe, heard a noise beside him and he turned to find Geneva standing close enough to brush against his arm. She had returned her clothing to an acceptable state, although the white blouse, which he had chosen for its aesthetic rather than practical value, was now torn and soiled. Macalester sighed. Did everything he touched become dirty and sullied?

Geneva was staring at the lump of humanity that had been Orin, her green eyes wide and glazed. Quickly Mac stepped between her and the sight, wishing he could as easily blot the memory of the last few hours from her mind. She stared up at him, not quite meeting his gaze. A tear worked its way from her eye and left a glistening trail to the crest of her cheekbone. Macalester made a move to brush it away, wanting to touch her pale, smudged cheek, but he was quickly reminded that his hands were secured behind his back.

Chapter Sixteen

They rode throughout the night and into the following day at a steady, deliberate pace, without stopping. They did not travel fast, which was just as well for Geneva's healing legs. All that was required of her was that she remain in the saddle. Lennox led both her bay mare (the one Macalester had given to the doctor), and Macalester's roan by the reins, leaving her and Macalester behind him to wonder at his plans.

Macalester rode to her left and a little behind her, sitting erect upon his saddle with his broad shoulders squared and his hands remaining bound behind him. Geneva did not want to stare at the outlaw, but she found she could see him if she stared straight ahead and allowed her peripheral vision to encompass him. She could feel his gaze upon her, as well. It was not as satisfying a sensation as she had envisioned it might be, three days ago on the Arkansas River, when she thought she would gladly see him dead. In fact, it made her feel very heavy, as though a fat little man were sitting upon her chest, urging her to cry.

At the start of their bizarre odyssey with the forbidding bounty hunter, Geneva, racked by pain, terror and outrage, had submitted to the man's terse, emotionless commands without even thinking to question them. Even Macalester, normally talkative, had nothing to say, either to her or to their custodian. But after a dozen or more hours of staring at the back of the man's dirty suede vest and misshapen, stained bowler hat, Geneva, who had done a lot of thinking and recovering, decided the time had come to break the silence.

"Mr. Lennox." She congratulated herself on the clear, even tone of her voice.

He did not answer her.

"Mr. Lennox!" she tried again, louder.

"What?"

He had not moved. Not even the brim of his hat had bobbed. At first she did not even realize he had answered her. It so startled her that she had to gather her wits and remember her carefully planned speech.

"May I know what you plan to do with me?"

She hoped her emphasis on the final pronoun was adequate to convey her meaning to him. She did not wish to have more discourse with the murdering bounty hunter than necessary.

"Happens I believe you, ma'am. You ain't Macalester's wife."

Her relief was so sudden and so thorough that she very nearly fell off of her horse. She drew in a breath and plunged on. "Then—you'll let me go?"

He still did not grant her a look. "Nope."

Geneva felt her face drain of blood. "Why not?" She choked out the words.

"Happens I believe Macalester on that score, too," the man told her, with neither glee nor rancor. "Not even

181

Macalester's *that* good a liar. 'Sides, Even if he is lyin', it won't take much trouble to look into. Just means a couple a days' detour to Fort Worth on my way to Austin."

Geneva felt the familiar well of despair within her, which had never been far away from her since her terrible discovery in Little Rock.

"Kill me now, then," she said. "I'd rather die than go back there willingly!"

"I would, ma'am, 'cept I expect you ain't worth nothin' dead."

Lennox called to his animal to halt and dismounted, his buckskin leggings stretching against the pull of his long, sinewy legs. With a quick, easy gesture, he tied the extra pairs of reins to the pommel of his saddle, then allowed the animals to graze the sparse growth of the forest floor. He approached her mare. Geneva knew he intended to help her down, but she did not want him to touch her. She did, however, have one additional question to ask him, which she did from her saddle.

"Why did you kill all of those men?"

The question escaped in a whisper, like the air being slowly released from a child's balloon.

"Funny question for you to ask." He made an expression that might have been taken for a smile.

She looked him in the eye, and he her. He had startling eyes, like those of a wild animal. In the midmorning light filtering through the thinning box elders, they were a most peculiar shade of mustard.

"What do you mean?" She forced herself to return his cold, empty-eyed stare.

"I don't much cotton to rapists," he told her, neither blushing nor hesitating. "Besides, what's it to me if somebody finds the bodies and blames *him*?" He gestured to Macalester with his thumb. "Get down, now. You, too, Macalester. We'll rest a spell."

Geneva was not even a little impressed by his reasons. She sat resolutely erect upon the mare, crossing her arms before her tattered blouse. "I refuse to cooperate."

Lennox smirked. "No, you don't. Because if you do, I'll—"

"You'll what?" she interrupted, feeling the hairs stand at attention on the back of her neck. "You'll kill me? Go ahead! I told you I'd rather die than go back. And I know you to be capable of killing people. So please, be my guest."

"If you ain't the mouthiest woman I ever saw!" He shook his head slowly. "No, I ain't gonna kill you. You misbehave, and I'll kill *him*." He gestured again to Macalester, who still had not said one word.

What angered Geneva the most about Lennox's response to her defiance was that he turned on his heel and walked away from her immediately after he'd said it. This left her with the impression that he knew she would not want that unhappy event to take place, even when she herself might not have considered it a bad trade at one time.

But no. Watching Lennox walk away from her, collecting wood for a fire, she knew, hating herself, that she could not sign Kieran Macalester's death warrant. Feeling an ache that started in the back of her neck and crept, like an encroaching tide, throughout her limbs and her entire body, she climbed slowly down from the placid mare.

She scarcely noticed the soreness in her legs and congratulated herself on having done a proper job of binding them. The dressing should probably be changed. With what? she wondered gloomily. It was probably best left alone, she decided. At least it was clean. She did not even look at Macalester, who dismounted, with some awkwardness, from his sweating roan.

Lennox untied Macalester long enough for the latter

to relieve himself, then immediately tied him again, this time securing the subdued outlaw's ankles as well as tying a noose about his neck with the other end firmly knotted to a strong young maple.

"I'm flattered that you think me so dangerous," Geneva heard Macalester say to Lennox as she returned. Lennox was testing the knot on the maple.

"Shut up, Macalester." Lennox walked away from him.

Geneva took several steps away from the campsite before she was halted in midstride by a challenge from Lennox.

"Where d'you think you're goin'?"

She fixed a cold look on him. "I have a bladder, too, you know," she snapped, and did not wait for a reply before continuing about her business.

"Watch out for snakes," Macalester supplied helpfully as she ducked behind a tree.

Go to hell, she thought, but said nothing. She did, however, kick the grass and debris at her feet before proceeding.

Upon her return, she noticed that Lennox had opened a can of hash and produced two plates and a spoon. Crouched by the small fire he'd built, he divided the meager fare between the two plates and set them near the fire to warm. As revolting as the stuff appeared, it did remind Geneva that she was hungry. Ravenously. She realized, looking at the plates, waiting an eternity for them to warm, that she would have eaten the sole of her own boot, if she could have gotten it off quickly enough.

She watched Lennox roll himself a cigarette, waiting for some kind of sign from him. He took a twig from the ground, held it in the fire, then used it to ignite the cigarette. Lennox seemed amused by her scrutiny. He gestured to the plates with the hand that held the burning butt between thumb and forefinger.

"Go 'head. It ain't gonna improve none."

She approached the fire, keeping one eye on the wiry, buckskinned man who smoked and watched her with unblinking yellow eyes. Stooping, she reached out for both plates.

"That one's mine."

He so startled her that she nearly knocked both of them over into the fire. Lennox, seeming not to notice, gestured with one hand to the plate with the spoon on it.

Geneva bridled. "What am I supposed to eat with? My hands? And what about Macalester? He—"

"You can stick your face right down in the plate, far's I'm concerned," Lennox interrupted her tirade, his voice a notch louder and a shade harder. "As to him, I don't feed dead men."

With that, he reached for his plate and snatched it out from under her gaze. He retreated to a place a little away from the fire, easing himself to a reclining position. She stared in amazement as the man proceeded to eat as though she and Macalester had magically ceased to exist. She was about to make further remarks when she heard Macalester's voice behind her.

"There's a spoon in my saddlebag, Gen."

Macalester's gentle, bedroom baritone. For a moment, the sound of it made her throat tighten. Without looking at him, she found the spoon he had promised. She took it and the plate of tepid hash and sat on the ground by the outlaw, avoiding his eyes, although she could feel him looking at her. She scooped a spoonful and held it out to him, but he shook his head.

"You go on and eat," he said to her quietly, so quietly that Lennox could not have heard him. "I'll eat whatever's left."

She could not prevent herself from looking up at him.

185

His dark eyes were tired but alert, penetrating her very soul, yet revealing nothing whatever about his own emotions. She resisted a compelling urge to touch his beard-roughened cheek.

Geneva could easily have wolfed down the entire plateful, over-salty yet otherwise tasteless as it was, but she stopped herself halfway through. Macalester, with her help, ate with the same enthusiasm, although her hand trembled maddeningly and some of the stuff was spilled. They shared water from his canteen, spilling that as well, and Geneva wiped both of their mouths with the corner of a blanket, there being a lamentable shortage of linen napkins.

"Thank you," Macalester said, barely above a whisper.

She met his gaze again. He was smiling with his wide mouth, creating dimples in the corners, but his eyes did not share the expression. In fact, contrary to the reckless conformation of his lips, his sable eyes appeared to be, for a fleeting moment, profoundly sorrowful, until he somehow masked their emotion and put up the invisible shield once again. Geneva started. For a fleeting instant, she saw before her the dashing, strongly sensual California attorney who had gallantly offered her his cape at Delmonico's in the rain. The image vanished, and Kieran Macalester knelt, tied like an animal, on the ground before her. She swallowed hard, looking away.

"You're welcome."

She had something to tell him, something she did not want Lennox to hear. She sat by him for a time, hoping that Lennox, a dozen feet away, would disappear for a few minutes. The bounty hunter, however, merely wiped his plate with a handful of leaves and returned it to his saddlebag, along with the plate she and Macalester had shared.

"Get over here," he ordered her in a short bark.

I don't much cotton to rapists, he had told her.

Not wanting him to guess her trepidation, she held her head a notch higher. "Why?"

"Now," he said in nonanswer, his right hand poised over his holstered Colt.

She got up and moved three or four feet toward him.

"You wanna be tied down on this blanket over here, or right there in the dirt?" His eyes had narrowed and his words quickened. She continued over to the bedroll, standing at last two feet from him, close enough to smell that same sickening wet animal odor she recalled from that night in Memphis.

"What about Macalester?" she asked. "Let me at least give him a blanket."

"Why the hell are you so worried about him?" the man grumbled, looking down at his hands.

Geneva's heart pounded. The man was jealous! Perhaps he didn't even realize it himself; if not, so much the better. She would have to proceed cautiously. She could not let him know that he repulsed her, nor could she allow him to believe she could ever be anything to him. His jealousy empowered her, yet at the same time placed her, and Macalester, in danger. Just how much danger depended entirely upon Lennox's degree of infatuation.

She did not answer Lennox. Instead, she picked up a blanket and wadded it up as she strode over to Macalester, who now appeared perplexed. Apparently he, too, had marked something unusual about Lennox's response, although he perhaps had not worked out its meaning just yet. Geneva knelt beside him, her back to Lennox, and placed the blanket on the ground.

"I spoke to Dr. Thorpe before we left the campsite." She barely mouthed the words to him. "He saw Lennox gun down those men. At least you won't be blamed for that."

Macalester did not react in any way, and she stood up as he lay down upon the blanket.

"Thanks, Gen," he murmured, closing his eyes.

"We're in Texas," Lennox announced late the following day. They had crossed the Red River that morning. Until that time, Geneva had not known a horse could swim. She fervently hoped she would never have the firsthand experience again. Her clothing was still damp, and she had taken a chill. Her throat felt scratchy, and she had the sniffles. Further, there seemed no hope of getting warm anytime soon, as Lennox demonstrated no sign of stopping, and all of their things had gotten wet. She shivered atop the mare, suddenly thinking of Roanoke: the warm, cozy hotel room, Macalester's worried look and the performance that had won those things for her.

Plodding along behind Lennox with Macalester in the rear, she tilted her head upward toward the sky, hoping to catch direct rays of the late-day sun. Looking at the sun often induced a sneezing fit in her, and that might be enough to encourage Lennox to halt.

She did sneeze, five or six times. Neither man issued so much as a "bless you." Annoyed, she tried coughing. Still no response.

Short of falling off her horse, which she had no intention of doing, she could think of no other way to stop the caravan save one: To ask.

"Mr. Lennox," she called, orchestrating a blend of imperiousness and supplication in her tone that satisfied her. "Could we please stop for a few minutes?"

The bounty hunter did not look at her. He merely pulled up short. "Why?"

"Mr. Lennox." She managed a gentle reproof, even a

blush, if he cared to look. "Must I tell everything?"

Silence followed for half a minute. "Make it fast," he growled, like a bear disturbed in its sleep.

Geneva began to shake, badly. A harmless deception was one thing. Attempting to trick a man who made a career of hunting desperate criminals was quite another. Marshaling her resolve, Geneva clumsily dismounted. She dared not glance at Macalester, who was watching her from his horse, lest she lose her nerve. She stumbled over a tree root in her haste, and walked as far into the woods as she dared before choosing a spot.

Chapter Seventeen

Macalester grew restless on the roan. His wrists were raw from the chafe of the rawhide thongs securing them, and they burned from sweat and dirt. He craned his neck trying to follow Geneva into the woods with his eyes, but he lost her at last, fighting an unreasoning apprehension. She was up to something. He didn't know how he knew that, exactly, and if anyone were to try to pin him down, he knew he could not defend his belief. Maybe it was the way she had avoided not only his eyes, but looking at him altogether.

Her scream, a sound with which he was by now all too familiar, pierced the peaceful late afternoon, causing Lennox, heretofore as still as a cigar-store Indian, to vault from his saddle in an instant, drawing his Colt.

"Get down, Macalester!" he ordered, backing off in the direction Geneva had taken. "On your belly!"

Macalester was in the dirt before the words left Lennox's mouth.

"Help!" The terror in Geneva's quivering soprano was real. "There's a snake! He's—he's making a noise—"

Macalester watched Lennox disappear into the woods, his running step fading into silence.

He waited.

And waited.

His heart hammered. *Where the hell were they?*

Presently he heard footsteps again. Light. Erratic. Peering hard into the woods, he could perceive nothing.

"Lennox?" he called at last, tentatively. "Geneva?"

Geneva Lionwood appeared before him, as though, like a wood nymph, she had materialized from the evening mist. Profound relief quickly gave way to doubt in Macalester's mind.

"What the hell happened?" he demanded in a much quieter tone, struggling to sit up.

She did not help him, and she did not reply. She was pale, except for a bright red circle on either cheekbone, and she was trembling. Her green eyes were wide and glazed.

"Where is Lennox?"

Macalester's voice sounded hard in his own ears. Geneva still did not answer. From the folds of her black skirt, stained with the mud of the Red River, she withdrew Lennox's big Colt, holding it like an artist's tool rather than an instrument of violence. The sight of it, and its import, stunned him, momentarily, into silence.

"Geneva, what did you do?"

The question barely escaped in a whisper.

In reply, she shook her head. "I hit him," she said, her tone lacking body. "With a rock. I—"

She paused and stared at the gun, as though bewildered by its presence in her hand. He thought she might drop it, as one would drop a hot potato, or a poisonous snake.

"What, Gen?" he prodded, fearing her answer.

191

"He's dead, Mac," she said tonelessly. "I hit him with a rock. The same way I hit you with that lamp."

Macalester shook his head.

"But you didn't kill me," he reminded her gently. "You knocked me out. You knocked Lennox out, too, didn't you? Good gir—"

"He is dead," she repeated, her eyes betraying her disbelief. "I killed him. He—I—" She faltered, her expression oddly resembling a small child who has done, by accident, a terrible thing, and fears the inevitable punishment.

Macalester thought quickly: Geneva was not herself. He saw at once that he needed to take charge of the situation as quickly as possible, a difficult task to accomplish with his hands bound behind him, and her with a loaded gun in her inexperienced hands. Difficult, but not impossible. He rallied, standing with some effort.

"Geneva, listen to me," he said slowly, looking into her frightened green eyes. "Untie me, and I'll go have a look at Lennox. If he's dead, we'll have to bury him. If not, we'll have to tie him up quick before he comes to."

He offered her his back, looking over his shoulder at her. "Come on! Hurry up!"

Whatever spirit had possessed her for those few minutes had fled. The life returned to her features, animating them with amused triumph. She laughed with no trace of hysteria.

"How stupid you must think me!" she exclaimed, folding her arms before her. "To believe I'd release you only to have you take me prisoner again!"

Macalester longed to seize her by the shoulders and shake her. He could not recall ever feeling more helpless in his life, and it was not a pleasant sensation. He tried again, composing his features into an unworried look as he faced her.

"Geneva, this won't work," he told her patiently, clenching his fists behind his back. "We're miles from the nearest town. You're afraid to ride the horse. Do you even have any idea of where you are?"

His remarks, rather than causing her to reflect upon her situation, seemed instead to anger her. "Of course I do," she retorted, her green eyes narrowing in contempt and bitter amusement. "I'm in the center of Hell, on my way out. Where's the money?"

Macalester saw a ray of hope. Without betraying his thoughts by so much as a faint grin, he raised his chin and leveled a hard look at her.

"Look for it," he taunted her, taking a step backward.

Geneva glanced for a moment at the gun in her hand, and seemed to think better of it. She tossed it to the ground some distance away and approached him with a bold step, faltering only slightly before she stopped in front of him. She stared steadfastly at the breast pocket of his shirt as she deftly unbuttoned it and slipped her fingers inside. Macalester stood perfectly still, barely breathing. He perceived a slight tremble in her hand as she withdrew her empty head from the pocket. He waited. She tried the other breast pocket with the same result. She hesitated, looking at the pockets at the hips of his jeans. He felt a grin tease the corners of his mouth.

"Go ahead, Gen," he dared her, sensing her weakening resolve. "It's in one of them. Take your pick."

She scowled, but did not look him full in the face. With a measure of defiance, she extended her index finger. At her touch he felt, against his will, a rush of raw desire. He shook himself mentally: that was a sure way to get into trouble.

Her fingers edged into the pocket where the money rested, folded into a small rectangle beside his scrotum. He regarded her unblinkingly, but she would not meet

193

his gaze. She was breathing in short, shallow gasps, and he swore he could hear her heart pounding inches away from him—unless that was his own heart.

In a swift, sudden movement, he hooked the heel of his right boot around the back of her legs and leaned into her, forcing her to the ground and himself on top of her.

"Unh—" She gasped for breath on the ground, the wind having apparently been knocked out of her. She writhed and struggled beneath him, but his weight was too much for her.

"Mac." She sobbed. "Please—I can't breathe—"

"Reach behind my back," he ordered her in a harsh whisper, trying desperately, under the circumstances, to keep his mind on his mission. "Untie my hands."

With a small grunt she pulled her hands free from beneath her.

"I think you broke my arm," she whispered reproachfully, sliding her arms around his, finding the ropes at his wrists.

"You'll be lucky if I don't break your neck after this, Mrs. Humble," he growled, staring hard into her wide, frightened eyes inches from his. "Now work on those knots! Quick!"

He felt her hands work awkwardly. She made a sound of dismay, still gasping. "Mac—I can't—they're—"

"Do it, Geneva!" His bellow echoed in the trees. She turned her face away from his as if trying to escape. She bit her lower lip and fumbled with the knots again, breathing hard. Her body was warm and trembling beneath him, and he felt her breasts pressed against his chest and her heart beating like a caged wild bird's. At last he was able to pull his wrists apart, and he flexed his cramped hands as he brought his arms around. He placed each hand on the ground beside Geneva's narrow, shuddering shoulders. She looked up at him again, her fear evident in her wide, green eyes. Her lips were dry and parted. She wet them with the tip of her pink tongue.

"Wh—what are you going to do to me?" she whimpered.

He swallowed hard. He knew what he wanted to do with her. Staring down at her, watching the tendons in her slender white neck strain and her throat bob once, he allowed himself a moment of desire. He brushed his cheek gently against hers, triggering a treacherous memory. She was soft, and she still smelled, faintly, of jasmine . . .

He stiffened. Was he out of his mind?

Releasing her from his hold was one of the hardest things he had ever done, not only because of his unreasoning desire, but also because his shoulders and arms ached from countless hours forced in the same position. He rolled off Geneva, laying beside her on the ground, faintly amused that her panting breaths were in time with his own.

"I can't blame you for trying," he allowed at last, gulping air. "Did you really kill him?"

It was therapeutic to fix his mind upon a fresh topic.

"Don't you think I recognize a dead man when I see one?" she snapped irritably, still breathless.

Rueful, Macalester got up, brushing the dirt from his clothing. His wrists, he noted, were gouged from the rawhide and mottled with dried blood. They burned like hell.

"Show me." He ignored her sarcasm, pulling his sleeves down to hide his wounds from her sight.

She led him to the spot in the woods where she had stood with her back plastered to the rough trunk of an old oak tree. She had waited for Lennox after her scream, and rammed the heavy, jagged rock against his head just behind his right ear as he had leaned over to find her snake. Lennox lay where she had left him, with deerflies buzzing and crawling about his clothing. His face was pressed against the forest floor; his eyes were closed. He did not move.

Macalester knelt beside him and touched the prone bounty hunter's neck with four fingers. His eyes met hers, confirming her belief. "He's dead, Gen." His voice was quiet with awe.

Geneva felt as though she might be sick. She forced herself to look at the bounty hunter whose life she had taken, the man who had rescued her from certain rape, or worse.

"I didn't mean to kill him, Mac," she said, remembering, oddly, flashes of her childhood when she had committed some infraction and had faced her father, or mother, or both, and told them "But I didn't mean it!" as if the words themselves were a mystical incantation, and that she could undo the damage merely by giving them utterance.

But Lennox was dead. He would not rise and walk, pat her on the shoulder and tell her it was all right, that they could go on from there as if nothing whatever had happened. Lennox would never walk again.

And she had killed him.

Her legs evaporated beneath her and she sank to her knees. "Oh, God, Kieran." She choked back a sob. "I've killed him! I killed a man!"

He was beside her, his hands gripping her shoulders. She did not look at him. Her gaze was compelled by the lifeless form before her, the body she had, in one desperate, impetuous gesture, robbed of life.

Kieran Macalester looked on, filled with conflicting emotions. Geneva's actions had saved his freedom, if not his life. No doubt she had not intended for Lennox to forfeit his life, but there it was. It would do no good to allow her to brood on the awful truth with the dead man before her eyes. He got her on her feet and grasped her shoulders, turning her toward him.

"Stop it, Geneva." He kept his tone firm and even. "It's over. He's dead. He killed a few men himself, in his time. More than a few."

"But that doesn't mean he—"

"No, it doesn't mean that he deserved to die," he interrupted her patiently, anticipating her remark. "What it means is that all things come 'round full circle, in life. It was Lennox's time, that's all. Hell, I hope—" He found her, from somewhere, a ghost of a grin. "I hope that when it's my turn, I get to die by the hand of a beautiful woman. It sure beats the hell out of being shot in the back by a half-crazy old bounty huntcr!"

She did not even smile at his morbid humor. Instead she gazed at him, hard. As if he were a half-finished painting she was trying to understand.

"How many people have you killed in your life, Kieran?"

The woman asked the damnedest questions. He shifted his weight and released her shoulders, meeting, just barely, her gaze.

"I never killed anyone." He glanced at Lennox again. "Never had to. I expect I may, one day, though."

Why in the world would he think of Garland Humble?

Chapter Eighteen

The forests of easternmost Texas were replaced, quite suddenly, by grassy prairie. The sun rose and set three times, finding them at last in Irving, a bustling little cowtown not more than forty miles from Garland Humble's place. Geneva, numbed by her failure to free herself from her abductor, had long ago ceased to trouble herself with her surroundings, or even with speech. It was over. She had no will remaining to resist Macalester's efforts any longer. She decided, after leaving Lennox behind in a shallow and unmarked grave, that it would be best to concentrate what little energy there was left in her on surviving Garland Humble and planning escape from him. Again.

She sighed brokenly, drawing Macalester's corduroy jacket about her shoulders. It was a chilly October twilight, and she elected to remain on the mare while Macalester went into the only hotel in town to see about rooms. Irving reminded her, unpleasantly, of Fort

Worth, and she shuddered inwardly at the thought of the following day, of facing Garland Humble after a long period of self-imposed exile.

"Come on, Gen." Macalester was beside the mare, his arms outstretched. "I got us a room."

She allowed him to help her down from the saddle, sliding easily into his arms. He held on to her for a moment or two longer than necessary, but she willed herself, successfully, to remain impassive in his tentative embrace. She had learned long ago, thanks to Humble, the skill of disassociating oneself from one's feelings— an invaluable asset where Garland Humble was concerned. Far more valuable than her unfortunate tendency to cry. Crying had never found any favor with Garland Humble. That was why her gremlin had been such a handy companion.

"Gen, for God's sake, it's been three days. Say something! Anything!"

Macalester's whispered plea bounced off of her like a deflected arrow. She looked up at him briefly. His dark eyes betrayed his worry. She fancied she knew his motivation: It would never do to return to Humble with defective goods.

She found herself in a small room with an even smaller bed. It featured faded floral wallpaper that was no doubt intended to lend charm and homeyness, but only served to enhance the shabbiness of the accommodation. There was, however, a bathtub, and Geneva allowed herself the luxury of a soak, accepting Macalester's diffident offer of soap and an hour of privacy.

Macalester quitted the room with a measure of relief and anxiety. Geneva had been more than acquiescent since the ghastly episode with Lennox. She had, in fact, been wraithlike in her daily activities. With a heavy heart, he made a stop at the telegraph office, where he wired Humble, alerting him to their imminent arrival in Fort Worth. Then he ambled across the street in darkness to the saloon. He entered the brightly lit and noisy establishment, careful not to look any of its denizens in the eye as he made his way to the bar. He found a spot and squeezed in between two young cowboys whose backs were to one another. He ordered a beer from the big, bald barkeep, then thought better of it and added a double whiskey to his original request. The bartender provided both wordlessly, and Macalester put up his six bits.

He was tired. Exhausted. In less than a month, he had traveled from Fort Worth to New York and back, in a variety of conditions. He had masqueraded among the very highest of New York society, had been taken prisoner and had escaped. He had buried a man. He had found his heart, and had lost it. Quite a full calendar, he reflected, closing his eyes. At least he would have a lot of stories to tell Billy.

But he wouldn't tell Billy everything.

Cradling his beer in his left hand, he downed the whiskey, welcoming the slow burn flowing like molten lava down his parched throat and into the pit of his empty stomach. It was a good feeling, that burn. It helped him to ignore, for a time, the ache in his heart that had tormented him since that night in Memphis, when he had allowed Geneva Lionwood to seduce him. The ache, in fact, that bore her very name, as though it was a wound upon his soul. He thought it likely, taking a long draught of his warm, foamy beer, that the wound would be a long time in healing.

He was aware, presently, of a pair of eyes monitoring him. He realized, to his wry amusement, that the eyes were his own, staring at him from the cloudy mirror behind the bar. He smiled briefly, then the smile faded. Looking at the lines in his face, he felt aged. He felt as old as he ever had, and he wanted another whiskey.

Badly. He missed her already, and she had not even gone from his life yet.

He closed his eyes, not wanting to look any longer upon the man who had wrought such devastation upon himself. Upon the man who had ruined the life of the captivating and profoundly unhappy young singer who was at this moment soaking in the bath at the hotel. For he had ruined her life, perhaps in ways he did not even realize. *Garland Humble is a monster,* she had said, without passion. She had merely stated it as unequivocal fact, as one might quote the price of a piece of goods, or remark upon the weather.

A monster. What could she have meant? She was theatrical, of course. Dramatic. Many men beat their wives. He imagined Garland Humble would be capable of such abuse, and that Geneva Lionwood would be capable of embellishing the fact. He was dismayed to find that the idea of Garland Humble beating his young and distressingly lovely wife was like a steel spike through his chest.

He took another draught of beer. It had turned bitter. He pushed himself away from the bar, leaving half of his beer, and departed the saloon, unable to endure the bright and bawdy ruckus any longer. In his dark humor, he much preferred the comparative gloom of the night, covering the town like a canopy.

There was a restaurant across the street from the hotel. It was a warm, homey-looking place with blue-and-white checkered curtains in the windows. He went inside, famished, and ordered chicken and dumplings and a big dish of fruit slump. He washed all of it down with coffee, then ordered a second platter to take to Geneva, his "wife who's at the hotel. She's sickly," he explained to the proprietor, a tall man of ample proportions with a gray mustache and a jolly smile. Having given Geneva her hour, and more, he made his way back to the hotel with a small basket containing her dinner.

Geneva used long, firm strokes with a damp cloth, brushing her clothes to remove as much of the dirt as she could. She would face Humble the following day, and she was damned if she would do so looking like a tumbleweed. Her legs, to her surprise, seemed to be healing nicely, to the point that it would no longer be necessary to bind them. With any luck, she might not even have scars to remind her of her ordeal. Visible ones, anyway. Her clean, damp hair was tied at the base of her neck, having been rolled in coils from her temples, and she had washed out all of her underthings, which now decorated every piece of furniture in the place like banners of surrender. She wrapped herself in a pleasantly clean, crisp bedsheet and wondered, fleetingly, what had happened to all of the clothing she had left behind in Little Rock. She wondered what had become of Camilla Brooks, bound for New Orleans, and the three hundred dollars.

She wondered what had become of the promising young singer who had taken a bow as Zerlina on the stage of New York's Academy of Music in September.

How long ago it seemed! Yet it had been less than a month. She could not quite forgive herself for what she saw as her foolish naïveté in trusting the charismatic and ruggedly handsome charlatan attorney who had turned out to be the outlaw Kieran Macalester. And she could not comprehend how her attraction to him, which she had thought to be superficial, could have left her feeling so desolate upon discovering the truth.

It had been a lie. All of it. From the enticing offer of the San Francisco Opera and Light Theater Company (she had thought it too good to be true!) to McAllister's—that is, Macalester's—faintly whispered declaration of love after their liaison in Memphis. And the pain

202

of that lie had, at last, been enough to cause her to murder a man, and to pitch her into a survival mode resurrected from her brief tenure as Garland Humble's resident wife.

Her mind, blessedly, was as active as ever, but she kept her own counsel, no longer trusting her interests to anyone but herself. Men had used and betrayed her before, from her first music master to Lord Atherton, and she had always made do, somehow.

But none of the others had ever tugged upon her heart in quite the same way as the engaging outlaw.

A sob caught in her throat until, by force of will alone, she pressed it down again. She envisioned her gremlin opening his box, and herself tucking the unwanted emotions inside. These last few days, the gremlin had become her boon companion. But as payment for his services, he exacted the toll of her silence. She rendered it willingly.

If she had no further discourse with Macalester, she could not be seduced by his lies again.

"I brought you some supper." The outlaw's soft baritone was just above a whisper.

Geneva started. She had not heard him enter. She abandoned her suit, clutching the ends of the sheet tightly about her as she turned to face him. His angular features were devoid of emotion, but his dark eyes monitored her steadily, as though he might be waiting for something.

What?

Geneva looked at the basket, unable to maintain the gaze that made her painfully aware of her nakedness beneath the sheet. If he were of a mind to, he could take her, here and now.

And the worst of it was, she did not really think, remembering his love in Memphis, that she would object.

He waited, watching her as if he had not seen her for

a very long time. At last he set the basket on a chair and proceeded to take from it a tin plate, utensils and a red checkered napkin, as well as several small tin pots. He set the vessels upon the small table beside it.

"Chicken and dumplings." Macalester's voice had a definite buoyancy to it, no doubt due to his good humor at being so near his goal. The notion made her angry, until the gremlin came forth again and trapped the bubble of emotion in his box. Without a remark, Geneva sat down at the table on the solitary wooden chair, knotting the sheet over her left shoulder, and began to serve herself.

It was the best meal she had ever eaten, no doubt improved considerably by the steady diet of cold beans, hash and Macalester's coffee that had sustained her through the last three days. Chicken had never tasted so succulent, nor dumplings as savory. The fruit slump rivaled the finest desserts she had ever enjoyed at Sherry's. And the coffee was a vast improvement over Macalester's.

But then, trough water would have been.

She giggled at the thought before she could prevent it, and Macalester was beside her in an instant.

"What's so funny, Gen?" He crouched beside her until his eyes were level with hers. He rested his left arm along the back of her chair. She felt it press against her shoulder blades. It was like iron. His right arm rested on the table beside her plate, the long fingers of his hand splayed out flat as though he meant to restrain the furniture. A faint smile she could only call hopeful played at the corners of his overly wide and sensuous mouth, and she felt his warm breath upon her bare shoulder. His gaze held her captive. There were words on her tongue that yearned to be loosened, and his grin seemed to pry them forth.

"What will happen to me, Kieran?"

Had she spoken? It did not even sound like her voice. Macalester's grin faded to a rapt expression. He did not reply. She looked away again, hoping to conceal her confusion from him. She felt his warm, gentle fingers upon her chin, and at his touch she wanted to cry. He turned her face toward his own and she found that his dark eyes had imprisoned her once again. She had no will to break away a second time.

"I swear I won't let anything bad happen to you, Gen," he whispered, and his words, comforting though they might have been, were taken by the unforgiving gremlin almost as soon as they left his lips. "I'm taking you back, but I swear I'll help you get away again. Do you believe me? Say you believe me! Sweet Jesus, this is the hardest thing I've ever had to do . . ."

She felt the strength and warmth of his big hand upon hers where it rested in her lap, and she watched as Kieran Macalester closed his eyes. His dark lashes glistened with unshed tears.

The gremlin swallowed up the words, and her hope, but not, she suspected, his pain.

Geneva slept late, and Macalester was gone in the morning when she awoke. His absence did not trouble her. It seemed to be a habit of hers, sleeping late, and a habit of his to venture abroad before she even woke up. He had probably gone out to fetch the horses from the livery and to see about breakfast. She washed herself and dressed in her newly cleaned clothing, glad that she had been able to refresh herself for this, the last leg of her journey. She was ready to meet Garland Humble again. She had changed, she knew, since he had last seen her. She doubted very much that he had, except for being three years older.

The knock surprised her, until she deduced that it was but another of Macalester's attempts to get her to speak. Thinking to outsmart him, she merely opened the door.

But her caller was not Macalester.

Three men stood in the hallway, dressed in trail clothes that still bore the dust of their journey and Stetson hats of varying colors. She looked into each of their faces—none of them was any older than Macalester—but they yielded nothing with their blank expressions.

"Geneva Lionwood?" the man in front, with blond hair and a bronze mustache, addressed her.

"Yes. What—"

"Macalester sent us," the leader explained tersely. "His job is finished. We're here to take you to Mr. Humble."

"*What!*"

Her stomach knotted and her mouth went dry. Her escorts, as one, shifted their weight to their opposite legs, yielding no further clue.

"We have forty miles to cover, ma'am, so get your things and let's hit the trail."

She was so stunned that she could not move. The outlaw had betrayed her—again!

Sweet Jesus, he had said. Sweet Jesus, indeed. Her backbone went rigid.

"I have nothing," she told the man coldly. "Mr. Macalester has seen to that."

She walked from the room in as regal a gait as she could muster, summoning her gremlin at the same time. Willing her trembling hand to be still, she closed the door behind her, damning Macalester's soul to hell for all eternity.

The men flanked her, with the blond leading the way. He turned, however, in the direction of the hallway opposite the stairs, drawing Geneva up short.

"Wait," she exclaimed, a sudden apprehension seizing her. "That's not the way to the—"

A strong pair of hands seized her arms in a savage grip from behind, and a wet cloth was jammed over her nose and mouth. The scream never left her lips.

Chapter Nineteen

Macalester bought sweet rolls and coffee for breakfast. He was in a raw and savage humor, which he attributed to a terrible night's sleep in a lumpy old chair that was about as soft as a skinny whore, and to the fact that he was relinquishing custody of Geneva today in Fort Worth. He hoped breakfast with her would improve his mood, but he doubted it. Reproach and distrust were ever in her green eyes, and were all the more intolerable because he so richly merited them.

A lie was a funny thing, he had discovered lately. For one thing, lies were so easy to tell. He had left many of them scattered upon the landscape of his past like bad seeds, lies that had stayed behind and had never touched him again. After a lifetime of lying, though, he had finally been brought up short by one, had finally told a lie that would remain with him all of his life like a hideous deformity. He remembered Geneva's conversational remarks about her penance for the lie she had told in Roanoke, but Kieran Macalester was neither a religious nor a superstitious man. He was, however, beginning to believe that lies brought with them their own punishment, and the bigger the lie, the greater the weight of its penalty. And his lie to Geneva Lionwood had only begun to take its due.

The door to the hotel room was not locked. Carrying the basket from the restaurant in one hand, Macalester pushed the door open and took two bold steps inside before he realized Geneva was not there. He felt his face drain of color. He quickly closed the door and stepped back, holding up his arm to fend off the blow he expected from behind, a blow like the one he'd taken in Little Rock.

But there was none forthcoming.

Where the hell was she?

He dropped the basket and ran from the room, fairly flying down the stairs in a thundering gait that caused the clerk, an elderly man with thinning gray hair and thick round spectacles, to scowl. Macalester could not even pretend to be abashed at his reproof.

"The—my wife," he panted, willing himself to think, and to make sense. "When did she go out? Did she say where she was going?"

The small, wiry man behind the counter looked over the rim of his glasses, pursing his small, dry mouth to a pucker. "Your wife ain't been down 'tall," he answered in a high, thin tone that suggested that Macalester had, perhaps, lost his mind. The outlaw grabbed hold of the oak trim on the counter, because he knew the man would protest if he reached across and seized his stiff shirt collar.

"Is there a back way out?"

The man shook his head firmly, pointing to the staircase lately descended by Macalester. "One way up; one way down."

The window?

Macalester doubted it, even as he ran outside and scanned the building. There was not so much as a rain gutter beneath the lone window of their room, or anywhere else around the building. Macalester found himself running: to the stage depot, to the livery, to the restaurant and back to the hotel. No one had seen her.

No one.

Macalester was out of breath, and his heart raced as he stumbled back into the room. He threw himself face down upon the rumpled bed upon which she had slept. *Geneva,* he thought, aware of a faint trace of her jasmine scent upon the sheets, *where the hell are you?*

If she had not left the hotel, he reasoned, rolling over to his back, she must still be there. But where? He got up again and looked out through the sheer lacy curtains at the window onto the now-busy main street of the small town. He needed a plausible excuse to go from door to door of the hotel looking for her. The idea seemed ludicrous to him even as he thought it, and the plan would probably get him arrested for disturbing the other patrons . . .

Below his window on the street in front of the hotel, two men lifted an awkward and amorphous bundle into the back of a buckboard. In spite of his anxiety, he was amused by the spectacle of the men struggling with the bulky thing wrapped loosely in burlap.

The men suddenly looked familiar to him, especially the blond with the dark red mustache. He forgot about Geneva for a moment, staring hard at the man, trying to remember where he'd seen him before.

Humble's foreman! That's who he was!

Why, he wondered, scratching his chin, was Humble's foreman in Irving, so far from home? He considered the men thoughtfully. They were fussing with their bundle like it was a load of peacock's eggs. The bundle, he mused, allowing his imagination free rein, could have been a person.

The realization was like a shower of ice water: that lousy, no-good, double-dealing son of a bitch! Macalester bolted from the room. Just outside his door, he met a third man, but only for an instant. A thunderous blow caught him full on the right side of his face, and a shower of orange sparks in his brain quickly faded to blackness.

The pain moved in small waves, like the ripples on a slow-moving river. He was lying down. There was something cool on the side of his face, and slowly Macalester gathered his consciousness from its far places like calling small children in to supper. The images came together and he recalled, finally, a face outside of his door and then the orange sparks. Abruptly he opened his eyes.

Billy Deal sat on the lumpy old easy chair he'd pulled over to the foot of the bed. His big, dirty boots were propped negligently on top of the ecru coverlet, soiling it with Texas dust. His hands were folded upon his chest in the manner of one accustomed to waiting comfortably, and his azure eyes twinkled merrily under his crop of corn-colored curls. His baby mouth, under a brand-new full golden mustache, grinned.

"Howdy, Senator!" he chirped, laughter in his voice. "What the hell hit you? Humble's wife?"

Macalester, trying to focus his eyes and his comprehension, did not immediately respond. With great effort, he propped himself up on one elbow, removing the damp washcloth from his face with the other hand.

"What the hell are you doing here, Billy?" he grumbled, not wanting to think about Humble's wife for the moment. "And what's that thing on your lip?"

Billy blew off a breath, like a surfacing whale. "Humble kept a pretty close rein on me," he reported tersely, ignoring the second question. "They got careless last night. I heard Tyrell, the foreman, talking with Humble about Irving. I guessed you'd sent him a telegraph from here, so I slipped out, grabbed my horse and found you in this shithole with your ugly face stove in."

Macalester lay back against the flat pillow, frowning. It didn't make sense. Any of it. Unless—

He slammed the heel of his hand into his forehead. Telegraph. How could he have been so stupid? Well, the damage was done, for now. Best not to act too hastily from here on out.

"Billy." He rubbed the corners of his eyes with his thumb and forefinger. "Is there any chance that Garland *let* you get away?"

It was Deal's turn to frown. "What are you getting at?"

Macalester didn't answer right away. He was reviewing the mission in his mind, trying to come up with another reason why Geneva Lionwood would disappear without a trace and Billy Deal would materialize within twenty-four hours of one another, even if he left Humble's foreman and his gargantuan headache out of the equation. It all added up to the fact that Garland Humble was lower than Armadillo shit, and about as fragrant.

"Did Humble ever say anything to you about his wife? About why he wanted her back?" he asked, staring at Deal's boots.

Billy's hands arced and came to rest behind his head. "Humble didn't say more'n a handful of words to me about anything," the younger man declared, but his tone was thoughtful. "What the hell's goin' on, Senator? You smell a rat?"

Macalester grimaced. "A great big fat one," he affirmed, meeting his partner's inquisitive gaze. "Named Garland Humble. Listen, Billy. I want you to stay here and wait for me. I have to get out to Humble's place to collect the ten thousand, and—"

"But where's his wife?" Billy interrupted. "You know he won't pay if you're not delivering the goods!"

Macalester had started to rise, and in fact had actually gotten one foot off of the bed, but the core of Billy's observation stopped him cold. He met Billy's frank, blue-eyed gaze with a sort of wonder. "What did you say?"

Billy held out his hands, not at all annoyed, it seemed, to be repeating himself. "Humble isn't going to pay you if you're not bringing his wife." He pronounced each syllable carefully. "So where is she, Senator?"

Macalester said nothing. The beauty and treachery of Humble's master plan was slowly revealing itself to him: The old spider intended to do him out of his bounty by taking Geneva from him, then holding Macalester to the letter of their agreement. And speaking of letters, he felt inside of his shirt for the parchment envelope and withdrew it. He quickly checked the contents, feeling only a little foolish. He was discovering, to his dismay, that nothing was beneath Garland Humble.

The thought of Geneva in the hands of the spider made him shudder.

"He'll pay," Macalester said finally, more to himself than to Billy. "Every cent he owes, and maybe a little bit more than he figures."

He met Billy's steady gaze, filled with a new and grim determination.

"You stay here in Irving, Billy." He shrugged off the dizziness as he got to his feet. "Take this letter over to the post office and mark it 'special delivery.' I don't aim to give old Gar a chance to change his mind. Anyway, it might be best if you keep out of Humble's way for a while. I can wire you if I need your help."

Now Billy was mystified. "Need my help with what?"

Macalester did not feel like explaining, and not just because he couldn't spare the time. He waved an impatient hand and moved to the washstand to escape the younger man's scrutiny.

"I promised Geneva I'd help her to get away from Humble again." He concentrated on the water he was pouring into the basin. He closed his mouth, finding that the very mention of her name caused him discomfort and made him feel exposed.

Behind him, Billy was silent for a moment. *"Geneva?"*

Macalester closed his eyes. Why was it always so easy to forget how perceptive Billy was? He rallied, forcing an indifferent tone to his voice.

"Geneva," he repeated, feeling the knife of her name twist in his gut so hard that he almost recoiled with the pain of it. "She claims Humble treated her badly in the past, and she's afraid of—"

"Whoa, Senator!" Billy's voice was low with amazement. "Maybe you'd better start from the beginning. I got a feeling this is a damned interesting story!"

Macalester did not trust himself to look at the younger man. "Oh, it's interesting, all right," he growled, splashing water into his face. "But a sight too long to go into, just now. I got to—"

"Shoot," Billy interrupted in a cajoling way. "Humble ain't goin' nowhere. And I been holed up in that fancy dungeon of his for near a month now. I could use a good tale. Tell me all about you and . . . Geneva."

He said the name in a leering way, as if peeling fancy lace stockings off a shy young whore. Macalester curbed his sudden impulse to collar his partner and shake him until his neck snapped.

"Dammit, Billy," he retorted irritably, patting his face dry with a towel. "There's nothing to tell! Except for tangling with a lah-dee-dah English lord, running into

Lennox—remember him?—taking a couple of knocks to the head, getting caught by a wildcat posse and spending two or three days tied up like a piece of beef."

Macalester threw the towel onto the washstand hard enough to rattle the basin. He found his comb and worked on his unruly sienna locks, thinking, as he blocked out Billy's grinning reflection in the mirror, that he'd rather be in a dentist's chair than conversing with an astute Billy Deal just now.

"For such a good liar, you're doin' a mighty pitiful job of it at the moment," his partner allowed broadly, and Macalester, feeling his face grow warm, could hear the laughter in Billy's voice.

"Go to hell," he muttered, still combing hair that was already in place so he did not have to face the mocking younger man on the other side of the room. "I'm not lying."

"Boy, she musta got to you, but good," Billy declared, sounding more amazed than amused. "Maybe you ain't lyin', Senator, but you sure as hell ain't tellin' the whole truth, either!"

Macalester sighed. "I'll tell you all about it sometime," he said after a long moment, avoiding his own eyes in the mirror. "It's just—I can't talk about it. Not right now. Not yet."

His candor seemed to embarrass his friend into courtesy.

"Sure, Mac." Billy Deal sounded mollified. "I didn't mean to rib you on it. I guess you're entitled to your feelings, like everybody else."

This unexpected consideration for his feelings was almost worse than the teasing. Macalester felt his throat tighten, and he swallowed several times before he dared to speak again.

"I have to go, Billy," he said finally. "Wait for me here. Give me two days."

He faced his partner at last, his features carefully bland. Billy was regarding him with a thoughtful, probing expression, and he hoped he was equal to it.

"You sure you don't want me to come along?" Billy tested.

Macalester felt his jaw tighten. He shook his head. "I can handle Humble. You just concentrate on keeping out of trouble. And mail that damned letter, before something happens to that, too. I swear, I just don't seem to have any luck when it comes to holding onto things."

Billy's grin was like the quick slash of a sharp blade. "Maybe you just ain't been holdin' onto 'em tight enough."

"Or maybe," Macalester mused, "I just haven't been holding onto the right things."

Without waiting for an answer, he pushed off.

Geneva was convinced that she had died and was on her way to Hell. There was a rough, stifling blanket wrapped tightly about her like a shroud, and it was suffocatingly hot. All around her was the relentless racket of wooden wheels creaking and groaning like satanic instruments of torture. All that was missing were the agonized screams of the victims. And inside of her was the numbing grief of betrayal. *Sweet Jesus*, she thought, tearing at the image of Kieran Macalester, the great liar, in her mind. *Sweet Jesus*.

A sudden jolt rolled her onto her back, hard. She groaned, then started at the sound. Did the dead have voices? Perhaps she was not dead, after all. Through the pinholes of the woven cocoon about her she could see light beyond her confinement. She felt weak and light-headed, though, and unable to marshall her wits to free herself.

If she had the strength, or the breath, she realized

tiredly, she would have screamed. Still, she did manage to wriggle her arms loose and to struggle briefly against her bonds. After a few tries, the wrapping had loosened measurably. Encouraged by her success, she fought on until at last she had uncovered her face. She gulped in several breaths of cool, sweet air as she shielded her eyes from the sudden light with her arm.

Presently her eyes adjusted to the raw, unforgiving light. She perceived that she was lying on the floor of a wagon, a buckboard. A buckboard that was moving at a good clip, for a buckboard. Above her were trees. A forest, like Arkansas and eastern Texas. She frowned. There were no forests such as this anywhere near Humble's place that she recalled. She remembered suddenly, like a door opening, the three men who had come for her at the ramshackle hotel in Irving. With some effort, she rolled over and pushed herself up on the heels of her hands, feeling as wobbly as a baby lamb, or a drunk. If only she could still the spinning in her head!

Before her eyes, on the seat of the buckboard, were the backs of two men hunched over, their hats hiding their necks and hair from view. They appeared to have no notion of, or concern about, her presence.

Such was the magnanimous hospitality of Garland Humble, she thought.

"You, there!" She summoned her most imperious tone and was annoyed when it came out little better than a whimper. "I'm hungry, and thirsty. Stop this wagon at once!"

Simultaneously, the two hats moved, and their owners stared at her for a moment. Their faces told nothing of their ages or intellect. She was equal to their scrutiny, but somewhat abashed when they merely turned their faces forward again without so much as a nod of acknowledgment. By God, someone would answer for this abominable treatment!

217

"Stop, I say!" She tried again, and this time her words were supported by a stronger tone.

"They take their orders from me, ma'am." A high, nasal tenor with an unmistakable Texas twang addressed her from behind. She turned to see the blond man rein a mottled gray-brown horse up beside the wagon and keep pace with it. He wore a dark kerchief over his nose and mouth, hiding from view the dark red mustache she remembered. His ridiculously large and nauseatingly filthy ten-gallon hat must at one time have been gray, or even white, but was now as mottled as the spirited animal he rode.

There was something ruthless and frightening about the man's frank, expressionless stare, all the more unnerving because she could not see the rest of his face. The kerchief, while in itself hardly ominous, gave the man the aspect of an outlaw.

An outlaw like Kieran Macalester.

"Who—who are you?"

"Tyrell," he replied briefly. "I work for Mr. Humble."

His words were muffled by the kerchief, but she was able to make them out. She coughed then as a sudden cloud of dust came her way on the light breeze. Tyrell said nothing.

"Did my husband order you to suffocate me in that?" she demanded, glaring hard as she gestured to the bundle of burlap on the floor of the buckboard.

"Your husband ordered me to do whatever was necessary," he answered, holding his horse back with a firm hand on the rein.

Geneva stared at him, taking a mental step backward. Whatever was necessary . . . Why did that phrase frighten her?

"Macalester won't let you get away with this," she heard herself say. "If you, or Garland Humble, or any-

218

one else thinks they can prevent that mercenary from collecting his payment—"

"Macalester won't be coming after us." Tyrell cut her off laconically, adjusting the brim of his hat with a gloved thumb and forefinger as he surveyed the trail ahead.

She was filled, inexplicably, with dread. "What did you do to him?"

"That's not important," the man assured her. "Only thing you need to know is I got me a full bottle of chloroform here, if you're plannin' to give me any trouble."

I plan to give you as much trouble as you can manage, she thought with a disdainful sniff.

"You're not as smart as Macalester, then," she interpolated, as though apologizing to Tyrell for assuming that he might have been.

Tyrell laughed. "Maybe I'm smarter," he retorted.

The driver snorted. "Yeah, and maybe I'm Billy Deal," he said to his companion in a low tone.

"Shut up, Wes!" the mounted man snapped in annoyance. Returning his attention to Geneva, he added, "If Macalester's so smart, why's he out cold in Irving, and why're you on the road with us?"

So Tyrell had lied to her in Irving! Macalester had never sent him! She kept herself in check: It would not do to let this bucolic trio guess how much, or how little, she knew. The driver and his companion were chuckling as well, apparently amused by their leader's humor. She sat back against the side of the wagon feeling helpless, a feeling she hated. The untended wood dug mercilessly into her shoulder blades as the buckboard bounced along, and she seized the burlap from the floor, wadding it up like a pillow behind her. Tyrell, to her bitter amusement, remained on his pony pacing the wagon, as though she might require strict guarding. Where would she go? she wondered, considering the

219

man, who looked about Macalester's age.

Macalester! Why could she not stop thinking about him?

"Why aren't we going to Fort Worth?" she said then conversationally, as much to evict Macalester from her thoughts as to catch her audience unawares. She did not know for certain that they were not headed for Fort Worth, but she thought it a good ruse to discover the truth.

Tyrell was undeniably startled by her question. Geneva pretended not to notice, even after he had lagged several yards behind while the wagon pressed on.

"Who says we ain't goin' to Fort Worth?" he called after her, then spurred his pony to catch up.

She kept her triumphant smile to herself. *You just did, you fool*, she thought, shifting her position uncomfortably.

"Can't we please stop?" she pleaded in nonanswer, sensing that time, somehow, was her ally. "We've been traveling for days, and I'm starving."

"We ain't been on the road but a coupla hours," the driver argued without turning around, revealing to her that they had only left Irving that morning. Briefly she thanked the Lord for the stupid men Humble had, in his typical arrogance, sent for her.

"Shoot, Wes, she ain't no sack a beans; she's a lady!" the passenger chided him, slapping his partner's arm with the back of his gloved hand. "Hey, Tyrell, let's us stop for a few minutes. Won't do no harm. 'Sides, I got some business to take care of, m'self."

Geneva turned an expectant gaze upon the leader with, she hoped, just the right amount of wistful supplication in her face. Tyrell seemed to avoid looking at her, but he reined his pony with a look of disgust.

"I swear, Lope, you're worser than a old woman," he declared, dismounting.

The driver, Wes, applied the brake and pulled the pair to a halt.

Geneva climbed out of the wagon with difficulty. She was stiff and sore, but she had no desire to be touched by any of Humble's men, even if it was only to be helped down. She walked about a bit, acquainting herself with the aches and bruises in her legs, back and neck. The man Tyrell had addressed as Lope did, indeed, lope off into the woods with all possible speed, for purposes about which she did not care to conjecture. She herself headed off toward the trees in another direction, but was halted by the strident command of Tyrell.

"Don't get any notions, now, Mrs. Humble," he ordered her. "I'll give you a canteen and some jerky for the trip so you can eat in the wagon. I don't aim to stop again before nightfall, so take care of your business. And don't think you can wander off." He wagged a dirty, gloved finger at her.

She scowled at him, but did not answer. Ignoring his offer of a canteen, she made her way a short distance into the woods, debating the wisdom of trying the same trick she had used, with too much success, upon Lennox. While arguing the merits of such a rash course with herself, she was startled by the sound of gunfire coming from the area of the wagon.

She held her breath and counted half a dozen shots. Her first thought was Macalester. Had he caught up to them after all? The notion pleased her, yet at the same time alarmed her: Humble's trio of bumpkins would be far easier to outwit than the outlaw, who seemed to know her as well as, or better than, herself. Scarcely daring to breathe, she plastered her back to a broad oak tree and waited, straining to make out voices or any other noise that might yield a clue as to what was happening back at the wagon.

She did hear voices presently, strange voices speak-

Carole Howey

ing in an exotic and unfamiliar language. She listened hard for a reply from one of Humble's men, but heard nothing but more of the foreign tongue spoken in a harsh baritone. Indians? she wondered doubtfully, yet at the same time chilled by the prospect. Not likely, she told herself. She remained very still, burning to look, but not daring to move.

She heard the deliberate tramp of heavy boots making their way through the trees. By the sound of them, they were coming closer to her position. She shrank against the tree, feeling the rough bark dig into her back, wishing she could disappear. It occurred to her that whoever it was, he was looking for her. It was a most unsettling thought, especially in view of the fact that the hunter had doubtless already killed or wounded at least two men.

The sound grew closer, perhaps less than ten feet away. The steps were slower, though, as if the unseen menace might be about to give up his search, or about to seize her. She tried to moisten her lips, but her mouth was as dry as sand. *Please, God*, she thought, paralyzed by fear, *please let it be Macalester*. Her breath sounded loud in her ears, like the wind. The hunter had to know she was there. . . .

Suddenly a dark figure passed by to her left, not a tall one, but terrifying nonetheless in shades of black, a costume that looked like Osmin's from Mozart's "Abduction from the Seraglio." She gasped in surprise and wonder. The figure in black spun around, staring right at her with coal black eyes set in a tawny face partially covered by more black veiling. Geneva nearly fainted from terror but forced herself to maintain the man's stare.

He shouted at her in words she could not understand, which was going some, because she was fluent in Italian, German and French. Fear vanished, replaced by fascination.

"Who are you?" she asked, unable to muster more than a whisper.

The man did not reply, probably, she thought, because he did not understand her language any more than she did his. Suddenly, he reached out and seized her arm with a strong, savage grip, shouting in the same incomprehensible gibberish he had used before.

"How dare—" She pulled away from him, but he held her fast, yanking her after him with alarming strength and purpose. She pulled harder against him, crying out, striking his arm with her free hand. She broke away at last and fell to the ground from the momentum, but the man quickly seized her by the waist and flung her over his shoulder, ignoring her cries and the flailing of her fists upon his back.

"Put me down!" She kicked and struggled as hard as she could, to no avail. "Damn you, put me down!"

In moments, they emerged from the woods and the man dumped her, like a sack of flour, onto the ground. The impact made her dizzy. She opened her eyes to a spinning sky and four dark faces with black eyes like the first, except that two of them wore white. She tried to speak, but she could not. Instead, she rolled onto her side.

Within arm's length was Tyrell, sprawled on his face, hatless. His blond hair was dyed crimson with blood, the wound like a blossoming flower at the back of his skull. It was then that she fainted.

Chapter Twenty

Macalester drove the roan hard, hoping to catch up with the wagon, the men and Geneva before sunset. But darkness came quickly in October on the prairie, and he was forced to stop after only a few hours of riding. Lying on the hard ground as he stared up at the canopy of stars, he wished that Billy had come along. Billy would have provided distraction from his gloom. Instead he was alone, with no relief from his thoughts of Geneva Lionwood in Garland Humble's hands.

He was worried about her. He cared about her, more deeply than he could ever have imagined caring about another human being. Bone-weary and aching, he could not make himself comfortable for thinking about her.

He supposed he loved her, although prior to this adventure, he had had precious little experience with the emotion. All that he really knew about it now was that it hurt like hell, and that it had robbed him of his ability to reason. What man in his right mind would ride into Garland Humble's stronghold alone and challenge him for his own wife?

He was off again as soon as the sun rose, having caught snatches of sleep fraught with unpleasant dreams only half-remembered, certain that he would overtake Humble's foreman and his precious cargo by midmorning.

But he did not.

It was only a little past noon when Macalester saw Humble's place in the distance, and there was no sign that the road in between had even been traveled upon recently. His nerves were frayed, and now doubt preyed upon him like a relentless parasite. He was not a tracker. Was it possible that Tyrell had not brought Geneva back to Humble after all? Had he second-guessed Garland Humble wrong? There was no way to be sure. All he could do at this point, he realized, was to ride calmly into Humble's and play along as pleasantly as he could in the hope that Humble himself might reveal his plans. That, in itself, would take some doing: He felt like choking the truth out of the wily old millionaire with his bare hands. Thinking it might still come to that, he willed himself, in the half-hour remaining before he reached the house, to be calm, level-headed and alert.

The place was quiet, for midday. There was no sign of another living thing. The working aspect of Humble's huge spread was centered in a remote location, making the huge mansion seem even more isolated from both humanity and reality. Of course, Macalester reflected, dismounting, all of this desertion could be Humble's doing, as well. He felt, hitching the tireless roan, that all of the windows were actually eyes, and they were all watching him. He commanded himself. Humble had him spooked, which was no doubt exactly what the old man intended. Macalester took several deep breaths while he strode in an easy swagger up the half-dozen steps to the veranda, then to the front door. He did not knock, electing instead to seize the highly polished brass levers of the dark green doors and open them both, admitting himself, without scraping his dirt-caked boots, to the magnificent marble foyer.

"Humble!" he called, pleased by the clear, even tone in his voice. "Where the hell are you, you double-crossing old skinflint bastard?"

From a doorway at the far end of the foyer, Hallis appeared. He was wearing a starched white apron tied across his chest and a disapproving frown on his as-cetic, hawklike features.

"Mr. Humble is not at home," he said coldly, holding a silver tray, which he had apparently been polishing, across his aproned chest like some prissy shield. The sight was comical. Had Macalester not been so angry, or so wary, he might have laughed. He moved toward the scowling butler in a slow and deliberate gait.

"You and I both know better, Alice." Macalester used Billy's nickname for the butler, hoping the inference was not lost on Humble's faithful minion. His tone, he knew, was dangerously congenial. "Where is he? Or do I take this place apart looking for him?"

"Hallis might scare at that kind of talk, Macalester, but I know you too well."

It was Humble, somewhere behind him.

"Bring us brandy, Hallis. Come in, Mac, and stop be-having like a bully in my house."

Macalester took a swallow of air and faced Geneva Lionwood's elderly husband. Garland Humble, in a gray tweed suit that must have cost a pretty penny, sur-veyed him with a sharp scrutiny that made the hairs on the back of his neck stand on end. He admired, in a detached sort of way, Humble's ability to entice his prey

226

into his web with disparaging words spoken in an affectionate tone. He had to force himself to remain where he was, so powerful was the lure.

"I'm happy right where I am, Gar," he insisted quietly, not smiling, not even blinking. "I want to know why you sent Tyrell and his boys to Irving."

Humble's gaze flickered once, indicating to Macalester that the older man had not intended for him to discover that. So far, so good. Macalester continued to monitor Humble steadily. Humble hesitated, then spoke in a lower, more formal voice. "Tyrell was my insurance," he said finally, meeting Macalester's stare coolly. "I had to be sure she wasn't going to sweet-talk you into anything at the last minute."

"Especially since you let Billy get away," Macalester added, still watching him.

To his surprise, Garland chuckled, his bulk quivering like blancmange. "Not much gets by you, does it?" he declared, beckoning the outlaw with a beefy, outstretched hand.

Macalester still resisted the venomous Humble charm. "It occurred to me," he said, not responding to Humble's question, "that you might be trying to do me out of the ten thousand dollars you owe me."

This seemed to make Humble irritable. "Get the hell in here, Mac," he growled, frowning. "I'm tired of standing out here arguing with you."

The older man turned as if presupposing that the outlaw would follow. Macalester still did not move. "I've taken a sight too many knocks in the head this last month on account of your wife, Gar, and I don't intend to line up for any more. Just let me have my money."

And let me see Geneva, he almost added, but stopped himself just in time.

Humble paused, then faced him again, his blue-gray pig eyes narrowing and his small mouth, almost lost in

227

the steel-gray beard around it, pursed and tight.

"As I recall, the deal was that you were to bring her here to me," the old man intoned slowly.

Macalester smiled acidly. "Don't even think it." He folded his arms across his chest. "Your wife may be good company, and pretty to boot, but I earned every penny of that ten thousand in the last month, and I'm not leaving here without it."

As Macalester had intended, Garland Humble seemed satisfied by his words. He'd had to allow his attraction to Geneva. To deny it, by word or omission, would have been a sure signal to Humble that he was not telling the truth.

"She's more than pretty," Humble amended, nodding slowly. "She's beautiful. She's gifted. She's bright. And she's almost as good a liar as you are."

Macalester, eyeing his adversary steadily, felt his face drain of color. What did Humble know?

"She's a better liar than I am," he corrected Humble, finding a grin in spite of his mounting apprehension. "And a damn sight better actor. She tell you how she got me off the train at Roanoke?"

Humble stared blankly for half a second. Then his porcine features became animated. "Yes," he chuckled. "Yes, she did. Come on, Mac, let's have that brandy. You must be parched."

Macalester *was* parched, and his feet very nearly carried him forward into Humble's study. But he detected a false note in his host's buoyancy and remained fixed for another moment.

"What I still can't figure," he went on, still grinning, "was why I believed that story about her old, sick mother. Of course, it could've been those big green eyes of hers, filling with tears."

Humble waved a hand impatiently. "I told you she was good," the old man fairly snapped. "Now let's—"

Macalester did not hear the rest of his sentence. He was chilled with triumph. His arms unfolded and went to his sides, his right hand grazing his gun.

"You haven't even seen her, have you, Gar?" he prompted quietly, not blinking.

Garland Humble's eyebrows met like gray storm clouds over his angry eyes. "What the hell are you talking about, Macalester?" he demanded in a low, reedy tone. "Tyrell and Lope—"

"Tyrell and Lope and whoever the hell else was with them wrapped Geneva up like a Christmas package and rode out of Irving yesterday. If they were headed back here, I would have caught up to them."

Humble's stare became hostile. Macalester did not move.

"What are you after?" Humble wondered, barely above a whisper.

Macalester shrugged. "My ten thousand," he answered lightly. "And just to satisfy my natural curiosity as to why you lied to me about wanting your wife back here. And why it's so damned important to you that I drink brandy in your study."

"You know something, Macalester?" Humble mused, nodding faintly. "You're a sight too smart for your own good."

"Save it," Macalester snapped. "I only want two things out of you right now, Humble, and one of them is the ten thousand."

"And the other?" Humble inquired as though the first was of little consequence.

Macalester drew in a hard breath. "I want to know where you sent her."

The words left his lips before he could prevent them. But it was not his words that betrayed him, he knew.

"Halfway to Hell, I hope," Humble muttered, looking away at last, and Macalester knew that the man had not

229

even intended to say that much.

Macalester felt the gun in his hand, chilled by the dark sentiment. *He is a monster.* Geneva's words, simply uttered, echoed like a curse. Garland Humble was smiling again, but it was a bitter smile.

"So she got to you," he remarked, sounding sad and a trifle envious. "I'm not surprised, although I'd hoped you were too smart for her. You're a fool, Mac, if you think you could ever have had her for very long. Geneva is a selfish and spoiled trollop, with staggeringly expensive tastes. She's capricious and fickle. I can tell by that look on your face that you know exactly what I'm saying, don't you?"

Macalester was mortified. Humble had somehow turned the tables on him. Again.

"I've tried myself for three years to forget her." He slid his hands into the pockets of his trousers. "But she's a disease damned near impossible to shake. So I figured if I worked it out so she was really gone, to a place where I'd never have to hear about her again, never even know whether she was alive or dead, it would really be over. I made it so she won't be able to dance on my grave and come around to claim all of my money when I'm gone, after running out on me."

Humble's pronouncement left Macalester cold as ice. The old man was serious. *He moves people around like pieces in a chess game,* Geneva had warned him.

Where, the outlaw wondered, had he moved Geneva?

Macalester rallied, pulling a reckless grin out of the ruins of his hopes. "Now that sounds more like you, Gar," he declared, congratulating himself that he even managed a laugh. "You're a man who likes to hold on to what he has, including people. You don't care about Geneva. You never did. It just galls you that she got away from you. You just can't stand to part with anything, can you? And I expect, in some way, you think

230

of me as one of those possessions, too."

Garland Humble did not answer him right away. He merely stared at Macalester, his eyes as glassy and as empty as death itself. Presently Macalester realized the old man had withdrawn his right hand from his pocket, and in it was a small derringer.

"Well, Hell, Gar," Macalester said softly, feeling his own heavy Colt poised in his hand. "I can't just let you stand there and shoot me, now can I?"

"And I can't let you go after Geneva," the other man said faintly. "So you'll have to shoot me. Of course, if you shoot me, you'll never find out what happened to her, will you? Looks like we've reached an impasse, Mac."

Macalester felt oddly detached, as though watching the drama unfold from another part of the room, or as if it were a picture in a museum, complete with a heavy, ornate frame. He did not think for one minute that Garland Humble would hesitate to shoot him where he stood, with or without further provocation.

He also sensed that the next one of them who spoke had lost.

Garland Humble's barrellike chest rose and fell, and his breathing grew labored. Macalester felt as though he himself had frozen to the floor. His booted feet had not moved in several minutes, and he wondered, fleetingly, if they would ever move again by his own direction. He heard his heartbeat, surprisingly slow and regular, as though the organ was blissfully unaware of the proximity of death. He did not fear death, he realized, nor even the act of dying. The only thing he regretted, deeply, was that he would not see Geneva again.

No doubt of it, he thought, feeling a faint grin tease the corners of his mouth. He was in love with her. At least he could take that with him. Maybe it would be enough, in the eyes of whatever God there was, to cleanse him of his terrible lie.

Humble's stare became vacant, as though he was looking at something beyond Macalester, or perhaps as though Macalester himself had abruptly ceased to exist. A loud clatter broke the stillness at last. Glancing down, Macalester saw the derringer on the black-and-white marble floor. Humble's hand flexed once. Macalester saw it tremble just before the old man pressed it to his chest. Humble looked surprised, then shocked. Before Macalester could quite make out what was happening, Humble staggered forward, first with one leg, then the other. Then he fell to his knees, hard.

"Mac—" Garland's blue lips formed the name three times before any sound actually emanated. Macalester still could not move, although he suddenly wanted to. It seemed an invisible wall had gone up between himself and the afflicted man, preventing his comprehension of the situation for another moment. Then Humble fell forward onto his face, and Macalester heard his own voice break the stillness.

"Hallis!" he shouted, holstering his gun as he found his legs and sprang forward. "Hallis! Come quick!"

Macalester knelt beside the prone man and turned him, with great effort, onto his back. Humble was still breathing, but the breaths were shallow and rapid. His nose was bloodied. He'd probably smashed it on the floor when he fell. He tried to moisten his cracked blue lips with the tip of his dry tongue. He regarded the younger man with a weak, pleading look. Macalester was stunned by the unexpected pity he felt for the suddenly helpless, and apparently dying, man.

Hallis appeared and dropped the tray with the brandy bottle upon it. The service fell to the floor with a loud crash. Macalester, irritated, glanced up at him.

"Does he have medicine?" he challenged the mortified butler tersely.

Hallis nodded.

"Then get it!" the outlaw ordered. "And send someone for the doctor. Hurry up, Hallis, or he's a dead man!"

Hallis disappeared.

"Don't you die on me, you ornery son-of-a-bitch." Macalester tapped on Humble's pale and papery cheeks. "Not before you tell me where Geneva is!"

Garland's puffy eyes fluttered open, and his lips moved soundlessly. Eager, Macalester bent his neck and pressed his ear near Humble's face.

"Go to hell," he heard the old man rasp.

Hallis returned and, with badly shaking hands, held a small brown bottle out to Macalester. Hallis, Macalester noticed with some disgust, seemed to be virtually useless in an emergency.

"The doctor, Hallis!" he reminded the mute butler sternly. "Get the doctor!"

The smaller man nodded and disappeared again. Surprised at his own calm, Macalester deftly uncorked the bottle and shook one small white pill into the palm of his hand. Humble, still struggling for breath, watched him from the floor. It was an odd sensation, to see the ruthless and powerful Garland Humble utterly helpless, waiting for his life-saving medicine.

Macalester closed his hand on the pill, staring hard at the fallen millionaire.

"I wonder," he said quietly, "if you'd rather die than tell me where she is."

"You bastard!" Humble mouthed.

Macalester's only emotion, staring down at him, was a profound hope that the old man would live long enough to tell him what he wanted to hear.

"You taught me everything I know," Macalester assured him. "Now where is she, Gar? You don't have a whole lot of time, judging by the color of your lips."

"Galveston," Humble struggled, closing his eyes. "Give me . . ."

Galveston! Why the hell would he send her there? Macalester wondered, mystified. Well, no time to ask now. He held tightly to the pill.

"One more thing." It was a struggle to prevent himself from giving the wretched hulk his salvation, but he managed. "The money. Where is it?"

Too late. Humble had passed out again. Macalester muttered a brief curse under his breath and slipped the pill between Humble's dry lips. He got up then, leaving Humble on the floor where he was.

Galveston. Could Humble have been lying? Macalester wondered, staring down at the pale, virtually lifeless bulk on the floor. Possible, he thought. But not likely. Garland Humble, who knew the price of everything and the value of nothing, would not gamble with his own life.

Macalester stirred himself. Time was short. He abandoned the unconscious, or dead, man in favor of a search of the study. The first place he tried was Garland's enormous rosewood desk, which he had once heard Garland refer to as his "Louie Katorze." Macalester had no idea what that meant. The desk was, in his opinion, garishly ornate and impossibly cumbersome, typical of the ostentatious trappings with which Garland Humble enjoyed surrounding himself.

The top drawer was locked. Macalester withdrew a sword-shaped letter opener from a crystal well on the desk and pried it open, leaving a deep, jagged gouge in the tender wood.

Macalester could never understand why rich people like Garland Humble would leave so much cash lying around the house, where anyone could just come in and steal it. He did not bother to count it out. He merely stuffed two bundles of bills into his shirt, leaving the rest. There was a time when he would have taken it all, he mused, allowing himself a bitter smile as he closed the damaged drawer on several additional bundles of wrapped greenbacks.

Hallis was kneeling over Humble in the foyer when he returned, fussing in a most annoying and ineffectual manner.

"What do you know about Garland's business in Galveston, Hallis?" he challenged the butler, whose gray head jerked around. Macalester was surprised that the man's sharp eyes were wet.

"Mr. Humble sent his foreman to Galveston to meet a man." Hallis frowned as if trying to recall. "A foreigner, I believe."

Humble hadn't lied, after all. So nice, reflected Macalester, glancing at Humble's motionless, amorphous mass, to discover unexpected qualities in one's business associates.

"A foreigner?" Macalester challenged him, mystified. "From where?"

Hallis waved his hand, returning his attention to his master. "Arabian," he replied impatiently. "I believe Mr. Humble was purchasing horses."

Macalester stared, trying to analyze. What connection could there be between Geneva Lionwood and Arabian horses? The more he thought about it, as he headed back to Irving for Billy, the less he liked the sound of it, although he could not fathom why.

Chapter Twenty-one

A cold rain accompanied Kieran Macalester and Billy Deal out of Irving, but Billy was glad to be going anyway. He didn't minded telling Mac that he'd worried some in the day and a half the older man had been gone. He'd seldom seen his partner in such a grimly determined state, and never over anything involving a woman. The Senator was quiet, too. Abnormally so. Although, Deal reflected, watching puffs of steam issue from beneath his own new mustache and dissipate in the steady rain, the weather was not much of an inspiration to one's eloquence, even Mac's.

But the weather, he suspected, had little, if anything, to do with Mac's taciturn humor.

Mac rode a little ahead of him, his back ramrod straight. His poncho flapped about his boot tops and rainwater ran in a stream off the back of his hat as he cantered the big roan along the muddy road. He'd returned from Humble's early that morning without saying much. He'd merely handed him a bunch of greenbacks and indicated he was going out to provision them for a hard ride. Billy had guessed that right along, but there was something about the way Mac had avoided his eyes as he told him that made Billy refrain from questioning his partner further at the time. But all of that had taken place several hours ago. Billy's stomach was growling for lunch, and he had a yen for hot coffee and conversation.

They'd put about twenty miles or more behind them, and at the rate Mac was pushing, they'd make Galveston Island in two days' time. A train, with all of its stops in between, could not make it any faster than that. And he was damned if he'd go on riding in the rain without even the diversion of a little conversation; he didn't care what might be on Mac's mind. Enough was enough. With a "G'yip" and a nudge with his heels, he urged his own gray gelding ahead until he was pacing his partner.

"Hey, Mac, you got any jerky? Mine's all wet."

The ruse, he knew, never fooled Mac, but it always got his attention. The older man laughed briefly. It was a hollow sound, though, like the report of a shotgun in a box canyon.

"The hell it is." Mac's hooded eyes scanned the road before them. "What's on your mind, William? I got time for three questions."

He reined the roan to a trot, slow enough for a brief dialogue.

"Hot damn, three whole questions?" Billy teased, hoping to lighten the mood a little. "I got time for about a dozen answers!"

"Two, now," Macalester amended, shrugging the rain off his shoulders. "That was one."

Billy allowed the laconic jest to pass without reacting. "What happened at Humble's?" he asked bluntly.

Macalester glanced at his partner and saw at once

that Deal was serious. He answered the younger man with neither omission nor embellishment. Deal remained silent during his reply and for several minutes thereafter.

"What do you suppose they plan to do with her?" Billy wanted to know next. Billy, Macalester was somewhat amused to note, was choosing his questions carefully. He began to dread the final question.

"I don't know," he replied, aware of the uneasiness that had not left him since his parting conversation with Hallis. "That's what worries me. I wouldn't put anything past Gar, after this."

They covered another half a mile before Billy exercised his right to the final query.

"What, exactly, happened to you, Mac? On this job, I mean? I never seen you like this before."

Macalester sucked in a hard breath, held it, then let it out all at once, still not looking at his partner.

"Ask me another question," he said.

"Aw, come on, Senator!" Billy sounded annoyed. "You said three questions. That's my third. I spent a month of my life holed up in Humble's fancy-ass prison, and now you got me chasin' some skirt halfway to Bejeezuz when we should be gettin' set to winter in Mexico, and I guess I'm entitled to know why."

Macalester stared at the wet, matted dark hair of the roan's mane. Billy, he knew, was entitled to an answer. Given his own admittedly odd behavior, and the demands he was making, he knew he certainly owed the younger man that much. But, damn it, he was— ashamed. There was no other word for it. He was appalled by his own behavior, from his arrival in New York to the night of madness in Memphis when he'd lost his will to stay away from Geneva. Behavior that, he realized to his chagrin, would have made him and Billy laugh before. But somehow, some way, something had happened to him. And that something, he knew, feeling the ever-present tightness in his breast, was Geneva Lionwood.

"Did you ever meet anybody," Macalester began, seeing her so clearly in his mind's eye that he ached to touch her, "who made you wonder about everything you thought you knew, as if suddenly the sun came up in the west one morning instead of the east? Somebody who made you wish, just being near thcm, that you could live your life over again in a flash and be somebody, really be somebody, in their eyes? Somebody who could make you feel like the biggest, smallest, smartest, dumbest, highest, lowest son-of-a-bitch that ever drew breath, just by looking at you sideways? Somebody who could turn you inside out, string you up, slice your heart into little paper dolls and beat you like an old carpet, and make you wish they'd beat you some more?"

"By 'somebody,' I guess you mean a woman." Billy sounded cautious. Macalester smiled to himself: Billy knew when to walk on eggs around him.

"No, I don't just mean a woman," he retorted, feeling his face grow warm. "I'm talking about *the* woman. Did you cver meet *the* woman, Billy?"

Billy laughed, a trifle nervously, Macalester thought.

"Well, hell, sure, I met a lot of women," he answered easily. Too easily. A man who had found that woman, Macalester realized, could never be easy again, until she was his.

"It's not the same. Not the same at all." He shook his head slowly, wondering at the change in himself since a month before. It was as if he'd found something, something so vital, so fundamental to his existence that he could not begin to comprehend how he had lived without it all of those years. And, having lost it again, he wondered hourly how he could be expected to continue drawing breath . . .

239

His face was wet. He put his head back, looking up at the slate-gray sky, welcoming the raindrops that would camouflage his tears.

"I have to get her back, Billy." A quick sigh caught him off-guard. "I promised her I wouldn't let anything bad happen to her. She's a smart woman. Damned smart. And resourceful, too. Hell, with everything she's been through in the last month alone, I'd say she could handle just about anything. But that scares me, too. She's so capable, what the hell does she need me for?"

The two horses plodded along in the mud for a time.

"Same reason you need her, I imagine," Deal offered at last.

Macalester smiled, ruefully.

"I don't know." He used his damp kerchief to wipe his face. "I told her the lie of my life, and I don't think she'll ever forgive me for it. I owe her, Billy. I owe her big. She was the one who got rid of Lennox. She killed him. It was an accident, but it happened. And that's my fault, too. She'd never have had to kill him, if it hadn't been for me. When I think about it, I've fouled up her life in just about every way possible, and I'm damned it I can come up with even a shabby reason why she should ever want to forgive me, let alone love me. So I have to do this, Billy," he wound up, feeling so bad again that he wished he'd never brought it up. "I can't even think about how she feels about me. I just know I couldn't live with myself unless I did everything in my power to help her now. Does that make any sense?"

Macalester sure hoped it made some sense to Billy Deal, because he didn't feel as though anything made any sense to him, not since that night in Irving when she had gazed at him with those big green eyes of hers and spoken the first words she'd said in three days: *What will happen to me?*

How could he have known when he promised her

nothing bad would happen that her husband would have made some wild plan for them both at which he could only guess?

"What the hell is that?"

Macalester stared at his partner. Billy, craning his neck, was squinting at something in the road ahead. Macalester followed his stare and saw a buckboard stopped dead around a bend in the road with a man lying in the mud beside it. The horses were gone, and in the back was a big brown bundle. The bundle moved.

Macalester's heart skipped. With a nudge and a cry, he spurred the roan to a gallop, forming a wordless prayer as he bore down upon the wagon. He pulled the roan up short, dismounting even before the animal came to a stop. He heard Billy's gray gallop up behind him, but he was already in the back of the wagon, reaching for the saturated burlap bundle.

"Gen! Is it you? Are you all right?"

He pulled the burlap with a final quick jerk and was crushingly disappointed to find not Geneva but a man, huddled, with the look of a scared rabbit on his unshaven face.

"Don't hurt me," the man whimpered. Macalester recognized him at once as the last face he'd seen in Irving before waking up to Billy Deal's. Before the outlaw quite knew what was happening, his own hands were fast around the man's scrawny neck, and he was shaking him like a hapless rag doll.

"Where is she?" he demanded, his hoarse shout thundering through the soaked woods about them. "What happened to her? Damn you, answer me!"

The man made a choking sound, and his eyes began to bulge out of their dark, sunken sockets. His head lolled as though his neck was broken.

A strong, firm hand took hold of Macalester's arm, causing him to release the man abruptly. "He can't tell

241

you nothin' if he's dead, Senator." Billy's voice was the quiet voice of reason.

Macalester stared hard at the cowering figure before him, panting for breath. He wanted to kill the man, and he would have, had Billy not intervened.

"Tyrell's over here," Billy offered, and Macalester still did not look at him. "And another fellow. They're dead. Shot in the back of the head. A real mess. I'd guess they've been here a day or more."

Two dead men and a live coward. But Geneva? She wasn't here. She wasn't dead. He'd know it, somehow, if she were. Wouldn't he?

"All right." Macalester panted, eyeing the man in the buckboard with disgust. "What happened here? Where is she?"

The man pulled the wet burlap about himself again with badly shaking hands, not taking his eyes off of Macalester.

"We stopped for a rest," he stammered, his voice no more than a squeak. "I went into the woods to do my business, and next I know, there's shots. I got down and looked around, and saw these—I don't know—devil men. I never seen anything like 'em. They was all in black, with these black things on their heads and faces, and they was jabberin' in some language I couldn't make out. Wasn't no Injun that I ever heard. Then I hear the woman screamin', and I kept real still. They carried her off, I reckon. Humble's gonna be mighty pissed. We was supposed to pick up thirty Arab horses after we took her to Galveston. I don't know what we're gonna do. Hell, Wes is dead, and Tyrell . . ."

The man was rambling, but the import of his recitation struck Macalester like a mule kick to the balls. Garland Humble meant to trade his wife to a bunch of heathen white slavers for a herd of horses. Macalester had heard of such atrocious doings before, but he had never known of it himself, and had therefore never believed it.

But he believed it now.

The next thing Mac knew, the wet man in burlap was out cold on the floor of the wagon with a river of blood gushing from his broken nose. His own knuckles throbbed.

"Feel better, now?" Billy's voice, somewhere behind him, had a laugh in it, but it was a bitter laugh.

"Let's get the hell out of here."

"I'm right behind you, Senator."

Macalester, Billy knew instinctively, would gallop the roan to death and shoot another man for his horse, if he had to, to get to Galveston now. Whoever and whatever this Geneva Lionwood was, he mused grimly, climbing into his own saddle, hc hoped she was worth what it was going to cost.

Chapter Twenty-two

The roan and the gray were lathered and sluggish. Macalester guessed, leading his animal through the dusk to the livery, that he and Billy had covered two hundred miles in two days. The horses were near dead, and he was pretty beat himself. Even Billy had grown surly, so much so that all conversation between them had ceased several hours before and was not likely to resume. Not, at least, until they'd had a hot meal. Macalester would have liked a bath and a rest in a warm, dry bed as well, but they had reached Galveston. There was no time to rest. Not when he was so near to his goal.

The air stank of salt marsh and the sea. Macalester hated the smell. He was unaccustomed to it, and it had always made him a little sick. Billy, on the other hand, stood straight and tall and filled his chest with the noxious stuff, vowing he should have been a sailor.

The man at the livery stable treated them like a pair of criminals, and Macalester suspected that it had to do with the condition of their horses. He did not care. Most things had ceased to bother him in the last forty-eight hours, including his own comfort. The rain had only lasted a day, and that in itself, Billy had declared, was a good omen. Cold, unrelenting rain was a regular event at this time of year along the gulf. Rain, sun, wind; it was all the same to Kieran Macalester. Since Irving, the days and nights had become one unending string of gray hours, counted as one would count the rings in a hangman's knot.

Galveston. They were here at last, and Macalester found renewed energy. Having stabled the horses, he began to formulate a plan of search for the missing diva. Galveston was a good-sized town, but its ranks ebbed and swelled with the arrival and departure of ships on the gulf. Galveston was, after all, the port through which much of the state's raw goods were shipped and finished ones received. It should be simple enough to identify a cargo of thirty Arabian horses and to locate their ship of origin.

"Let's take a short walk to the harbormaster, William," Macalester invited, trying to inject a bounce into his step that he was far from feeling. His boots, at the moment, felt as though they were filled with buckshot.

Billy Deal stopped him dead with a look of such amazement that he felt his face grow warm. "Tonight? Mac, I'm beat!"

"We'll take a cab, then." Macalester looked down the darkened street at the row of gas lamps and the traffic of wagons and buggies so he did not have to meet his partner's gaze. Beside him, he heard Billy Deal laugh wearily.

"You don't give up, do you, Senator?" he declared incredulously. "I ain't goin'. I don't care if you carry me all the way down to the dock on your back. I'm gonna find me a hotel, a bath, a saloon and a whore, in that order. And maybe I'll squeeze a steak or some gulf shrimp in there, somewhere. This is your little picnic, remember? I just gave you my itinerary; you'll know where to find me if you need me. Mind a word of advice?"

Macalester shrugged, hooking his gloved thumbs in his belt as he rocked back on his heels. Billy's handsome face looked haggard.

"Do the same," the younger man said in a terse, weary voice. "They couldn'ta got to town no quicker'n us. Hell, they're prob'ly still on the road. A night's sleep'll do you no harm, and we can start fresh in the morning."

There was a warm, heavy pressure on Macalester's left shoulder. It was Billy Deal's hand, firm and sure. The weight of it nearly overwhelmed Macalester with weariness and something even worse. He shook off the feelings, though, slapping his partner casually in the chest with the back of his hand as he edged away from his grip.

"I'll be along in a bit. Get us a room over there." He found Billy a brief grin and gestured to a small sign across the street, advertising clean rooms with bath plus hot water, two dollars a night. "It won't take me more than an hour. Just don't bring any lady friends back to the room. I'm not in any mood to be sociable."

Billy grimaced with no hint of amusement, however wry.

"You don't say," the younger man offered in a rude tone. "Go 'head, Senator. Wander off down on the docks by yourself. Get yourself shanghaied. When you wake up pukin' your guts out on some steamer bound for the East Indies, just don't say I didn't warn you."

Billy ambled away, showing his own saddle weariness in his limping gait. Kieran watched him go, wanting to call him back, wanting to apologize for not caring about his feelings, or about anything. But the words

246

would not come. He stood on the street for a full minute watching until Billy disappeared into the hotel. He turned his back on comfort and headed in the other direction.

The harbormaster was gone for supper and would not return for an hour. The clerk was pouring over a tower of manifests, and was unwilling, if not unable, to impart any information to Macalester regarding cargos, arrivals and departures. He did, however, suggest the Sailor's Rest saloon on pier three as a possible source of information. Macalester thanked the man and aimed himself in that direction, thinking a beer would go down real easy right about then.

The street was dark and trafficked by men in pea jackets and small pancake hats. Macalester, in his brown Stetson, felt conspicuous. Indeed, he drew a few stares as he strode along the waterfront to the accompaniment of waves lapping at the pylons, the odd caw of a gull and the lonely, far-off ring of a buoy bell out in the harbor. God, the stench of barnacles and rotting sea life and air heavy with salt mist was disgusting! How did these men tolerate it every day of their seafaring lives?

The reek of tobacco and sour beer in the saloon was a welcome change for Macalester. The Sailor's Rest was a small place, tucked away between two warehouses on the pier, off the street. A perfect location, the outlaw mused, surveying its seedy-looking denizens, for a shanghai such as Billy had mentioned. He had best be on his guard.

The barkeep provided him with a bottle and a glass, and Macalester paid with one of the greenbacks recently liberated from the tight fist of Garland Humble. He felt the curious stares of the handful of patrons in the place. Even the barkeep, a tall, solid-looking man with red-blond hair, a ruddy complexion and a bushy mustache of the same color regarded him with something approaching suspicion, his ice-blue eyes steady and unblinking.

"You lose your way, cowboy?" He poured Macalester his first shot of whiskey. Macalester considered the man and swallowed the drink. He allowed the liquid fire to settle in his stomach and watched the inquisitive bartender pour a second glass before he responded.

"I wish to hell I had," he replied without smiling. "I'm looking for a shipment of thirty Arab horses, and ships like that don't navigate the Trinity to Fort Worth. You wouldn't know anything about it, would you?"

The bartender considered him, his stare yielding no clue. At last he cocked his head slightly to one side and crossed his big arms, covered with golden hair, before his white-shirted chest. Macalester swallowed the second drink.

"I might," he conceded briefly, glancing once to a far corner of the room. Macalester did not turn around. He had assessed the room upon entering, and recalled a large shadow in that area belonging, he assumed, to an equally large man who apparently had no desire to be seen in the light. Macalester did allow a faint smile on his wide mouth, then.

"Remarkable how money improves a memory, isn't it?" he said whimsically, shaking his head. "Well, hell. It ain't my money."

He withdrew a fiver from his pocket without revealing its several bigger brothers.

His audience stiffened. The big man's arms dropped to his sides, and his stare became hard. "I don't like your mouth, cowboy. Now get the hell out of my place."

This was an interesting ruse. "And what if I don't?"

"Abel!" The barkeep bellowed, not taking his eyes off of Macalester. "This fellow's leaving. Help him out!"

Macalester was wondering what kind of a show he should put on when he felt a large, crushingly strong

Steal Me, Sweet Thief

hand grasp the collar of his corduroy jacket from behind. To the accompaniment of the bored and amused stares of the few patrons of the Sailor's Rest, Macalester protested as his assailant half-pushed, half-carried him a few steps to the door. He braced himself for what was to follow.

No sooner had the door closed behind him than he felt the rush of a blow to the side of his head, a blow he ducked just in time. Raising his fists, he turned quickly on his attacker, who proved, to his dismay, to be even bigger than he'd expected.

It was dark, and he could not see Abel's face. He was not even certain he wanted to. He had hoped to overpower the man and force from him the information he sought, but he thought, as he took a dizzying swat to the temple, that he would do well merely to keep out of the fellow's way. He considered reaching for his gun but decided that, as the greatest effect of the weapon was visual—in his hands, at least—its value would be considerably diminished by the fact that it would be nearly impossible to see in the darkness.

He ducked a telegraphed punch and riposted by hurling himself into his opponent's midsection. Abel merely took a half-step backward, as though stepping out of the way of a passing lady.

Shit, Macalester thought.

Suddenly another pair of hands pinned his arms to his sides and yanked him backward. This unexpected turn of events gave him cause for alarm: His alternate plan had been to put up a struggle, then to feign unconsciousness to see where his assailant would take him. This new wrinkle in his plans might mean, he realized as he struggled against his new captor, that he might not, after all, get the chance to pretend.

The first blow to his midsection knocked his wind clear back to Irving. With the second he felt a rib crack,

249

and he doubled over in time to take a mighty swat to the jaw that set off a fireworks display in his brain. With the force of his will alone, he clung to consciousness and braced himself for the next blow, although where it would fall, he hadn't a clue.

Even as he expected a punch, he heard a loud thump. Opening his eyes, he saw the massive bulk of his attacker fall prone on the pier before him, a virtual mountain of useless flesh. He looked up in surprise and was able to make out a familiar outline holding the muzzle of a Colt whose butt had, no doubt, recently rendered Abel unconscious. His arms were suddenly freed, and he heard the running footsteps of the other party fade into the darkness. With a sigh of relief, he flexed his arms and gingerly felt his bruised side.

"Are you all right, Mac?" Billy's voice was terse, and he was breathing hard.

Macalester nodded, gulping air before attempting to speak.

"Yeah," he said finally. "Thanks, Bi—"

His words were cut off by a punch that caught him full on his chin, sending him rocketing backward against the wall of the warehouse. He slid down the wall until he sat hard upon the pier, and it was a moment or two before he realized what had happened. He could not even muster the energy to be angry.

"What the hell was that for?" he grumbled, rubbing his aching chin.

"For bein' stupid," Billy answered him vehemently, working the fingers of his right hand. "Now come on. Let's get the hell outta here."

He stood over Macalester, extending his arm to help him up. Macalester took it and, with a grunt, got to his feet unsteadily. No doubt about it, he thought, considering Billy's deadly serious, if shadowy, features. He was getting too old for this sort of thing.

"You hit him hard?" He gestured to the prone body.

Billy shrugged. "Hard enough, I guess. You wanna talk to him?"

Macalester nodded. "Here, help me."

With no small effort, the two men dragged Abel's lifeless bulk to the wall of the warehouse, where they sat him up. His huge head lolled to one side.

"Wait a minute." Billy disappeared, and in moments he returned with a fire bucket. He leaned way over the side of the pier. There was a splash and Billy came up again, the bucket heavy with seawater.

"Good thing it's high tide," he remarked, straightening. "Get out of the way."

Macalester obeyed.

With a heave, Billy Deal emptied the contents of his bucket upon Abel's face, drenching him. Something moved across the big man's chest. Billy reached for it and held it up in the dim light, laughing.

"How 'bout that? A crab!"

He tossed it over his shoulder, and the creature splashed back into the gulf, no doubt confused by its brief ordeal. Abel stirred and sputtered the salt water from his mouth. Macalester knelt beside him, slapping at his fat cheeks to encourage his revival. He did draw his gun then, and he placed its muzzle against Abel's ear so the fellow could not mistake the sound of a clean, cocked Colt.

The man's eyes opened wide, reminding Macalester of a one-armed bandit in a gaming hall. He grinned at the analogy.

"Damned if this ain't the unfriendliest place I ever saw," he declared softly. "I dislike having to shoot a man, my first day in town."

"Come on, Senator, this ain't a social tea!" Billy was impatient. "Get what you want, so we can feed this big ol' boy to the sharks."

251

"No, no," Abel protested feebly, his mass quivering. "I'll tell you whatever you want to know."

Macalester, in a lazy, calculated way, forced the tip of the Colt's barrel a little way into the man's ear. Abel reacted by drawing up his bulky shoulders.

"Thirty Arab horses," Macalester prompted. "We want to know where the ship is, and who bought 'em. And anything else you might know about it," he added, thinking that in all of the excitement, he might have forgotten something.

"The *Corvallis*," the man stammered, panting like a winded dog. "Pier twelve. She's been here almost a month, and her captain's fit to be tied. He was supposed to discharge them horses and take on new cargo, and now his orders are to take the nags to Biloxi, and a boatload of furriners with 'em."

Macalester pondered this. He did not doubt the man's story, but there was still plenty of margin for error. And if he missed Geneva somehow, he feared he would not get a second chance.

"You looking to fill out her crew?" he asked then.

"Damn, Mac, you ain't thinkin' of—" Billy's amazement trailed off in the darkness.

"I might be," Macalester mused, before returning his attention to his oversized audience.

"She's short a man or two," Abel offered, rubbing the back of his head, probably where Billy had hit him.

"When does she sail?"

"Tomorrow, I think. What the hell'd he hit me with?"

"My finger," Billy supplied, pacing.

In spite of himself, Macalester grinned. "When, tomorrow?"

"Train's due in at the yard sometime after midnight. She'll sail with the next tide after that. Prob'ly around daybreak."

Time. There was no time. Cursing under his breath,

Macalester thought quickly. He and Billy could check out the train and its passengers. If they located Geneva, they might be able to get her before she was taken to the ship. If they could not, then they'd all be taking a short cruise to Biloxi. Macalester stood up.

"Got any rope, Billy?"

"What're you gonna do?" Abel ventured.

Macalester couldn't be sure, but it sounded like the man was trembling. He let out a hard breath. "You broke my rib, you son-of-a-bitch." He sighed, shaking his head. "I'd like to kick the shit out of you. The sharks won't much care what you look like."

"You'll mess up your boots," Billy observed, casually looking up and down the pier.

"Hmm." Macalester scratched his cheek. "You have a point. But these old boots ain't worth much, anyway."

"That's true," Billy allowed. "I see some rope."

He was back in a minute with a length of heavy hemp, and in a few minutes more, they had the man nicely trussed.

"Well?" Billy winked at his partner. "Over the side?"

Macalester considered the man, wondering why he and Billy enjoyed tormenting people with threats they had no intention of carrying out. Just like when he'd threatened to scald Gen, or told her he wouldn't mind dropping her on the road, and of course he'd had no such inclination.

Geneva. The very thought of her drove a spike into his gut and brought a quick burn to the back of his eyes. Quickly he shook his head, looking for a fresh topic upon which to fix his mind. With a flick of his wrist, he removed the kerchief from around his neck and deftly secured it across the frightened man's mouth.

"I won't see you again while we're in town, will I?" He looked directly into the man's wide pig eyes. "Because if I do . . ."

Abel shook his head from side to side like a mournful steer caught in barbed wire. Beads of sweat had formed on his balding brow, in spite of the shower of seawater he'd enjoyed. Macalester nodded in satisfaction.

"Good. Let's go, Billy."

Billy muttered under his breath the whole way to the train yard.

Chapter Twenty-three

The train jolted to a stop, awakening Geneva from a weird dream instantly forgotten. Groggy, annoyed, she got out of her bed and listened at the locked door for a clue as to the delay. Outside she heard nothing. Some time passed, and Geneva began to wonder if her captors had forgotten her.

Hakim was her jailor but not her master. The sultan was her master, but she had not yet met him. She didn't want to. Hakim, his man-in-charge, was chilling enough. He was not a large man, but was, in his trim white suit and turban, nevertheless a commanding one. The fellow he most often commanded was Abdul, a distressingly large man with a propensity for pantaloon trousers and a garish gold sash. The two had attended her infrequently in the little, locked train car since her imprisonment.

Hakim spoke, but seldom to her. Abdul never spoke at all, and she'd learned that it was because his tongue

Carole Howey

had been cut out. She suspected he'd been gelded as well. Those were sufficient reasons for her to behave herself, until she devised a practical means of escape. Since she was kept locked in at all times, she'd decided the best thing to do was to hide somewhere in the car, lead them to believe she had escaped, then slip away while they were all out searching for her.

She was alone now. The train had stopped. There was a bench settee running half the length of the car on one side. Geneva tried the seat, hoping to find it to be a hinged storage compartment. It was. Elated, she scrambled inside the dusty, unused space and pulled the lid closed on top of herself, settling in so she could peek through the thin space beneath the bench seat, straining her neck and back in a most awkward and uncomfortable position. There, motionless, she waited.

After a time, her patience was rewarded. Two men entered the room. She could not see their whole figures, but through her horizontal line of vision she could see the white of Hakim's suit and the gold of Abdul's sash. They paused, and she watched as they turned. Hakim spoke, using an imperious and unmistakable tone, even if she could not understand the words. Geneva's heart pounded so hard that she wondered why the two men did not seem to hear it. She held her breath, watching the white and the gold move quickly about the room, rifling its furnishings. Suddenly the gold sash disappeared from view. Feeling a trickle of perspiration glide along the small of her back, she turned as quietly as she could, trying to see where he might have gone.

Presently her vision was obstructed completely, and she realized, stifling a gasp, that Abdul was standing directly before her position. If the gap had been just a bit wider, she could have poked her finger out and touched the dark cloth of his pantaloon trousers. She heard Hakim bark another brief command, and the gi-

256

ant moved again. The lopsided duo left the room, exhibiting no great haste or vexation. Geneva bit her lower lip, deciding on her next course of action.

She waited another minute. The men did not return. Cautiously, she lifted the lid of the bench and listened. Hearing nothing, she climbed out and shivered. It was like emerging from a coffin. Soundlessly, she tiptoed to the door and pressed her ear against it. Outside, at some distance, she could make out voices, although she could not determine what was being said, or even whether the language being spoken was English. She tried the door lever tentatively.

It was unlocked.

Her heart leaped at this unexpected boon. She pushed the door open, at first a crack, then a narrow wedge. Outside, it was very dark. Her eyes adjusted to the blackness, and in moments she could see there was a freight car stopped beside them. Slipping out, she closed the door quickly and quietly behind her. The stench of creosote mingled with an unfamiliar odor she could not quite place. On the other side of the train was an open space. Lights glowed in the distance on shadowy structures like yellow globes, sending glistening reflections on the straight rows of rails stretching before her eyes like silent regiments. Again, she heard the distant sound of voices and running feet nearby. She flattened her back against the door, hoping to be invisible in the darkness to searching eyes.

A minute passed.

She heard the distant cry of a bird. A gull. It was then that she recognized the heretofore unfamiliar smell: the sea! At once excited and frightened, she mastered an urge to jump from the train and run, although the lure of freedom, so near at hand after such a long time, was suddenly very powerful. The gull called again in a mocking laugh. *I am free*, it seemed to taunt her, *while you hide in shadows from men who would make you a slave.*

She swallowed hard, even though her mouth was dry as sand. There was a rushing to her right. The sound of running. In the darkness, she saw shadowy figures flit past her hiding place, between her position and the freight car. She had to move. Her impulse was to head toward the light, but she quickly rejected the foolish notion. She needed the cover of darkness and shadows to succeed, and she needed to do what her enemies would not expect.

Geneva had never been close to the wheels of a train before, and the idea scared her. It was but a few feet to the freight car beside her, though, and if she could slip under the car and hide between its huge metal wheels, she would have a better vantage of her surroundings while remaining unseen. She knew she could not remain where she was.

She listened hard. The sounds of voices and of movement were far ahead of her, some distance up the track. She would not have a better opportunity. Slowly, she edged toward the steps, feeling rather than seeing her way.

The first step down was much farther than she had expected. She poked her toe downward, reaching for the second step. She found it at last, congratulating herself on being one step closer to her immediate goal. She risked a glance up ahead, craning her neck so she could see past the corner of the car in front of her. She could apprehend nothing but the long columns of the two trains, which seemed to meet somewhere in the darkness. Resolutely, she stepped down again, and she was pleased to find it was easier to move.

Her next step took her to the ground. The heel of her shoe sank into coarse gravel with a loud and unexpected crunching sound. Geneva recoiled at the noise, then waited, one foot upon the earth, literally sunken into it, the other poised upon the bottom step. It was an awkward pose, and a precarious one: Suppose the train began to move suddenly? Her two hands upon the guide rails, she shifted her weight to the foot sunken in the gravel—she already felt moisture seeping into the seams of the cheap boot—and in another moment she stood with both feet sunk into the wet ground.

There was no help for it. The noise, in her ears, was like a loud alarm rattle. Quickly gathering her skirt into her hands, she took several crunching steps away from the train car that had been her gilded cage and pressed her back against the hard, splintery wood of the freight car across from it. She took a deep breath, willing herself to think only of her freedom so near to being a reality, and she ducked under the car, nearly tripping over the track in her haste.

She was breathing so hard that her chest began to ache. Crouching low beside a great iron wheel, she peered hard into the darkness. Presently, Hakim approached in advance of four or more black-robed associates. Abdul, to her mild surprise, was nowhere in evidence.

In the clipped, imperious tone Geneva could not fail to recognize, Hakim issued what sounded like commands. The men scattered like provoked beetles, except for one who, with Hakim, idled by the train not five feet from where she was hiding. Her fear gave way to annoyance at her predicament: What were those fools doing there? Her feet and legs began to cramp, and she desperately wanted to get out from under the train, but now she dared not move—not, at least, until Hakim and the other man went away again.

So she waited.

And waited.

The two sentries paced in a random fashion, more in

idleness than order. She monitored their legs as they passed close by her position, counting their steps to pass the time, pace her breathing and take her mind off the painful cramping in her legs.

All at once two large, indistinct forms fell from above her, one each upon Hakim and his minion. Startled, yet fascinated, Geneva watched as the new assailants easily overpowered the two men. Who could they be? she wondered, transfixed by the silent spectacle. She remained still, observing. It would not do to reveal herself, or to call attention to her presence, especially as she had no notion as to the motives, much less the identities, of these two new and unanticipated players.

Presently, their quarry overpowered and immobilized upon the ground at their booted feet, the new shadows straightened.

"I think I broke my damn foot jumping from that boxcar, Senator," she heard one terse male voice accuse, just above a whisper. "You think these good ol' boys know anything?"

"They know," the other man answered in a low, brief growl she recognized at once. She grew so dizzy that she very nearly fainted.

Kieran Macalester!

She tried to call out, but no sound came forth from her vocal cords, which were paralyzed, like her limbs, from sheer relief. She managed a muffled cry, a choking sound, and willed her legs to propel her out from under the shelter of the freight car. Stumbling in the darkness toward the voice, she barely heard the sound of metal against leather that was the drawing of two guns from their holsters. She straightened, still unable to see anything but two tall shadows.

"Gen!"

Kieran's whispered ejaculation had a ring of amazement. She felt his hands grasp her arms as though he might be picking some rare and delicate fruit from an exotic tree. She almost fainted from relief, from terror—she did not care to analyze its origin any more than she cared how it should come about that Kieran Macalester stood before her in the darkness of this strange place, with danger all around them.

"Gen," he whispered again, pulling her close in a desperate, rough embrace. "Gen, Gen . . ."

She could not see him, but she knew the feel of his arms around her and the softness of his cotton flannel shirt beneath her cheek. And he smelled, wonderfully, of leather and of horses. She did not have to see his face. It was enough to know he was there, with her.

She pushed away from him suddenly and swung a sharp blow with her open palm against his bristly, unshaven jaw. How dared he show up here after allowing Humble's men to take her away and subject her to the horrors of the days that followed?

There was an amused chuckle behind her, and she remembered the second shadow.

"What was that for?" Kieran released her abruptly, sounding stunned.

She saw him lift his hand to the cheek she had struck, and her own cheek burned with the pain of the blow she had dealt him. How could she answer him, when she could not even form a cogent reason for herself?

"For takin' your sweet ol' time, Senator; what else?" The chuckling voice behind her supplied the answer in a low tone. "What woman likes to be kept waitin'?"

"Mac, take me away from here. Please. Quickly!" Geneva could not even feign an interest in the man whom she knew only as a shadow and a gently mocking voice. She only knew that she felt exposed, out of her hiding place, in spite of the darkness, and would not feel safe until she was far away. Without wasting another word, Kieran Macalester took her hand in his own, and they moved together toward the rear of the train.

They had not taken more than a few steps when Kieran suddenly released her hand. Dismayed, Geneva turned in time to see the ominous bulk of Abdul, who had already subdued the two outlaws by some unknown means, and was even now planting a large sandaled foot squarely in the center of each of their backs as they lay face first on the ground. Powerless, she watched in new horror as the two men strove uselessly to free themselves from the feet of the impassive giant. The sounds of their struggle to breathe under his crushing weight were awful. She did not know what to do, and in the moment she needed to formulate a plan she was seized roughly from behind by several pairs of hands.

"You insult His Highness's hospitality." Hakim's high, nasal voice rebuked her from a few feet away. "And what has Abdul caught? A pair of mice?"

"They—let them go," Geneva managed, giving up her struggle against the men who held her fast. "I escaped on my own. They just happened by."

"You lie!" Hakim railed at her, brushing dirt from his costume as he moved beside her.

"It's the truth!" she insisted, hoping to keep her feelings hidden from the sultan's counselor. "I was hiding when you came with Abdul, and when you left the car, you neglected to lock the door. You must let them go!"

"And why must we do this?" Hakim challenged her disparagingly

Abdul had already withdrawn his long and fearsomely curved sword from its sheath at his waist, and he appeared to be considering which head he wanted first. Geneva forced herself to remain calm.

"Because," she said coolly, her gaze compelled by Abdul's weapon, "the bodies will be found, and you'll be detained for questioning. The authorities won't allow the sultan or anyone else to leave the port until they find the murderer. It is wisest to let them go."

She restrained herself from going on, sensing that further argument would only convince Hakim that she was lying to spare their lives. She prayed that Hakim, no doubt the only person present other than the two outlaws and herself who spoke English, could not detect the desperation in her voice.

She turned her carefully blank stare to Hakim, scarcely daring to breathe. He was regarding her keenly. With doubt, or merely disdain? There was no way to tell. After a minute, he shouted a few brief commands to the men who held her arms. The result was that they half-led, half-dragged her away, back to the train car where she had been imprisoned. She dared not betray her interest in the outlaws by pleading further for their lives, certain, with a horrible, sick feeling in her stomach, that to do so would ensure their doom.

Chapter Twenty-four

The *Corvallis* was a sailing steamer built for cargo and passenger service in shallow coastal waters. She was a long ship, but not especially fast, especially in a headwind. Her sails were furled; she chugged along through choppy gulf waters on steam alone. The sky was boiling gray, and the horizon blended ominously with the sea all around them.

Three or four days to Biloxi, the first mate had said yesterday. Dumping another bucket of garbage over the side, Kieran Macalester gagged and by force of will alone prevented himself from retching again. In the hold, Billy was tending thirty skittish Arabian colts and fillies, and was whistling as he did so. Billy displayed no tendency at all to motion distress, whereas Kieran had discovered very early in this mission of folly that he himself had best spend as much time as possible topside: It was only in the heavy, whipping salt wind that he had any hope of keeping his seasickness at bay, as it were. Every minute on board, he was unpleasantly reminded that he didn't know diddly about the sea.

He cursed himself hourly for his carelessness in Galveston, carelessness that had resulted in Geneva Lionwood having been snatched away from him, and in his sorry state now in gulf waters with noxious duties and the perpetual, unrelenting revolt of his stomach. When he found Geneva again, and had somehow got her off of this hell-bound vessel, he vowed to himself, he would personally take her anywhere she wanted to go, so long as it did not involve boats. Afterward, he would never let her out of his sight again, if he could help it.

So far, he had not found her. The passengers were quartered up front, in cabins above deck. The crew, about twenty men, of which he and Billy were now a part, were quartered below, in the stern. His duty would be over at eight bells, whatever the hell that meant. He and Billy would slip away after that, and find some way into the passengers' quarters without attracting attention.

Macalester hoisted another bucket of slop over the side and was nearly knocked over by a mammoth wall of green-gray water. The wind blew half of the sorry-smelling mess right back on deck. Muttering a brief curse, the outlaw seized his mop and began to clean it up. The mop was heavy with seawater. Every push reminded him painfully of his broken rib, and of those bruised by the unknown boulder of a man who had crushed him under his feet in the Galveston trainyard. He cursed again at the memory, still feeling the grit of the gravel in his mouth. He had had Geneva. She had been in his arms.

And in the next moment he had been eating dirt, and she was gone.

But not before saving his neck. Again.

Damn, he thought, mopping the stuff up.

Carole Howey

His mop fell on the strangest pair of shoes he'd ever seen on a man: white, all pointed and decorated with elaborate gold brocade, like some whore's outlandish slippers. He very nearly laughed at the sight. He looked up from the shoes, scanning the long, voluminous gray robe cloaking the man before him, who stood more than a head shorter than he, in spite of his white turban. Macalester would have recognized him by his build alone, but the turban clinched it.

It was the man he had jumped on from the train roof not forty-eight hours before in Galveston.

"Howdy." Macalester waved the fingers of his left hand, standing the mop beside him like a staff.

The man stared at him hard, his small dark eyes and etched features seeming to memorize Macalester's every feature. Macalester met his sharp gaze evenly. The man could not possibly connect him with the events of that night. It had been darker than the black hole of Calcutta and the man, he was certain, had never seen him. And of course, he and Billy had already been face-first in the dirt by the time he had revived.

The man stared at him for another minute, an icy stare suggesting that its sender thought himself too high and mighty to share space on this earth, let alone this ship, with the likes of an ignorant deckhand. Macalester mastered a sudden urge to empty another garbage bucket in the haughty man's direction, even as the object of his animosity turned from him abruptly and retched heartily over the side.

Macalester, fighting his own queasiness, felt a measure of satisfaction at the sight. The sea, he reflected with bitter amusement, truly made equals of all men. He went about his own distasteful chore with considerably greater vigor thereafter, watching, as he worked, while the strange little man made his way in a weaving step back along the port gunwale and paused every now

266

and again to empty the contents of his stomach. Macalester made a note of the location of the doorway through which the man disappeared, then completed his task, his discovery strengthening his heretofore failing constitution.

"I don't want to meet up with that big sumbitch again," Billy muttered, his back pressed against Macalester's own as they approached a corner in the dimly lit corridor. It was really no more than a short, narrow passageway lined on either side with the doors of individual cabins. The air was heavy, and faintly smoky, with exotic sweet spiciness.

"Me, either." Macalester's whispered reply was laconic. "Shut up, or you'll guarantee it."

Night had finally come on the gulf, and Macalester and Billy had been relieved of their duties for eight hours. He had eight hours to look for Geneva among the foreigners. He pressed his face against the unpainted planks at the corner of the corridor, peering around the side, trying to see without revealing himself. What he saw did not please him. He retreated a step, motioning to a curious Billy with his index finger pressed to his lips.

"He's there." He barely mouthed the words to his partner. "Guarding a door. Must be hers. I'll need a distraction."

Billy beamed. "Wait here," he mouthed.

The younger man withdrew before Macalester even had a chance to caution him. Well, he thought, he'd never had to play nursemaid to Billy before this; there was no reason to start now. He waited, risking another glance into the corridor, hoping, briefly, that nothing untoward would prompt anyone to emerge from a cabin before Billy had executed his portion of the plan. The giant remained, an impassive and solitary guard.

267

Macalester pulled back, waiting, counting each breath as if it were an hour. He brushed his sleeve across his brow once.

From around the corner, a short distance away, he heard a ringing sound, like a silver dollar rolling along the floor. What the hell was Billy doing? The big oak tree of a man would never fall for such an easy trick as that. Or would he? Macalester peekcd once more around the corner in time to see the giant's large foot disappear around the far corridor.

Quick as a cat, Macalester emerged from his own place and was by the untended door in an instant, even as he heard a dull thud from the void into which its sentry had lately disappeared. Praying the thud was Billy's doing and not the giant's, he inserted a long nail into the lock on the door, daring neither to knock nor to call out, lest he attract unwanted attention. He had not troubled to invent an excuse for himself or Billy in the event they should be discovered. In fact, he could barely focus on the comparatively simple act of picking this shabby excuse for a lock. The idea that Geneva Lionwood might be on the other side of the door occupied the major part of his conscious thought.

The lock yielded even as Billy strolled into view from around the corner, his black shirt and trousers augmenting his devilish appearance.

"Move it, Senator," he recommended in a whisper, drawing his Colt as he edged toward Macalester's position with a quick glance at every door. "We ain't got all night. Go kiss your lady love good night. I'll wait here."

Macalester dealt the younger man a grimace. He did not even know for sure that this was Geneva's cabin. Trust Billy to make a joke of everything! Without answering, Macalester opened the door, first a crack, then, discovering that the hinge was soundless, wide enough to poke his head inside. The room was dimly lit by a single lamp, but he was satisfied that the figure on the small bed was Geneva. His heart tightened. He slipped inside and closed the door behind him.

The room was small and stuffy. There was not even a porthole. It was like a prison. Macalester moved quickly to the bed, reining in a shudder. By the pale golden light of the lamp on the table beside the bed, he looked upon the slack, sleeping features of the woman he loved, unable to resist touching her soft pale cheek with his finger.

Her eyes were closed, her dark, full lashes making crescents upon her cheekbones. Her mouth, small and pink, was slightly open, and her abundant dark curls were strewn upon the whiteness of the pillow like a rich warm blanket with which he longed to cover himself. He knelt on one knee beside her, content, for the moment, just to be near enough to hear her shallow breath, gentle as a spring breeze. Her small, fine hands clutched the blue coverlet to her neck. She looked, he noted with no small relief, as though she had been treated well enough. Encouraged by the thought, he patted her cheek gently.

"Gen," he called to her, scarcely above a whisper. "Gen, wake up. It's me. Mac. Kieran."

To his surprise, she did not stir. He thought, for a capricious moment, that she might be feigning sleep just to annoy him. He had to admire her spunk. He felt a brief smile tug at the corners of his mouth.

"Come on, Gen." He tickled her neck gently with his fingertip. "Don't tease me. Not now."

Still, she did not react. Puzzled, he tapped her cheek more briskly and spoke her name as loudly as he dared.

"Geneva! Wake up!" he commanded. "It's me! Kieran!"

At last, slowly, her eyes opened, her lids fluttering like

the wings of a sluggish butterfly. Her green eyes looked dark and strange, and she looked at him, he realized with a shock of apprehension, without seeing him.

"Geneva! It's Kieran. Kieran Macalester! Don't you—" He gulped, hard. "Don't you know me?"

She continued to stare at him without moving, without blinking. Overcome with desperation, he seized her shoulders and shook her.

"Gen, what is it? For the love of God, Gen—"

She blinked once, slowly. Her lips moved, but she did not speak. Her eyes seemed to focus on him at last. He relaxed his grip, but he did not let her go.

"K—Kieran . . ."

Her voice was no more than a whimper. He felt sick, and it had nothing whatever to do with the motion of the vessel.

"It's me, Gen." He lifted her to an upright position, putting his arm about her to hold her up. "What's the matter, honey? Why can't you wake up?"

There were three soft knocks upon the door. Go away, Billy, he thought, glancing once in the direction from which the sound had come.

"Head." Geneva groaned softly, trying, to shield her eyes with a clumsy hand. "Hurts. Tired . . . so tired . . ."

Kieran took hold of her hand and pulled it gently away from her face. Straightening her arm, he noticed strange blue bruises on the soft white flesh on the inside of her elbow.

"What's this, Gen?"

He looked from the bruises to her face and watched with growing apprehension as her lovely features clouded with confusion. She looked away from him, but he caught her chin with his hand and drew it toward him again. She did not resist him. When she met his gaze, he could see that her eyes, those lovely green eyes that had looked upon him with such infinite trust on the train to Roanoke, had filled with tears.

"Hakim," she whispered, her small voice shaking. "He—I—"

A sob stopped her. He felt like there was a big, sharp, heavy stone in his own throat.

"What, Gen?" He found his voice at last. "Did Hakim do this to you? What does it mean?"

She seemed to struggle with her answer, as though some unseen power held her back. Confused and frightened by her strange behavior, he held her more tightly, wanting to take away her pain with his embrace.

"A drug," she said faintly. "Laud—laudanum, I think. I—I'm scared, Kieran. Help me!"

Laudanum. The word was a curse. What had they done to her? What had he allowed to happen to her? He wanted to be sick.

Her eyes were wide, but still glazed and unfocused. The green in them was almost entirely eclipsed by the blackness of her pupils. He held her limp body tenderly to his breast, wanting to take her with him at once, to remove her from this awful place.

Billy knocked again. Macalester filled his lungs with the sweet scent of her jasmine before he released her.

"We'll reach Biloxi the day after tomorrow," he said, training her wandering gaze to his own again with a firm but gentle hand upon her chin. "I'll come for you and take you off the ship. We're stuck here for now. We're in the gulf, out of sight of land. You have to hold out until then, Gen. You can do it. I know you can. I—I have to go now, before they come and find me here. You'll be all right. Do you understand? You'll be all right . . ."

He held her again, realizing that he was babbling on more as an excuse to remain with her for a few moments longer than to offer her any real assurance. That, he knew with sickening certainty, was far beyond his limited capabilities. She did not want him to leave. He could tell by the way she held his sleeves. Clutching at him, the way a drowning person would grasp at a rope. He hated leaving her, but he had to, or there would be no hope of liberating her at Biloxi.

He bent his neck to kiss her lips. They were cool and dry, and they responded only slightly to his own. *Laudanum!* He shuddered, stroking her dark hair tenderly. *What have they done to you, Geneva? What have I done to you?* When he broke away from her, he could not look into her eyes. He could not bear the emptiness in her eyes, or the pain that emptiness would inspire in him.

"I'll be back for you, Gen," he said, not even sure she was listening any longer. "I'll get you out of this. I swear it."

She drifted off into her deadly, drugged sleep again before he even finished speaking.

Chapter Twenty-five

Geneva was cold. She felt as though a fire had gone out in the room some time before. Beneath the blankets, she shivered uncontrollably in her thin nightdress, and her head throbbed like the churning of a great unruly engine.

Kieran had been there, and had gone. She remembered that much, but she recalled nothing further about his visit. She remembered, too, that she was in terrible danger, but she could not remember from whom, or why. She could not even muster concern. There was an agent insulating her against extremes of emotion, driving even her gremlin away, and she had ceased to trouble herself with her own welfare.

But she was cold. So cold. Her feet were like blocks of ice, and she shivered as though her very core had extinguished itself. A fire. She needed a fire. Hakim could make one, or Abdul, but they had been there only a short while before, and would not return for several hours. In that time she could imagine herself slowly freezing to death, and she could not allow that to happen. Kieran was coming for her.

The thought took her by surprise, and yet she suddenly remembered it as clearly as if he had just now spoken the words to her. Perhaps he had. He would come for her, he said. Tomorrow.

But when had he said it?

A fire. She needed a fire. She was freezing. Clumsily, she got out of the bed, stumbling as the pitching of the ship carried her slight body off balance. The blankets, she thought. They were such pretty colors. Would they burn in pretty colors as well? The notion intrigued her drugged senses. The very idea of all of those colors flickering brightly in a brief conflagration struck her at once. It was a sight she desperately wanted to see. She gathered the bulky things into her arms and dropped them into the middle of the floor. A bonfire. A nice, big bonfire. She imagined a bright, colorful bonfire sending its curls of blue and red and orange into the blackness of the heavens, and she imagined herself dancing around it, like some half-wild gypsy.

The lamp by the bed was full of oil and would start the fire nicely. She picked it up and with careful, concentrated effort removed the glass globe around the tiny flame. The globe was hot. It burned her hands, but she barely noticed it: The flame fascinated her. She had never realized, before now, that fire was alive. It breathed and moved, expanding and contracting in a teasing, sensual way. Captivated, she put her hand into it. The sudden shock of the burning pain made her drop the lamp and back away, cradling her injured fingers in her good hand.

The flame from the lamp quickly spread about the pile of blankets, spawning lively little offspring. Geneva watched as the brothers and sisters and cousins of flame tickled and teased one another like bratty children at an unwieldy family reunion. *More,* they seemed to hiss, greedily. *Give us more; give us more. We are hungry. Feed us*.

Geneva fed them. The room was slowly filling with gray-black smoke smelling of burning, salt-cured wood. She fed the hungry children with her pillow, and the nightstand, and, with some effort, the thin mattress from her bed. She was warm, now, gloriously warm. Hot. The heat from the fire singed the passageway to her lungs with her every breath, and soon there were children all around the room. Nieces, nephews, cousins, playing leapfrog and hopscotch and tugging impatiently at one another.

A crash upon the door tore the barricade from its hinges. Many children were crushed as the giant entered the smoky chamber. Geneva felt him lift her from her bare feet; could feel his beefy arms through the thin nightshift that she wore. She fought him, kicking and biting. He wanted to take her away from the children, and she had so enjoyed watching them play . . .

Fire! she heard many voices shout. And other shouts, strange words from foreign tongues that meant nothing to her. Hakim's voice was among them, but she could not see him. The corridor was thick with smoke, although the children seemed not to have emerged from the room as yet. Through the column of smoke the giant carried her, and she wept for the children she would see no more, and her burned hand hurt her again.

The giant crashed through another door and they were outside. It was gray and wet. And cold. Men were running about the broad deck of the long ship, shouting. Gray smoke wafted heavenward like a mighty sacrifice to pagan gods. The giant set her down on the deck and disappeared. She huddled against the damp gunwhale, hugging her bare arms to herself. Why had he taken her from the warmth? Despairing of ever being warm again, she got onto her hands and knees and crawled back, unnoticed by the dark figures that darted about her, calling to one another, creating a rich fabric of chaos.

The children had grown and spread, and another generation had sprung up about them. The entire corridor was ablaze, awash with a warm and crackling light. The children were laughing at the pitiable attempts of the men to deprive them of their sustenance. Geneva laughed with them, her eyes stinging, her throat burning. She allowed the gentle smoke to curl around her like a soft cocoon, sealing her into its warm and deadly embrace.

When Kieran Macalester and Billy Deal came up from the hold, the entire passengers' berth was a tower of flame. Off the port bow, the coast of Louisiana watched in the misty gray autumn twilight, too far to render assistance in battling the flames. Kieran broke into a run at the sight of the conflagration, ignoring Billy's exhortations to stop. He slipped once on the wet deck, cursing as the wind got knocked out of him. He scrambled to his feet again and ran, wondering why the deck of the *Corvallis* had not seemed this long to him before. He forced his way through the bucket brigade, ignoring the shouts and curses of its members wanting to enlist his help.

The wall of heat from the flames nearly pushed him backward. He looked around before continuing on his mission of folly, trying to determine whether Geneva might be among the ragtag assemblage of refugees huddled against the starboard gunwale. He remembered the previous night, when he'd found her in her room. She had barely recognized him. How could she, in such a state, realize the danger she was in? He seized one of the buckets passing near him and poured its contents over his head, lest he provide the fire with more fuel. The man from whom he had snatched it cursed him as he handed it back, but Kieran ignored him and made for the fiery archway, calling to Geneva in a loud and desperate voice.

The place was an inferno. Holding his arm before his eyes like a shield, he stumbled through the flaming corridor, unable to see. How could she still be in here? he asked himself, fighting a growing desire to turn and run from the flames. How could she still be in here, and be alive?

"Geneva!" he called again, and coughed as he gasped a lungful of hot smoke. "Geneva!"

He tripped on something and fell face first beside it. The air was clearer down there, and he saw a blackened bundle beside him, huddled upon the floor like a pile of dirty laundry. He took several breaths of clearer air, then reached for the bundle with a sooty hand. No sooner had he touched it than it uncurled itself like a blossoming flower before him.

It was Geneva.

Relief and dread partnered in him as he gathered her quickly into his arms. She did not move. With little effort, he picked her up and headed back through the smoke and flames, back in what he hoped was the direction from which he had come.

He could not have gone more than a few feet into the burning part of the ship, for in moments he was outside with his small but precious bundle. Even the salty wet air tasted good, although every breath burned him all the way down inside his aching chest. There were shouts all around, and someone doused his back with another bucket of water. He held tightly to his cherished burden, carrying her away from the fire, away from her prison.

277

A strong hand seized his arm abruptly.

"This way, Senator." Billy's voice was low and swift. "I got a lifeboat all ready to go."

Macalester did not reply. He allowed himself to be led, fairly dragged, unnoticed, across the deck to one of the dinghies. With but a moment of hesitation, he lifted the scrap that was Geneva into the boat. The stabbing pain in his side reminded him sharply of his injured ribs, but he stifled a gasp and clambered in himself, falling hard to the wooden floor of the small craft. The boat swayed on its winch, and in moments Billy himself climbed in. In an expert fashion that bewildered Macalester, he began lowering the vessel into the water alongside the *Corvallis*.

"Where the hell did you learn all about boats?" Macalester managed to wonder aloud, in spite of his aching chest and throat.

Billy, hauling away at the rope with astonishing vigor, seemed pleased by his partner's surprise. "You don't know everything about me, do you, Senator?"

"I guess I don't," Macalester replied, trying to sit up.

The boat landed with a splash in Cat Island Sound, and Macalester fell back again from the shock, muttering a curse.

"I sure hope to hell you know what you're doing," he said, feeling that familiar queasiness edge up on him as the little boat rolled and pitched in the dark waves alongside the *Corvallis*.

"Relax." Billy pulled in the line. "See to your lady friend back there. She looks poorly, Mac. I swear, I never thought I'd see you come out of that hellhole alive, much less with her!"

Macalester did not answer. While Billy positioned himself in the stern and lifted two long, heavy oars into their fittings, he made his way forward to Geneva, who still lay exactly where he had placed her. It was getting

278

dark, and it was hard to see, but he gently uncurled her limbs until she lay upon the tarp. She looked burned, but not as badly as he might have expected. Her clothing was destroyed: burned, or shredded, it was impossible to tell which in the darkness. He felt her neck and pressed his ear to her sternum. Her heart was beating, and she was breathing.

"There're some blankets and other stuff up there," Billy called to him in a clear, almost merry voice. "How's she look?"

Macalester felt around and did, indeed, find blankets and several tins of water, among other staples. Billy, bless his heart, had apparently been planning this little cruise from the very start.

"She looks bad," he heard himself report tonelessly, opening a tin of fresh water without taking his eyes from her smoke-blackened form. "But I guess she'll make it."

I pray she'll make it, he thought bleakly.

"Oh, she'll make it, Senator," Billy predicted with another laugh, extending an oar to push off from the port bulkhead of the *Corvallis*. "She'll want to slap your ugly face a few more times 'fore she's through with you. Count on it."

Macalester could not help smiling. *She will at that,* he thought, bathing her face gently with a soaked bit of his shirt. *And I'll kiss her hand when she does.*

"She needs a doctor," he said, pleased to see so much of the blackness yield to white, untouched flesh as he continued to wash her. "How far to Biloxi, Skipper?"

"Biloxi, hell," retorted Billy from the stern, breathing hard as he pulled on the heavy oars. "We're headin' for New Orleans. I figure we're—uh—" he grunted again with exertion—" 'bout halfway between the two. Maybe a day. And I may as well tell you up front, Senator—" he paused to pull again—"I mean to winter in New Orleans. Find me a plump little quadroon and stake out a claim till March or April. And after this, you owe me, so don't try to talk me out of it. Soon's you can manage it, I'd appreciate you grabbin' that other set of oars."

Macalester did not reply. He pressed a clean piece of wet cloth against Geneva's cracked, dry lips and lifted her head, bracing it against his knee. With one hand, he plunged a dipper into the water tin and held it to her lips.

"Drink, Gen," he urged in a quiet whisper, although he was almost certain she was unconscious. "It's water. Fresh water. You're safe now, honey. Billy's going to take us to New Orleans."

She answered him by swallowing once. He pressed his lips to her forehead before covering her with a blanket and joining Billy on the oars. The exercise was excruciating, but it was nothing compared to the torture of thoughts of what would happen after they had reached New Orleans.

Chapter Twenty-six

"I hate comin' into town like a damned half-drowned water rat," Billy Deal declared, although his declaration came out in an exhausted whisper. Twilight settled over the Crescent City and the lifeboat from the *Corvallis*, a deep, rosy orange bleeding to violet. Kieran Macalester's body felt as if rusty iron spikes pierced his lungs with every breath. He no longer had any feeling at all in his back or his shoulders. These had long since ceased to feel a part of his being. He wished, surveying the reclining, immobile figure of the injured and abused soprano in the prow, that he could say the same about his heart. He pulled for one last time upon the heavy oars that had, along with Billy's, brought them to the barnacled pylons of this quiet dock in an otherwise bustling port. The lifeboat bumped gently against the dark brown clusters.

It was low tide. There was a wooden ladder descending from the pier above into the shallows of the Pontchartrain, its wooden rungs hung with wispy white shreds of some unknown plant life, stranded by the receding water. It was no small task, but Kieran managed, with Billy's help, to lift Geneva's slight body out of the prow and up the five or six steps of the ladder onto the dock. Kieran, under Geneva's limp but inconsequential bulk, heaved a broken sigh of relief as his feet stood once again upon solid ground.

A trio of stevedores strolled past, their labors apparently ended for the day. Kieran avoided their eyes, hoping they would ignore him. They did not.

"Hey, watcha got there?" one man called genially, his drawl as thick as Spanish moss. "A mermaid?"

"A half-dead one." Billy, behind him, answered the man in a reedy voice. "There a doc around here someplace?"

The three men, dark brown from long exposure to a near-tropical sun, exchanged perplexed glances. Kieran endured their curiosity as they approached, but he held Geneva closer, drawing the blanket about her to shield her from their stares. He wondered, in an abstract and detached way, if wild animals protecting their young felt the way he did. He wondered further, feeling Garland Humble's greenbacks pressed against his sternum, how he and Billy would muster the strength to fight these burly and robust individuals, should they be of a mind to beat and rob them.

Fortunately this seemed not to be their intention, whether because they were in fact honest men, or because they judged that three worn-out, ragged refugees obviously suffering from exhaustion, exposure and possibly one or two additional maladies could not possess anything of value, Kieran did not know. Nor did he care to speculate. Like a mute pack animal, he followed the men, along with Billy, lagging behind their annoyingly lively pace but steadfastly refusing offers to share his burden. Geneva was his burden, and he would not, if he could help it, ever share her with anyone again.

Around the corner from the warehouse at the mouth of the pier, the marketplace seemed to be winding down business for the day. Awnings were being drawn over shop stalls, tarps strewn over crates of fruits and vegetables. Baskets of fish, left too long in the warm October sunshine, were sold off wholesale for bait as fishermen prepared to head out to gulf waters for the night. Last minute bargains were struck with vendors by menials, mostly Negro ones, who no doubt would hurry home and add their finds to the evening's jambalaya. Kieran realized, glancing about himself at the aromatic produce, crates of squawking chickens and squealing pigs, and ropes of link sausages hanging from cypress rafters, that he was savagely hungry.

"Sisters of Mercy Hospital is yonder, up on Paris Avenue." One man pointed a big, beefy finger in a vague direction.

Another snorted. "That a fine hospital, do you like lice."

"A doctor," Kieran heard himself say. "Just a doctor. No hospital."

There was a doctor several streets down, they said, gesturing vaguely southward. The men then went their own way, glad, it seemed, to be quit of such dour company. Because he had no better idea, Kieran Macalester followed their direction, coming at last to a long, two-story clapboard structure that boasted CLINIC on its only painted surface. Doubtful, but too exhausted to search further, Kieran instructed the unencumbered Billy to knock and to try the door.

Dr. Beaumarche was not in at present, a very correct, dusky little domestic assured them, not taking her black eyes from Billy's face. He would make his rounds shortly. She ushered them past a large, busy ward to a

room that was spare but clean, with four neat, empty
beds, one in each corner. There was one window, and
it was clean, and there were plain white curtains fram-
ing it. The room smelled faintly of fresh-cut pine.

Kieran laid Geneva upon the bed nearest the window,
in the far corner of the room. The domestic returned
with a basin of clear water, a cake of white soap and a
pile of soft, white towels, and fell to helping him un-
cover and bathe the woman upon the bed. Kieran discovered very quickly that the serving woman possessed
far greater skill in the area of nursing than he, and in
spite of his desire to care for Geneva, he gradually allowed her to take over completely, although she had
given no indication that he was in the way. In no time
at all, the woman had completely stripped away the old
blanket and the smoky, singed remains of Geneva's
nightdress, and had washed her skin clean of dirt and
soot, while he and Billy had stood by in relative helplessness.

"Melusine!"

A deep and mellifluous bass voice echoed through the
place, emanating from the area of the ward. Kieran
turned his head simultaneously with Billy at the sound.
Together, they watched a tall and erect figure enter the
room with grace and a dignity that, Kieran was certain,
would have accompanied him even without his finely
tailored gray linen suit and crisp dove-gray bowler hat.
The man's age was indeterminable. He might have been
thirty, or sixty.

"Melusine, what have we here?"

The man's words were strangely yet pleasingly accented, not Creole, or Spanish, or French, exactly. His
tone was refined, and demonstrated, to Kieran, a high
level of education.

And he was as black as bituminous coal.

His obsidian eyes, set in his carved features like black

pearls in an onyx sculpture, regarded Kieran and his partner expectantly.

"This is a Negro hospital," the doctor remarked.

Kieran felt the measure of the man and the comment like a powerful blow. "She needs help *now*," he said firmly, his glance straying to Geneva's limp form. "You can't turn her out!"

"I turn no one away," was the stern, mildly rebuking response he got from the man, who did not move a muscle. "I merely point out the fact. Now then. Your wife?"

Kieran swallowed, still tasting smoke in his mouth. "She's burned," he replied briefly, wanting to tell the man the whole story, but unable to form the words. "Help her. Please."

"There is a tale behind this, I am certain," the doctor volunteered after a long moment, considering the outlaw with a slow nod. "One I am most eager to hear. But now is not the time."

He turned to the woman in black, who seemed to wait upon his word.

"Make up two cots in my consulting room for these gentlemen, Melusine. Show them the bath, and send a messenger to my home asking cook to send a supper for four. I think I shall be working late tonight."

The doctor shed his jacket, tossing it carelessly upon one of the empty beds. He removed his gold cufflinks and rolled up the sleeves of his starched white shirt even as Melusine ushered the weary outlaws from the room.

The waterfront was a ceaseless buzz of activity. Camilla Brooks was restless, waiting in the carriage Dr. Beaumarche had hired for their afternoon outing. Why he insisted on visiting his clinic on his only free afternoon was a complete mystery to her. But then, many things about the handsome Dr. Beaumarche puzzled her.

He would, for example, haggle with a merchant over the price of a loaf of bread, then hand the same loaf over to a ragged little street urchin, wordlessly, without waiting for a "thank you."

Dr. Beaumarche was the only Negro man she'd ever known who had an education. He'd come from Africa by way of France, where he'd been trained as a physician. He had appeared one evening at The Hall and, after hearing her sing, had returned every night.

She liked having a beau, a real gentleman who treated her like a real lady. She'd used some of Eve Lyons's three hundred dollars to improve her wardrobe, and some of it to bribe the manager at The Hall to listen to her sing, at first. Of course, it had only been a short while, but so far things were going even better than she'd hoped. Especially after Dr. Richard Beaumarche had become interested in her.

Her boredom and annoyance and the midday sun finally got the better of her patience, and she jumped down from the hired rig, pulling her rosy pink satin skirts after her. She avoided a puddle in the cobblestone pavement, tiptoeing around it in her black kid shoes, and admitted herself to the building Beaumarche called his clinic.

Inside was a long, low room crammed with crying children, old women, sick and injured Negroes of every age and description. Two gray-clad nurses, Negro, of course, moved among the metal cots like mother birds feeding hungry chicks. They glanced up at her, then continued about their endeavors, not interested in her, or too busy to be. But Beaumarche was nowhere in evidence.

This was how the quiet but merry doctor, whose age she had been utterly unable to determine, plied his trade. Her heart swelled with pride at the thought, and she decided, on the spot, that she would be his wife. But where was he? She made for a closed door at the far end of the room, thinking that to be his private consulting room. She entered without knocking and came upon him changing a dressing. He had removed his charcoal-gray jacket, and it hung on the back of the caned chair upon which he sat. He glanced over his shoulder and, upon seeing her, his handsome features registered alarm.

"Camilla! I mean, Miss Brooks! I—please, leave. This is not—" His accented bass trailed off unconvincingly. She smiled as she peeled off her long white gloves to help him.

"Dr. Beaumarche," she began, thinking she'd never flirted in a clinic before, "I—"

The rest of her remark died upon her lips. It was a white woman whose dressings the doctor was tending.

The import of her discovery struck her like a runaway milk cart: If word of this were to get out, the gentle doctor could be in serious trouble. For perhaps the first time in her life, Camilla Brooks was stunned into a profound silence. Dr. Beaumarche had ceased his labor and was regarding her steadily. She could feel his gaze upon her even as she continued to stare at the scrap of a woman who lay unconscious upon the white sheets of the cot.

"Two men brought her here three days ago," Dr. Beaumarche said, his concern apparent in his quiet voice. "She is burned. She had been heavily dosed with opium. And they had spent nearly two days in a lifeboat getting here. All three of them are suffering from exposure. The men are in back." He gestured to another door leading, Camilla supposed, to the rear of the building.

"I could not turn them away, Camilla. And to move

her—" he gestured to the wispy figure on the cot—
"might kill her. We must keep this secret, Camilla. Their
lives depend upon it. My life depends upon it. Do you
understand?"

Camilla, however, had stopped listening. She stood
above the young woman on the cot and stared down at
her, unable to believe her own eyes.

"Eve," she whispered, rooted by the sight of her companion from the flatboat and the Arkansas woods, who
very obviously had suffered much misfortune since.
"Eve Lyons!"

"What did you say?" Beaumarche challenged her in
a whisper. "Do you know this woman?"

Camilla felt a lump in her throat, recalling their brief
chance meeting that had resulted in friendship.

"Eve is the lady I met on the flatboat," she replied,
overcoming a desire to cry. "We got to help her, Richard! She saved my life!"

Camilla worked the afternoon at Dr. Beaumarche's
side, and the doctor seemed more than glad of her gentle assistance.

Geneva lay still for a very long time without opening
her eyes. She saw images in her head, and she was not
certain whether these were real or illusion. The most
vivid of these was of fire, a golden conflagration. The
next was of pain. The pain was a real and palpable
thing, like embracing a pillow made of long, sharp nee-
dles. But the pain was all around her, a prison for her
body as well as her mind. Every breath she drew, every
swallow, burned and stabbed her. She did not remember her life without pain.

"We must not use the morphine, Melusine," she
heard a deep, unfamiliar voice opine in gentle remonstrance. "See her arms. Morphine is a poison, if used to
excess. It merely replaces one pain with another."

She wanted to speak. She wanted to plead for the drug to assuage her suffering, to release her from the imprisonment of pain. She wanted the drug, or she wanted to die.

There was something gentle touching her cheek, and for an instant the pain vanished, unable to stand against the tenderness.

"Gen." Another voice spoke, a voice she knew. "We made it. You're going to be fine. Can you hear me, Gen?"

Then she slipped into dreams. Awful dreams, dreams of such startling clarity that she thought them to be real. Terrible things happened in these dreams. Bizarre things. People changed into animals. Flowers became large and deadly insects. Nothing was what it seemed. Reflective, she thought, in her more lucid moments, of what her life had become, since boarding that train in New York with R. Hastings McAllister more than a month before.

She had no idea how long she remained thus, hovering on the fringes of dreams and death, steeped in pain. She knew only that she awoke one morning and opened her eyes at last, aware that the pain had eased. And that, after a long and blessedly dreamless night of sound sleep, she had finally awakened to the world she had come perilously close to leaving.

"Well, what do you know?" a deep, unfamiliar voice mocked lightly. "Our celebrity has decided to join us this morning. Welcome to New Orleans, Miss Lionwood!"

A tall man of perhaps thirty stood over her with his thumbs tucked into his belt. His eyes, the startling and intense blue of a clear autumn sky, surveyed her with some amusement. His was a handsome face, with its dimpled chin and a nose sculpted with great care atop a full golden mustache. Billy Deal, she thought, but was unable to form the name with her lips. She opened her mouth, but could not persuade a sound to come forth. She swallowed. It was as if there was a knife in her throat.

Billy Deal seemed to sense at once that something was wrong, for his blond brow furrowed over his narrowing azure eyes. "What's wrong? Can't you talk?" The humor vanished from his voice.

Geneva stayed her panic and tried again. Her throat yielded no sound.

Billy Deal flashed her a quick grin, and she thought at once of Kieran Macalester.

"Wait here," he told her, but his buoyant tone rang false. "I'll find the doc."

Wait here, she mused. *Where else would I go, with no clothes and no voice?* She noticed, for the first time, the white gauze bandages covering her arms like a second skin. She could feel the same about her feet, and the soft cotton lawn of a delicate nightgown from her neck to her knees. She drew the clean, fragrant sheets of the small bed up to her chin, willing herself to think of nothing.

She was startled by the abrupt advent of a large black man, followed by Billy Deal.

"This is Dr. Beaumarche, Miss Lionwood," the younger man explained. "He fixed you up real good when we brought you here two weeks ago. I'll just bet he can fix this, too. Don't you worry about a thing."

Billy Deal disappeared again, and Geneva watched the big, well-dressed, dark-skinned man intently. He had kindly eyes, but just now he wore an expression of regret upon his features, broadcasting the fact that he was not pleased by Billy's generous assurances.

"Good morning, Miss Lionwood."

Geneva liked his voice. It was as deep as a lake, laced with a rich, unidentifiable accent and as soothing as a gentle breeze in an exotic tropical tree. She wanted to reply to him, to thank him for all he'd done so far, but still could not coax a sound from her throat.

"You have caused quite a stir in our little hamlet, I must tell you," the doctor went on, palpating her throat with big, gentle fingers. "It seems as if half of the country has been looking for you, and suddenly you have turned up on my doorstep. Open your mouth, please."

Half of the country? Looking for *her*? Beaumarche's words astonished her, and she wished he would tell her more. Blessedly, he did.

" 'Where is Geneva Lionwood?' " he intoned, chuckling as he looked down into her throat. "It has been in all of the papers. Your disappearance nearly over-shadowed the opening of the Metropolitan Opera House in New York City. Of course, no one knows you are here. Yet. And it will remain so, until you or one of your mysterious friends reveals your whereabouts. And Miss Brooks has proven remarkably adept at keeping a secret."

Camilla! Geneva's heart leaped. Her excitement must have shown on her features, for Dr. Beaumarche smiled down at her benignly.

"Miss Brooks showed much the same enthusiasm when she saw you. She is a singer herself, you know. She performs nightly at The Hall. Your throat looks fine." He sounded both encouraged and puzzled. "Are you quite sure you cannot speak?"

Geneva nodded, realizing that she was terrified to try again, lest she find that her voice was gone for good and all. Dr. Beaumarche sat back in the caned chair, crossing his arms before his chest, regarding her with pursed lips.

"Perhaps rest is what you need," he pronounced finally. "And a chance to regain your strength. You are going through quite an ordeal, but the worst of it may be behind you. The laudanum has worked through your system, and your burns have healed nicely. Good food and sunshine may be all that is yet required, and fortunately both are in abundance here in New Orleans. Of course, we must remove you to a suitable hotel as soon as possible."

Dr. Beaumarche stood up, straightening his collar and pushing his silver-rimmed spectacles up his broad, black nose. "You are a fortunate woman, Miss Lionwood." he declared. "But you have a long recovery yet ahead of you."

Geneva's heart swelled with renewed gratitude for the man. "Thank you," she mouthed, but did not attempt to give body to her words.

He regarded her with a steady, unsmiling gaze.

"It has been my pleasure, Miss Lionwood. Now please rest. I believe your voice will return. I will look in on you later."

She was alone. She realized, surprised, that she wanted very much to see Kieran Macalester, to convince herself that the nightmare of the past few weeks had ended at last. She wanted . . . She wanted many things from Mac, she realized with a quick pang of sadness. Most of which she would probably never get.

Her next visitor was not the outlaw but Camilla Brooks, looking prosperous and effervescent in a gown of fuschia and white, complete with an intimidating piece of millinery to which she was equal. Geneva, while admiring the couture, could not help but experience a stab of jealousy: Here she was with nothing but a borrowed nightgown to call her own, her hair in God alone knew what state, still wrapped in bandages like an Egyptian mummy to shield her healing burns from infection. And there was Camilla Brooks, looking as though she'd just stepped from the display window of New Orleans's finest dressmaker. However, steeped as she was in her own mire of problems at present, Geneva perceived at once that Camilla's attire was more for another's benefit than for her own.

"Lordy, gal, didn't you get to New Orleans the hard way after all!" Camilla declared after they embraced in greeting. "And in the comp'ny of two handsome men! Soon's you can talk, I want to hear all about it from you. Mr. McAllister and Mr. Doyle, they tole us their side. But I 'spect your side is much more interesting."

Doyle. So Macalester and Deal were still using aliases. That explained why Deal was with her when Mac was not: They could not risk her awakening without one of them present, lest she reveal their identities to the doctor, or to Camilla. But now, of course, as long as her voice remained locked in her throat and her hands wrapped in enough gauze to render them useless, their secret was still safe.

For a while, at least.

Camilla remained with her for better than an hour, prattling on about her budding musical career, her growing relationship with the doctor and New Orleans news in general. Geneva loved listening to her. It was comforting to hear another woman's voice after what seemed an eternity among men, and it was wonderful to be reminded, as she gazed at Camilla's heartbreakingly lovely dress, that beautiful clothes and gentle things still existed in the world.

Her life had been challenged by such ugliness of late that she had very nearly given up hope of retrieving any beauty from it at all. And then Camilla had come, just when she was most earnestly needed. Geneva was suddenly crying, but they were tears of joy and relief. Camilla misunderstood them, rushing forward to hold her in her arms and comfort her.

"Don't cry, honey." The younger woman soothed Geneva, stroking her tangled hair. "Everything gonna be fine now. Dr. Beaumarche, he a fine doctor. He gonna make you all well again in no time; see if he don't. And that McAllister! I can tell he gonna take real good care of you. He ain't hardly let you outta his sight, since Richard fixed him up. I expect he think you a big pile a gold, the way he watch you. No ma'am, that man ain't gonna let nothin' happen to you, that's sure."

Not, at least, until he has collected his compensation, Geneva thought, adding a bitter tear or two to her happy ones. *I am his pile of gold, at least until the next one comes along.*

Chapter Twenty-seven

Camilla left her. Geneva was sorry to see her friend go, and the small room darkened appreciably after the lively young woman departed.

Geneva grew restless. The pain, except for her throat, had faded to a memory, and she found herself wanting to move. Gingerly, for she had no sense of her strength or condition, she drew back the coverlet of the bed and lowered her gauze-swathed feet to the floor. She stood up, trying her balance. She blacked out abruptly and sank back down upon the bed until her vision cleared. Then she tried again, slowly.

A few cautious steps took her to the window. Beyond the curtains and the imperfect glass, she perceived the daily activity in the alley, distorted, as if viewed through a filter. She was reminded, unpleasantly, of her drug-induced dreams, and she wished she had not ventured out of her bed.

"Gen!"

She recognized the velvet baritone at once and became painfully aware of her sorry state. Maddeningly, she felt tears sting the back of her eyes again, tears of frustration and shame. She fought them, though, successfully. Kieran Macalester, she knew, had seen her under circumstances far worse than this.

She turned to him, and even as she did, he dropped his parcels wrapped in brown paper and string and ran forward, not stopping until he had enfolded her slight, pliant body into a strong, almost painful embrace.

She had forgotten what it felt like to be held so close to him, to feel the strength and the hardness of his lean body pressed so closely against her own. To hear his heart against her ear and smell the wonderful scent of leather and of the outdoors and of him, and to feel his hand in her hair. She found herself holding on to the front of his dark green flannel shirt with her gauze-thickened fingers, closing her eyes and allowing the reality of Kieran Macalester to lift her gently into his powerful arms and carry her back to the bed, where he sat down with her upon his lap, cradling her like a child.

"Gen," he murmured, kissing her forehead and her temple. "God, it's so good to hold you like this! I thought I'd never—" He broke off suddenly, as though he did not want to think about the rest of his statement.

She tried to answer him. Her mouth formed the words, but her throat was dormant, as though that part of her was still asleep. She pushed away from him, although she made no move to escape from the throne of his lap, and she looked squarely into his probing dark eyes.

"I—" She mouthed the word, and even managed an awful, guttural sound, but then she placed her hand against her throat and slowly shook her head.

"I know," he whispered, his tone gentle but his angular features etched with concern. "Billy told me. But it'll come back, Gen. Believe it. There's no god so cruel that he'd take that from you. Not after everything else you've been through."

Her arms were around his neck. Although she did not remember putting them there, she did not wish to remove them. He was with her, her savior and her nemesis. No matter what his motivation or his ultimate design, she confessed to herself in that moment a love so great that she had not known its like before, nor would she, she suspected, ever know its like again.

His face was inches from hers, and she studied it for a minute. He allowed her to, remaining perfectly still while she examined the faint lines at the corners of his eyes, the conformation of his dark eyebrows, straight and uncompromising, the turn of his amusingly small nose and the fullness of his wide, faintly smiling mouth with its dimples at either corner. She touched her own lips with the tip of a finger protruding from the gauze, then touched his with the same finger. She watched as his eyes began to burn with a fire from somewhere deep within him. When her lips met his and she felt his mouth yield to hers, she knew, trembling in his hungry embrace, that he was the only man who could ever make her completely happy.

He responded to her kiss with a wordless murmur, a growl of desire. She felt his hand upon her jaw, his fingers teasing her earlobe as he held her in thrall. He tasted wonderful, like a sweet dessert of which one could never have enough. She wanted to touch him. She wanted to feel his soft sable locks between her fingers like fine spun silk, but she could feel nothing but the bandages. The sensation reminded her, with a cruel jolt, of her circumstance. She pulled away from him, confused and embarrassed. She felt his soft chuckle begin as a gentle rumbling in his chest.

"I know," he whispered, holding her close to him.

"You don't feel very desirable right now, do you? Honey, you'd be desirable to me in sackcloth rags with your hair cut off. But we can wait. See all those packages? I bought you some new things, Gen. Camilla helped me pick them out. You'll get better, we'll move into a hotel, and . . . we can wait."

Geneva snuggled against him, warmed that he knew her so well, and not wanting to think beyond the picture his words painted. She sat thus for a long while, gaining strength from his very presence. He told her, in soft, gentle tones, the tale of his odyssey from Irving, but for the most part the words simply flowed by her like a lazy stream on a summer afternoon. The sound of his voice alone was a greater comfort than any drug or balm he might have offered.

"Oh!" he exclaimed presently, startling her. "I almost forgot. Take a look at this!"

From his back pocket he produced a rolled-up newspaper, perhaps twelve pages thick. Obligingly, she sat up and watched him open it to the third page. Folding the oversized newsprint back, he held it before her to highlight the headline of a two column item that read:

Soprano Still Missing

Geneva seized the paper from his hands, holding it clumsily with her gauzed fingers. She read with interest:

Soprano Geneva Lionwood, reported missing in these pages three weeks ago, may have been abducted. An Important Person who has asked that his name be withheld has come forward with information which points to foul play. Colonel James Mapleson of the New York Academy of Music confirms that a Mr. McAllister, allegedly representing a San Francisco opera company, appeared shortly before Miss Lionwood's disappearance; the same person mentioned by the Unnamed Source.

Authorities are now investigating the possibility that Miss Lionwood may have been taken west. Reports that the soprano, whose last appearance at the Academy of Music in Mozart's *Don Giovanni* as Zerlina commanded sterling reviews, may have been seen in Roanoke, Virginia, and even in Memphis, Tennessee, are still unconfirmed.

"It would be a great tragedy if this fine artist is not found," Mapleson has responded to this most recent information. "She is an asset to opera in America."

Henry Abbey, who fired Miss Lionwood from *Faust*, which premiered on October twenty second to less-than-favorable reviews, is no longer under suspicion in Miss Lionwood's disappearance.

Geneva, scarcely able to believe what was on the page before her, read the article three times.

"Well? What do you think?"

Kieran's question startled her. She had forgotten he was there, that she was, in fact, sitting on his lap. She felt lightheaded. Euphoric. *A fine artist*, Mapleson said. *An asset to American opera.* Mapleson! The same man who had upbraided her for her curtain call! And—she nearly laughed at the notion—Henry Abbey had been suspected of foul play in the matter!

Public praise from Mapleson was an honor she had never before enjoyed. It made her want to thank him personally, although he was nearly two thousand miles away. Then another thought occurred to her: If her disappearance from New York was news even in New Orleans, it must have made headlines elsewhere, as well: Chicago, Philadelphia, Denver, San Francisco, St. Louis . . .

"Gen!" Macalester's lusty laugh jarred her. "You look

299

like you've seen the very devil! What are you thinking?"

She was looking at him, but he seemed strange to her all of a sudden, like someone she had never seen before. Five paragraphs in a newspaper had thrust her right back into the world of Verdi and Mozart, of Abbey and Mapleson and the ritual mysteries of opera. A rite to which initiation was closed for Kieran Macalester.

"Hotel St. Pierre," Kieran announced as he strode into the small room at the clinic he had been sharing with Billy since their arrival in New Orleans nearly two weeks earlier. "On Rampart Street. A suite for Geneva and a room for us. Adjoining."

He flung himself onto the low cot, which yelled in protest, and loosened his collar. He'd needed a new suit to be presentable at the St. Pierre, and one for Billy as well. With all of the clothes he had bought for Geneva, and the two weeks in advance he'd paid at the St. Pierre, the money he'd taken from Humble was bleeding out as if from a mortal wound.

Billy glanced up, surveyed him for a moment, then returned his attention to the newspaper he'd been reading.

"There've been some mighty strange sounds comin' outta that room," the younger man informed him. "I think your lady friend is finding her voice. Either that, or the end of the world is comin'."

Mac closed his eyes with a sigh, rubbing the bridge of his nose with his thumb and forefinger. In the last five days, he had seen Geneva once, and it seemed to him that if she'd had her way, he would not have seen her then. He was annoyed and, yes, hurt. Camilla Brooks came and went from the Lionwood sanctuary like a privileged guest, and he felt like he was being quarantined from her company. *She not ready to see you*

300

yet. Camilla had shrugged when challenged. *Give her time.*

Time.

When Beaumarche cleared her to be released from his care, Mac had hoped to resume their relationship where they had left off in Little Rock, before she'd found that damned letter. Certainly she'd seemed receptive enough, sitting on his lap for better than an hour on the afternoon when she had first recovered. But then something happened. A change had taken place in her, starting with that item he'd shown her in the newspaper.

He sat up abruptly, startling Billy into looking at him again. Billy folded his paper at last and tossed it to the floor. "You gonna ask her, Senator? Or you gonna let it ride?"

Mac grimaced, scratching the side of his neck where the stiff collar itched. "Damn it, Billy—"

He checked himself: Billy wasn't trying to be a pest, he realized with chagrin. Billy just wanted to be sure Geneva would not turn around and accuse him of abducting her when she at last came forward about her whereabouts for the last seven weeks. Macalester doubted she would do such a thing, but where Geneva Lionwood was involved, he had learned, the only thing that was certain was uncertainty. And after all, he *had* abducted her, or at least lured her under false pretenses. He liked to believe that her feelings for him would cancel out any desire for retribution, but in the final analysis, he simply did not know her mind.

Then, of course, there was the problem of broaching such a topic. If she did, as he hoped, entertain feelings for him that were akin to his own for her, his asking such a question would hurt and offend her, especially after all she'd been through on account of him.

He was in the midst of a sigh before he realized it.

"If you ask me," Billy was speaking again in a slow and thoughtful way, "that newspaper article opened up a whole new can of hash for your lady love. She's thinking maybe her life isn't shot to hell after all, and maybe she can start her career up again, now that she sees she matters to people."

Macalester directed him a hard look. "I didn't ask you," he said pointedly.

"No, you didn't," Billy agreed, unruffled. "But you're no fool, Mac. You thought about that, too. You just didn't want to admit it to yourself."

"Now why in hell would I care, if she wants to keep on singing?" he retorted, feeling his face grow warm. "She can sing anywhere she wants, any time. All I want is to—"

His voice caught, exasperatingly. All he wanted was to be with her, another useless ornament dangling from her arm. Like that irritating Blaine Atherton. Only Atherton was a lord, and a rich one, at that. Who the hell was he? An outlaw, nearly broke and without prospects.

"What?" he heard Billy prompt him quietly. "What is it you want, Senator? If you know, you're way ahead of most folks, myself included."

"I want a wife," Kieran heard his own voice say after a time, but it sounded odd. Far away. The way he imagined his voice might sound to God, if He was listening. "I want to be able to put my feet under a table at the end of an honest day's work and have a sweet, gentle woman put a tasty supper in front of me on a dish that's made of something other than tin. After supper, I want to bounce my babies on my knee, tell them stories and tuck them into their own beds. I want to sit by a fire and talk with an intelligent woman who's got an opinion about everything, even if I don't agree with it. Then after we're all argued out, I want to leave my boots under her bed and make sweet love to her all night, if she wants it. And I want her to want it."

He felt there must be more, but when he thought about it, he'd really said it all. The only thing he'd left out was the woman's name.

From the next room came the cascade of a prolonged *obligato*, followed by a peal of melodious laughter.

"Ordinarily I'd say you weren't asking much," Billy opined, and Macalester avoided his bright blue eyes. "But to put Miss Geneva Lionwood into that picture . . . It's a little like lockin' a puma in a henhouse, if you take my meaning. I guess you'll either have to change those dreams, or find somebody else to share 'em."

Restless, Macalester got up from the cot again. The room seemed to have shrunk, suddenly, to the size of a cigar box. He felt Billy's eyes upon his back as he took three steps to the window, staring out through the gauze curtains. The sun was shining, even though it had drizzled all morning, the raw, chilly mist of the gulf in November. From next door, the sound of scales, ascending and descending, in a soft, even soprano, could be heard.

"I think you're right, Billy," Macalester said slowly, at the end of a breath.

There was a long time, then, when neither of them spoke.

"So what're you gonna do?"

The very question he'd been asking himself ever since he'd first discovered he was in love with Geneva. And, he realized grimly, his jaw clenched like a sprung bear trap, he wasn't any closer to an answer now than he had been in Memphis.

You're a fool, Mac, if you think you could ever have had her for very long. He heard Garland Humble's voice echoing in his memory like the rebuke of a stern patriarch. Maybe he was a fool. Maybe Geneva was, as Garland had declared, a spoiled and selfish trollop with staggeringly expensive tastes. But even if both were true, and he had his doubts, that did not change the hard fact that he loved her more than his liberty. More, even, than his own life.

He drew in a big breath and allowed an answer to Billy's thoughtful question. "I'm going to escort Miss Lionwood to the Hotel St. Pierre this afternoon and let her tell them whatever she pleases. You're welcome to stay behind, if you like."

Behind him, he heard Billy sigh heavily. "Promise me, Senator: If I ever fall in love with a woman like you fell for Humble's wife, you'll shoot me in the head and put me out of my misery."

"I don't think your friend Mr. Deal likes me very much." Geneva adjusted the brim of her black hat trimmed with lace and netting. Kieran sat across from her in the hired carriage, pleased by the results of his shopping excursions with Camilla Brooks. Geneva looked ravishing in the midnight-blue satin gown, and she wore its accompanying black velvet cape with regal élan. She was looking out of the window, her face still pale and thin, her features utterly devoid of expression.

Mac laughed once, softly. Her green eyes questioned.

He couldn't take his eyes from her. He could be quite contented, he realized as the carriage took them across town to the French Quarter, simply to look at her just as she was today for the remainder of his life.

"Billy?" he asked. "Sure he does."

Geneva did not appear convinced by his words. "Then why didn't he come with us?" There was no hint of a smile on her heartbreakingly lovely face.

Mac studied her. Of course Geneva would prefer, if it was her intention, to turn them both in at once. After all, the reward for such a coup would be manifestly greater, and she would not then have to concern herself about retribution from the party who had avoided capture. He shook himself. His imagination was getting the better of him.

"Billy thinks," he began lightly, still watching her, "that you might decide to turn me in for kidnapping you when we get to the hotel."

Her expression did not change. "Oh? And what do *you* think?"

Kieran weighed her question. "I think if you did, you'd be perfectly justified," he said finally. Then he said nothing more. She had already made up her mind, he knew, as to whether or not she was going to report him to the authorities. And he had made up his, as well: If she did turn him in, which he tended to doubt, he deserved it, surely. He would accept his fate and spend the remainder of his life at hard labor doing penance for his lie, and for being foolish enough to have fallen in love with her in the first place.

"That doesn't answer my question." A smile tugged briefly at the corners of her pretty pink mouth.

He traced, in his mind, the outline of her curved lips with the very tip of his index finger. "I guess it doesn't," he agreed, a grin of his own making its way slowly across his face. She considered him, her smile fading again. "You don't know what I intend to do, do you, Kieran?" she said softly, and he was taken aback at the bold perceptiveness of her observation. He shook his head.

"No, I don't, Gen." He was unwilling to dissemble further. "All I know is I've learned enough about you in the last six weeks not to be surprised by anything you do."

"And you're willing to escort me into the St. Pierre, knowing all of this?"

Mac bit his lower lip, weighing her words against her tone. "I made a promise to myself," he began, after allowing a reflective moment, "when we got to New Orleans. I swore I'd stand by you no matter what, for as long as you wanted. Maybe longer, if I thought you might come to harm. I figure I owe you at least that much."

She stared, and he did not avert his gaze. It was Geneva, finally, who looked away, her green eyes moist. "Pretty words," she offered, a faint trace of pink tinting her otherwise pale cheeks becomingly. "But what do they really mean, coming from a liar?"

It was Mac's turn to look away. Her words cut him deeper than any blade. He supposed it was because he had earned them.

Chapter Twenty-eight

The St. Pierre was not a fine old New Orleans establishment. It was new, sumptuous almost to the point of garishness, and not the least bit charming. From its white marble columns and floors to its gold leaf and Irish crystal chandeliers, the St. Pierre looked its part: an architectural monstrosity built with carpetbagger money. It had been purchased from its financially strapped owner by Horace Tabor, a Denver mining millionaire, and its lavishly appointed suites could be had for a fraction of their worth until the new management took over. Kieran had learned of this through the newspaper and other sources, and it was for this very reason that he had selected the St. Pierre as their new home.

He watched Geneva from the corner of his eye as, her arm linked in his, they moved through the bright foyer toward the front desk. Mac felt her fingers tighten upon his arm, and he pictured himself, for a fleeting moment, walking up thirteen steps to the gallows. He found the image amusing in a macabre sort of way and realized that he was, oddly, experiencing otherwise no emotion whatsoever.

Geneva's steps faltered slightly, but no one except him could have noticed, even though he perceived that every eye in the place was on her. She recovered at once, not looking at him, and they completed their journey to the desk.

"M'sieur, M'dame." The young clerk addressed them. "How may I serve you?"

"Rooms for McAllister," Mac heard himself say, his voice sure and steady.

The clerk's plain, scrubbed face brightened. "Of course, M'sieur McAllister," he murmured, his eyes straying to Geneva with an expression of unabashed admiration that made Mac want to throttle the fellow.

With a quick, practiced gesture, the clerk presented them with the register, a pen and an inkwell. Mac watched Geneva reach for it, bewitched by her graceful and deliberate movements. She handed him the pen when she was through, meeting his gaze for an instant. As he signed, he noticed she had written, on the line above, "Geneva Lionwood." Kieran returned the young man's pen and the register book, waiting for the next thing to happen. Beside him, Geneva made no remark.

"Very good, M'sieur, Ma—"

Mac watched in amusement as the man's eyes, staring at the book, grew wide.

"Mademoiselle." The clerk's lips moved several times before the quivering sound actually came forth.

Geneva's smile was beatific.

There followed a commotion as the clerk loudly beckoned an absurd number of porters for the purpose of carrying their comparatively few belongings. The clerk himself then presumed to see them to the staircase with an unceasing stream of flattery and gush directed at

Geneva, who said nothing. As they started up the stairs, Kieran noticed, lazing against a white marble pillar beside the stair, a lone figure in a dove-gray wool suit. He realized, staring into a pair of cobalt-blue eyes, that it was the sartorially splendid Billy Deal, his gray derby set at a rakish angle, grinning at him, and offering a conspiratorial salute.

Telegraph messages began arriving with impressive regularity, along with flowers and gifts and visitors. The manager of Opera New Orleans was among the first, after a news reporter, offering Geneva the lead in the season finale. He had scheduled *Il Trovatore,* but informed her that he would be happy to accommodate her with whatever role she cared to name. He left her suite without a signed contract, however: Geneva preferred to make New Orleans squirm for its slights to her in the past.

Blaine sent a breathtaking diamond choker, which she promptly assigned Mac to pawn. It commanded a handsome price, and she was able to hire herself a personal maid and a private secretary. She was quickly turning the St. Pierre into her headquarters, and its willing staff into her private army. This was Mac's laconic assessment, and she had laughed with delight at it.

She saw little of the outlaw in the maelstrom of days following their arrival at the hotel; she was too busy with practice, interviewing vocal coaches and responding to the many new demands upon her time. Camilla and Dr. Beaumarche were the only visitors allowed complete access to her, although she was certain the hotel only tolerated this circumstance because of her position. The St. Pierre's business could only profit by her presence, and it was to their dubious credit that they were wise enough to recognize that fact. Their indulgence meant increased revenue, even if it was a direct contradiction of their unwritten policy against Negroes in any but a menial capacity.

Dr. Beaumarche exhorted her to rest and to take in fresh air. It was too soon after her ordeals, he cautioned her, to overtire herself with so frenetic a schedule as she had begun to keep. She heeded him with one ear, making a mental note to ask Mac to take her for a drive through the park that very afternoon. That is, after she had interviewed Maestro Durand.

They drove half a dozen blocks in the hired buggy in the November sunshine, and Kieran had spoken barely as many words to her. He was pretending to concentrate on his driving, but she knew he was sulking. She could tell. His very square jaw was set in a hard line, and his dark eyes stared determinedly at the cobblestone street before them, even though Geneva had worn her most fetching new gown of emerald-green taffeta with a matching picture hat and a plaid jacket.

The afternoon was bright and almost warm. It reminded her, wistfully, of a September afternoon in New York not long ago. She'd been driving with Blaine, who was angry at the attentions she'd recently lavished upon a young Italian tenor understudying Maesetto at the Academy. Blaine's jealousy had amused her and had made her feel powerful. It was a sensation not unlike the one she was experiencing at this moment. Only somehow, with Kieran Macalester cast in the role of the jealous, possessive lover, it was a far more satisfying one.

"It is a lovely afternoon," she observed contentedly, resting her head against the back of the cushioned seat. "I'm glad I decided to take Dr. Beaumarche's advice. I've been working too hard these last few days. What about you, Mac? How have you been passing the time?"

"Mostly wondering what you've been doing that kept

you holed up in your sanctuary like a hermit," he retorted, his strong hands tightening perceptibly on the reins.

He still did not look at her. Geneva smiled to herself. It seemed so long since she had last flirted, and it was a glorious sensation.

"Oh." She waved a hand and contrived to sound bored. "My troubles aren't really worth telling. But at last I've found a suitable vocal coach and rehearsal pianist, and Adele has gotten my correspondence well in hand. Now I can concentrate on the business of singing again."

"That's great, Gen," Mac remarked, as though it was anything but. "You'll excuse me if I don't dance a jig for you."

"My, aren't we surly!" she exclaimed petulantly. "Perhaps you should just turn around and take me back to the hotel."

"Perhaps I should." He faintly mimicked her.

But he continued on his course away from the St. Pierre. Geneva was pleased, but not surprised, that he did not call her on her gambit. She wanted to play, and he was such fun. Such a long time had passed since she'd had any fun.

"You know, you really should tuck in your lower lip. Your pout is very unbecoming."

Mac reined the buggy to an abrupt halt, jolting Geneva and causing her to cry out, holding her hat with one hand.

"Damn it, Geneva!" he snapped, turning to her at last, his imposing features dark with anger. "Do I look like that fancy-assed Lord Atherton who showed up drunk on your doorstep at the Biltmore?"

Someone behind them shouted an assault of French invective. Geneva could not hear all of it, but she did recognize an exhortation to move their vehicle, among other choice remarks.

"No, you don't," she replied coolly. "Nor do you look like Garland Humble. But you are starting to behave like him."

The day darkened even as she mentioned her estranged husband's name. She hoped she had hurt Macalester by her simile. He pursed his wide mouth, but seemed determined to maintain her gaze. She tried again for a reaction

"Forgive me. I forget, occasionally, that you are not a gentleman, and that you have no schooling in the art of flirtation!"

Without waiting for him to reply, she gathered her skirt in her hands and began to climb down from the buggy.

"Geneva, get back in here!"

His tone, luckily for him, was more in the nature of a request than an order. She leveled a hurt look at him, already half-outside of the buggy, her hands gripping the sides. He held his arm out to her. Behind them, more disgruntled drivers voiced their irritation.

"Please?" he added, with an inclination of his head that caused a lock of sable hair to tumble into his eyes. The combination was irresistible to Geneva. Without undue haste, she resumed her seat. Mac, apparently satisfied, picked up the reins again and chucked to the dapple-gray gelding. Geneva pressed her lips tightly together, determined to force him to speak next.

Mac guided the buggy hack onto the park drive. The magnolias clung valiantly to their leaves and the chrysanthemums obliged with a glorious golden display. The park was quiet this weekday afternoon, and Kieran managed to find an even quieter corner of it, where four swans glided regally among the lilypads on a small pond. He reined the hack to a gentle halt and applied the brake. Geneva still did not speak, although the beautiful surroundings sorely tempted her to do so. She stared at the swans, envying them their idyllic, uncomplicated existence.

Presently she felt a warm, gentle pressure on her gloved hands, folded demurely in her lap. Startled, she looked down to see that Mac had placed his own hand on top of hers. This intimate and unexpected gesture caused her to look up at his face. His dark eyes were sober and compelling, and she felt trapped by their sincerity. She opened her mouth, then closed it again, clinging to her determination to remain silent until he spoke.

"I've missed you," he said simply.

I've missed you, too, she realized, but could not bring forth the words. Her desire to tease and to flirt had vanished with that one simple, earnest phrase.

"Oh." She was unable to confront his penetrating gaze any longer. She felt as though something was tugging her in two different directions at the same time, and for some reason it made looking at him painful.

"Gen, there's so much I need to say to you." His baritone was a gentle, soothing accompaniment to the peaceful autumn afternoon. "I feel as if a hundred years have gone by since I first saw you in New York, and yet it seems right now as though I hardly know you."

The long-necked swans preened themselves like vain young girls.

"We're not running anymore," she observed, wondering at the conflicting emotions that realization wrought in her. For weeks they had lived in isolation, with only one another to turn to for comfort and help in times of peril. It had been the natural thing to do. But now they were back among civilization again, and nature would, perhaps, demand that they behave in an entirely different fashion.

"That's true," he agreed at the end of a long breath. "At least, you aren't. You know, I've lost count of the number of apologies I've made to you since that day in Little Rock."

She felt a lump in her throat, and her eyes filled with unshed tears. She swallowed the lump, but the tears remained, waiting.

"So have I." She recalled, painfully, one occasion in particular when she'd called him the sorriest man she'd ever met.

A pair of young lovers strolled into view along the far bank of the pond. Geneva watched as the young man, no more than a boy, really, slipped his hand shyly into the girl's. She, in turn, looked about, mortified, but ultimately yielded to both of their desires.

"To my knowledge, you never accepted a one of them."

Mac's words were soft. Wistful. His hand was still on hers, and she felt his fingers tighten around her own.

"I didn't know it was that important to you." She tried for a natural tone, but managed only a whisper.

"It—" He paused, clearing his throat. "It is, Gen. I—it is."

She was afraid to look at him. She was afraid of the emotion she might at last see revealed in his dark eyes, an emotion she'd long wished for but suddenly dreaded to name.

"Then I accept them."

She had stopped short of forgiving him. She did not know if she could ever do that, even though he had followed her from Irving to Galveston and beyond. Even though he had rescued her from the fire and from slavery, or worse. After all, he had been largely responsible for her troubles, he and Garland Humble.

"Does that mean you'll have time for me now?" Mac's

voice was as quiet as the swans' graceful ballet on the pond.

She searched for an easy answer to his question and discovered there wasn't one. Her schedule, her very life, if the past week was any indication, was shortly to become more full than at any other time during her brief career. Her disappearance had created, to her amazement, a sensation. A demand for her. She needed to capitalize on that demand to ensure her future in opera. His apologies, and her acceptances thereof, added not one iota to her time, not, especially, having lost precious weeks of practice. The demand for her celebrity would quickly fade, she realized, if she could not support it with vocal and musical excellence. She withdrew her hands from his, and he pulled away as well, seeming to sense that the time for retreat was upon them.

"My time," she began slowly, searching for words that would not hurt either of them, "is not my own to give right now, Kieran. I have an obligation to my art. I study. I practice. I perform. I negotiate my engagements, since I have no manager yet. Opera is my life. My very essence. It is who I am. It's the one thing, the only thing in this life that I can't live without.

"Garland didn't understand that. He was attracted to me for my voice, and my talent, and yet when he married me he meant to keep me all to himself. A prisoner to his devotion. A bird in a gilded cage, just like the song. I knew I'd made a mistake from the moment I married him."

"You didn't love him, then?"

Kieran's question was unapologetically direct. She could not help smiling, still not trusting herself to look at him.

"He was the first man to have shown me kindness without placing expectations upon it. I know this sounds silly, but I did love him, in a way, for that. But

I was young, and I couldn't see that the expectations would come later. I spent six months trying to correct my error, but neither of us would compromise. The more I tried to break away, the tighter he held on."

She stopped herself. Why was she telling him these things? Kieran Macalester had not asked her to marry him. Mired in sudden confusion, she fell silent. On the pond, the largest swan rose up, flapping his great white wings in a menacing display against a common stray goose that had intruded upon the tableau. The goose quickly retreated.

"So he never hurt you?" Kieran sounded surprised. And, strangely, very far away.

"Not in the physical sense, no," she replied with greater calm than she felt. "I never said he did. What he did was more on the order of locking me away, like a criminal. Or a madwoman."

"There are some women who wouldn't have minded being locked in such a prison."

"Not this woman," she declared in a soft breath.

She felt, all at once, his gentle fingers caressing the back of her neck. The sensation caught her unawares and caused a stirring along her spine, into her loins.

"I'm having a little trouble with that picture myself," he averred, his laugh quiet and thoughtful.

She barely heard him. The motion of his fingers on her neck was both soothing and exciting, and she closed her eyes to allow herself the full enjoyment of it. She heard the creak of well-oiled leather, and she knew he was going to kiss her. The notion filled her with giddy anticipation.

His mouth found its fit over hers in an instant. It had been so long, it seemed to her, even though it had been but two weeks, at most, that it was like the very first time. He tasted each lip, tugging gently upon them with his own, and the strength of his wide mouth was tempered by his restrained passion. She wished, as her hand found the hair curled over his collar, that he would not stop. That his kiss would go on and on just as it was, neither deepening nor receding. It was a kiss that promised unnamed pleasures, the promise in itself being as much pleasure as her body could handle decently.

Presently his kiss ceased. She waited, eyes closed, for another. When he did not renew his activity, she opened her eyes, undeniably disappointed. She found him studying her intently. His face, unsmiling, was inches from her own.

"I just want a little corner, Gen," he whispered, his dark eyes commanding her gaze even as his urgent words turned her inside out. "A little room of my own in your busy life."

She would have promised him anything if he would only kiss her once more. And she was not sure she wanted to promise. *A corner,* he said. How could she even yield a corner, when she had no idea which one he would demand? And which she was prepared to part with?

She sat up, directing her stare to the pond again. "I can't, Kieran. I can't promise anything. And I don't know if I would even if I could. Please don't ask me. I can't exactly explain it to myself, much less to you or to anyone else. But I can't. Please, take me home now."

"Is it Humble?" His voice had a hard edge to it. "Or Atherton?"

She resisted an urge to plant her face in her hands.

"Yes." She groaned. "No. I mean . . . It's more than all of that, Kieran. How can I make you understand? It's Mozart and Verdi and Gounod. It's the Metropolitan, and Covent Garden, and La Scala. It's things I couldn't possibly begin to explain to you, if I had a lifetime to do it! Please, just—just take me back now. It's best if we forget we ever had this conversation. It's best if we never discuss it again, at all."

"I have the feeling it's even simpler than that." All of the softness was gone from his address. "I think it's Memphis and Little Rock and R. Hastings McAllister. It's Camden and Galveston and Lennox. I can't change what's happened between us, Geneva. Not the bad, or the good. But just remember: Neither can you."

The sterling November afternoon was tarnished beyond reclamation. He did not speak again during the half-hour drive back to the St. Pierre, and Geneva was unable to do so because of the great weight in her chest pressing painfully into her heart. He was right in a way, she knew. But far from simplifying matters, those names he mentioned evoked a far more complex series of emotions in her than any she herself had uttered.

Chapter Twenty-nine

The price of the *New Orleans Times-Picayune* had gone up a penny. Macalester found the additional coin in his pocket and accepted the twelve-page tabloid from the newsboy outside of the St. Pierre, folding it under his arm without looking at it. Geneva had gone directly inside without further remark, and he was glad. He did not have the strength to exchange further words with her.

Billy was getting ready to go out as Macalester returned to their room. He was whistling off-key, the only way he knew how, a tune resembling "Little Brown Jug" more than any other as he tied a crooked knot about his collar. He had been seeing an actress and was no doubt preparing for another of his romps. The light-hearted anticipation he never failed to exhibit on such occasions normally amused Macalester, but this evening he found it intolerably annoying. Billy took one look at Macalester in the mirror, his blue eyes merry.

"How was the funeral?"

Macalester sent him a look he hoped was withering and tossed the newspaper on the bureau.

"Very funny."

He had intended to say nothing to his friend about the dismal climax to his afternoon. He had every intention of carrying on with his activities as though nothing was bothering him. But somehow, seeing Billy so cheerfully involved in his toilette for a night of sparking robbed him of his self-control. His fingers pulled clumsily at the buttons of his jacket and he nearly ripped the garment, turning it completely inside out as he tore it off and flung it on the bed. Billy was watching, but Macalester didn't care. It didn't matter. Nothing mattered. He shoved his hands into his pants pockets to prevent himself from throwing something else. Maybe Billy. He stared at the floor, unwilling to look at his friend.

"When are you going out?" he asked finally, in a hostile voice.

"Damn, Senator, I'm sorry all over hell, whatever it was I did!" the younger man declared in a mockingly contrite tone. "I'm leavin' here just as soon as I can. I guess you applied your usual charm to Mrs. Humble, and that's why you're back here so early, grouchin' like a grizzly bear?"

Macalester did look angrily at Billy then, angrier than he had a right to be. Knowing that didn't make it any easier, especially when his friend called Geneva by her married name, which Billy knew he hated. And worst of all, he could not even contrive a response to his annoying friend, except to continue glaring.

Billy's lips pursed in a thoughtful expression. "You wanna tell me about it?"

"No."

"Fine."

Billy continued fiddling with his tie and resumed his

whistling. Macalester watched him, not moving from his place. His fists were clenched so hard that his fingernails were digging painfully into the hardened palms of his hands.

"She doesn't want me, Billy," he heard himself say dully, before he'd even intended to speak.

"Smart woman."

"Thanks!" Macalester snapped, looking up sharply. "Thanks a lot, Billy! I'll remember your kind words, the next time you're puking your guts out after some pour sap calls you out!"

Billy Deal faced him at last, his blue eyes like ice. "Well, damn it, Mac, at least I wasn't stupid enough to—"

He stopped abruptly, as though someone had shouted "Enough!" The room was still for a full minute. Macalester could hear his heart thumping as if each beat were its last. Finally, he could no longer sustain Billy's unswerving, annoyed gaze.

"Did she turn you down?" Billy inquired finally, judging, apparently, that Macalester's temper had been mitigated, at least for a time.

Macalester felt as though the words were going to pour forth whether he wanted them to or not, so he decided to let them come out a little at a time, hoping to stem a gushing tide.

"Not exactly." He shook his head.

Billy made a face.

"What the hell does that mean?" he demanded. "Did she slap you?"

"No," Macalester retorted, feeling a little uncomfortable about the conversation.

"Did she let you kiss her?"

He felt himself blush, and he wondered why. Billy had seen him in bed with whores, and he Billy. Why should Billy's comparatively mild question cause him embarrassment this time?

"Yes," he answered, unwillingly remembering her sweet, reciprocating mouth.

Billy, to his surprise and chagrin, chuckled.

"If she hasn't said 'no,' it probably means 'yes,' Senator." Billy sounded so sure of himself that Macalester stared in wonder. "You just have to find the right way, and the right time, to ask, that's all."

Macalester considered his friend, who was cleaning his even, white teeth with a cedar splint. Billy, unquestionably, had had a great many more liaisons than he, but there had not been a serious attachment in the lot. Ladies—women, really—came and went in Billy's life like daily bread. Satisfying meals, soon forgotten. Macalester had sat at that table a few times himself, but this was different. It wasn't so much that Geneva was like a banquet to which he had not been invited. It was more like she was a well, and he hadn't even known he was dying of thirst until he'd met her. He had the feeling that Billy was still way out in the desert somewhere, looking for his own oasis.

"I don't know," Kieran said at last, shaking his head. "It's like I took something from her without permission, Billy. Just when I feel like she's within my reach, she slips away from me again."

Billy appeared puzzled. "Come again?"

Macalester grimaced. His own emotions were in such a morass that he wasn't at all sure he could explain them, not even to himself.

"Forget it, Billy," he said dismissively, sitting, then reclining on the bed, aware of a sudden profound and overwhelming weariness. "Go out. Have a high old time. Just toss me that newspaper so I don't have to move again."

Billy considered him, placing his hand on the folded

tabloid on the dresser. "Why don't you come with me, Mac?" he urged presently, sounding pleased by his sudden inspiration. "I'll bet Andrea can dig up a friend for you, and we can all light up this old town together. Just like old times. How 'bout it?"

Billy's idea held no appeal for Macalester, but he did not want to hurt his friend's feelings.

"Not tonight." He leaned back against the pillows, crooking his arm behind his head. "I'd be lousy company. Go on out and have a good time. I'll work things out. It may take me some time, but—I'll do it."

"Suit yourself." Billy shrugged his arms into the sleeves of his jacket and tossed the paper to the bed, looking about the room. "Where the hell is my billfold?"

Macalester knew Billy was not asking him. With one hand he picked up the newspaper and flipped open the fold. The words on the front page leaped out at him.

"God, Billy!" he exclaimed, sitting bolt upright again as he stared in disbelief at the paper before his eyes. "Roberts has pardoned us!"

"What!"

Billy sprang forward, seizing the tabloid from his partner's grasp. As his blue eyes scanned the paper, Macalester got up from the bed and moved beside him, reading:

Governor Oren Roberts of Texas signed a proclamation granting amnesty to notorious outlaws Kieran Macalester and Billy Deal on Thursday, a controversial move rumored to have been instigated by his political cronies. Roberts, whose term expires next November, said his decision was motivated by pleas from lawmen around the state who have encountered violence, and numerous false claims from countless bounty hunters for the five thousand dollar reward previously offered for each man. The move was designed, he said, to save lives and the taxpayers' money.

The article went on, but Macalester stopped reading. The rest of it was unimportant to him, and was probably a lie, anyway. Some men who made a career of lying, he reflected bitterly, were called politicians.

"Well, what do you think of that?" he said softly, feeling as though an immense yoke had been taken from his shoulders.

"I think I want a drink," Billy replied hoarsely, sounding completely serious for once "Join me, Mac?"

Macalester felt the younger man's hand upon his shoulder.

"I want to go tell her," he heard himself say, even though he'd had every intention of accepting the invitation when he'd opened his mouth.

Billy met his stare with a look of such profound understanding that Macalester was stunned.

"Go ahead, Mac," he told him, nodding slowly. "You and me have had a lot of drinks together, and we'll sure have plenty more. Go on. Go tell Geneva. And good luck."

To his surprise, Billy stuck his hand out. Macalester accepted it with a firm shake.

Then Billy was gone.

It was with some reservation that Geneva accepted Kieran's unexpected invitation to dinner, after the dismal result of that afternoon's outing. She ignored her secretary's disapproving look, though, and accepted his arm as he escorted her down to the hotel dining room. They were seated at once at a secluded table in an alcove surrounded by huge bromeliads in terra cotta pots. Geneva took the chair offered her by Macalester, wondering why she was there. It had been her intention to keep her distance from the outlaw, and two feet of white damask was not quite the distance she had envisioned.

He took his place across from her, and it was very obvious by the deep, appealing clefts in his cheeks that he was trying to suppress a smile. She admired, as always, the easy grace of his movements and the air of self-assurance he never failed to exhibit. He was, she admitted to herself, allowing a small spark of pride, a commanding presence. What a pity that fate should have decreed him an outcast.

"I had an interesting piece of news waiting for me when we got back to the hotel this afternoon," he began after ordering an expensive bottle of Champagne from an approving waiter.

He was not even trying to suppress his smile, now. His wide mouth displayed his fine teeth and the dimples with which she was by now achingly familiar. She had not the faintest idea what he was talking about.

"Oh?" she offered politely, looking about the room at the other patrons, unable, for some reason, to maintain his scrutiny.

"Have you seen the *Times* today?" he questioned her, drawing her attention again.

"No. What have I missed?"

In reply, he reached into the inside breast pocket of his black dinner jacket and withdrew a piece of newsprint, torn at the edges and folded into a small rectangle. He held it out to her, seeming to monitor her every move. Curious, she took it from his fingers and unfolded it.

The import of the article struck her like a blow with a silken glove.

"I—" She folded the paper again and handed it back to him, feeling a strange fluttering in her breast. "I'm happy for you, Kieran," she said, hoping she sounded natural to him. "I'm happy for you and Billy."

Kieran reached across the table, but took her hand instead of the paper she offered to him. His firm gesture startled her into meeting his gaze.

"Do you know what this means, Gen?" His fingers massaged hers in a most distracting manner.

She could not answer him. Her voice had fled.

"Miss Geneva Lionwood."

It was an abrupt, raspy tenor voice that distracted her from Kieran's urgent question. There appeared at once beside her a short, impeccably dressed man of perhaps fifty. She withdrew her hand from Kieran's quickly, not sure whether she was annoyed by the intrusion or grateful for it.

"My name is Horace Tabor, Miss Lionwood," the man proclaimed, bowing. "I own this hotel. And one or two other things." He laughed at his remark, as though he thought it a good jest. "May I join you and your escort?"

With an odd sense that this had all happened before, Geneva glanced at Kieran. The former outlaw was scowling.

Horace Austin Warner Tabor did not wait for her permission. An eager waiter brought him a chair and another bottle of Champagne, an even more expensive one than Kieran had selected. Within moments, their secluded little table became the focus of attention throughout the crowded dining room.

Horace Tabor wanted to talk opera, and when the diminutive, stocky millionaire spoke, one had no choice but to listen, or flee. The subject being opera, Geneva chose to listen. Macalester also opted to remain, but he chose to scowl, as well, reminding her sharply of Blaine Atherton at Delmonico's when a certain R. Hastings McAllister had intruded upon their evening.

Geneva found herself fascinated by the older man's knowledge of and devotion to the art, and by his casual talk of his connections in Chicago, St. Louis and Philadelphia. He was building the newest and most fabulous opera house in all of the country, bar none, in Denver. It was his intention, he assured her, to concoct an offer that would result in her leading an ensemble of the finest singers ever assembled to perform in, and to fill, that facility. And Horace Tabor spoke with such bold authority that it was impossible for her to doubt him.

Geneva tried to temper her excitement. After all, she had been duped before, and not that very long ago, by similar extravagant promises. But the images Tabor conjured for her at that little table like some master magician were as compelling as they were real. The only dark spot in the evening was Kieran Macalester, sullen, yet obstinately remaining at the table like some glowering specter, even after the other diners had departed and he, Geneva and Tabor were the only ones left in the place.

It was obvious to her that Kieran had no intention of yielding the arena to the Denver tycoon. Geneva found that notion, against her will, to be very exciting.

Tabor at last retreated, with the promise of seeing her on the following day with an offer in print. Kieran escorted her up to her room without speaking, his arm tense as she held it. She offered a remark or two about Horace Tabor, his generosity and his persistence. Kieran, not surprisingly, said nothing. He paused at her door, but she did not release his arm.

"Kieran, wait," she said, breathless from more than just the climb up the stairs. "I think I might faint. Stay with me for a moment."

She leaned her back against her door, feeling very warm as he stared down at her with a serious, even forbidding, countenance. She had never seen him look more magnificent. She drew in several hard breaths, but found, to her surprise, that breathing was not getting any easier.

Suddenly he was kissing her, his strong, hard mouth drawing an unexpected fury of desire from her like a firestorm. She seized his lapels and held him to his purpose, feeling deliciously out of control.

He stopped quite as abruptly as he had begun, and disappointment stabbed her sharply. She felt a deep blush surge into her cheeks, and she could not meet his steely gaze.

"Goodness," she managed to murmur at last. "I—I'm afraid I may have drunk too much Champagne. Would you—" Did she dare ask it? "Would you help me inside?"

She felt his fingers on her chin, purposeful, but not bruising. In a moment, she was looking into his eyes again, and he would not let her look away. Her cheeks burned.

"You're not drunk, Geneva," he told her in a low, dark tone. "You're not even tipsy, not any more than I am. I'll help you inside. But if I do, I'm not leaving until the morning, so just make damned sure it's what you want."

Geneva, imprisoned by his intense sable eyes, swallowed hard. It was exactly what she wanted. It was exactly what she had always wanted. Her right hand fell away from his lapel and behind her back to the door lever, and in another moment they were inside, in the dark sanctuary of her room.

Chapter Thirty

The light of the full moon bathed the suite in an eerie, pale white glow, like a dream from which she could not, would not awaken herself. Kieran had touched something deep within her, something that had stripped her of sense and reason and had left her only with the desire to feel him around her and inside her. He took her mouth again in the sanctuary of her room, and she yielded to him gloriously, trembling as his tongue tested her.

She pulled on the end of his tie. It gave way with no struggle and she cast it aside, working at the buttons of his shirt. In moments she uncovered his chest and she pressed her hands against its hard, warm surface, caressing the contours and loving the feel of the soft hairs upon it. He moaned softly in response to her touch, his kiss becoming more fiercely urgent. Her breasts strained against the green taffeta, and she wanted him, desperately, to undress her.

But he had already begun. His hands had found the buttons on the back of her dress bodice, and the kindly buttons loosened with ease. With his help, she slid her arms from the sleeves and the dress fell to the floor, forgotten. His lips burned a trail along her throat to the very swelling of her breasts, and her breath caught in short little gasps as she felt the first stirrings of a sweet climax in her loins.

"Geneva," he murmured in a low growl, his tongue finding the cleft between her breasts. "My sweet . . . my love . . ."

Her hands found his face and traced his very square jaw before losing themselves in the soft thickness of his sienna locks. The lacings of her corset were loosened by his deft fingers. She wanted him to touch her, and that want was a palpable thing. In moments, there was nothing but darkness between them, and an instant later, not even that.

He carried her to the bed, laying her upon it and himself on top of her. He was heavy, but not crushing. His weight was as thrilling as the bold exploration of his tongue and his mouth. He got up from her, and she shivered with the sudden cold of his abandonment. He lit the small lamp by her bedside and she blushed again, knowing she wore her desire as plainly in her face as he did in his, and that she had no secrets from him. He gazed down at her, his bold stare lingering on her bared breasts, then again on her ivory silk garters and stockings. A slow, sensuous grin played upon his wide, slack mouth and in his adoring dark eyes. He parted her legs with an idle gesture and sat down on the bed between them. She found herself panting in anticipation, unable, unwilling, to move.

"This," he whispered, fingering the garter lazily at her thigh, "is what I wanted to do in Roanoke."

He undid her garters and, with agonizing slowness,

rolled the stockings down each leg, one at a time, revealing the smooth, white skin beneath. When he was finished, he caught her left foot firmly in his hand and kissed the inside of her ankle. She heard a soft moan, and she knew it was her own voice. She thought she would go wild.

He worked his way with kisses from her ankle to the inside of her knee. He paused there, gazing at her with that faint, drowsy smile she loved. She felt the wetness between her legs begging him.

"Shall I continue?"

She nodded. "Yes," she urged, her voice weak and trembling. "Yes. Oh, yes. Please. Oh, God . . ." And his lips completed their journey along the inside of her thigh to that soft, moist, tender place awaiting him. He drank from the well of her desire until she thought she would explode, and then she did. It was as if thousands of little pieces of her shimmered and danced and fell at last to the bed, where they slowly formed themselves back together again.

He was on top of her, and she wanted more. He pierced her and she cried out, astounded by her body's thrusts that complemented his own, and by the sweet instinct that had possessed men and women since the beginning of time itself. Her legs held him to his design, and he went on, and on, each of her sobs of joy seeming to inspire him. Her climax crescendoed like a battery of tympany, and Kieran, groaning, throbbed inside her until at last he lay still, spent. She kissed his ear and his neck, relishing the salt of his satisfaction.

"Gen." He sighed drowsily, not moving. "Gen, Gen, Gen . . ."

Geneva thrilled at the sound of her name in his hushed baritone. She tried her own voice, and it came forth in a tranquil whisper.

"Kieran," she murmured, raking his hair gently with trembling fingers.

His hair was so soft, so fine and so abundant. She played in it for a long while, twirling it about her fingers. Presently he eased off of her, rolling onto his back with a shuddering sigh. He pulled her close and she nestled against his shoulder, losing herself in the caress of his hand as his fingers stroked her breast.

"What are we going to do, sweet Gen?" she heard him ask at the end of another sigh.

The question troubled her. She did not want this perfect night defiled by nagging thoughts of tomorrow. She stroked the faint, dark stubble on his jaw with her finger, feeling a quiver of desire wash through her again, like a gentle but persistent breeze rustling leaves in a dense forest.

"We're going to make love again," she told him, turning his face to hers with the same finger. "And again. And again."

She punctuated each repetition with a kiss on his lower lip. Thus it began afresh, and several times more, until Kieran drowsily told her she'd best put on a nightgown, or neither of them would get any sleep that night.

The sun was bright by the time Kieran heard the knocking. He carefully disengaged the sleeping soprano's arms from about his shoulders and moved her leg off his before rolling naked out of her bed. He stumbled toward the door half-asleep, cursing under his breath as he stubbed his toe on the bedstead.

"What is it?"

"A message for M'mselle."

It was Adele, Geneva's secretary. Her tone was chilly and clipped. He guessed it was because she recognized his voice.

"Slip it under the door, Adele," he told the woman,

keeping his voice low. "She's asleep."

There was a stiff silence on the other side of the door. Then a white parchment envelope appeared at the seam at the bottom.

"M'sieur Durand will be here at ten o'clock," Adele informed him, and he heard the rustling of her skirt as she walked away from the door.

Kieran stretched before stooping to retrieve the note. He had gotten precious little sleep in the night, but he nonetheless felt invigorated and better rested than he had in ages. It was a new day. He was a free man, and he was in love. How lucky, he mused, turning again to the bed upon which he and Geneva had wrought such celestial havoc the night before, could one man be?

Geneva's dark auburn curls were strewn carelessly about the pillows, and her fine lawn nightgown was caught up high on her legs, revealing that soft, firm, white flesh he had so delighted in mere hours before. He smiled, feeling the glow of awakening desire as he approached her again, tapping the envelope against his fingers. He propped the note up against the lamp on the nightstand and sat on the very edge of the bed by her side. With a gentle hand, he brushed a lock of hair from her throat and replaced it with his lips. He kissed her neck softly, loving the yielding of her skin to the gentle pressure of his mouth. He tried another place on her neck, and another, and finally he kissed the hollow just above her breastbone, and he heard her utter a soft cry.

A surge of need swept through him at the sound, and he slid his hand up along her thigh, under the deliciously flimsy garment she wore.

"Gen," he called to her softly, finding her hip bone, her softly curved belly and, finally, the firm, tender roundness of her breasts. "Wake up, Geneva. Wake up and love me again."

He felt her gentle hand at the back of his neck, pulling

his head down to hers as a sleepy smile played upon her sweet mouth. She giggled like a naughty schoolgirl, and the giggle gave way to a sigh as he took her mouth with his own. This morning it was quick and urgent, almost as if she knew she hadn't much time. But he didn't mind. He imagined, lying beside her afterward, that there would be many, many, many ways of loving Geneva in the days and nights to come, and that belief was every bit as satisfying as the act itself.

"There's a note for you, Gen," he said, rubbing the stubble on his chin. "On the nightstand. And Adele said that fellow Durand is coming at ten."

"Did you answer the door like that?" Geneva teased, and he started at the touch of her hand to his groin.

"Of course," he rejoined, chuckling. "Adele fainted. She's probably still on the floor."

Geneva punched his hard bicep playfully. "Liar!" she teased.

Kieran cringed inwardly at the word, even though it had been uttered in jest. Geneva, too, seemed to fall silent afterward. Presently, she sat up and retrieved the note. The quiet while she read was too unnerving for him. He got up and collected his clothing from around the room, wondering how the glow from so brilliant a night could so quickly fade in the unforgiving light of morning. When he turned around, she was folding the note into a pink calico notion box. He waited, hoping she would volunteer its message. It became clear, shortly, that she had no intention of doing so.

"Who's it from?" he inquired, keeping his tone light.

She glanced at him, not smiling. "Horace Tabor," she replied blandly. She said nothing else.

Kieran digested this, pulling on his rumpled pants. "What's in the box?" He tried not to sound too curious.

She granted him an enigmatic look. "That's where I keep my men," she told him with a half-smile. "Blaine is in there. And Abbey. Mapleson. All of the notes and telegraphs I've received here in New Orleans."

Kieran found her a grin, in spite of his sudden uneasiness.

"It must be nice having all of those men at your fingertips now," he offered. Then he was silent, putting on his shirt, buttoning it.

Geneva did not answer. Instead, she walked briskly to the door and opened it a crack. "Adele, please have Harriet draw me a bath. Tell her to hurry. Mr. Tabor is coming up, and I want him to wait, but not too long."

"Tabor!" The exclamation came out before he could prevent it.

Geneva narrowed her eyes at him. Was he intending to be difficult now?

"Yes," she replied shortly. "I must ask you to leave, now, Kieran, or—"

"Or what?" Kieran's voice rose in pitch. "Or he might think there's something between us? We can't let *that* happen, now can we?"

She rolled her eyes heavenward, then stared at him again. His dark eyes returned her gaze with the same unreadable expression she'd become accustomed to, and it angered her.

"You selfish, insufferable oaf!" she flung at him, wishing the words were rocks. "How do you dare to speak that way to me after everything that's happened? After what I've been through on account of your loyalties, and your greed? Horace Tabor is coming here in half an hour to offer me the chance to put my career back together! By what right do you presume to sabotage my future?"

She saw Kieran blink, and she knew she had hit her mark. She waited for his answer. He seemed to be looking past her as if at some distant mirage, clenching and unclenching his very square jaw.

"Are you telling me—" Kieran's next words were low and deliberate—"after last night, that there's no place for me in your future?"

After last night: The sweet memory stormed her reason. She could still feel his arms around her, his bold, gentle touch caressing her. She could almost feel him inside of her. She trembled at the memory and choked back a small cry of desire. She realized at once that she was in danger, in terrible danger of losing sight of her ambition and of failing to fulfill the promise of her talent and training. She realized that a word from Kieran Macalester might very well make her forget all of those things that had once been so important to her, but seemed at this moment to be so elusive and intangible as to be no more than a wild fantasy.

"There are things I must do," she answered him simply. "For myself. And they are things I must do alone."

"Alone?" His voice was hard. "Or with Horace Tabor?"

His meaning infuriated her. She clenched her fists in the folds of her nightgown.

"Horace Tabor," she said through her teeth, "is the chairman of the Tabor Opera House. He's offering me a contract in black and white, Kieran. Not the pie-in-the-sky arrangement offered me by a bogus San Francisco attorney on behalf of a nonexistent company. There's a measurable difference between the two!"

"Not to mention several million dollars!" he retorted hotly, his face red with rage.

His words hurt her, as much because the idea had occurred to her as because it meant he suspected her of mercenary qualities. It wasn't Tabor's money she wanted; it was the opportunity he was offering.

But how could she explain that to a man who had always seen opportunity in terms of dollars—and someone else's, at that?

"Kieran, be reasonable!" She tried to keep her hurt and her anger in check. "What do you expect me to do? Tell Horace Tabor, 'No, thank you. I prefer to go chasing around the country after an outlaw—excuse me, a pardoned outlaw—than to open your opera house and headline half a dozen productions?'"

Macalester tried to order his response, but realized bitterly that his answers sounded shabby and hollow, even to him. What, after all, was the professed love of a thief and a celebrated liar when compared to the genuine offer of a millionaire who would make her, at the very least, the star of Denver? Even if he did have his amnesty, he was penniless and without a future. Before him stood a woman who would be heiress to a king's ransom. That alone would have been enough to place her totally beyond his reach, but combined with her formidable abilities as a performer, she might as well have been on a distant planet. He found himself, to his dismay, staring at the floor.

"What happened last night," Geneva went on softly, so softly he thought his heart would break, "must never happen again, Kieran. I admit there's—a physical attraction between us. But that isn't enough. It's barely anything. It certainly isn't enough to throw away a career."

So it was merely a physical attraction on her part. Did she assume the same was true for him? *Liar*, she had called him. Would it, he wondered bleakly, make any difference to her, if she knew the truth?

He drew in a deep, painful breath. It was as if steel bands were clasped about his chest, preventing him from taking in quite enough air. She was watching him. He made himself meet her gaze once again, and he forced the pain and disappointment from his face.

"I suppose it's over, then, isn't it, Gen?" He congratulated himself on a light and even tone. He felt as though his insides had been ripped from his body by a sharp-clawed predatory bird who was devouring them before his eyes. *Please say no*, he begged her silently. *Please tell me it's only begun!*

Geneva could not deny the lump in her throat as she returned Mac's steady, measuring gaze. Her heart was not comfortable with her statement, which was really only a tiny lie: She had confessed to a physical attraction, and that was real enough. What purpose would be served by admitting to a love that could only result in bitterness and failed dreams? Or worse, in the realization that he hadn't ever really loved her at all? *Please give me a sign*, she entreated wordlessly. *One word. One look.*

The small space between them might have been a bottomless chasm filled with silence.

Her sigh hurt deep in her chest. "I suppose it is, Mac."

Kieran wanted to seize her by the shoulders, to shake her, to kiss her as he had kissed her in the night, and would never kiss her again. And if he stood there looking at her for another moment, he feared he would do just that. And he could not. It would earn her rebuff, if not her disdain, and he could not bear either result.

"Good-bye, Geneva," he got out, although he could manage no more than a whisper. "I'm sorry for everything. And I won't trouble you again."

He took his jacket from the bedpost. When he turned away from her, he felt as if he were leaving a part of him behind in the room with her. A large part. He did not know what part, exactly, but he did know he was going to miss it.

Badly.

Geneva watched Kieran amble out of her life in his lazy, long-legged gait that was just shy of a swagger, and she wondered numbly if she would ever find the will, or the strength, to love another man the way she loved Kieran Macalester. Or if she would decide, after a time, that it simply wasn't worth the anguish.

By the time Horace Tabor arrived, her tears had stopped. The gremlin had once again taken up residence in her heart.

Chapter Thirty-one

In December, Geneva was in Chicago singing Violetta when she read the news that Garland Humble had died of a failed heart. Horace Tabor was amused when she confided to him that she had been Humble's wife, and he set his lawyers to work immediately to secure her inheritance for her, in spite of her protests. She didn't want Garland Humble's money any more than she had wanted him, but she suspected Tabor was guided by purely selfish motivations: If he was building up to ask her to marry him, as she suspected, he would consider himself even more fortunate to be marrying an heiress.

But of course, he could not know that she would never marry again.

The new year, 1884, saw her celebrate in St. Louis with a critically acclaimed Gilda in *Rigoletto*. Horace was not traveling with her, having returned to Denver to settle a dispute regarding his opera house. Geneva took her bows onstage every night, and every night she remembered, with a heaviness not even the gremlin could absorb, the flowers thrown at her feet on the stage of the Academy of Music, with the single word "Delmonico's" on the note attached.

February was cold and wet, even in New Orleans. Billy Deal, miraculously, had met and married a widow. Thanks to her inheritance, he opened a music hall and casino just outside of the French Quarter, where Kieran Macalester faithfully got drunk every night. He played poker every night, too, winning enough to keep him going, but not enough to earn him any ill will from the other patrons.

In March, a man came into the place to meet the famous Billy Deal and Kieran Macalester. He was vice president of the Union Pacific and Southern Central Railroads, and he had an unusual and attractive proposition to put before the two men. He wanted to make them consultants for passenger and cargo security, at excellent pay. Billy promptly left the music hall business, kissed his pretty, pregnant wife a fond farewell, and dragged Macalester out of a bourbon bottle and into a new suit of clothes to pursue this lucrative and amusing new adventure.

April meant the end of the opera season, and Geneva attempted Senta in *The Flying Dutchman* in Philadelphia. But hers was not a dramatic voice. The reviews were lukewarm at best, and she damaged her voice besides. Horace did not seem to mind, wiring her from Denver that all would be well, and that October in Denver would give her renewed popularity and exposure in *La Traviata,* a role perfectly suited to her. She was assured an entire season in Denver, with the option of closing the season for Mapleson in New York. The colonel had already petitioned her for the following year at the Academy of Music, and the stages of Europe still teased her.

In May, it was announced that Henry Abbey was fired from the Metropolitan for a lack of critical successes coupled with financial devastation. Blaine, Lord Atherton, returned to England under a cloud of scandal involving a young actress, and Geneva Lionwood decided to retire for the summer to New Orleans, hoping to regain her voice—and other things she had lost.

Camilla Brooks finally persuaded the reserved Dr. Beaumarche to the altar in June. Geneva was honored to attend their wedding, even as she was cripplingly disappointed to find that Kieran Macalester had gone to parts unknown. July and August were stiflingly hot and uneventful. Geneva refused entreaties from Horace Tabor to come to cool Denver, electing to rely on Dr. Beaumarche's care and Macalester's return to the Crescent City. The first was a success, the second a dismal failure.

The first rehearsals for *Traviata* began in September. Denver was a disappointment. Its only resemblance to the major eastern metropolises, contrary to Tabor's boasts, was the opera house itself. At least Horace had not misrepresented that. Its acoustics favored Geneva's fully recovered lyric voice, even if its garish design was an offense to the senses. Her dressing room not only bore her name but would accommodate, she was sure, a small family comfortably. Best of all, Tabor had lured the Academy's own wardrobe mistress: Audrey Stancil immediately became, once again, her confidante and her confessor.

On October the fifth, one year to the day after Geneva had left New York City with R. Hastings McAllister, the *Denver Sentinel* reported the engagement of soprano Geneva Lionwood, shortly to inaugurate the Tabor Opera House as Violetta, to millionaire Horace Austin Warner Tabor.

*   *   *

"I'm spoken for, ladies." Billy's decline sounded only a trifle reluctant to Macalester. "But my friend the Senator might be interested. Ask him."

Kieran was forced to look up from his newspaper. Before him stood two young whores whose combined ages he doubted equaled his own. One of them had hair the color of Geneva's, the other, luminescent green eyes. Some part of him was amused by the irony that two women together could not begin to compensate for the one. It hurt to look at them. He waved them on wordlessly with a careless hand, then returned his attention to the *Denver Sentinel*.

"Shoot, Mac." Billy sounded disappointed. "Since I can't indulge anymore, would it kill you to at least give me the pleasure of knowin' that *one* of us was enjoyin' himself?"

Macalester put the paper down and surveyed Billy without smiling. He glanced at the full glass of bourbon on the table before him, then picked up his paper again. He had sworn off drinking since he and Billy had accepted the peach of a job from the Union Pacific, but he still made a practice of ordering a glass at every saloon he entered and having it sit before him, untouched. It reminded him of his shortcomings. Today, however, he was mightly tempted to yield to its temptations.

Billy issued a heavy sigh. "I swear," the younger man declared, "it's like you got nothin' better to do than sit around saloons and chase away female comp'ny. Why don't you just go see her, and get it over with?"

"Why don't you just shut the hell up?"

" 'Cause I got to talk for both of us these days." Billy, Macalester noticed with some resignation, was not intimidated by his touchy humor. "She's still eatin' you up, Mac. Face it. The only way you'll ever get her outta your system is if you look her right in the eye and tell her exactly what's on your mind."

Macalester rolled his eyes in supplication to the Almighty. "Not another chapter from Billy Deal's book on advice to the lovelorn!" he pleaded mockingly, but could not as easily put aside the familiar gnawing sensation in his gut.

"Yeah, well, I figger I'm performin' a public service." Billy settled back in his chair until it creaked, joining his hands behind his curly blond head. "Years from now, you'll thank me, when you finally get over Geneva Li—"

Macalester suddenly found himself on his feet in possession of the lapels of Billy's charcoal-gray jacket, staring into Billy's faintly amused blue eyes.

"You wanna hit me, Mac?" the younger man challenged him in a whisper. "Go ahead. But it won't make you feel no better. This is the third time we been in Denver in two months, and I'll bet you think I don't know where you disappear to every night after supper, do you? You better do it, Mac, and do it now. Or she's gonna marry that Tabor fella, and then there won't be nothin' either one a you can do about it."

Macalester felt exposed. No, he hadn't realized Billy knew where he went every night when they were in Denver. He'd thought it was his secret, haunting the streets near the enormous opera house, wanting to catch a glimpse of her, yet terrified at the same time. Suppose she saw him? What would he say to her? But he had been spared finding out.

"The place opens tonight," Billy went on, even as Macalester felt his fingers relax their deathlike grip. "There's a rehearsal at three."

"Two." Kieran corrected, then felt a warmth creep up his neck as Billy grinned knowingly at him.

"You could just make it," the younger man encouraged, straightening his clothing with no hint of rancor.

Macalester picked up his chocolate-brown Stetson. "You coming?"

Billy sat down and shook his head once, taking Macalester's full glass of bourbon in his right hand. " 'Three's a crowd,' " he intoned, raising the glass in a toast. "Here's to ya, Senator."

"The flowers are wrong," Audrey announced flatly as Geneva pulled the neckline of her costume lower over her powdered and pushed-up bosom.

Geneva could not bring herself to care. She stared at her reflection in the full-length mirror trying to conjure something. Nervousness. Excitement. Trepidation. *Something.* She had sealed off her heart for so long, she supposed, that the gremlin to whom she had entrusted its care was unwilling to relinquish his claim.

"I'm sure they'll be fine, Audrey," she remarked indifferently. "How many people in the audience, do you suppose, will know?"

"If even one does, it's too many!" Audrey snapped so peevishly that Geneva granted her full attention at last. "You forget, Miss Lionwood, that I take as much pride in my work as you do in yours!"

Geneva accepted the rebuke in silence, watching as the vexed older woman pulled camellias out of a broad, flat box, camellias of such size and perfection that Geneva gasped in wonder.

"My God, they're beautiful!" She examined one, holding it close to her cheek to feel its softness and inhale its gentle fragrance. She would not have believed it possible that such perfection could exist in the mile-high hamlet.

"They're beautiful," Audrey allowed, grumbling. "But they're all wrong! They're supposed to be in a chain I can attach from here to here—" She gestured from Geneva's right shoulder around to the hem of the sumptuous, scandalous dress, her wrinkled features a study of vexation. "Hand me that box of pins over there. I expect I can do something."

"I expect you can," Geneva murmured, holding the single flower to her cheek while Audrey began her labors. Its sweet aroma triggered a vague memory she was loath to name, or to abandon. No sooner had Audrey finished than a knock disturbed them.

"If that's Horace, I don't want to see him now," Geneva stated in a low voice, affixing to her ears the pearl earrings he had given her earlier as a memento of her Denver debut.

Audrey gave her a look. "I wonder why you ever do," she huffed, then responded to the knock.

"Miss Lionwood's flowers," the messenger reported wearily. "From Mr. Tabor."

Geneva frowned.

"You're too late," Audrey told him, no doubt annoyed that she'd just spent half an hour fiddling with the wrong flowers. She took the second box anyway and shut the door with her backside before depositing the new offering in the center of the floor. These camellias, Geneva noticed as she opened the box, were properly arranged, but possessed nowhere near the degree of beauty of their predecessors.

"Where could these have come from then?" Geneva mused aloud. Mystified, she searched the empty box. Her fingers found a small white card under the paper. Her hands trembled as she opened it.

You're not the type for camellias, but I suppose you must have the best.

It was not signed.

The gremlin very nearly toppled from his perch upon her heart.

"You have a secret admirer," Audrey observed, looking over her shoulder.

346

Geneva did not answer. She was remembering the tall specter in Blaine's box at the Academy. She remembered, barely, to breathe.

"Or maybe not so secret?" Audrey peered into her face, her gray eyes narrow with suspicion.

Still, Geneva could not speak. A sob welled up in her chest and caught in the back of her throat, where it remained like a stone stuck in a pipe. She thought she saw, from the corner of her eye, a small gremlin slip quietly from the room. The backs of her eyes stung, suddenly, with unshed tears.

"Geneva! What's the matter with you?"

"I—" She choked on the word. "I can't do this, Audrey!"

"Of course you can!" the wardrobe mistress reproved, aligning Geneva's shoulder seams. "Jitters! I never saw 'em on *you* before. This is your Violetta, dear. Get down there, now, and sing your heart out!"

It was as though someone else's legs carried her down the stairs to the stage. Choristers bustled to their places, Flora and Alfredo exchanged a fond embrace, and the wistful strains of Verdi's overture filtered through the curtain. Geneva discovered, just as the curtain went up on the Denver premier of *La Traviata*, that she was still holding one of the perfect camellias beside her cheek.

Chapter Thirty-two

She had done it. Somehow, she had remembered every cadenza and staging, every cut and cue. Or perhaps she had not remembered them so much as she had forgotten everything else. The enthusiastic audience demanded, and got, a dozen curtain calls. Horace Tabor stood on the chair in his box—otherwise how could he have seemed so tall?—and applauded the loudest of all. He could not have seen the tall, shadowy figure behind him in the doorway; not as Geneva saw it. With each reappearance onstage, she expected the ghost to have disappeared, but he remained, stoking her memory and haunting her reason.

When she finally managed to escape, alone, to her dressing room, she was exhausted. Drained. And she was shaking so badly, she thought she must be ill. She wanted to lie down on her chaise, in the lavender nightgown, her costume for the death scene, and go to sleep, although she knew she would not be able to do so. Her

348

dressing room was quiet, almost unbearably so. It added to her sense of detachment. *This could not be happening,* some part of her realized as she sat at her mirrored dressing table. *None of it was real . . .*

"Hello, Gen."

The specter had returned. Kieran Macalester's tall, lean, broad-shouldered outline suddenly formed in the background of her mirror. She stared at it for a long moment, wondering if her ears might be deceiving her, or if his appearance might not be some cruel trick of the light. The phantom, or mirage, or whatever he was, took two steps more into the room and she could see, in his reflection, the work of the year since their parting.

His features, always angular and stark, remained as they had been indelibly imprinted upon her memory. The lines were deeper than she recalled, though, and she could apprehend tiny folds at the corners of his dark eyes, eyes that still monitored her as though at any moment she might, as Camilla Brooks had once suggested, turn to gold. The smile on his generous mouth was a faint imitation of the wide, reckless grins so painfully clear in her memory, and there were traces of silver threading the otherwise sable hair at his temples. The shiny locks were still slightly longer than was fashionable and combed back off his face. She could almost feel them between her fingers.

"Kieran Macalester." She managed a light, if faintly mocking, tone, not daring to face him, lest he prove to be a phantom after all. "To what do I owe this honor?"

Kieran's courage had failed him at the rehearsal earlier. The sight of her after a year, commanding the stage as if the place had been named the Geneva Lionwood Opera House, had been somewhat more than he had been prepared for. But his determination returned by the time the curtain had gone up on the premier, and was reinforced by the sight of her encircled by the embrace of his camellias in the opening scene.

Geneva looked thinner than Kieran remembered. Her features seemed more sharply etched, and yet somehow softer. He could almost feel the stare of her dusky-green eyes upon him like the gleam of smoky emeralds. He blinked, his eyes remaining closed for a moment, allowing her melodious voice to wash over him like a golden wave.

"You sounded wonderful tonight," he said, opening his eyes but otherwise not moving. "Even better than I remembered."

Kieran's compliment lacked the effusiveness of Horace Tabor's brand of praise, but it made her feel freshly bathed nonetheless. She did not respond to it, however, for she did not trust herself to speak.

"Did you like the flowers?" His gentle baritone sent an undeniable quiver through her breast. She arched an eyebrow, hoping to seem indifferent.

"Oh, were they from you?" She dabbed at her makeup with cream and a soft cotton cloth. "They were lovely. Of course, I get so many. Horace, you see, sends them daily, usually without a note. I am curious, though, as to how you arrived at the conclusion that I'm not—how did you put it?—not the type for camellias?"

She hoped, for some reason, to hurt him with that, but he reacted only with a faint, fleeting grin. Damn him.

"You're engaged to marry Tabor."

He seemed determined not to respond to any of her questions, so she decided to treat him in kind. "Yes." Of course, it would have been nice if her lips were not so traitorous.

Kieran took another step closer. He was only five feet away from her, and his eyes, in the mirror, commanded her gaze.

"Do you love him, Gen?" His quiet voice snapped her

350

heart in two, like peanut brittle.

He doesn't deserve an answer to a question he has no right asking in the first place, she told herself, placing her fists on the dressing table before her. But she wanted to answer him. She wanted to answer in the affirmative. She wanted to embellish her response and to watch him recoil with the pain of it. But in the end his steady gaze, as always utterly unreadable, compelled if not the truth, then something close to it.

"He could make me happy, if I let him," she replied finally, then realized she was no longer looking at him.

Kieran longed to span the breach separating them, to gather her into his arms and to reacquaint himself with the feel of her after a long year of drought. He thought he might die if he had to stand there for another minute without touching her, but he managed to compose himself again.

"That doesn't answer my question." He slipped his hands casually into the pockets of his trousers so she could not see him clenching them.

Geneva's cool gaze in the mirror rebuked him. She wiped the last of the makeup from her lovely features and shook her chestnut curls about her shoulders. He ached to touch them.

"I haven't seen you for nearly a year." Her voice was a soft, silken cord, choking him. "Do you really believe you deserve an answer? Why do you want to know?"

He closed his eyes, feeling a familiar frustration settle on him like a cloud of black soot. Why couldn't he tell her? He had told her once, a very long time ago, in Memphis, when he was R. Hastings McAllister. He had told her again in Arkansas, when it could have been argued that he would have told her anything just to make her go along with him. But why couldn't he tell her, here, now, that he loved her? Why couldn't he just come out with it?

He knew the answer to that, but knowledge was not, in this case, power: He had lied to her. It had been a long time ago, in another life. But he had lied. And she, as far as he could tell, had never forgiven him for it, even though his lie had been the catalyst for her success. No matter what he might tell her, no matter how earnestly he might frame his declaration, she would always nurse a doubt, would always believe he might lie again. He opened his eyes and discovered that he was staring at the floor of her dressing room. It was littered with clips and pins. The glint of them hurt his eyes.

"I want you to be happy." He formed an answer for her, staring at the back of her chair. "Will you be, Gen?"

Damn him! She was on her feet, sending her chair tumbling over. Facing him, she abandoned all attempts at restraint.

"If you were so concerned for my happiness," she hissed, "why didn't you say so in New Orleans? Why did you let me go as if I were no more important to you than a—than a stick of wood? Why has it taken you a whole year to decide that you cared so very much for my happiness?"

She could not keep the tremor from her voice, or the tears from her eyes. She had not cried in so long, and this was the hardest cry she could ever recall having. It hurt her, down in her chest. In moments she was crying into his lapel, and his strong arms were around her, warm and sure.

"Damn you!" she sobbed, her fists striking his unyielding chest with little strength and even less resolve. "Damn you, Kieran! I hate you! I hate you! I—"

Kieran did not heed her words. He had her in his arms again, where he'd wanted her for so long he could not remember. He held her close, feeling her heartbeat. Feeling her soft hair against his cheek. Feeling her sobs choke him, and his own face become wet. He somehow found her lips with his own, and they were salty and sweet.

She did not fight him. Her fists were clutching his jacket, not hammering away at him, and her mouth surrendered to his. Her sobs became sighs, sweeter music to him than any she had sung onstage.

"Gen," he murmured, his voice breaking even as his baritone sent a ripple along her spine. "Gen, Gen . . ."

The year fell away as if it had never been. Geneva allowed her emotions to rush in, like a bursting dam, and she was shocked to discover just how much she had kept hidden away. She loved him. She wanted to feel his long, strong fingers comb through her hair, his powerful, lean body against hers. She wanted to hear his luscious, velvety voice murmur her name, again and again. But she wanted more than that: She wanted to hear him say he loved her. He had said it a long time ago, and she had dismissed it. Now she longed to hear it once more; thought she might die if she did not. She tore herself away from his splendid mouth.

"Why did you come here, Kieran?" she demanded breathlessly as he kissed her throat, his lips burning her like sweet fire.

His dark brown eyes were inches above her, and he probed her very soul. For once, those eyes were windows rather than mirrors, and the emotion she perceived in them was almost more than she could bear.

"Because I couldn't keep away from you any longer," he whispered swiftly, as though he needed to speak before he lost his nerve. "I'm wrong for you, Geneva. I know that. But I also know that I love you, more than anything else in the world. I needed to tell you. I needed for you to know, before you ma—"

She pulled on his lapels and drew his mouth to hers again, reveling in the knowledge: He loved her. Everything else was unimportant. He had followed her to

Denver, just as he had followed her from Irving to Galveston and New Orleans. His love was a real and tangible thing, a thing that had a life of its own.

"Say it again."

"I love you, Gen," he repeated, gazing at her with a new wonder.

The words, it seemed, had released him from his prison. He realized the moment he spoke them that it was not so important for her to believe them, just now, as it was for him to utter them. It never had been. His discovery was so simple, yet so overwhelming, that he felt like laughing. Why hadn't he seen it before?

"I love you," he said again, his terrible burden lessening with each repetition. "I love your eyes and your mouth. I love your temper and your sweet, sweet voice. I love your brain and your wit. I love the way you cry. I love holding you like this, and I love being in the same room with you after all this time. What about you, Gen? Do you love me? Or am I in this alone?"

He was holding her face in his hands, his thumbs making gentle circles on her cheeks. She took hold of his wrists, feeling her heart swell in her breast as she searched his tender, earnest dark eyes.

"We're in it together," she breathed, trembling. "I love you, Kieran Macalester. God help me."

He kissed her again, the sweetest, gentlest kiss of all. He enfolded her to his breast, and she knew, with a certainty that was bliss, that she belonged nowhere else. Her own arms encircled his neck, and her right hand played in his soft sable locks as his kiss deepened. She felt her legs weaken beneath her as his tongue probed her mouth, slowly. He was in no hurry.

In the time it took to draw a breath, he had lifted her into his arms, still commanding her mouth. She had left the earth, and she never wanted to return to it. He carried her to the chaise and sat down, holding her upon his lap like a cherished treasure.

"Let's lock the door," he murmured, teasing her ear-lobe with the tip of his tongue.

"I—" She couldn't think clearly with him behaving that way.

"What?" He took her lobe gently between his teeth.

"Oh, Kier . . ." He found a spot, right behind her ear, that made her forget what she had been about to say.

"Don't talk," he whispered, then nipped her ear yet again. "Don't—" Another nip. "Even—" A third, longer one. "Move . . ."

She willingly obeyed. Presently, the bright noonday sun burst forth from a shroud of black clouds. Again. And again. An amazing phenomenon, made still more incredible by the fact that it was nearly midnight, and there were no windows in her dressing room.

Kieran's lips moved along her neck to her collarbone, leaving a burning trail. She wondered, through her swelling desire, if they had left a glowing red mark as well as evidence of their passage.

The pearl earrings Tabor had given her tickled her neck and reminded her, suddenly, of her fiancé.

This had to stop. She could not think, and she had to. Reluctantly, she pushed herself away from Kieran, but could not summon the will to get up from his lap.

"I have to tell Horace," she told him, focusing on his face. His ardor was evident in his rapt features.

A notion crystalized in Kieran's mind.

"Marry me," he urged her, surprised by his own impulsiveness.

By the look on her exquisite features, he knew he had surprised her as well.

"Marry . . . you?"

He shrugged, and a grin coaxed the corners of his mouth. He could not take his eyes off her. "Why not?" he countered, sliding his arms down about her nicely rounded hips. "Billy got married, you know. I can't let him get too far ahead of me, can I? Besides, it's the only way I can be sure I'll know where you are all the time."

"You—you won't try to stop me from singing?"

He laughed softly. "Darlin', I wouldn't stop you from singing and dancing naked, as long as I knew you were coming home to me every night!" he declared, knowing he meant it. "Hell, I'll even be your agent, or your manager, or your bodyguard, or any other damned thing you like. The Union Pacific doesn't own me, and I have no deep-seated prejudice against having an extraordinarily talented wife. As long as she doesn't mind having a broken-down old ex-outlaw for a husband."

Her slow smile warmed him like a fine old cognac.

"I'll hold you to it," she warned, wagging a finger at him. "Not the naked part, of course. But the singing—"

"Anywhere you like," he affirmed. "New York, San Francisco . . ."

"London? Paris? Milan?" She sounded doubtful.

"The moon, if it makes you happy," he finished, taking her chin between his thumb and forefinger, wanting to keep her there forever.

Her green eyes became wet, and the wetness made him want to crush her in his arms.

"I do love you, Kieran. I do!" She breathed the confession, placing her hand over his in a possessive gesture that made him realize, with only a tiny bolt of fear, that his hand really did belong to her, and it always had. It had merely taken him until now to realize it.

He was an idiot.

But maybe he was not as much of an idiot as he'd been a year before.

Epilogue

A cool, steady breeze blew off the ocean. The sun was setting over New York Harbor, its rosy orange glow sending a small pang of regret through Geneva Lionwood Macalester: They would not see the azaleas this May. Above her, the steam whistle of the *S.S. Columbia* signaled its departure from harbor waters into the open ocean. Several far-off horns responded as though bidding them farewell. They were lonely sounds, and they reminded Geneva that she was leaving behind the security of an established career for the great unknown: The conquest of Europe. She wondered, in an abstract way, if the ancient Carthaginian general Hannibal had felt as she did, before attempting to cross the Alps with his elephants. It was a terrifying prospect, but an exciting one, also. Nor was it the only such contradiction in her life at the moment.

"I couldn't find yours, so I brought you mine."

She felt the heavy, comforting warmth of Kieran's

357

opera cape envelope her as surely as his strong, gentle arms encircling her waist as he stood behind her on the deck. Satisfied, she leaned against him and felt his lips graze her temple.

"How do you feel?" she asked him, watching the wake spread behind them. "Have you been sick yet?"

"Shh," he warned her. "So far, so good. How about you? Happy?" His hands softly traced the gentle swelling of her abdomen.

"Mmhmm," she murmured, feeling a familiar thrill at the warmth of his voice.

He chuckled "Scared?"

"Mmhmm."

"They'll love you, Gen," he told her, his arms tightening around her. "I hear Paris is crazy about pregnant sopranos. Milan can't get enough of them. And London—"

She laughed in spite of herself.

"I won't be pregnant anymore by October," she reminded him, holding onto his arms with her hands. "Besides, I'm not worried about my singing. Not much, anyway. I'm thinking about the baby. He'll be born in Europe, Kieran. It may be a year or longer until he even sees his own country."

"Or she," Kieran amended. "I almost hate to say it, but I keep hoping it's a girl. Girls are so much easier to raise."

"Am I proof of that?" Geneva was doubtful.

"Your point is well taken, my love," Kieran agreed, turning her toward him. "However, I can hardly consider myself a standard of excellence for a boy to emulate. I'm sure you agree."

"I consider you," she said, settling her arms about his neck like a wreath, adoring his sensuous smile, "to be the most wonderful man I have ever met."

"Considering some of the men you've met, that's hardly an endorsement."

"You know what I mean!" she chided him.

He laughed again, and she could not testify to it, but she thought she detected a rare trace of a blush in his otherwise swarthy cheeks. "I know. Do you really think so?"

She nodded. "I also think I'm making another in my long string of mistakes in telling you so."

He bit his lip in a self-shaming expression. "I can always count on my wife to keep things in perspective, can't I?" Kieran punctuated his rueful declaration with a kiss on the tip of her nose.

Geneva felt the warmth of his cloak and his love around her. It was very nearly enough to drive away her troubling thoughts, or at least make them seem foolish. Very nearly, but not quite.

"What is it, Gen?" her husband asked her while she was still debating the necessity of even bringing it up. She found him a smile.

"Nothing," she said dismissively, not quite convincing herself. "It's just—oh, nothing."

" 'Nothing' looks like it's making you unhappy." Kieran probed her face with a faintly worried look. "Are you all right? Maybe you should sit down."

Against her will, she laughed. "Are you speaking as my husband or my manager?"

"Whichever one you'll listen to," he retorted, only sounding a little agitated.

Having just completed a matinee performance of *The Marriage of Figaro* at the Academy's season finale hours before their departure, Geneva was amused by the notion that fifteen minutes of standing on the deck of the *Columbia* could cause her distress. She patted Kieran's cheek and shook her head.

"I'm fine, Kieran. I just—" She couldn't hold it in any

longer. She sighed. "I'm frightened. I can't help it."

He took hold of her hands, holding them tightly before him.

"Of what, honey?" His voice was quiet and urgent, and his eyes worried. She found herself, curiously, wanting to comfort him.

"Every other time in my life when I've been happy, and hopeful, I've been disappointed," she whispered, afraid to speak too loudly, lest she awaken perverse spirits. "And I've been so happy with you since October, and now with the baby coming . . . I'm just afraid something's going to happen to spoil it. It sounds silly, I know. But I can't help it, Kieran. I—I keep thinking I just wasn't meant to be this happy."

"Gen." He took her in his arms and held her close. "Why didn't you ever tell me before?"

"I thought you'd laugh," she murmured into his breast, aware of a sense of relief that she had finally confided in him.

She felt him push her back, gently.

"Look at me, Gen."

She obeyed, and found him regarding her with the tender gaze in which she had taken refuge almost since their first meeting. Her fear waned at the very sight of it.

"Are you happy right now? Right this minute?" He held her face in his two hands.

She nodded.

"Then why let the threat of something that may never happen take that away from you? Honey, we had all of our bad times at once, and they're way behind us now. I found out that everything in this life that I thought was important all came down to you, and as long as I had you, there wasn't anything else I couldn't handle."

He stroked her cheeks with his thumbs, and she trembled at the strength of his quiet conviction.

"I love you so much, Gen," he whispered, although she did not need to hear his words to know it was so. "I want you to believe we deserve this. I don't care how many times you've been disappointed, or hurt, in the past. The point is that it *is* past, and we have so much more to look forward to in our future. Because no matter what happens, we have each other."

She was happy. Happier, even, than she had realized. Kieran's handsome, rugged features broke unexpectedly into a slow smile, as if he could read her very thoughts.

"Will you believe me if I tell you every day?" He was teasing again.

"And every night, too?" she prompted coquettishly, stroking the lapel of his shirt with her finger.

He nodded, arresting the finger and placing a soft kiss on the tip of it. "If you must have a sad ending," he told her, suppressing a chuckle, "write an opera. You can do it during the summer, while I'm out walking the baby along the Seine."

Geneva almost laughed at the idea, then thought the better of it. "Why not?" She warmed to the suggestion. "Imagine! I can write it about us. The handsome, charming outlaw and the brilliant, naive young singer—"

"You can't write it about us," he interrupted, shaking his head.

"Why not?"

"Because our story will have a happy ending."

She kissed him soundly, with the glorious certainty that their happy ending had only just begun.